CW00433348
with love
from Me
July 1994

SANDRO AND SIMONETTA

BY THE SAME AUTHOR

A DANCE FOR THE MOON
THE PANDA HUNT
WHY DIAMOND HAD TO DIE
KHALINDAINE
TROUBADOUR
FOND AND FOOLISH LOVERS

SANDRO AND SIMONETTA

RICHARD BURNS

BLOOMSBURY

First published 1992

Bloomsbury Publishing Ltd, 2 Soho Square, London W1V 5DE

A CIP catalogue record for this book is available from the British Library.

ISBN 07475 12531

10 9 8 7 6 5 4 3 2 1

Printed in Great Britain by
Clay Ltd, St Ives plc

The author gratefully acknowledges the assistance of the Arts Council of Great Britain and the Royal Literary Fund for financial support during the writing of this book.

**FOR MY FATHER:
WILLIAM BURNS,
PAINTER,**

*La cara e buona imagine
paterna*

1498

I used to be mad. I can picture the madman I was, see him on an autumn day. Bright light flattered the Arno's waters and left cold shadows between buildings. It was the fall of the year we burnt Savonarola, and the last day of sun of that year. Little of the sunlight entered the room: some made seams round ill-fitting shutters; a little more seeped its way up the stairs from where it sprawled, a widening oblong, through the street door below. Sandro the Mad, the man I once was, lit a candle and rummaged through the gloom. Savonarola had declared looking-glasses to be tools of the Devil, but they are painters' tools too and Sandro had been allowed to keep one for reasons of his trade. Though that trade was declining, and his reasoning likewise, he knew there was a glass in the room.

The hunt was slow and awkward. He used his crutches to poke through his possessions or sweep them aside, and at the ferrules' clumsy prodding a plaster hand crumbled, revealing the fingers' wire frame; a vase broke, and the bristles fell from an old brush to make a scatter of hogshair on the dusty boards. He dug further through the heaped relics of his life, disturbing the spiders, disinterring a mouse's corpse that was a plug of grey fluff with a tail. A pile of books toppled; Sandro sneezed in the dust. He could have opened the shutters, let the sun aid his search, but he was too impatient.

The looking-glass, excavated at last, was opaque with dust. Its backing flaked at the edges and it rattled in its brass frame. He cleared the dust with his finger and examined himself by candlelight. A looking-glass is the Devil's tool and vanity the curse of Florence, if Savonarola had been correct, but despite this and his wandering mind Sandro saw little in his glass to make him vain. He had not looked at himself for a long time, and what was now mirrored before him he neither recognized nor liked. Although the candlelight itemized his features, reducing them to shiny highlights of chin and cheekbones, forehead and nose, he could not ignore the shaded shafts that creased his flesh, the black scabs beneath his thinning hair, the way his lips withdrew into almost toothless gums. Simonetta, glimpsed in the crowd by the Orsanmichele, still looked as young as the day she had died; Sandro's face was ruined by time and he was not sure she would know him if they met.

Resting his crutches against the table he eased himself into a chair. With the looking-glass in one hand and the candle in the other he sought ways to improve his appearance. By raising his head he could reduce the number of chins beneath the sparse bristles of his beard, but the same pose only emphasized how meagre his neck had become; he tried holding the candle by his ear, so that half his face would be lost in romantic shadow, but the flame set fire to his hair – in his mirror he saw glowing twists of wire that burnt out quickly, and he suffered the cattle-branding smell as it singed – and had to blow it out. After the flame the room was darker than ever. He sat in the darkness and worried. Even if she does recognize me, he realized, how can she ever love me?

But rest was impossible: he had seen the woman he loved for the first time since her death more than twenty years earlier. He leaned over from where he sat and opened a pair of shutters. The shutters let in as much sound as light: noises which had previously been muffled, street vendors' cries, the rattle of looms, the tolling of many church bells, were swept into his room on a beam of dusty sunlight. Sandro lived the other side of the city then, the other side of the river; wherever one stands the Florence skyline is an arrangement of familiar features, Duomo, campanile, palazzo, but his old house on San Miniato also overlooked the tilted squares of a thousand crimson roofs. That day, however, Sandro was oblivious of the city. He thought only of Simonetta. She had been dressed as a youth when he saw her, but he had painted her face so often that he had recognized her at once. Her features – the pallor of her skin, the brightness of her eyes, the tilt of her smile – haunted his derangement. He must find and declare his love.

His head slumped into his hands. God has given me a second chance; Death has voided Simonetta back into my life, yet, he asked himself, how can I announce my love? She will despise me. A shuffle of feathers made Sandro look up. He saw a pigeon perched on his window ledge, but it flew off when it met Sandro's eye. I scare even the birds, thought Sandro.

He sat in a silent blizzard of dust and sunlight. There has to be a way, he decided, to confront her without frightening her. His eyes, which had adjusted to the brightness outside, peered once more into the gloom. Of course! Nature has made me old, but Art can make me young again; the skill which has preserved Simonetta's beauty on a dozen panel paintings can surely serve me now.

As rapidly as his legs allowed he pushed his table and chair under the window to take advantage of the light, then assembled the other things he would need. Most of his materials were in the studio on the Via Calimala; only one among the paintbrushes he found in his room was supple enough to use, but one would be enough; pigments were also a problem, for though he had the basic ingredients, copper and sulphur and lead and earth, he had neither walnut oil nor egg to bind them. He despaired, then brightened. I have oil for cooking, and flour.

The paint he mixed was thick and clumsy, but sticky enough to cover any surface. He wedged his looking-glass firmly on the table, resting it on two books and using a third to make sure it did not slide. He worked steadily and, holding his head so still in front of the glass that his shoulders and neck hurt at once, began to cover his features and restore the youth he had lost, taking the red he found in his eyes and returning it to his lips, the blue he found in his lips and returning it to his eyes. The surface was greasy and the paint reluctant to take, but Sandro was content. He did not fool himself: he knew that his painted face would never convince Simonetta by day, but hoped it might fox her by moonlight or torchlight; he ignored the way the paint did not fix properly to begin with, the way it resolved itself into little balls of colour that would not set, and simply worked the surface till it was covered.

His work continued. He painted from the memory of how he used to look when Simonetta was first alive, and as he painted he daydreamed, imagining what he would say to her and she to him when they met. The autumn day drew to a close. His mind wandered. He thought first about the pigeon at his window, and then about the specks of starlings crowding the dusk and making fluid patterns round the tower of the Palazzo della Signoria. More birds live in Florence than men, Sandro considered, yet I rarely see birds' corpses, and, when I think about it, this surprises me. Sometimes I have money, he thought, and I still sleep on a feather mattress. The mattress is many years old and is leaking, but the feathers it leaks and that tickle my sleep are pristine. Even if birds' bodies decompose quickly, the feathers should survive: Florence's squares and streets should be awash with feathers, should choke on them. Where are these uncountable feathers? I can only guess, he decided, that, when the time comes for them to die, the birds go elsewhere.

The starlings still circled the tower. Their formation was always altering. At times the birds seemed to choose a leader and follow him in a column. At other times they were a dense cloud, a ball of bone and feather. Occasionally all sense of pattern seemed to disappear, yet as he watched Sandro learnt that the disappearance of order was illusory, no more than the signal of another order yet to come. He turned back to the business of painting his face, and as he did so he tried to imagine the place where birds would go to die. It would be an island perhaps, in the sea to the west, and should a man make a landfall there each step would involve a crushing of tiny bones, a sweeping aside of deep drifts of feathers.

Sandro finished retouching his features at last and sat back to ease his stiff neck. He admired the face in the glass, then pulled himself up on his crutches and hobbled through the cluttered room. The stairs creaked beneath his weight. The ground floor was a storeroom, and though the casks were mostly empty and rats had nibbled the grain there were still cockroaches for him to disturb as he limped towards the street. He locked the door behind him and started towards the city, insecure on cobbles coated with refuse and dung.

On the table the looking-glass was still propped between books, and painted on its smooth surface was the picture of a healthy young man. Only the eyes had received no paint, and they mirrored and mocked the dark room.

1502

I am much recovered now, thank you, and not unhappy in this place where you find me, although at night I am disturbed by the screams. Listening to the screams, it is hard to tell torment from pleasure, hard to distinguish the anguish of those chained in the long room from the exuberance of the man who thinks he is monkey. The screamers' motives make little difference to the sound, or to me. Delighted or desperate, the screaming keeps me from sleep.

I cannot draw by candlelight any more – my eyes are weak, perhaps ruined – so I use the hours when sleep is denied in prayer or, as now, in writing. To occupy myself tonight, and to please Fra Agostino, I have decided to embark on this, the story of how I came to be in this place. My candle attracts insects. Sometimes a cricket or clattering cicada is trapped in my cell and goes mad, hurling itself against the walls and ceiling as though it were contaminated by the same noisy craziness that afflicts so many of those in this place; often it is a moth that dances in the light, throwing spasms of shadow around the cell until it singes its wings for love of the flame and falls damaged on to the table. Most madness here is of the cicada kind, a lunatic abandon, but I am moth-mad, for I ruined my wings for love. My father owned a copy of Lorenzo Ghiberti's memoirs. Ghiberti was a simple man, for all the beauty of his sculptures, and his life was simple too, yet his book is readable and enjoyable; Fra Agostino insists that I, who knew the most famous writers of our time, and whose moth-madness has been far from simple, can write a better one. Perhaps, though I am not so ambitious to think this the story of my life. Rather it is the story of my love.

Around me, my city. The madhouse is close by Santissima Annunziata, the church of the Annunciation, and Michelozzo's dome dominates the view from our cloistered court; on the other side is the monastery of San Marco, where Savonarola was once prior, and its tower, the bell removed after Savonarola's fall, casts its morning shadow over our yard. My city and I have grown old together: we shared a golden age of growth, passed into a time of madness, and have now reached a quiet dotage. Yet the skyline has barely changed between the time when I walked through the snow with my father, to be apprenticed to Fra Filippo Lippi, and now, when I sit in the cell in the dark and my pen teases out my memories. I am sometimes helped to the roof. The monkey-man chatters in his tree alongside. My weak eyes are troubled by the sun, but I do not need to look to know that to the north are the city walls, spacing the bold square towers, and beyond are the hills, dotted with buildings and sheep, any more than I need to see the dome of the cathedral, the campanile, and the tower of the Palazzo della Signoria, clustering in spikes and curves to the south. I have my city charted in my head. Nor do I find it hard to populate the city with memories, to see myself as a young man walking through snow on the way to begin my apprenticeship, or in my madness following love's ghost. The three of us – painter, madman, old man who writes – trace our separate paths through the city to where we converge on these pages.

1465

White flakes fell from a slate grey sky. It was forty years ago. It was less than a mile from here. My father and I, in middle age and youth, reached the door of Fra Lippo's shop. 'Lippo!' my father cried. 'How's the head?' I found this joviality, this eagerness to be everybody's friend, embarrassing and slightly nauseating.

'Mariano di Filipepi! Good to see you! The head's fine.' The friar was broad in beard, in belly, in smile. 'How's yours?'

My father laughed, perhaps a little uncertainly. 'There's not a wine bottled can stop me the next day.' This may have been true, but I had seen his bad temper that morning, when he had complained at every noise and gagged at his rice broth. His face was pale beneath the heartiness still.

Filippo's laugh easily topped my father's. 'There's not a wine bottled can stop me the same night. I had them both again after you'd gone.' He neither looked nor talked like a man of God, yet he painted like an angel.

'What? Both of them?'

'Why not? One on my face, one on my cock: shame to waste the fee.' Filippo was loud and cheerful: the assistants in the shop laughed obligingly. The painter looked at me. 'This the son of yours you told me about? How old you say he is?'

'Twenty years this Michaelmas,' said my father. 'I know he looks younger. He was often sick as a child, held him back.'

I not only looked younger than my age, I felt younger. With three older brawnier brothers I who had always been the baby of the family now found that, wherever I was and whoever I was with, I always felt myself to be the youngest there.

'Sandro,' said Mariano. 'Meet Fra Filippo, Florence's greatest painter.'

I knew Fra Filippo's reputations – his reputation for womanizing almost equalled his reputation for painting – and had seen his pictures in many churches. The paintings were smooth, beautiful and serious; Fra Filippo was none of these things, but the eyes he ran over the young man, assessing and enquiring, were blue and fresh, indecently innocent. 'You sure he's yours, Mariano?' he asked my father.

'You suggesting something?' my father asked in turn, but without rancour. I believe he was in awe of his famous drinking companion. 'Sandro's a funny little runt, we know, but he's mine. You'd better apprentice him now, pay back the insult you threw my wife.'

The friar turned back to me. 'Can you draw?' His breath was a loam of wine and garlic.

'Drawing and dancing is all he ever does,' my father complained. 'His brothers, they drink a bit, whore a bit. They pretend I don't notice, I pretend I don't notice: at least they're doing what comes natural. But this one, he's more girl than man.'

'Angelo!' called the friar. 'Paper! Chalk!' All assistants are known as *garzoni*, boys, but the title can be misleading; this assistant, bulky, swarthy, and several years older than I, who fetched the materials and dumped them on a table, was clearly a man. I looked on nervously. 'Right. Let's see what you can do,' ordered Fra Filippo.

'Now?' I asked. There were many people about.

'Of course now,' said my father, impatiently; he was anxious to please Fra Lippo, and anxious I should please. My father usually scorned my drawing; that he suddenly seemed to be encouraging it gave me a sense of drawing's worth. But, though given confidence by this thought, I had no idea what to draw. There are too many things in an artist's studio – assistants preparing colours and boards, heaped pots tufted with balding brushes or dribbling streaks of bright paint, a floor that is spattered with colour like the bottom of a rainbow bird's cage, easels on gawky legs – for the choice to be easy. At home I drew birds and flowers; there was nothing so friendly, so straightforward, to draw at Fra Lippo's shop.

The friar seemed to understand my problem. 'It doesn't really matter what subject you choose. You work with your right hand? Draw your left.'

In fact I can draw almost as well with either hand, but I did as I was asked: I sat down at the table and looked at my left hand, flat on the wood with the fingers spread. I had rarely studied it before, and never so closely. It was a weakling's hand: I had been told so often. But it had a good shape to it, an elegance my father's hands, tanned the colour of his hides, never had. I started to draw on the smooth buff paper. The red chalk was unhelpful to begin with. At home I used the scratchy nib which my father kept to write his *denunzia*, his tax returns. Unaccustomed, I found it hard to make precise lines with the chalk, and as I copied the outline of my outspread fingers on to the paper I felt resentful: this was my chance to prove what I could do, and they had cheated me by giving me a stick of French chalk.

I stopped drawing. This lumpen pose of my left hand was as boring to look at as draw. I altered the attitude, turning my hand on its back, curling all but the index finger in and leaving that one outstretched to point at the heavens. Now it was the hand of a saint that I drew, or that of an angel. I crossed out my first picture and started again.

The second picture was much livelier. I found I could enjoy the smooth passage of the chalk across the paper now, the ease with which shadows are smudged. I wondered if I should be allowed a brush dipped in white lead and gum, to paint the highlights of my knuckles and nails, but before I had worked the drawing to anything approaching completion the friar stopped me. 'I'll take him on,' he told my father. 'You'll pay his board?'

'Of course,' sighed my father. It is the usual arrangement. 'How much?'

'We can sort that out later. He doesn't look like he eats a lot. You brought his clothes?'

'I'll have them sent on. You're sure you want him?' It seemed my father, though happy enough to get rid of me, could not believe anyone would want to take me.

'He's no hand but a good eye,' said the painter. I have two hands, I thought, one of them reproduced on the buff paper Lippi is holding; I also have two eyes. 'We might make something of him,' continued

Fra Lippo. 'Nothing special: he's no Masaccio. But an assistant? Why not?'

Masaccio had been a prodigy, a full member of the Arte dei Medici e Speziali by the time he was 20; he was dead before he was 30. I knew his frescos in Santa Maria Novella, as well as those he painted with Fra Lippo in the convent of Santa Maria del Carmine, and did not particularly like them. The figures seemed old-fashioned and solidly human to me in my youth; I have always had a taste for lightness, for angels. But, though Fra Filippo painted wonderfully graceful angels, I knew Masaccio had been the friar's master and hero, and was not so foolish that I spoke.

My father left, hugging me with surprising force: it was not the strength of the squeeze which surprised me but the strength of the emotion. We were too dissimilar, my father and I. We had too little in common. Perhaps, I thought – and it was a curious thought to begin my life away from him – he cared for me more than he knew how to show.

I spent the rest of the day with the friar, being shown round the shop, the bottega. There were four apprentices and five assistants. I was introduced to them all but the names did not stick in my head. Both the apprentices, though they had been in the bottega several years, looked younger than I: 20 is very late to start. Someone asked me about this. 'I had a lung infection a few years ago, and couldn't work; afterwards I worked with my brother Antonio, who beats gold, but he thought I was better at drawing things than making them. And my father knows Fra Filippo, which is why I'm here.' A concise life, and about all there was to tell of my existence to that point. But my health had recovered, and I considered I was ready at last for life and for work.

Not that there seemed to be much work to do in the shop at that time. Two assistants were gilding an impressive wooden frame; one was covering wooden panels with linen and gesso; the other two, and the aprentices, were painting *cassoni*, wedding chests which would be sold in the market, poor work for a master's studio but all that is to be done when times are hard. Fortunately the friar was full of energy and was enthusiastic about everything, so no one was worried about the shortage of commissions. 'Something will turn up,' said Fra Lippo, and I believed him. 'Meanwhile,' he added, and I believed this as well, 'there's a huge amount you must learn.'

I was told how much. I would be taught to grind colours, to use glue, to fasten the linen to the panel, to prime it with gesso, to scrape and smooth it, to make reliefs in the gesso, to put on bole, to gild, to burnish, to make tempera with water and egg yolk, to make Flemish glazes from pigment and linseed or walnut oil, to lay on grounding colours, to transfer by pouncing through pricked lines, to sharpen lines with the stylus, to indent, to colour, to ornament the panel, and finally to apply the varnish. And afterwards, I was told, I must go on to the different and much more difficult techniques of fresco. I felt a kind of panic: I did not know half the terms, much less the techniques they describe. But Fra Lippo was already moving on to other subjects. He talked of schemes of perspective, of foreshortening, of the relative merits of various chalks, of silverpoint, of the use of willow charcoal, of size, of cartoons. He described the various paintings we were expected to produce, the Annunciation, the Nativity, the Adoration, the Madonna and Child, the Flight into Egypt, the Agony, the Passion, the Deposition, the Lamentation, the Entombment, the Resurrection, the Ascension, the Assumption, and the variations within the variety. One of the easel paintings there then was an Annunciation, showing Mary's response to the Archangel Gabriel: there are five stages to the Annunciation, I learnt, from her 'conturbatio', her initial shock at finding an angel in the house, to her eventual 'meriatio', or pleasure that she has deserved God's favour; this painting showed the 'humiliatio' of her submission to God's will. Although Fra Filippo was a bad priest and a worse scholar he was knowledgeable about such things. And finally I was told where I should eat and sleep, and the ordering of my day, from drawing water at dawn to checking that no fires still burnt before we slept. It was a relief to hear something I understood.

In the evenings we were to eat at a long table, assembled from smaller tables, which ran the length of the shop; as we ate our meal that night my brother Giovanni came with my clothes. There was snow on his shoulders and boots, and when I looked out into the evening I saw fat flakes that rocked as they fell. I was happy to see Giovanni. We did not look like brothers: he was ten years older than me, solid like our father, and though short he was even broader than Fra Filippo; he looked like one of the barrels he sold for his living.

But Giovanni had always been good to me, and I believe his visits and prayers had saved my life when I was sick in my childhood.

It seemed that everyone in Florence who has a taste for wine knew Fra Filippo, the unholy friar who painted such holy pictures. 'Lippi!' called Giovanni. 'How are things going?'

'Botticello! What are you doing here? Is the whole Filipepi clan calling in on me these days?'

All his friends called my brother 'il Botticello', which means the little cask, a description of his trade and his appearance. 'How's my little brother doing?' asked Giovanni.

'Sandro's fine. We'll talk of him later. You'll have a drink with us? Get some wine inside you, man; warm yourself up. Has the snow begun? And how are you and your new wife settling?'

'The house is cold but we're still hot,' said Giovanni, using a phrase newly-weds often used in those days. 'How are you and your family?'

'Lucrezia and young Filippino are still in Prato. I daren't bring them here while old Buti's still alive.' All Florence knew this story then: how Fra Lippo Lippi seduced the daughter of Francesco Buti, how Francesco wanted the friar put to death, and how even Cosimo de' Medici, even the Pope himself, had found it hard to soothe the situation. 'And anyway, I wouldn't want a woman round all the time. Or a child. Too inhibiting.'

'There are compensations to taking a wife,' said my brother.

'It's cheaper to sleep with a wife than with a prostitute,' admitted the friar, pouring more wine into the goblet from the jug.

'Is that all that matters to you? What about companionship, love, comforts?'

'You've only been married five weeks,' teased Fra Lippo. 'Wait till it's five years.' He drained the goblet and handed it to my brother.

'Five years! Fifty years!' A strong man talking tenderly is impressive, and I was proud of Giovanni. 'What do the years matter when you're in love?'

'No one stays in love for fifty years,' said the friar.

'We're not all like you' said my brother. Sometimes Giovanni seemed older than our father: he had more confidence, less need to be what others expected; our father wanted to be thought cheerful and manly, whereas Giovanni simply was these things, without need of artifice or display.

'You're none of you so different,' replied the friar. 'Some men let their women put a tether round their bollocks, others don't, but we've all got bollocks none the less.'

'Love isn't just screwing.' Giovanni emptied the drinking cup and one of the *garzoni* took it from him.

'Screwing isn't just love, you mean. Love gives the screwing zest, but so do other things. The worry her husband might catch you, the thrill of taking a virgin, the shape of a well-turned thigh.'

'I can't talk to you about these things,' said Giovanni. I was given the empty goblet and the jug but I passed them on and listened. 'You don't understand. You speak as if you despise women.'

'Not at all,' said the friar. 'Don't think I've not been in love. I've been in love with half the women in Tuscany. I've given years of my life to love. But as you get older you'll realize there are better ways to spend your time than to write sonnets beneath your beloved's window – not that I can imagine you doing that, Botticello! – and sighing at the moon. What is this thing called love? You see a girl in church, gorgeous profile, enticing waist. You follow her home, pick flowers and fights for her, promise you'll die for her. Oh, that's love! But if you'd turned the other way that day in church you might have seen her cousin, golden curls falling on a pearl-white throat, breasts a man would give up drink for, and you'd have fallen in love with her instead. The world is full of women worth loving. I don't despise women at all. I simply refuse to believe that any one is so much better than the rest: a man in love despises all women except his beloved; I divide my respect equally between all women. And give my cock to any who'll take it.'

'You see! I was right! I can't talk to you about these things!'

The friar laughed. 'Your dad said that your brother dances,' he said.

Giovanni accepted the change of subject. 'He dances beautifully,' he said, which was embarrassing. 'Me and Dad, we lumber. Sandro's got grace.'

'Then he must dance for us now,' decided Fra Filippo, and I did not seem to have much choice.

Jacopo, one of Fra Filippo's pupils, was persuaded to play the lute. The dinner plates were pushed aside. Fra Filippo helped me on to the table. 'Lads!' he said. 'You've met Sandro Filipepi. His brother, il Botticello here, says he can dance. So Sandro's going to entertain us. Aren't you, Sandro.'

I stood on the table. All the apprentices and assistants were dining in the shop that night, and all were watching me. Jacopo strummed some notes, the opening of 'Abelard'; I missed my introduction and had to wait as he played through the verso. Some of the assistants jeered, but at least I had time to compose myself. I wished I had taken the wine.

As the music came round for me again I prepared my position, hands above head in the French manner, for this was a French tune, and counted myself in. One, two, three: step. The table was a good place to dance. My foot made a satisfactory slap as it landed, a beat that led into the next step. I danced better than Jacopo played. To begin with I followed the rhythm of his music, but soon he was playing to the more rigorous beat of my feet. The others clapped in time, and clapped louder when the dance was done. I bowed, jumped down from the table, and bowed again. Giovanni gave me a hug. 'You were good,' he said, 'and don't let anyone tell you otherwise.'

Fra Filippo held my hand above my head as though I were a victor. 'Il Botticellino!' he christened me, and the name, though soon shortened, stuck.

Afterwards I sat with Jacopo. He was a few years older than I and his father was a saddlemaker; he had nearly completed his apprenticeship and had already done some work on his own for the Pitti family. 'I expect you'll enjoy it here in the shop,' said Jacopo. 'The studio is friendly and Fra Filippo is a good man to work for: he expects a lot from us but he's always fair. Watch out for Angelo though.' Jacopo's eyes indicated the heavy young man who had brought me chalk and paper. 'He's the senior assistant. When Fra Lippi's away Angelo likes to think he's in charge: he can't paint but his fists are big.'

'Is the friar away often?' I did not like the sound of this. Angelo had led the jeering when I messed up the beginning of my dance; he had turned away in contempt while the others clapped at the end.

'All the time. Lippo's excuse is that he has to finish the murals he's painting in Prato, but he admits to us that the murals are all but done. He used to take some of us lads with him, but now he only goes to visit his woman and his son so he leaves us behind. It's better when he's here.'

'There seem to be a lot of people working in the shop,' I said.

'Well, he'll always take apprentices; he needs the money.' I was saddened: I had thought there was honour in being apprenticed to the studio of the famous Fra Filippo. Jacopo must have seen my expression. 'Not that he takes on just anybody,' he added. 'Only the best.'

Whether this was true or not it was a comfort. 'Is there a lot of work at the moment?' I asked, making conversation; I already knew the answer.

'It's not like it was before Cosimo de' Medici died. Fra Lippi was a great favourite of old Cosimo's. We had more work than we could cope with then. Fra Lippi kept getting into trouble because he wasn't doing enough of the work himself: people paid for him to paint and all they got was me, or worse still some incompetent like Angelo.' I noticed Jacopo's voice was very low. More than the description, the lowered voice emphasized that Angelo was dangerous, drew attention to the discrepancy between Angelo's skills and his fists. 'Did you see old Cosimo's funeral?'

When Cosimo had died he had asked to be buried without fuss. But Florence does nothing without fuss. We enjoy display too much: displays of wealth, of piety, of grief. 'I went to San Lorenzo with my brothers,' I said. 'But we couldn't see much.'

'We didn't see the procession either,' said Jacopo. 'But afterwards Andrea del Verrocchio asked Fra Lippi if we would help the men from his shop move the memorial stone into place. It was hard work, and Verrocchio's lot are more used to humping marble than we are. They started insulting us, nothing serious, saying we were weaklings and women, until Angelo hit one of them. It worked, it shut them up, but we were in church. And more than that, Cosimo hadn't been dead long and his spirit was only a little way over her heads. But Angelo doesn't think about that kind of thing. He doesn't think at all. His fists rule his head, not the other way round.'

Giovanni came over to me. The wine had made his cheeks and nose red. 'I'd best get back to the missus,' he told me. 'You be happy here,' he ordered. 'Work hard, listen to what the friar tells you, and remember, if you want me I'm not far away.'

Sometimes Giovanni seemed more a father to me than my real father had ever been. I walked with him to the door. 'Give my love to Donna Nera,' I said, referring to his wife. We stepped outside. The snow had stopped falling and lay on the ground, crisp and flat. Fra Filippo was also leaving, going drinking with a couple of the *garzoni*; the dread Angelo, I was sorry to see, did not go with them. I let the friar and his companions get up the street as I did not want them to witness my emotion, then I hugged my brother. 'I'm glad you came,' I said.

'Don't get cold,' said Giovanni. 'And look after yourself.'

'You too,' I told him. I watched his broad frame walk away. The snow forced him to tread more slowly and carefully than usual, which made him look older than he is, made him look like our father. I returned to the shop. The crust on the snow crunched underfoot, giving easily, exposing the softer powder beneath. It was like walking on tiny feathers, on brittle bones.

'We'd better get to bed,' said Jacopo when I got back inside. 'Fra Lippi sometimes comes back later, and he'll be angry if we're not asleep. He doesn't like us to stay up too late.'

'He stays out late,' I mentioned. 'He's famous for it.'

'He doesn't have to work as hard as we do. And he doesn't like the fire burning too long. Costs too much. Are you coming?'

'I think I'm meant to put out the fire.'

'Leave that to Angelo. He's in charge with Fra Lippo away. And tending the fire's all he's good for.'

There was a small gallery above the shop and the apprentices slept there on straw beds. But before I could climb the ladder a hand landed heavily on my shoulder.

'Where are you going?' Angelo asked me.

'To bed,' I said, surprised by the question. Where else would I go?

Angelo laughed. I turned to face him. Were his parents joking when they gave him that name? He was a fearsome angel. 'Not yet you're not. You've got to be admitted.'

'Admitted?' I knew what he meant – every apprentice must be initiated, and when I entered the shop of my brother Antonio I had been forced to drink a flagon of wine – but I was playing for time.

'That's right. You've got to drink our piss.'

'No!' I had been lucky at Antonio's, and knew it. My brothers had suffered: when Giovanni had started as a wine broker he had been shoved into a large cask and rolled into the Arno; when Simone had begun his apprenticeship as a tanner his hair was first shaved and then pasted, haywire, back on his scalp. But to drink piss: this initiation seemed the worst of all.

'No?' asked Angelo.

I looked round for Jacopo but, though like the others who were left in the shop he was watching Angelo and me, he was keeping well away. 'You can't make me,' I blustered.

'Are you for the Party of the Hill or the Party of the Plain?'

The change of subject surprised me, but talking politics seemed better than drinking piss, even though the politics were as bad-tempered as Angelo. I had no great loyalty to either side: I just wanted to say what would cause me least trouble. 'The Party of the Plain,' I said. This was the faction which supported Piero de' Medici, Cosimo's son; the Medici palace is on the plain, next to San Lorenzo. Cosimo de' Medici had been a friend of Fra Filippo, so it was likely that those in the friar's studio would be Medici supporters.

My assumption was more reasonable than Angelo was. 'Typical,' he sneered. 'A weakling like you would support a weakling like Piero.'

There was justice to this, I thought. My father had never let a day go by without reminding me of my own lack of strength, while Piero, who suffered gout and arthritis, was virtually a cripple. On the other hand, there was nothing to be gained by agreeing with Angelo; if I did not stand my ground I would prove myself a greater weakling yet. 'The Medici have been good for Florence,' I said, repeating what half Florence was saying.

'Cosimo maybe. Piero isn't fit to govern. Florence needs a real man,' argued Angelo, repeating what the other half of Florence said, the half who supported the Party of the Hill. The hill in question was across the Arno, for those who opposed the Medici were based in the Pitti palace on its rise above the river.

'A man like Niccolò Soderini?' I wondered.

'What's wrong with Soderini?' asked Antonio. 'At least he can walk!'

I did not know much about Soderini actually, and my question was asked to buy me time, but at least Angelo's answer had given me an opening. 'So can most people. It doesn't mean they're fit to govern.'

There was some approval of this answer among our small audience. The friar had worked for most of the great families of Florence, so his studio was more familiar with the notables than I was. There were sketches of many of the *popolo grosso*, the big people, the people of wealth and power, in the shop around us, half hidden in the dusk. Piero de' Medici's sons, Lorenzo and Giuliano, looked down from an easel behind my cowardly friend Jacopo; Niccolò Soderini, proud and determined, was drawn full length on the opposite wall; the head of Niccolò's brother Tommaso, who like Piero de' Medici was married to one of the Tornabuoni sisters and who was therefore with the Party of the Plain, lay on a nearby table; Luca Pitti, whose home was the focus of the Party of the Hill, looked across from a neighbouring easel. If I must drink piss, at least it would happen before a distinguished audience.

Angelo eventually thought of an answer. 'At least someone who can walk is better than someone who can't,' he said at last.

'Oh,' I said casually. 'I don't know. They say Pius II was a wonderful pope, yet he could barely walk and had to be carried everywhere on a litter.'

The blow broke my nose. I could feel the bone shift and splinter. I fell on to an easel which staggered under my weight. The easel collapsed, I collapsed, and Angelo sat on my chest.

No one came to help me, and despite strange sensations in my head, as if, though it were pouring blood, it actually contained more blood than usual, I could still hear Angelo's voice through the heavy pulse. 'How's that feel then? You want more?'

I shook my head in case he was offering me a genuine choice. He wasn't, but this time the swing of his fist was restricted by the way he sat on me and less damage was done. Or perhaps it only seemed less: perhaps my senses were still sated by the first blow.

'Now who's right? Medici or Soderini?'

I found it hard to say anything. His weight on my chest made breathing awkward; the pain in my face did the same for my thinking. 'Medici,' I whispered. He lifted my shoulders from the floor and slammed my head down. My eyeballs were bursting with brilliant colours, and next – it seemed this happened immediately, though time must have passed – I was awake and outside, being tumbled in the snow. In the dark, against the snow, my blood was black and ugly. 'He's coming round,' announced Fra Lippo, bending over me, shoving another ball of snow aross my face. 'Are you all right?' he asked.

'I'm all right,' I told him. It was true. I could cope with the blood. I could cope with the pain of my broken nose. I could cope with the snow that was pushed in my face and slid down my clothes. I could cope with anything, for anything, I had already decided, is better than drinking piss.

1466

Except that a modern apprentice learns to use oils as a medium for his paints, in addition to egg tempera, the training I received was not so different from that of a painter today. I rose at cock-crow. Water had to be fetched, fires lit, food prepared. Twice a week we went to the church of San Lorenzo, to give our thanks to God and the Medici. San Lorenzo is the Medici church, where Cosimo is buried and his descendants worship. On Sundays the whole family was there, Cosimo's widow the Mona Contessa, Piero with his wife Donna Lucrezia and their sons and daughters, and a number of cousins and nephews; on Wednesdays only the women attended. The peace of the church contrasted with the rest of my hectic week, for not only did I have the usual chores of an apprentice, but, perhaps because I was older than is usual when I began my studentship, or perhaps because I had a soothing way with tradesmen, I was often sent out to haggle for credit while my manual jobs were given to others. This was a trying if useful aspect of my education with Fra Lippo.

In the morning, after the *garzoni* had eaten, they cleared the tables and opened the shop. Jacopo had finished his apprenticeship while I was in the first months of mine, and he took charge of our instruction. We spent some hours learning drawing techniques – Fra Lippo insisted that a painting should be thought of as a series of shapes, each strongly outlined and distinct, and organized in the most simple and lucid manner the subject allows, so good drawing was essential – and being shown the rudiments of colouring, before getting on with more humdrum tasks around the workshop, heating the water, cleaning the brushes, scrubbing the tables.

I was happy there, and though Angelo continued to trouble me at the beginning of my time he did not stay long. Although his hero Niccolò Soderini won the election and became Gonfaloniere nothing much changed in Florence; the Gonfaloniere is in office only for two months, and when Soderini's time was up at the beginning of 1466 he had become so unpopular that most of the city had an unofficial holiday to celebrate, while Angelo had a fight in a tavern. We did not see Angelo for two days, and when he returned both his eyes had been blackened. 'Somebody been giving you a lesson in politics?' I asked him.

'It's not over yet,' he replied.

Nor was it. In March Francesco Sforza, the duke of Milan and Piero de' Medici's closest ally, died, leaving his peculiar son Galeazzo Maria as his heir. The Party of the Hill, chastened but not defeated, felt that Florence should drop its friendship with Milan and side itself with Venice. After all, they argued, Venice is a republic like Florence, and the republics should stick together against the nobles. With Venetian help, Soderini, Luca Pitti and their friends plotted to get rid of Piero de' Medici.

Perhaps Angelo knew of the conspiracy: he left our shop, and the painter's trade, and joined Soderini's household. I occasionally saw him, dressed in Soderini colours, carrying messages across the city. He ignored me completely when we met, which suited me well.

Those left in Fra Lippo's studio were pleasant enough companions. Gentile was incompetent but keen, and did not mind the nasty jobs such as cleaning hardened egg white from the bowls or grinding the tough white marble to make pigments for fresco work. Giovanni had red hair. Tullio was good-looking, gave his girl a baby, and had to leave his apprenticeship for better paid work. I cannot remember the rest.

I worked hard and went out rarely. I worked all day and then half the night because, since I was a boy, I have suffered from threadworms, never managing to be rid of them for more than a few weeks, and they have kept me awake at night for as long as I can remember. Perhaps that is why it seems natural now to work through the night: in those days I spent the sleepless nights reading by candlelight or practising drawing; now I use them to write these pages, to relive the short period of my apprenticeship. There is a symmetry here. In many ways that was the most stable period of my life until my retirement to this madhouse. My education seemed to be progressing steadily, following the pattern Cennini had outlined at the beginning of our century: the first year should be spent studying, and practising drawing on small panels; after that should come the acquisition of skills, learning to boil size, grind gesso, and work colours; eventually, after these techniques are mastered, the apprentice should get experience of painting, embellishing with mordants, making cloths of gold, and working in fresco, until he is ready to produce his masterpiece and join the guild. A minimum of five years' instruction, and a maximum of thirteen. But two undramatic events on the same day ensured my formal training lasted only seven months.

First, Jacopo left the shop. This was no surprise: a studio needs only one master, and he had stayed so long after completing his apprenticeship only because he was saving for a bottega of his own. There was a party to wish him luck. Jacopo had taken a small property at the end of the street, and two apprentices; Fra Lippo's studio brought food to his shop, and wine. The night was long and drunken. Fra Lippo had invited some whores he knew, and had also brought a quantity of burnt wine, which I had never drunk before. The whores did not interest me, for I was a serious youth unwilling to spend my seed or money on a woman I did not love; the burnt wine did. The casks my brother Giovanni made, the casks that gave him the nickname that I proudly carry still, were used for storing wine. The staves were dove-tailed and bound with iron hoops; the wine was the red of our region, rich or vinegary according to the year. But, though I am named after a wine barrel, I am not a wine drinker; I do, however, have a taste for this burnt wine, called aqua vitae, vinum ardens, or sometimes even vinum sublimatum, and I acquired that taste that night. The burnt wine occupied my evening, though as far as I could remember even the next bleary day, much less now when all my memories are sporadic and disjointed, I did nothing outrageous. The same cannot be said of Fra Lippo who, climbing on to a table and attempting to mount one of the whores, slipped and broke his arm. He lay there screaming, his arm pinned beneath him while his member, embarrassed at finding itself exposed, slowly collapsed. Someone else laid his whore.

Our studio was late up the next day. Our heads were as foul as our tempers, and there would have been fights had we had more energy. My eyes were sore and my mouth was arid so I was not pleased when I got a message, via a barefoot boy with a knowing grin, asking me to go to Jacopo's new shop at once. The friar was not around, so my only problem in getting away was the pain in the front of my head.

The friar's absence, and the boy's knowing grin, were both explained when I reached Jacopo's. Fra Lippo was still there, sprawled on the floor with his hose round his knees, and cursing anyone who tried to move him.

'I'm glad you're here, Sandro,' said Jacopo. 'I found him like this when I got up. I think his arm is broken.'

'Of course it's broken!' said the friar, unusually if understandably bad-tempered.

'I want to get him a bone-setter,' continued Jacopo. 'But he won't let me.'

'Of course I won't,' said Fra Lippo. 'What do you take me for? A fool? My right arm is broken, my painting arm. Commissions are hard enough to come by as it is. If it gets out that I can no longer paint that'll be that, the end of the shop. No more credit, no more nothing. It might suit you, Jacopo del Sallaio, to get rid of a competitor, but I don't want to die in the poorhouse like Domenico Veneziano if you don't mind.'

Jacopo was shocked. 'I'd never . . . It didn't occur to me . . . I couldn't – '

'Couldn't what? Couldn't get rid of your old master like that? No, you probably couldn't at that. But at least you can see why I don't want a bone-setter.'

'There must be someone who could set your arm discreetly,' Jacopo said. 'You need someone. You'll lose the arm if you're not careful, and then what'll happen?'

'Who do you suggest?' asked the friar.

'I don't know.'

The friar cast his eyes upwards in mock despair, then winced in genuine pain. 'That's not a lot of use then, is it?'

'We've got to do something,' said Jacopo. My friend was understandably agitated. Apart from anything else, this was the first day of his new career, and he did not need a crippled friar with an exposed penis in the middle of his floor. But he also cared for Fra Lippo, as we all did, and wanted to help.

'I'll see if I can find someone,' I said.

'Pettro Negro,' decided Fra Lippo through clenched teeth. 'He lives in the Pigiglioso district behind here. He's not in the guild. He'll do.'

Painters, because the pigments they use come from the same source as the drugs apothecaries peddle, belong to the Arte dei Medici e Speziali, the physicians' and apothecaries' guild. If a guild member found out about Fra Lippo's accident it would be very difficult to keep it quiet. Jacopo may not have been the man to take advantage, but there were many painters in the city, in those tough times when Piero de' Medici seemed to be taxing even the tax on our taxes, who would gladly have spread the story that the friar could no longer work. So I headed for the back streets, looking for Pettro Negro, a man unfashionable and unscrupulous enough to fix the broken bone.

Behind the streets of tradesmen's shops are the homes of the *popolo magro*, the thin people, the hungry ones. Their houses are unadorned and unembellished, yet generations of slow growth, of piecemeal extensions to existing buildings, give them the organic complexity of northern cathedrals. One house is often built directly on top of others, its floors on a slant to accommodate differences of level; random balconies sprouting from the walls sometimes collect together in unstable galleries; broken shutters hang at the side of unglazed windows; the bunting of drying clothes gathers like a frayed tent overhead. I walked between buildings of scabbed stucco, wood, cheap brick. Mean moss spewed from holes in the wall, brown fringed with green, widening trails that diversified into flat dribbles of reeking liquid or wide oily sheets the colour and texture of seaweed. I did not know these streets well, and liked them less, but here, in the Pigiglioso, the flea-pit, is where I would find the bone-setter, a performer of messy abortions, a man to patch up stab wounds and dispose of dead babies. Thin children played barefoot by the slimy pools. 'Do you know where I can find Pettro Negro the bone-setter?' The children shook their heads. A fleshy matron leaned from a nearby window and emptied a stinking pot. Framed by tatty shutters she became a fat angel with damaged wings. 'Do you know where I can find Pettro Negro the bone-setter?' She spat and slammed the shutters. Two old men played chess on the wall at the edge of a well. 'Do you know where I can find Pettro Negro the bone-setter?' 'Check,' said one to the other.

The hour approached noon but the sun still avoided the gaps between these scrawny buildings. Sometimes I reached a main thoroughfare, a street I knew, the Via Larga or the Borgo Gola Noce, where the sun reached down, warmed the stones, made patterns on the church fronts, but when this happened I turned back into the dark alleys, the dim warren. The pain in my head was fading in that stinking gloom, which was a blessing. I looked for someone else to ask and saw, beneath a faded canvas canopy, a familiar figure counting coins. 'Angelo?' I asked, uncertain that it was him, uncertain I wanted it to be him, but needing help in my search.

'Sandro Botticelli.' Angelo had won a scar since last I saw him, and it pulled his thick lips up at one side. 'What brings you here? Not your usual haunts.'

'I'm looking for Pettro Negro the bone-setter.'

'Are you now?' Angelo carried a sword and played with it, flicking it out of its scabbard and letting it slide back in.

'Do you know where I can find him?'

'Yes.'

I waited for Angelo to continue; Angelo waited for whatever advantage his lumbering mind could get from the situation. 'Can you tell me?' I asked at last.

'Perhaps.'

'Will you tell me?'

'What's it worth?'

'Money? I haven't much.'

'A favour then. I do you this favour, you do me one some time. Fair?'

'I suppose so.'

Angelo nodded and spat to seal the bargain. 'Come with me.'

We returned through streets I recognized, past the well where the old men played chess, and into a grimy yard surrounded by buildings. 'Up there,' said Angelo. 'Top of the stairs. There's just the one door; knock and ask for Pettro.'

I expect I would have worked out the last of your instructions on my own, I thought. 'Thank you,' I said.

'You owe me a favour. Remember.'

I did not know why he was so insistent on this: he had not done so much, and talked as though he had saved my life. His scar distorted his expression, made it hard to read. 'I remember.'

'I'll leave you then.' He turned away, his sword clattering against the dirty walls. 'See you around.'

I climbed the dark twisting stairs. Dank smells lingered. Something I trod on gave underfoot, squelching. At the top of the stairs was the single door. I knocked. 'Pettro Negro?' I called.

Bolts were drawn back and a key turned. The door opened a short way and an elderly woman peered out. 'Yes?'

'I'm looking for Pettro.'

'Come in.'

The crone led me into rooms that were surprisingly well lit. I blinked the darkness of the stairwell from my eyes. Pettro's rooms looked out over the skyline, over the tumble of red roofs and the jumble of towers towards San Miniato, but there was no sign of Pettro himself. 'Son!' called the crone. 'Visitor!'

Pettro Negro waddled amiably out from behind a curtain. He wore no hose beneath his tunic, and the knees of his heavy legs were splayed as though he rode some invisible horse. 'What can I do for you?' he asked.

'My master has broken his arm. He wants the bone fixing.'

Pettro asked no names. 'Far from here?'

'No.'

He seemed relieved. His invisible long-suffering horse was doubtless just as glad.

'Eight florins then.' There seemed to be a fixed rate of charges.

It wasn't my money. 'If you insist.'

'I insist.' Pettro nodded, squeezing new chins from round his neck. 'Come on then. I'll see you later, Mother!' he called, picking up a canvas bag.

The church bells were striking for the hour after noon when we reached Jacopo's shop. The friar was still on the floor, but now with his hose intact, and Jacopo was trying to work. There was the familiar stench of size, like dead fish, in the room. 'I've brought the bone-settter,' I announced, and Jacopo looked relieved.

'I think Fra Lippo's asleep,' he said.

'Of course I'm not asleep,' said the friar, his eyes still closed. 'How could I sleep through this pain?'

Fra Lippo thumped the floor with his good arm to distract from the pain as the bone-setter rolled up a sleeve to examine the damage. 'Skin not broken,' announced Pettro Negro. 'I'll soon have it straight.'

'Is there any aqua vitae left?' asked the friar. His face was white except round his eyes. There it was green.

'No. Sandro drank it all,' said Jacopo, sheepishly, as though telling a joke he knew was not funny.

'Wine?'

'I'll send for some.' Jacopo called an apprentice, who hurried away and soon returned with a large jug. Fra Lippo snatched the jug and started to swallow greedily. Red lines like thin blood dribbled into his beard.

'That's enough,' said Pettro Negro professionally. He took the jug from the friar and finished the contents in a couple of gulps. His face was red and shiny already: the wine he spilt barely showed. From his bag the bone-setter fetched out a phial of powder. 'Mix this with water,' he told me. 'Make a thin paste.' I did as required. The substance that resulted was a kind of gesso or plaster-of-Paris. 'Ready,' announced Pettro Negro.

He took the friar's arm in his hands and started to twist. Fra Lippo gagged, breathed in sharply, gagged again. Pettro gritted his teeth and tugged harder. I can still hear the ends of the bone grate together; I gag myself as I write. Fra Lippo Lippi had been racked in 1450 for taking an assistant's wages, and they say he had joked with his torturers, asked that they did not stretch him too much as he couldn't afford new hose. He had been caught in a plague in Siena, almost starved to death in the quarantine, and laughed that it was the first time he had seen his penis in years. He was not laughing now. His eyes were screwed so tightly shut that the lids had disappeared between the wrinkles. He bit his lip so hard that blood welled between his few teeth. The bone scraped together again. The bone-setter sweated. The friar, it seemed, passed out.

'That should do it,' panted Pettro. Jacopo had turned away and supported himself on the table; I nodded weakly. The bone-setter dipped a rag into the paste I had made and then wound the wet rag round the injured arm. He did the same with several more rags. 'That'll hold him,' he said, tying the last of the rags into a neat knot. 'Eight florins please.'

Fra Lippo opened an eye. 'Not so fast,' he said. 'that's the wrong arm.'

We looked at one another, Jacopo, Pettro and I, and then back at Fra Lippo, who winked. 'Only fooling,' he said.

'Eight florins,' repeated the bone-setter.

I had no money; Fra Lippo carried no purse. Jacopo had to pay.

Fra Lippo was away from the studio for several weeks. Clients came and went, but none were surprised with the friar's absence. He was notoriously unreliable. If the clients were not worried, however, those of us in his studio were, and the tradesmen I had to visit each morning were starting to worry too. 'Fra Lippo's away on business,' I told them. 'Important commission. Lots of money. He'll be back soon.' Most of it was a lie, but I hoped the last part was true.

The friar eventually returned at the beginning of August, with his arm still useless, his 9-year-old son Filippino in tow, and a bag of coin at his waist. The bag of coin covered about as much of our debts as it covered his wide stomach, but we satisfied our most pressing creditors and then borrowed some more. 'The more I owe them,' said the friar, 'the more they have to support me. They know that if I go out of business they'll not get anything back, so it's in their interest to keep me in business.'

The problem with this argument was that Fra Lippo was already out of business, forced out by the injury to his arm. The friar took me to one side. 'Sandro,' he said, draping his good arm around me. 'I've been watching your progress. You're better than I expected: you're going to make a good artist, no question. How'd you like to work on something important?'

Of course I would! 'I'd be honoured,' I said.

'Good.' He led me to an unfinished panel, a Madonna and Child. The background, a vermilion curtain and a series of white arches, had been completed by Jacopo before he left us, and Fra Lippo had begun the ruddle underpainting of the figure of Mary before his accident, but her face and most of her draperies were no more than a blank space, while the Child was just an outline crossed with charcoal strokes. 'I want you to finish that.'

'Me!'

'Who else? Gentile, Giovanni, Andrea, Cristoforo? None of them could do it. But you, perhaps you can.'

I shook my head.

'It doesn't matter,' he said, sounding not at all disappointed. 'That's the end of it then. I should get some money for the lease on this shop. We can return the pigments we haven't used, which means our bill at the apothecary's won't be too high. I won't have enough to settle all your wages but that's the way of it, sorry.'

'All right,' I said. I recognized extortion when I heard it. 'I'll try.'

I have never tried harder, nor been tried so hard. Carefully, under the friar's direction, I worked on the figure of the Mother of God. We arranged clothes on a wire frame to get the draperies right. We used Tullio's handsome face, made suitably effeminate, for the model. Gradually the figure filled out. The blue robes, which were painted in the most expensive ultramarine drawn from the first soaking of the lapis lazuli, took on light when I touched the highlights with a brush of dry biacca. The face became luminous with a thin overpainting of tempera. I worked all the hours of daylight, and blessed the season for being summer, and Angelo came round.

'Nice work,' he said, barely looking. 'You owe me a favour.'

'Not now,' I said. 'You can see I'm busy.'

'I was busy when we met up last. I still did you a good turn.'

'It took you no time at all.'

'This won't take long either. I've a letter needs delivering.'

'Deliver it yourself,' I said.

He looked as crafty as his solid scarred features would allow. 'I'd rather you delivered it,' he said.

'Where to?'

'There'll be a man at the S'Gallo gate this evening. Be there at sunset. You'll recognize him by his scarlet turban. Give him this.'

If he wanted me there at sunset at least I would not waste any painting time. It was too dark to work in the shop well before the sun went down. 'If I must,' I said, and he handed me a sealed letter. 'And now we're quits. All right?'

'Fine.' He smiled and went. On his way out he swept a pile of colours and pots off a neighbouring table with a deliberate forearm, and smiled again.

I looked at the letter. There were several seals on it; it would be impossible to read it secretly, and anyway I was not sure I wanted to. I decided to deliver it, get it out of my life, and think no more about it. I managed the first of these resolutions with ease. The man in the scarlet turban was waiting at the gate, innocently cleaning his nails with the point of a knife. There were few other people about, and he was the only one loitering. I walked up to him and offered the letter. He looked at it, and at me, then nodded; the last I saw of him he was carrying it towards the livery stable at the back of San Zanobi. I went back to the workshop.

Fra Lippo was pleased with my Madonna, though not uncritical. 'The face lacks animation,' he decided. 'Can't you purse the lips a little more, make it look like she's about to say something to the baby instead of just waiting for it to shit on her knee?'

'I'll do my best,' I sighed.

At last I had finished, and the varnishing began. Others could do that; I was tired, relieved, and a little proud. The Madonna was not inferior to the rest of the painting: it looked like Fra Lippo's work and, though the face perhaps still lacked animation, there was a beauty and serenity there that was appropriate. We had a drink that night, and the next day the conspirators struck.

Piero e' Medici was out of Florence, ill as usual and recovering at his villa of Careggi, when Niccolò Soderini and Luca Pitti, with their followers, rode into the Piazza della Signoria and proclaimed that the Medici were criminals, to be exiled or executed, and that the Medici fortune was forfeit; what the conspirators did not know was that Piero had been warned of the conspiracy and, with his sons, was on his way back to Florence. While Niccolò gloated in the Palazzo della Signoria, and Luca worried in the Pitti palace, Piero arrived in the city and confused everyone by behaving as though nothing had happened. My work at the shop temporarily over, I was among the crowd outside the Medici palace when Luca Pitti, his naturally white hair looking like a jolt of fear, rushed in to surrender to Piero: Piero took Luca to a window and shook his hand in front of us all; though the followers of Niccolò Soderini were armed and on the street the conspiracy was already finished. There was little fighting. Soderini and his closest friends were exiled, and life in Florence returned to normal, which for me meant forging the friar's style and worrying that, in the round-up of conspirators, my function as a delivery-boy would be discovered.

I did not have long to wait. Tommaso Soderini visited the shop. This was not unusual, for Tommaso was a friend of Fra Lippo, but it worried me: though he was Niccolò's brother, Tommaso was no supporter of Niccolò's actions; he was also Piero de' Medici's brother-in-law, frequently with the Medici when they worshipped at San Lorenzo and an important member of the Party of the Plain, so when he came over to me and said, 'You're Sandro Filipepi, aren't you? I heard about the letter,' my stomach slopped into my throat.

'Letter?' I asked, wondering when the soldiers would be called in to arrest me. I hoped they wouldn't torture me before they killed me.

Tommaso smiled again, and left.

1502

That was a time of guilt, of guiltily forging my master's art and guiltily awaiting my arrest for treason; this is a time of confession. Fra Agostino is my confessor. He is good to me. They are all good to me here. 'Our Sandro,' they call me as I limp about the madhouse and, like the monkey-man, I am indulged. The monkey-man is tossed titbits and allowed to sleep in the tree in the centre of the courtyard; I am given pens and paper. The rest are restrained, locked in bleak cells, saved from tearing their flesh by chains, but the monkey-man and I, we like it here. The monkey-man adores his tree. He knows his way around it: the boughs are smoothed by his palms where he hangs; he has knocked off the twigs that might scratch him as naked he swings through the branches. He has simplified and polished the tree, moulded it to suit his needs. There is less evidence of my presence. I am too feeble to swing from trees. The straw palette and the crucifix in my cell are as they were when I arrived; I can fasten no drawings to the rough-plastered walls. Yet, like the monkey-man, I have made this my home.

It is not the most dignified existence. Some of my companions in this madhouse would count it a treat to drink their piss. They sit in their mess all day, naked and covered in sores, or are strapped to the walls by chafing chains. Flies lick from their sores. Their lives are monotony and anguish. Any variation will do. In summer the smell is strong. I receive few visitors in summer.

Even the stench does not deter Simone, my surviving brother, from visiting me, though all he comes for is to tell me to leave. 'Why do you stay in this madhouse?' he asks, more concerned for my dignity than I have the right to be. He is a year older than I, and his hearing is poor. He speaks too loudly.

My reply is always much the same. 'I'm too old and crippled to be much use out there,' I say, my voice not loud enough. He frowns, as though screwing up his face might make what I say audible. I continue. 'I'm safe here. I'm fed, I'm kept warm. I like it here.'

Whether or not he has heard me this time is irrelevant. He has heard me in the past. 'You can live with Gabrielle and me again,' he says, but I shake my head. Simone was always the steadiest of our father's sons, and made some money in his time in Naples, but I shared a house with him and his wife once before, in Savonarola's day, and would not want to repeat the experience. My devotion to God is no less than theirs, except in the demands it makes. Because of their piety I had to wear a hair shirt; because of their piety I committed two of my best paintings to the Bonfire of the Vanities; because of their piety I drank no burnt wine for four years, and the threadworms drove me mad. Besides, he has grown mean with age. At least in the madhouse I am allowed candles and can work on this memoir in the sleepless nights. But of course I say none of this, even though he probably would not hear me if I did, and simply smile and shake my head.

Actually, even if I wanted to live with them it probably would not be wise. His wife no longer likes me. She was fond enough – too fond – in the days before the moth got into my head, the days when I was famous and successful, but now, when my fame is almost gone and my success has vanished entirely, I cannot see Gabrielle wanting me in the house. Simone, in his loyalty to us both, has not noticed how little she likes me now, just as he never noticed how much she liked me before. A smile and a shake of the head is the only appropriate response I can make. Simone, his aged eyes as blue and innocent as Fra Lippo Lippi's, and with rather more cause, shakes his head too and smiles back.

I belong in the madhouse.

Perhaps it is because I belong here, or perhaps because I still have the instincts of a painter that, although I can look back on my life and see a kind of parabola, an arrow that climbs from my unpromising early years, arches across years of success and fame, and descends rapidly through madness to this place and this time, I am unwilling to describe events simply in the order that they happened. Events in a narrative happen one at a time. One word is placed after the next, one episode leads into another. A painting is apprehended completely and simultaneously. More often than it seems a parabola, my life seems to me like a painting. The young apprentice who fears arrest occurs alongside the madman who painted his youth on a mirror and the old man who writes this all down. When a fly crawls over a canvas I expect it takes in the details one by one, here a woman's foot pressing on the grass, there a pennon hanging limply from a lance; it can recognize the pattern in what it sees only when it flies some way from the canvas and looks back. And perhaps, should some scholar in some future age trouble to read the story of my love, he too will find only the details to begin with, the pennon and the foot. But the painter, the madman and I, we are fired like three arrows aimed on the same trajectory, and will land, thut-thut-thut, in the same place. We were launched by my love for Simonetta. We hurtle across these pages. Soon we shall converge in death.

And perhaps there is another pattern to my life. Like my city, which after ten years of war is still unable to recapture Pisa, I am weak and incapable of performing tasks that once I managed with ease; like my city, which is now no more than a pawn in the machinations of the emperor and the pope, a gaming piece in the contest between the kings of France and Spain, I have been marginalized; like my city, I was not always so negligible. This is the story of my love, not the story of my life. The story of my life must end with my death and I have no wish to tell such a tale, not here, not now. But remember who I once was. The Sandro of the golden age sat with the Medici, talked with Politian, Ficino and Pico, painted for Pope Sixtus; even in his madness he believed himself honoured by God.

1498

The madman trudged through the city. God, who in his jealousy had stolen Simonetta away, had returned her to him at last. He searched through darkened streets. The city, though clad in the velvet that night makes of stonework, the silk that night makes of brick, was recognizably the same as that the apprentice knew. The time of building was over. The differences lay mostly in the details. Wherever the apprentice would have found the arms of the Medici the madman would see only a chiselled ruin, an unadorned bare shield or the painted red cross of the republic. The front of the Palazzo della Signoria, the seat of Florence's government, held many torches in heavy iron brackets which were there to illuminate the decomposing head of some traitor or another, and by their light the madman could see Donato di Betto Bardi's vicious bronze of Judith beheading Holofernes; in the apprentice's day the statue had been in the Medici palace. The same artist's statue of David had also been removed from the palace to the Piazza, and stood on a column which towered over the madman's search for his beloved.

Hurriedly, Sandro the Mad crossed the deserted square. In lieu of citizens the leaves of distant trees seemed to have asembled there. The leaves were passive a long time, and then a demagogue wind blew and blustered, pushed them about the piazza, separated and reunited them. Disdainful as a tyrant, Sandro ignored the petitioning leaves, the rotting head, and made his way to the market by Orsanmichele. Set in the walls of the church of Orsanmichele are statues paid for and commemorating the craft guilds. Each trade has its own traditions, its own risks. My father was a tanner, smearing the dirt of dogs on to hides to cure them and spending his day in a fog of fat flies; my brother made casks, until a loose barrel crushed his legs and he died; lead miners grow slow and stupid, as though their heads and bodies have accumulated a weight of heavy metal, and their children are often imbeciles with gaping mouths and lolling tongues who cry 'Piero, Piero' to the winds. In my trade too we use much lead – in the preparation of primer for the canvas as well as for the biacca, the white we use for all except fresco painting – and I have heard it suggested that we too suffer in the mind because of this. Certainly, many painters have been mad. Paolo Uccello spent his later years not painting but working out more and more elaborate schemes of perspective, ways of showing the recession on increasingly awkward shapes, until his mind at last reached its vanishing point; the great German called Hugo van der Goes, whose altarpiece for the Portinari family made such an impression on us when it arrived in Florence in 1475, spent his last years in a monastery and believed he was Jesus Christ; Donato Bardi, who is known as Donatello, was insane in old age, kept his money in a bag suspended from the roof so anyone who wanted could help himself, and as a joke gave the farm he had earned from Piero de' Medici to a peasant; Leonardo da Vinci, in my opinion, has always been out of his mind; Sandro Botticelli, at that moment, rivalled them all in his lunacy.

It was a cold night. The church of Orsanmichele was shut up and locked. There were mercenary soldiers, of Paolo Vitelli's company, garrisoned in the city. They had been employed to recapture Pisa, but in September Guidobaldi Montefeltro, the duke of Urbino, had led a Venetian army against our eastern borders, where the troops of Ottaviano Rario messed up, and Vitelli's men had been recalled to help defend the city. The wind blew down from the Alps, through Lombardy, through Tuscany, through Sandro's cloak. The whores of the Orsanmichele retreated from the cold, retired to the warm scented comfort of the candlemakers' huts. The mercenaries left the walls unguarded and huddled round fires in the watchtowers or followed the whores. The candlemakers, the only craftsmen who work at that hour, manufactured six-inch columns of wax, and in the back of the stalls the whores and soldiers between them moulded similar shapes out of flesh. It was here I saw Simonetta, thought Sandro. She wore, in addition to men's clothing, the colours of the

Soderini family on her sleeve. Niccolò Soderini, who had earned me my broken nose, was long dead; his brother Tommaso, who had earned me much more, was dead too; the current head of the Soderini household was Piero, a pleasant, inoffensive man whose only offence in my eyes is that he favours Michelangelo too much. Sandro walked down the street of candlemakers. A fine rain began to fall but Sandro, obsessed, did not notice. He was looking for Simonetta and also, with equal lack of reason, looking for Angelo. Angelo had often gone with the whores; his thick masculine presence seemed to haunt the moonless street, but perhaps it was less his ghost than the accumulated ghosts of a hundred thousand such masculine presences, including that of my father and my mentor. The softly scented stalls were a place of women, where men were fondled visitors, but the streets of Florence, despite the feminine contours of Brunelleschi's dome, have always been a place of men. Sandro was getting wet in the rain. He would be very much wetter before the night was out, and the rain would have nothing to do with it, but meanwhile, in another time in the same city, the apprentice was in fear for his life.

1467

Fra Lippo chided me. 'Why can't you paint a smile for a change? It's meant to be a Nativity; it looks like a funeral.'

'I'm sorry,' I said, apologizing for my secrecy as well as my miserable paintings. I was ashamed to tell him why I was worried, for though my treachery had been small, it had not been inadvertent: I had known Angelo's loyalties well enough.

In fact, I did not believe it was important if my figures smiled or not. The quality of the painting seemed to matter little, either to me or anyone else. Nothing I did or could do counted for much. Fra Lippo, unable to paint, had lost interest in getting commissions, and as the new year began he was forced to let his assistants go. He would have said goodbye to the apprentices too, except our indentures had been paid in advance. We spent the days painting wedding chests and carnival floats; the only canvas I painted in the first part of the year was a banner to hang from a barber's shop! One day, as I was going up the stairs to the gallery, the friar called to me. 'Sandro! Have you a moment?'

I went back down to him. I was doing nothing else. There was nothing particular to do.

'This won't take long,' said the friar.

I was concerned. The friar's voice was serious, sad yet resigned: bad news was coming, a complaint about my work perhaps, or worse, news I was to be arrested.

Fra Lippo looked at me. 'I'm leaving Florence,' he said.

'Leaving?'

'For good.'

I was almost aghast. The shop was in a bad way, and so was the friar. Unable to work, he had been drinking, and though both his son and his son's mother Lucrezia were now living with him I knew he spent his nights whoring more voraciously than ever. But I had not expected him to leave the bottega, even less that he should leave Florence. Why should anyone ever leave Florence? Where else was there to go?

'Lucrezia and I are going to Spoleto,' the friar continued. 'They want me to paint some more frescos in the cathedral there. I don't intend to come back; I want you to take over the shop.'

'Me?' Now I was genuinely aghast.

'Tommaso Soderini will help,' said the friar.

'Tommaso Soderini!' Each shock was worse than the last, and I had run out of reactions. Was this some kind of veiled warning, or a cruel joke at my expense?

'He tells me he's taken quite a liking to you.'

What was going on? Was Tommaso playing with me as a cat plays with a mouse? Or did he really like me, in which case his loyalty to the Medici was in question? Whichever it was, I wanted nothing to do with it.

Fra Lippo, I was sure, knew nothing about the intrigues that obsessed me. In all Florence, he was the man least interested in politics: while other men conspired to change the government Fra Lippo was bedding their wives. When he saw my hesitation he mistook its cause. 'I know you haven't finished your apprenticeship. I'm sure we can do something about that.'

I barely considered this. I had more urgent concerns. I listened as the friar continued.

'You're the best apprentice I ever had,' added Fra Lippo encouragingly.

He had never told me this before. It was good to hear but inadequate to help me. Anything short of a public pardon would have been inadequate.

'Think about it,' said the friar. 'You can have the shop, and the apprentices. I'll maybe leave little Filippino too: I'll set the cost of his apprenticeship against the lease on this shop, so we'll be square. I know you and Filippino get on because I've seen you talking, and he's very keen to paint: it's time he started learning the trade.

Besides, I don't know I'd want to take him to Spoleto; he's so serious, so pious, it bothers me having him around. I don't know why but he thinks I'm wonderful, thinks I'm some kind of saint.'

'It's your pictures,' I told him, speaking without expression. 'He thinks your pictures are Holy.'

'Did he say that?' The friar sounded genuinely pleased. 'Isn't that charming!'

There was a silence while he considered, perhaps for the first time in his life, the compensations of fatherhood, and while my thoughts followed their less cheerful course. 'So?' asked Fra Lippo. 'You'll take over? I'm doing this as a favour to you, you understand? It doesn't make any difference to me, except I'd be better off if I sold the lease to the shop.'

'I'm – surprised,' I said.

'Of course you are. Talk it over with your brother. I've already mentioned it to him. And to Tommaso. Tommaso's coming round soon, promised he would. You can't have a better friend in Florence than Tommaso. I'm sure both he and Giovanni will help all they can. But I'll be leaving by Easter, so you haven't long to make up your mind.'

As he turned away I felt ungrateful. It was a wonderful opportunity. Fra Lippo wasn't to know that Tommaso Soderini was playing games. 'Father,' I said, out of reverence for his title, and out of affection too. 'I can't take up your offer.'

'Frightened?' asked Fra Lippo, curt, hurt.

'In a way. But not in the way you mean.' I explained, hesitantly but dutifully, about the letter, about Tommaso Soderini, about my fears. It was good to speak to someone about it, but if I had expected sympathy I was wrong. His reaction to my fear was good-natured contempt: if I was in trouble then so be it, but Fra Lippo, who had spent a lifetime in trouble, was not going to weep for me.

'That's it then,' he said when I had finished, and he referred to my chances of taking over the studio rather than to my story.

'That's it,' I agreed.

He left me then, and Florence three weeks later. The lease on the shop was sold and for a while I stayed with my brother Giovanni. But his house was small and his wife Nera resentful so, with nowhere else to go, I returned to my father's house in the Borgo Ognissanti. I carried a weight of worries with me as well as my equipment. When I arrived at my father's Filippino Lippi was waiting for me. His father had left him at the convent of Santa Maria del Carmine, where he had been a brother, but the friars, worried about taking on yet another Lippi, even one so apparently mild as Filippino, had sent him to find me. I felt I had become a kind of father, a virgin father.

My own father's house was not large, but as my brothers were married and my mother dead there was room for Filippino and me. I told my father some lie about Fra Lippo sending money on to pay for Filippino's keep, then climbed up the stairs to my room. I had been away sixteen months, and though I had never left the city in that time I felt as though I had travelled the breadth of Cathay like Marco the Venetian, fought battles and dragons, lost every time. Returning home was admitting defeat. My father had never shown much faith in my ambition to be a painter, and now I had proved him right. Yet I also felt comforted. I lay on the straw pallet in my room. The ceiling was as it had been, and so were the walls, the floor, the view from the window. I closed my eyes and slept.

These days I count myself old, which I am. It is not just the years that make me feel old, though I have almost sixty winters behind me, so much as the death of my friends. Filippino is the only one left, and he is in Rome as he has been for twenty years. I have seen him only occasionally since then, and the last time was under the most dreadful of circumstances. I shall not be seeing him again. He is infirm and will not leave Rome's ruined colonnades; nothing in Christendom could induce me back to Rome. Yet I miss him dreadfully. He is a fine man and a fine painter, yet perhaps it is the boy he once was I miss most – that serious, busy boy who nagged me from my bed, made me paint that day and the next, made me continue to work at my art – for in missing him I regret the passing of my own youth.

In the next month there was action. The exiled survivors of the Party of the Hill joined the condottiere Bartolommeo Colleoni and his Venetian paymasters in a final attack on Piero de' Medici. The city was unusually unanimous. Niccolò Soderini was a Florentine – there is no stigma to exile, as all Florentines of note are exiled from time to time – and he had his supporters in the city still, while

Colleoni was respected as well as feared, but the notion of Florence being in thrall to the Venetians was resented; Piero could justly claim to be fighting not only for himself but for the freedom of the city. Even I, in fear of Medici revenge, obviously safer should the conspirators win, felt no sympathy with Colleoni's invasion. We cheered Piero's mercenary army when it left Florence, and cheered louder when it returned victorious. Filippino and I went with my father to the Piazza de' Medici. It was raining steadily but the crowd was large. I had mixed motives perhaps in being there. I wanted to cheer Florence's deliverance, and I wanted to be seen to be cheering. It was unreasonable to assume that I would be recognized by Piero, much less pardoned on the spot. It was less unreasonable to assume that one of his agents might recognize me; after all, I had been recognized before. Perhaps I would be watched as I watched, and my evident enthusiasm for the Medici cause might earn me a pardon?

As it was, Filippino, on my father's back, was the only one who saw much of the proceedings. Benozzo Gozzoli had designed a triumphant arch of wood and painted canvas – I wonder if, suitably modified, it would have greeted Niccolò Soderini had he won? – and white flags bearing the red fleur-de-lis of Florence or gold flags marked with the red palla of the Medici drooped, heavy with rainwater, from all the balconies facing the square, but of the returning heroes I could see nothing. Just behind me a pitiable idiot called 'Piero! Piero!' too loud: his tongue seemed too big for his mouth, and robbed the words of meaning. By him a married couple, oblivious of the crowd, conducted a private argument, and their marriage dissolved as rapidly as a wedding cake would in that rain. In front of me two Dominicans, whose monastery of San Marco had been largely paid for by Medici money, consoled themselves for the soaking they were getting with the thought that they were escaping Vespers. A standard Florentine crowd, passionate, indifferent, or cynical, but always available to cheer a victor. And I, who cheered to atone for past disloyalties, was perhaps as typical as any.

A louder cheer suggested the victory parade was in sight. Several people started to climb Gozzoli's arch. I saw pennons and flags march above the crowd, and heard tambours, and then watched as the triumphal arch, the canvas sodden with rainwater, the frame threatened by the weight of spectators, began slowly and ominously to sag. There were shouts of panic. I saw a soldier, his red and white pennons still held in his hand, rise above the crowd on his rearing horse before being shrugged off. And then the arch crumpled, and several people were killed.

The parade was abandoned; Piero, we learnt, went to the house of his Tornabuoni relatives, and we went home, tired and wet. Some of those returning with us carried scraps of Gozzoli's canvas, artfully painted to represent marble but fooling no one now, as souvenirs. Everyone seemed satisfied by the day's events. Few mourned the tragic dead, fewer still recognized the tragedy. The only tragedy in Florence, then or now, is to be bored. Our problem today is that we, who once led the world, have ourselves become boring. The future has been washed down the Arno like Savonarola's ashes; it has turned to ash in our hands.

1468

The procession of months was interrupted less easily than the victory parade. Summer became autumn. A poor harvest was gathered. The leaves fell. Damp fallen leaves were a mulch; dry ones became filigree and feathers. The price of bread went up, so we ate many chestnuts that season. Winter came, and I went to the Duomo with Filippino and my father to celebrate the Christmas Mass. Piero de' Medici was absent from the cathedral, it was noticed, and there were new rumours about his failing health.

It was a bad time for me. My father never criticized. He went to work each dawn, returned home each dusk, as he always had, and in the evening we dined together. But we who had never been close became if anything more distant in that time. My inadequacies, my treacheries, and the cost of my incomplete apprenticeship made me uncomfortable with him. I owed him too much to love him.

Filippino was the happiest in the household. Life with his mother Lucrezia Buti in Prato had, I gathered, been difficult. Lucrezia, alienated from her family because of her bastard son, alternated between anxiously awaiting Fra Lippo's visits, and repenting the day she, a nun, had allowed herself to be seduced; sometimes, between the friar's visits, mother and child were hungry, living for days on acorns or flavourless soup boiled and boiled again from the same cabbage. We did not live richly in the Ognissanti, but we lived much better than that. Now Filippino was at school, and in the afternoons when school was out I taught him draughtsmanship, how to produce a smooth outline and where to put shade, how to see the world as shadow and light and reproduce it accordingly, and how to form figures in various poses. I did a little work on my own behalf at that time, a *cassone* for the daughter of a neighbour, a portrait of our butcher's son, but without indentures and without a shop I neither expected nor received commissions. My career, it seemed, was already over; my only relief was that with every passing day arrest seemed less likely. My crime would never be forgiven or forgotten, but perhaps I was too negligible to be worth a place in gaol.

In the spring of the next year a copyist who lived in Borgo Ognissanti died and, because I was able to read and had time on my hands, his widow asked me to help her put her husband's possessions in order. It was not easy. The poor man had clearly taken on more work than he could ever have accomplished, for the house was full of manuscripts. Sometimes it was unclear where the manuscripts had come from, sometimes it was unclear whom the copies were intended for, and after we had sorted everything out we were left with two books. We had the copyist's version of a vernacular translation of part of Virgil's Aeneid, and a manuscript of Alberti's treatise on painting written in an unknown hand.

It is hard, now that printed books are so common, to remember how unusual any book was in my youth. We saw prayer books of course, and Bibles, in church, but there were no books in most people's houses. The widow tried to sell the two books remaining, but the price she was offered was an insult so, as a reward for my help, she offered the Alberti to me. I suppose she thought, as I had once been a pupil to a painter, I would find the book interesting. But I had studied Alberti at Fra Lippo's shop – the advice the book contains is good but the theory is sometimes impractical – and anyway I was not sure I would ever be a serious painter again. I declined the Alberti; she insisted I took the Virgil instead. Dante placed Virgil in Hell, and Savonarola burnt Virgil's books, but I believe God put the work into my hands deliberately. In that slow underemployed season I must have read my fragment of the Aeneid a dozen times. It was as good an investment of time as any I have made, a preparation for better days to come.

On the half-days when his abacus school was closed Filippino liked to walk through the street of painters. There were some forty painters' shops in Florence at that time, and the most successful and important was Verrocchio's. My father and I both warned Filippino about Verrocchio's reputation with boys, but our warnings – which were made ambiguous by our embarrassment – were not enough to stop Filippino spending many hours at Verrocchio's bottega. And as it happened our warnings were unnecessary: Verrocchio was completely besotted with a pupil he had recently taken on, a handsome and conceited young man from Vinci, and was spending all his time trying to please his new apprentice; as an example of this, when the inexperienced apprentice had begged to take over an important commission, a Baptism of Christ, Verrocchio, against all sense, had agreed.

This young man of course was Leonardo, whose exaggerated reputation today is one of the few banes of my otherwise peaceful retirement. I have never understood what others see in Leonardo. As a youth he was vain, over-confident and incompetent, and nothing has changed. He has a certain facility with chalk and paint, it is true, and I am told by those I trust that the Last Supper he painted for the monks of Santa Maria delle Grazie in Milan is very beautiful, but his impatience and arrogance mean that everything he paints either falls off the boards or is incomplete: even this Last Supper, I gather, suffers these failings, and with any luck will soon slide off the walls and out of the room entirely.

In that spring of 1468, Leonardo was quite unknown, while what little reputation I had was as Fra Lippo's pupil. But Verrocchio, though foolish in love, was no fool in art. He had acquired a Virgin and Child which was meant to be by Fra Lippo, and with the advantage of expert knowledge had recognized at once that much of it was not painted in the friar's hand. Filippino brought the message. 'Verrocchio wants to meet you,' he said. 'Before sundown, at his shop.'

Verrocchio was alone when I arrived. He held the small panel of the Virgin and Child beneath a window and rotated it, exposing the brushwork to the low evening sun. 'You see the grain of the brushstrokes?' he asked, letting me look at the painting. 'Fra Lippo paints with a full brush. This drapery looks like his work. But the child and the face of the Madonna, though well painted, are clearly the work of another. Look at the way the shadow has been laid round the Virgin's eye.' I did not need to look 'Lippi would have done that with a single stroke, whereas whoever painted this has chosen to work the surface, and has even introduced a new colour between the flesh tone and the dark shadow. Rather effective, actually. But mysterious. It is common for the *garzone* to paint the drapery and the master to paint the flesh, but this seems to have been done the other way round. You were in Lippi's bottega: how do you explain it?'

'I can't,' I said.

Verrocchio laughed. 'Can't you? Then it's as well the friar's boy could. Young Filippino says you painted the flesh. He doesn't strike me as the sort who would lie.'

I was silent.

'Don't worry. I bought the painting believing it was by Lippi, but I don't think any the less of it when I find it was painted by you. The painting's the thing, not the man who painted it. Once we're dead, do you think anyone will care whose hand held the brush? Of course not! It is only when we're alive and living by our reputations that things like that count. Which leads me to a rather delicate matter.'

He went over to a large panel suspended on a wooden scaffold. 'I have a very talented pupil called Leonardo,' he continued softly. 'I am fond of the boy and want him to do well, and I'd like him to take credit for this painting. Unfortunately, as you can see, there isn't much credit attached to it at present. Not that I'm criticizing,' he added quickly, looking round as though fearing that the absent apprentice might overhear us. 'This angel is as beautiful as he is, and all his own work! But you can see the problem.'

I certainly could. All Leonardo's shortcomings were apparent in the Baptism of Christ picture. Verrocchio had provided the cartoon, and Leonardo was meant simply to paint the picture up. Instead, with his usual misplaced certainty in his own abilities, Leonardo had replaced Verrocchio's angel with another which, though quite pretty, was completely out of character; worse, he had tried retouching the egg-based tempera with a sort of oil paint of his own invention, and produced a surface that was completely unworkable. Tempera would not cover the oil, and the oil refused to dry at all. It was clear why Verrocchio was despondent. The entire expensive panel, taller than a man and almost as wide, looked as if it might have to be scrapped.

'That angel could make Leonardo's reputation, I'm sure of it,' said Verrocchio. 'But if the rest of the painting is no good I'll not dare show it and no one'll know how wonderful Leonardo is. Now, I could cut the panel down, leave just the angel, except Leonardo has his heart set on producing a big picture. Or I could help Leonardo myself. I'm sure there are ways I could sort out this mess. But if I did, the credit for the picture would fall on me, and I don't want that to happen. On the other hand, Sandro – I can call you Sandro? – no one's heard of you. Because you're a good painter, but not a master, you could give Leonardo a hand without compromising his reputation. I'm not a poor man; I'll pay you well, better than Lippi ever did; it's worth it to save that angel. Isn't it beautiful? Isn't he wonderful?'

'Charming,' I agreed. The angel had attractive features: the attitude was more interesting than was usual in those days, for the figure had its back to the viewer, with the neck bent to show slightly more than the profile of a soft and handsome face, and the hair was exceedingly well painted. But I did not, and do not, understand why Verrocchio was so particularly enthusiastic: the drapery was unnatural, all straight lines and angles; the expression on its face was more arrogant than devout. I have been in love, desperately so, but that did not blind me to my loved one's faults, though perhaps I was fortunate, for Simonetta had none; Verrocchio, infatuated, seemed truly to believe that this paltry angel was the apex of the painter's art!

'You'll take the work then?' he asked.

It was hardly the most flattering commission, but better than painting butchers' sons the rest of my days. 'How much is it worth?'

'Twenty florins.'

It was more than I earned in a year at Fra Lippo's. 'I'll take it.'

I started work the next morning. Verrocchio had a large studio – four or five apprentices, and twelve assistants – but they were mostly involved in sculpture, so, as Leonardo had not arrived, I was left alone. My first job, clearly, was to clean off the oil paint but, although it was not properly dry, and never would be, it was stubborn stuff. No solution I could find in the bottega would clean it, and rubbing it with a cloth only made it smear. In the end I used a knife, scraping the sticky paint off the linen-covered board as carefully as I could. Even then I was not rid of it; it clung to whatever it touched, including me.

I was suddenly thrown to the floor, and there was the angel standing over me, breathing heavily and colouring furiously. 'What are you doing!' the angel cried.

I still had the knife in my hand. The angel, Leonardo I presumed, saw it and drew a knife of his own. He was young, perhaps 17 years of age. I was older, heavier, and much less angry. Today, with long white locks and a wise white beard, he has the aura of a saint. Then he was an angel. But I swear it: he tried to kill me. He threw the knife and it hit me in the heart. It hit butt first. A better throw would have made a big hole in Florence's artistic reputation.

Two *garzoni* held him off while Verrocchio attempted to calm him. 'It's all right. Dear Leo, it's all right. Sandro is going to help you.'

'He's ruining my work!'

'Too late for that!' I shouted back as I got to my feet. 'You got there first!'

He pulled an arm free and swung at me. I stepped back until he was pinned down again.

'Leo, Sandro, stop this,' said Verrocchio. 'You've got to make friends.' There was more chance of St Francis shaking hands with the Devil, but I was not going to throw twenty florins away. 'That's better,' he said, as I smiled meekly at Leonardo. 'Leo, dearest, you must understand. Sandro is going to help you finish the painting.'

'I don't need help. His or anyone else's.'

'I think you do,' said Verrocchio, but it was a plea more than a statement. 'Sandro is a very good painter, and more experienced than you. He's willing to let you take the credit for the picture, and to give you the benefit of his expertise, because he admires your work so much. Isn't that right, Sandro?'

I counted each of the twenty florins in my head, swallowed, and replied. 'That's right.' I have never been so treacherous to anyone as I was at that moment to myself; for that treachery I deserved to be hanged.

The work was predictably difficult. For a while we tried to paint side by side, he in his oils, while I used the more conventional egg tempera, but although Verrocchio had, after tears from both of them, managed to persuade Leonardo to use a more reliable oil, his paints and mine would not blend, while our mutual dislike made our work unco-ordinated and difficult. We came to an unspoken agreement whereby I would paint in the mornings while Leonardo did his painting in the afternoon, but this, from my point of view, was not a satisfactory system. His oils could overpaint my tempera – sometimes he had obliterated a full morning's work by the time I returned to the picture – but the tempera could not overpaint the oil paints. Another problem, as far as I was concerned, was that I painted much more quickly than he, so that in the end I had covered virtually all the board except his precious angel; he preferred to devote himself to trifles, which meant that he touched parts of the picture only. And, as I could not correct his corrections, all I could do was try to accommodate them. The collaboration was not a success.

The only compensation to working with a man of such insufferable vanity is that he never feels under threat. I suggested another angel, next to his; he, thinking my second-rate angel would show his to its best advantage, agreed. In a sense he was right, for the angel I painted clearly offers his no threat; it gazes, eyes full of worship, at Leonardo's, as though regretting it is not so beautiful, and only someone who knows, which means only me and now you, would recognize the sarcasm in that glance, in the way my angel looks away from Christ and worships Leonardo instead.

It is, without doubt, a lousy painting. I felt little need to produce my best work if Leonardo was going to repaint half I did, while he was too inconsistent in either approach or application to correct all I left undone. The rocks and foliage are mere sketches – the tree on the left of the picture is a joke – and the water in which John and Christ stand is not a flat surface, as water should be, but slopes up to the right. I did not care. If I did not get the credit, neither would I get the blame.

When I was paid, which was a month or so after I finished working on the Baptism – I cannot say that the painting itself was ever properly finished, if only because Leonardo continued to make alterations after I had gone – I took my father, Filippino, Jacopo, and a *garzone* from Verrocchio's shop, Ottaviano, to a tavern. I felt more comfortable with my father now that I owed him less, and Ottaviano loathed Leonardo as much as I did, which made him an ally. We drank a toast to the summer evening, and another to the mosquitoes that bothered the dusk. We drank to the Duomo, the campanile, and the city walls. We drank to the Medici. We drank to all the *popolo grosso* families we could think of in Florence: Acciaiuolo, Albizzi, Alessandri Altoriti, Antinori, Barbadori, Bardi, Bentivoglio, Capponi, Cavalcanti, Colonna, Corsini, Daranzati, Giudici, Guadagni,

Guasconi, Guicciardini, Malespini, Martelli, Neroni, Pazzi, Peruzzi, Petrucci, Pitti, Portinari, Pucci, Riccardi, Ricci, Ridolfi, Rucellai, Salviati, Soderini, Spini, Strozzi, Tornabuoni and Vespucci. The tavern became crowded. We toasted the artists, Baldovinetti, Castagno, Gozzoli, Lippi, Perugino, Pollaiuolo, Rosselli, Uccello, Verrocchio. We drank the health of our party, time and again, which did nothing for our health but much for our spirits. I described Leonardo and Verrocchio for them. 'There were two men in Heaven, and the first says, "God's painting a picture," so the second one asks, "Is God a good painter then?" to which the first replies, "He's not bad, but the trouble is he thinks he's Leonardo."' 'Why is Leonardo like the campanile? Because Verrocchio's been up them both.' The conversation became more general; Ottaviano and Jacopo told jokes of their own. 'What do you do if a Venetian treads in shit? Wash the shit!' 'What's the difference beween a live Roman and a dead fish? You get a better price for dead fish!' We must have been a merry party; the jokes seemed funny at the time. We drank to the pope and the emperor, to the kings of Aragon, Castile, Denmark, England, France, Hungary, Portugal, Naples, Norway, Poland, Scotland and Sweden, to the dukes of Ferrara, Milan, Melfi, Savoy, and Sessa, to the marquises of Mantua, Monferrat and Saluzzo, to the counts of Anguillara, Arco, Avellino, Catanzaro, Campobasso, Fondi, Gorizia, Montella, Montorio, Piedmont, Poppi and Urbino. My father began a story about a nun and a student, got confused, began to tell it again; Filippino fell off his stool; I blinked, stared, and was suddenly sober. 'How's my old friend Sandjro Bodjicelli?' asked Angelo, swaying as he leant over the table.

'Hello Angelo,' I said. I hadn't seen Angelo since he had handed me the letter. I had assumed he was in exile, or prison, or an unmarked grave.

'And is that Jacopo? Nice to meet you again. Who're your other friends?'

'My father,' I said briefly. 'Fra Lippo's son Filippino. Ottaviano da Novellara.'

'It's good to see you. I haven't seen you since,' he hiccupped and puzzled – 'you delivered that Medici letter. Good djay's work that.'

He was not quite slurred enough. 'What letter?' asked Jacopo, to be friendly. 'I didn't know you had dealings with the Medici, Sandro.'

'It was nothing,' I said.

'Don't be modest,' said Angelo. He nodded seriously, confidentially, towards the company. 'I was meant to be working for Niccolò Soderini, but I was a spy! I was the one that warned Piero of the plot! Sandro carried the letter. He saved Florence.'

I had the feeling I had misunderstood. My companions seemed to be having equal difficulty following what Angelo had said, or at least, no one commented; I grabbed Angelo by the beard and pulled his head down to the level of my mouth. 'You were working for Niccolò Soderini?' A nod in reply. 'But you were a spy?' Nod. 'You warned Piero de' Medici of the plot?' Nod. 'I carried the letter?' Nod. 'I saved Florence?' Nod. I let go of Angelo's beard; his scar grinned, his mouth blinked twice, and he sat on the floor.

'Sounds like you're a hero,' said Jacopo.

'Really. It was nothing,' I insisted.

The others were all for more toasts, proposing the towns and cities, Alba, Amalfi, Ancona, Aquileia, Arezzo, Assisi, Asti, Bari, Benevento, Bergamo, Bobbio, Bologna, Brindisi, Cesena, Chioggia, Chivasso, Como, Cortona, Crema, Cuneo, Durazzo, Faenza, Feltre, Ferrara, Firenza: Florence, Florence, Florence. Distracted, I looked down. Sitting on the floor, propped against a bench, was Angelo. He saw me looking and raised a friendly hand.

'You silly sod,' I said, uncertain even then if I meant him or me. I raised my drinking cup and smiled.

1502

The madmen are at their meal. They are herded out of their confinement into the square, and friars walk among them handing out bread and milk. Only the monkey-man and I are not in chains. The monkey-man grabs a broken loaf and scrambles back to his branches; I take mine with – I hope – more dignity and retire on my crutches to my cell. My gums are sore again, and I have to soak the bread in the milk before I can eat it. Through the window of my cell I watch the madmen's banquet. Their nakedness emphasizes the differences in their physiques. All the various shapes of man are represented except the beautiful. Polished paunches hang over shrunken loins. Vast penises sprout between fleshless thighs. Rib-cages like bony fingers grab at feeble lungs. There are disfigurements here, withered arms and hunched backs, twisted spines and damaged legs. Yet the variety is not as notable as the similarity. Shaved against lice, their heads, though sometimes burnished, sometimes furred with dark stubble, ripen like grapes. They share the same furtive eyes, eyes that have been defeated by the sun and the earth. And, large or small, strong or weak, they each clench their food in the same anxious gesture and huddle the bread to their mouths with the same furtive hands. Perhaps this is characteristic of the mad; the madman who walked down the Street of Candlemakers, the man I used to be, clutched his vision of Simonetta that way, as though wary it might be taken from him.

1498

He scuttled from doorway to doorway, his crutches rattling the dark. A group of armed Swiss mercenaries strolled down the centre of the street, confident and incomprehensible, like an army of occupation. A fat whore with thin hair and thin lips stepped from a stall and spat on the wet cobbles. A girl, perhaps 9 or 10 years old, ran errands for the whores and learnt tricks of their trade. Sandro peered through the night at each of them, even the young girl, and each time he looked the certainty he would see Simonetta shrank a little more. After all, he reasoned through his unreason, why should she be here? The whores are of little use to her for all she might wear men's clothing. She would never descend so low that she would prostitute herself. He decided to try elsewhere.

Sandro hobbled round the corner and into the next street, where between darkened glassmaker's shops a mean oblong of illuminated rain showed an open door. Inside, steps led down to a low room, a drinking house. It was lit only by the flames of a small fire, and the ceiling and walls were black with smoke and grime. Wine drunkards sprawled among the litter. The fire could not hide the stench of vomit. Simonetta would not be here. A large man rose threateningly towards Sandro, lurched at him with neither malice nor balance, and collapsed at the foot of the stairs. Negotiating carefully, placing the crutches either side of the prone man's head and swinging his body over that of the other, Sandro returned to the street.

There was another tavern further down the Via dei Pandolfini, but Sandro was beginning to see the weakness in his plan. He believed the youthfulness he had painted in his mirror might deceive

Simonetta in the dark, yet he could hardly hope to find her in the night hours. The city is a different place at night. The buildings fold in on themselves behind shutters and the streets are abandoned to packs of dogs, packs of men. Simonetta's innocence – though married, her face was so pure that, like Venus in the waves, it was as though her virginity were daily restored – did not belong in the witch-black crudity of night, for all that her skin had the pallor of moonlight and her eyes the pale glimmer of stars. She was too pure for the spoiled dankness of darkened streets, he reasoned, and so, though he had seen her in the Orsanmichele by day, she would not, could not, be there at night. Except that she was.

Sandro stepped back, blinking away his disbelief with the raindrops. Simonetta was approaching, with two young blades, young toughs; they swaggered through the streets and swayed as they swaggered. Simonetta carried a lighted brand. She still wore the guise of a man, he saw at once, but Sandro could not mistake the full mouth, lower lip even fuller than the upper, with its promise of a kiss and its constant smile, nor the straight nose delicately pinched above the nostrils; even less could he fail to recognize the feline tilt of eyes that regarded the world affectionately, humorously, provocatively. He watched in amazement as she passed, her hair no longer braided but pushed beneath a brimless hat. She did not look out of place among her companions. Only one who knew her well would have seen through her disguise. He followed.

Each night in the madhouse I pray. I have even claimed that this book is prayer and confession aimed as much at God as at Fra Agostino or the unknown scholar. Yet at that time God seemed as unknown as the future to me. Throughout my life I have seen more evidence of the Devil's work than of God's. I have looked into lime-pits after the plague, where indistinguishable limbs melt yellow and black. I have visited a fallen city and seen men's bodies with their hearts cut out, their vegetable genitals stuffed like posies in their wounds. In the contado I have seen raped women who have been penetrated by steel as well as by flesh, bleeding a parody of their fertile lunar blood, crawling because of the shame as well as the agony. In Volterra there were pyres of skewered babies, several hanging from each lance, watched by soldiers who laughed and made jokes. It is easier to deny God than the Devil, for God moves quietly and the Devil makes all the noise. At that time, as deluded Sandro followed his love, Cesare Borgia, that Antichrist son of the pope who currently terrorizes the lands to our east, is said to have sodomized twenty male captives one after the other and then crushed each one's head with an ancient statue of Cupid until the child's stone flesh was awash with blood and speckled with brain and bone. And later, with his own eyes, Sandro was to see Borgia commit worse. God is all-powerful, all-forgiving. Yet He acts as though he despises us and delights in the Devil's work. Sandro approached his lost love and the Devil laughed at such easy meat. One of the braves turned round and peered at Sandro through the rainy night. 'There's a cripple chasing us!' he cried. 'Oi! Cripple! Piss off!'

'Maybe he wants something, Bernardo,' suggested another. 'You thought of that?'

'Hey! Cripple!' shouted Bernardo. He took Simonetta's torch and carried it over to Sandro, who stood still with rain running down his face. 'You want something?' The rain hissed as it hit the flame.

Sandro said nothing. Bernardo kicked his crutches away, first one, then the other, experimentally and with great concentration, like a boy plucking a spider's legs; Sandro fell blindly fowards and grabbed the brave for support; Bernardo dropped the torch, took the madman's thin wrists and twisted them; Sandro dangled beneath his trussed hands, was dragged a step towards a puddle, and then dumped. 'He didn't want anything,' Bernardo announced. 'But the bastard torch is sodden. Where we going to get a light this time of night?'

The pack surrounded Sandro now. They all wore Soderini colours. 'Look, Matteo,' said Simonetta's face, though the voice was strange and coarse. 'He's dirty.'

'Better wash him down then,' said Matteo. He pulled out his prick and pissed on Sandro. 'Better wash him down,' he repeated, in case anyone had missed his wit.

'Don't clean him up,' said Bernardo. 'He's not filthy enough for my taste. Dirty old men who hang round Orsanmichele and follow gangs of lads, they should be labelled for what they are.'

'All right,' said Matteo, slurring his words. 'Pissing reminds me I need a crap.'

Sandro shut his eyes. The brave squatted over the body in the puddle as his companions encouraged his efforts; the stools landed heavily on Sandro's back and he gagged at the stench. 'Rub his face in it!' said the voice Simonetta had used. 'That'll teach him to douse our torch.'

'I'm not touching him,' said Bernardo. 'Leave him there.' Eyes still shut, Sandro heard the ominous sound of splintering wood.

They left Sandro in the gutter and continued cheerfully on their way. He made no attempt to follow them, no attempt to move. His crutches were shattered. He did not understand. Was Simonetta testing him? Or had she failed to recognize him? And what was she doing in such company? The faeces slipped from his back when he moved and stank in the puddle beside him.

He felt anger at God, despised and desperate, the victim of some divine joke. He saw God's trick: Simonetta had been returned to earth, to Sandro, yet in some corrupt and transmuted form. He lay in the puddle, reeking of shit. There are only two responses to God's mischief, prayer or despair, and Sandro lay in the rain, trying each in turn, gaining nothing from either.

The night passed. Sandro, as passive as the shit, became a receptacle for leaves. In the bitter cold before morning he found himself waking through a splutter of bubbles and realized he had almost drowned in an inch of water. He crawled painfully from the puddle. His damaged legs refused his commands; even his frozen hand rebelled. He dropped again in the gutter, and the rain eased off.

He was found by another bunch of braves, another pack hunting something to divert them, something to deride. In earlier years, the years of passionate prosperity, the youths of Florence had causes to fight. The braves – apprentices, mercenaries, servants, and above all partisan followers of this or that cause – had no employment now, in the sad era after the Medici, after Savonarola. There were no causes worth fighting left. Florence was governed by consent rather than passion, and the consent was the result of apathy. The nubile form of the Duomo and the spiky male Palazzo della Signoria had in earlier years been proud, fertile and insatiable, incompatible lovers who had thrived on incompatibility. Now the twin spirits of the city had become just another elderly married couple. They had been together too long. The heaviness of shared problems had taken the zest from their relationship. Though more united than ever, because threatened from outside, they were no longer exciting company nor even concerned parents. They were old, fatigued, and aware of their mortality. Their children turned wild, and whereas before they had fought for their parents' favour now they just squabbled peevishly, quarrelled to fill the hours because their parents were too tired to cope. Every child needs an audience, someone it is worth making an effort for, but now the neglected children of Florence had only each other to impress. When a child tries only to please other children, to satisfy children's tastes, only its appetites develop. Nature teaches it to fornicate and to drink, and to resent its parents' neglect. Youth has energy, age has wisdom. Only when the two are combined can anything be achieved. Fornicating, drinking, resenting, the youth of Florence turned on their elders, turned on Sandro lying helpless in the gutter, and took their chance for revenge.

'Look at the smelly old sod,' said one of this vicious new pack. His voice was angry with wine.

Someone kicked Sandro in the ribs and his angry toe collided with shit. 'Yuk! Kill him.'

They might have done, had another not had a more amusing idea. 'Filthy bastard. Let's give him a wash in the river.'

'I'm not picking him up.'

'We don't have to. We can roll him.'

There was no one to stop them. There were not many people in the streets anyway, and though doubtless among that few there were several disgusted by the sight of a dozen youths kicking a frail old cripple, no one interfered. For the young, who had lost all faith in faith when Savonarola burnt, Sandro's was not a cause worth fighting, while for the old it was a cause already lost. And for the German-speaking Swiss soldiers, turning out of the taverns and brothels, the sight was just another confirmation of Florentine decadence, another reason to despise those they were there to defend.

Sandro was rolled through the Piazza della Signoria. His muddy body collected a smear of leaves. Dawn revealed the traitor's head on its pole. The ravens had eaten its eyes. Sandro saw the piazza in a tumble, a leaf's view of the city. He saw Donato's statue of Judith and Holofernes inverted, so that Judith had to strike upwards to cut off the poor man's head, and then the palace walls were above him, and it was the severed and treacherous head of the traitor he saw, lipless on the palazzo, reminding him of someone he once knew, until another roll showed him David on the column, and another gave him a sight of leather-shod feet as they propelled him on his way. Sandro was numb. The cold had leached feeling from him, but more than the cold was the thought that Simonetta had sanctioned what was happening, and more even than that was the thought that God too approved his humiliation. His prayers were made from habit rather than hope. The pack kicked him through the square, down towards the Ponte Vecchio; there they lifted him over the embankment wall and dumped him in the river.

The shock was immediate. They say there are men who can swim. I am not one. Even when my legs worked I never dared commit myself to water. I have never trusted water. It is pitiless. A more vivacious medium might feel sorrow for the poor man who drowns, but the brown waters of the Arno could not care. Sandro sank, dragged down by his already saturated clothes, the weight of water in his bandaged legs, and came to the surface in a flurry of bubbles and panic. He sank again, resurfacing downstream, and had no time to register that he had reached air again before he was down for the third time, the last. Does a drowning man see his life before him? Sandro saw nothing except black waters and chasing white bubbles, a swirl of darkness and then a miracle. For he was being pulled upwards, dragged through the grip of the Arno by a firmer grip on his arm. His head was out of the water. He could see the Ponte Vecchio behind him, its towers more precarious and impossible than ever. And then the oyster sky was in front of his eyes, and he lay on his back on a boat.

The boatman sat hard on his chest. Spewing up the river water was just another indignity in a chain of indignities, and Sandro felt no resentment. If this man wants to sit on me, he thought, then who am I to stop him? The weight of the man's fat arse hit his chest again, rocking the boat, and another billow of water shot from his mouth. Sandro breathed a noseful of air. It tasted good, which was a surprise for he thought he had passed the time when he could appreciate anything. He took another breath to be sure, and then another. There was no doubt. Breathing was a good thing to do. He closed his eyes hard, squeezing out the water, squeezing out the memory of the night. 'Are you all right?' asked the boatman.

Sandro considered a while, and decided he was. So charity does still exist, he thought, and there are still those who would help me. He lay on the boards of the boat. A clinkerbuilt boat is sturdy and sound but makes an uncomfortable bed. His useless legs could not move him, could not ease his discomfort. It did not matter. He lay there and found reason to give thanks to God.

1469

I made a decision, and nearly two years too late I went to see Tommaso Soderini. He was out. I returned the next day, and the next. Eventually I caught up with the grey-haired banker.

'Do I know you?' he asked as I stopped him at the steps of his palazzo.

'I was a pupil of Fra Filippo.'

'Oh yes. I think I remember.'

I nodded. 'Sandro Botticelli.'

'That's right,' he said, as though it were clever of me to remember my name. 'What became of you? Didn't Lippi tell me something about you.'

'He wanted me to take over his bottega when he left Florence. I was his best pupil. He said you might help me.'

'That was some time back! But wait a minute. Didn't you do us a bit of a favour once? Deliver a letter for Piero, or something along those lines?'

It was nice to be so clearly remembered. 'That's right,' I said.

'It's coming back to me now. Old Lippi thought you were good. What went wrong? No money?' I nodded glumly.

'Something like that,' I mumbled.

'And what became of you? I've not heard your name mentioned. Have you been working outside Florence?'

'No. I live in Borgo Ognissanti. With my father and Fra Filippo's son.'

'Son? I'd almost forgotten he'd got one. Well, it's been nice to meet you again. I must go now, I'm meeting someone. But good luck. And give my greetings to the friar's boy too.'

He started to move away, a flourish of dark cloak on the white marble steps. I had received something, confirmation that I had nothing to fear, but I felt I deserved more, deserved some compensation for the worry and the wasted time. 'I still paint,' I declared. 'I'm still good.'

He hesitated, and then turned round. 'All right,' he said, resigned. 'What's your name again?'

'Botticelli. Sandro Botticelli.'

I expected nothing from this unsatisfactory meeting, but perhaps it jogged his memory, for a few days later Tommaso came to my father's. My father was at work; our servant girl kept bowing at our distinguished guest and had to be shooed away like some over-friendly dog. 'I've been thinking,' he said, cutting through my muddled 'I'm honoured' and 'delighted' and the rest of the formalities. 'Lippo said you were good. Can you prove it?'

I showed him some figures I had been working on. He nodded. 'I don't know much about art,' he said. 'But these seem all right. I might be able to put some work your way. Are you educated? Do you read?'

'I can read,' I said.

'Good. Do you know the ancient authors?'

'I know a bit of Virgil.' What sort of work does he have in mind? 'But I don't read Latin, I'm afraid.'

'Don't apologize to me. I don't either. But young Lorenzo, Piero's son, is getting married soon. He wants some classical decorations. You know, in the ancient Roman style. It's good you've read Virgil. You might be the man for the job.'

Of course I am. But, 'I don't have a workshop,' I said.

'That's all right. I've spoken to Verrocchio; he said you can use his. He vouched for you too, by the way, when he told me where you lived. Are you interested in the work then?'

'Certainly.' To work for the Medici! The sun gilded the day.

The preparations for Lorenzo's marriage to Clarice Orsini lasted many months. In February, as I began work on the designs, there was a tournament in the piazza of the church of Santa Croce. I took

Filippino to the spectacle, and though we could not see much of the jousting we did see Lorenzo receive the prize, a silver helmet, designed by Verocchio, with a statuette of Mars in place of the plume. By the end of March my designs were ready and we began to work on the painting. Verrocchio's bottega was as large and flourishing as ever, which was as well. The decorations Lorenzo had in mind were certainly lavish, and I was not the only artist involved in the design, much less in the manufacture: we were to create a series of canvas arches, on structures built by Bernardo Rossellino; they were to be not dissimilar to the one by Gozzoli which had collapsed in the Piazza de' Medici, though everyone hoped they would be rather sturdier; monochrome, painted to resemble marble, and in the style of the triumphal arches of antiquity, they were to be decorated with ornate panels painted on to the canvas to represent niches, statues, and bas-reliefs of the story of the *Aeneid.* By the end of April everyone in the bottega was involved, intermittently, with the wedding decorations: everyone except Leonardo, who refused to have anything to do with it, or with me, and went round trying to spread disaffection. 'All this work. It's not art. It's simply pandering to a famous name,' he said. The accusation was just. But at least I have given my energy to Florence and the Medici, and not to the Duke of Milan as Leonardo did, much less to the infernal Cesare Borgia as Leonardo does today.

Tommaso may not have known much about art, but as Lorenzo's uncle he took a personal interest in our work. I found myself enjoying his visits. Not only was he knowledgeable about the world, but he gave us a respite from Leonardo's bickering. Had it not been for Verrocchio, more in love than ever it seemed, I think Leonardo would have ended in the well. So I was surprised when, on one of Tommaso's visits, in early May, I found myself agreeing with Leonardo.

'You know,' said Tommaso, pouring himself half a cup of wine from the flask Verrocchio kept for special guests, and topping the wine up with water. 'I envy you painters. It must be wonderful to have a skill that others appreciate.'

'You're a banker,' put in Leonardo. 'It must be wonderful to have money and privilege.'

'Would you rather be a banker?' asked Tommaso.

'I would rather work for myself than for others,' said Leonardo. 'I would rather choose my own subjects for paintings than have them foisted on me. I would rather paint beautiful pictures than waste my time on this trivia.' He indicated the decorations for Lorenzo's wedding, which Ottaviano was carefully labelling, with a sweep of his elegant hand.

'Really?' said Tommaso. 'And what do you think, Sandro?'

I thought. 'I don't consider this to be trivia, exactly. It's a job, and quite an interesting one. But to be honest, I agree with Leonardo about the rest. I'd rather paint beautiful pictures too.'

'Of your own choosing?'

'Oh yes. It's what every real painter wants. All of us, we spend hours ignoring things we would like to paint, painting things we would like to ignore.'

'Are we still talking about these decorations?' Tommaso asked.

'Of course we are!' said Leonardo.

'Sandro?' asked Tommaso, ignoring the interruption.

'No,' I said, 'I'm enjoying the work; I'll enjoy spending the fee. But I didn't become a painter thinking, "Won't it be wonderful to make decorations for a wedding, things that'll last a day and then be thrown away." I came into the trade because I wanted to make pictures.'

'Exactly,' said Leonardo. It was the first time he had endorsed anything I had said, but if that surprised me his next statement surprised me more. 'I want to make paintings that change the way we look at the world. I want to learn everything there is to learn. I want to understand the universe. I want to control the forces of nature.'

'I think perhaps you want too much,' said Tommaso quietly. 'Are you so ambitious, Sandro?'

'I'd like to be able to spend my time painting pictures, certainly, and have the leisure to paint them the way they should be done, instead of always being at a client's call. But I don't suppose I'll ever get what I want.'

'In that case, though you are so much less ambitious than our friend here, you want too much too,' said Tommaso. 'There's no point wanting what you know you cannot have.'

This was sanctimonious, annoying, and probably true. 'You might be right,' I conceded. 'But is it really so ambitious? All I want is to paint beautiful pictures.'

'No you don't,' corrected Tommaso. 'You want to get paid for painting beautiful pictures. There's a difference.'

'Not such a big one,' I countered. 'I don't want to be rich as the Medici. Money isn't important. I just need to make enough to keep going. If I don't get paid I can't buy the materials, the boards, can't pay assistants. That's what's so annoying: we ought to be painting and instead we have to spend our lives worrying about money.'

'I see.' He nodded understandingly. 'You want to argue with God then.'

'I didn't say that!'

'Of course you did. "Money's not important," you say! You're complaining that you need money if you're to do your work, but you might just as well complain about your need for food or sleep. Are food and sleep "not important" too?'

'At least food and sleep are natural. Money isn't: money's man-made, unnecessary.'

'You sound like a Franciscan friar. Do you want some wine?'

'No thank you. I wouldn't expect you to agree,' I replied. 'You're a banker.'

'Exactly. I'm a banker, part of a very misunderstood group.'

'A very rich group,' mentioned Leonardo.

Tommaso smiled at us. 'I take deposits from some people, make loans to others.' His fluency suggested he had said all this before. 'I give interest on the money loaned to me, charge interest on the money I loan out. You and the Franciscans can call this usury if you like: the Franciscans aren't the only order in the Church and there are plenty of clerics who pray for me daily because I've paid for new vestments or decorated an altar. And anyway, usury is just an ugly word for a straightforward transaction. Money's just a commodity, like eggs. If I bought eggs for five soldi and sold them for ten no one would complain: that's business. What I do is buy and sell florins: what we call interest is the price on what I give and receive. When somebody deposits a florin with my bank I pay them five soldi; when somebody else borrows that florin I charge them ten. The only difference is that if you sell me an egg for five soldi you never get it back; if you sell me a florin you get it back, and the five soldi as well.'

'What's that to do with anything?' asked Leonardo.

'You're not listening. Why do you need to eat and sleep?'

'Because Nature demands it,' Leonardo replied.

'Sandro? What do you think?'

'Because God made me that way, I suppose,' I said.

'And what do you eat?'

It seemed an odd question. 'Food: eggs, cheese, bread, pasta, meat. The same as everyone.'

'Don't insult the banker,' said Leonardo. 'I'm sure his diet is far more refined.'

Tommaso ignored him again. 'Who makes the food?' he asked me.

'God does,' I said.

'Wrong. Man does. Man plants the wheat, tends the animals, grinds the flour. God starts things off, makes the plants and animals, but man makes use of them. Who makes money?'

'You've just said. Bankers do, by charging interest. You've just shown how a florin can make an extra fifteen soldi.'

'So you were listening. Good: perhaps we'll make a businessman of you yet; we'll have to if you're ever going to come to anything. But – let's return to the argument – money grows in exactly the same way as corn. If you tend it, it flourishes; if you ignore it, it withers. Think of the parable of the servant who buried his coins. God made gold and silver just as he made wheat and pigs. He gave it for our use. That's the message of the parable of the coins. In making money work we are doing God's will. Money is part of God's way of things, despite what the moralists say. Money is neither good nor evil. It is neutral. The only time morality enters is when the money gets spent.'

'I follow all this,' I told him. 'But I still don't see what it's to do with us. We are painters.'

'Your complaint,' he said to us, 'was that painting occupied only half your time, and that grafting for money occupied the other half. But don't you see? You should be grateful for money; were there no money to worry about you wouldn't be able to spend any of your time painting; all your time would be spent growing food and making shelters for your heads. Florence is full of bankers; it's also full of painters. That's not coincidence, it's consequence: money made soon becomes money spent, and money spent on a good painting is never wasted. A good religious painting, such as my old friend and your old master used to paint, is the perfect investment. It's good for the soul – donated to a church, both its content and its existence help in God's eyes – and it's good for the body too, because there's no cheaper way to make an impression in this city of display than to be responsible for an attractive painting in a prominent position. I grow money for you, just as the farmers in the contado grow your food. Our labour liberates your art. So don't despise money, young Sandro, young Leonardo. If it wasn't for money you wouldn't be able to paint at all. You shouldn't complain about money, you should celebrate it; money isn't what constricts your painting, it's what sets you free to paint.' He added more water to his wine. 'You're both young, and you've a lot to learn.'

'We need patronage, not patronizing,' said Leonardo.

'You need to learn about the world. Above all, you need to learn to recognize its limitations, and to accept what you cannot change. Accept it, work with it, use it to your advantage.'

This may be so; it did not help me much. I was none the richer for knowing I needed to be rich. Leonardo was even less impressed by Tommaso's argument. 'You are teaching us humility, that's all. Why should I recognize my limitations? What's to say I have any? You grow money, and live well by it, and expect us to be grateful to you; we spend our lives painting pictures, live in poverty, and you expect us to be grateful to you for that as well. But for myself, I would rather be rich than grateful. Had I a tenth your money, or you a tenth my talent, we would not be discussing this, we'd be creating things of beauty and grace.'

Tommaso finished his wine. 'You see: again you're trying to change things that will not and cannot change. The world is as we find it.'

'And we may make it different by the time we leave it,' argued Leonardo.

'The folly, the vanity of youth! Certain things can be changed, and will be changed, though few of them by you. Most things will stay the same. That is the way things are.'

'Then the first thing I have to change is the way things are. It is as simple as that,' said Leonardo.

'You live in the clouds.'

'No,' said Leonardo. 'I live in the gutter. I stare at the clouds. That is why I am a painter.'

That is why I was a painter too.

By this time the painting for the arches was complete, and a team of carpenters took our work away. I found myself in the role of foreman to a group of men who knew far more about what they were doing than I could ever learn; I spectated rather than supervised. But it was satisfying to watch designs I had made turn into structures that towered over the joinery shop, and humbling to daydream that these were not modern arches of canvas and wood, built for the Medici wedding, but that they were marble, made for some Caesar, and would last for ever. Florence is a city of many wonders, but it cannot rival the magnificence of the ancients.

'Sandro Botticelli?'

I turned round. 'Yes?'

'I thought so.' The speaker was a well-dresed young man with a full mouth, a wide nose, and clever eyes: his ugliness was not repulsive, was even charming. He stood between two other men, better looking though similarly dressed. 'You look lost in thought.'

'I was,' I confessed. 'I was imagining these arches to be made of marble instead of paper. It's satisfying to watch the construction, disappointing to think that soon they'll all be destroyed.'

'Wasting all your efforts,' the young man sympathised, and I was about to agree when I realised who he was. I had not seen him for several years, since I stopped attending the church of San Lorenzo with Fra Lippo Lippi, yet although he had become a man in the interval I should have known those distinctive features.

'Lorenzo de' Medici!'

He bowed. 'I came to see how you were spending my money. Well, by the look of it. Keep the work up.'

'Thank you.'

'My uncle Tommaso tells me you have read Virgil. We must talk some time, when we're both less busy.'

'Thank you,' I said again. I was impressed he knew who I was, flattered he took an interest in me and shrewd enough to guess that he would be like this with everyone. His charm was not discriminate; like a blackbird's song it fell on all within range.

The wedding took place in June. The festivities lasted three days, and different decorations were used each day. The bride was staying at the Palazzo Alessandri. On the Saturday we erected the arches, seventeen in all, between the Borgo San Piero to the Medici palace. Bernardo Rossellino was in charge of the structures; I was there to repaint any canvas panels that got damaged. The work took all day and half the night. The next morning Clarice Orsini, on the white horse which was a present from the king of Naples, rode with a long procession of attendants to the Medici palace. A huge crowd came to enjoy the spectacle. I was among them, too involved to feel tired. Clarice wore glorious gowns of white and gold; and as she passed through the gate at the entrance to the courtyard an olive branch, symbol of fertility and peace, was lowered on to her head. A company of Flemish musicians played music by Pietro Aaron but could hardly be heard over the cheering. The wedding party went into the courtyard, where many tables had been erected. Although they dined in the open, we could not see them from the street, though we could hear the sound of trumpets heralding each new course in the banquet: game, poultry, cakes, savoury jellies, sweet jellies, sweetmeats, marzipan, and sugared almonds, washed down with innumerable trebbiano and vernaccia wines. We listened as the music changed, became music for the dance, and were happy to witness such richness.

The days and nights became a series of wonders. There were displays and performances, paid for by the Medici, in every district. Chinese gunpowder was exploded in a barrel suspended over the Arno and the night blew apart in a burst of coloured sparks. There were pageants, masques and revels, tourneys, dances and parades. Florence became a carnival. The rules of normal existence were suspended. Strange animals from Africa were led down the Via dei Calzaiuoli on chains. I saw a great grey beast with a tail at both ends, a long skinny creature with an impossible neck, a cow with a horn on its nose. Only the small horses with the plaited tails, painted in narrow stripes of black and white, were obvious fakes. Men ate fire and swallowed swords in the street. A woman, naked save long golden hair, sat in a cage full of bats. Horsemen rode by constantly, galloping the Medici arms, the palla on backgrounds of red, blue and green, across the city. The Palazzo della Signoria was closed and the Lions of Florence, released from their cage behind the Palazzo della Signoria, were encouraged to attack and eat dogs. And at the end of it, when the couple were wed and we were exhausted, someone had to clean up the mess.

The streets seemed purposeless when the festival was over, but they were not empty. There was straw everywhere. Paper, the rind of cheeses, and half-eaten breadrolls filled the alleyways. Two of our arches had been pulled to the ground already, for firewood, for souvenirs, or just for the fun of it, and the rest were damaged and precarious. In my role of redundant supervisor I watched as the rest were brought down. We took the remains to the Piazza San Croce, where the debris was being burnt, and tossed our efforts piece by piece into the flames. I stood at the side of the piazza while the clouds of oily smoke tumbled from the canvas and over the unfinished façade of the church; I stood in the gutter and watched the clouds.

After the wedding came the days when the dog star rises with the sun, the angry dog-days of fighting and brawling. In an earlier year the great Cosimo de' Medici had died on such a day, when the dust irritates Florence's streets and eyes and the sun warms every man's choler; in the summer of 1469, while I was at my father's home, news came from Spoleto that Cosimo's friend, my old master Fra Filippo, had given in to the heat of the season. That I was not surprised at the news made neither the fact of his death nor the thought of telling his son any less unpleasant. Filippino Lippi was a melancholy enough lad anyway. He was devoted to his father's paintings, visiting each church that displayed them on successive Sundays, and wanted to become a painter too. But he did not have his father's ready facility: he could not then understand how to be wicked yet paint pictures as noble and devout as those of his father; he believed he had to work all the time at being pious as well as skilled at the craft. I waited for him to return from church that day, and said a prayer for the dead.

Tommaso Soderini arrived, wearing the red cap of a councillor and causing the standard panic in our maid. 'Greetings, Sandro. Is young Filippino around? I heard that his father was dead, thought I'd pay my respects.'

'That's good of you. Filippino's at church. He doesn't know about his father yet; I only just found out myself.'

'I'll wait for him. How are things with you? I haven't seen you since the wedding.'

'I survive,' I said.

'Is that all? No work?'

'I do some things for Verrocchio from time to time. But nothing worth calling work.'

'Of course, the wedding was hugely expensive,' said Tommaso. For some reason all the bells in Florence started tolling outside, making conversation awkward. 'I don't suppose there are many commissions going at present.'

'What there are go elsewhere. Benozzo Gozzoli still gets most of the Medici work, though he's a Pisan and dreadfully old-fashioned. I thought I'd get something from the decoration of the Court of the Mercatanzia, through Verrocchio, but they gave the job to the Pollaiuolo brothers; Mino da Fiesole has been given the tomb of Count Ugo to do.'

'I'm on the Council of the Mercatanzia, though not on the committee in charge of the decoration. I'd heard Verrocchio was certain to get it.'

'What happened then?'

'I haven't been told.'

'Maybe Verrocchio let Leonardo da Vinci do the sketches,' I suggested.

'Wht harm would that do? He's a strange young man, that Leonardo, but you can't deny his talent.'

'Oh, I agree Leonardo draws very prettily. But he's completely impractical. The commission was for a series of seven pictures of the Virtues to decorate the wainscoting; Leonardo will have given them fifteen angels on horseback, a study of a fallen rose petal, and half a dozen mourners dressed in dark grey. There'll be no goldleaf, because Leonardo doesn't like gold on a picture – neither do I, actually, but clients seem to – so to keep the cost up he'll specify first quality ultramarine for the underpainting!'

'That's not what happened!'

'Probably not,' I agreed. I felt tired, and it was hard to talk over the bells. 'It's just an informed guess. I know what Leonardo's like: talented, but too ambitious. He doesn't know what clients want.'

'You're not doing so well with clients yourself,' Tommaso pointed out.

'No one asks me to. There's only you and Verrocchio in this entire city know I'm here.'

'I do my best for you, you know,' he said over the tolling bells outside.

Before I could reply Filippino returned. The boy wore a black scarf round his hat. 'Ah, Filippino,' I said. I indicated the black scarf. 'You've heard.' I was relieved I did not have to break the news to him.

'Filippino,' said Tommaso, solemn and formal. 'I was so terribly sorry to hear about your father. He was a great man.'

'My father? Has something happened to him?' Filippino took off his hat, more out of respect for Tommaso than for the dead.

'You're wearing mourning,' I pointed out.

'Piero de' Medici is dead,' said Filippino.

There was silence in the room, contrasting with the tumult of bells outside. Tommaso and I wrestled with Filippino's news; Filippino had his own grief. I got up and collected a cup, poured some wine. I added no water. 'Drink this,' I told Filippino.

'When did my father die?' Filippino asked after he had drunk. A circle of red wine made a moustache where no hair had yet grown.

'I don't know for sure,' I said. 'Last week, I think.'

Filippino nodded.

'What about Piero?' asked Tommaso.

'Today. This morning. I was at Santa Maria Novella. They interrupted the Mass to tell us.'

It was our turn to nod. 'They would,' said Tommaso. He thought for a moment then looked up alertly. 'Sandro can you do me a favour? Can you take a message to the Pitti palace for me?'

'I don't know. What do you want me to say?'

He thought further. 'Tell them to meet me at the convent of Sant' Antonio. As many of the family as possible. We must show solidarity.'

I worried. 'You're not going to try anything silly?' I asked. After all, his brother had tried all manner of silly things. 'If you've conspiracy in mind, I'm having no part of it.' Power would surely pass to Piero de' Medici's son Lorenzo, I reasoned; the Pitti and the Soderini may have other ideas, but I was pretty certain that most of the city would want another Medici in charge. Piero had not been popular, but had been allowed to rule; young Lorenzo, in contrast, was loved throughout Florence, for his extravagance if nothing else. I had no intention of being on the losing side, and anyway, having seen him often when he was younger, and having actually met him face to face, I felt loyal to Lorenzo myself. It would do Florence no harm to have a cultivated man leading us, I considered, rather than a banker.

'Don't be a fool,' said Tommaso, curtly cutting off my thoughts. 'Lorenzo is my nephew. I wouldn't hurt his inheritance, and anyway I've no desire for power. All I want is that everything goes smoothly, and I want all the *popolo grosso*, including the Pitti family, to be with me when I invite Lorenzo to take over his father's position.'

'If that's all,' I decided, 'I'll be happy to help.' I certainly would! We were talking about the Pitti and the Medici, the richest and most important patrons in Florence. I could not refuse this chance to make myself known to them. 'Filippino, are you coming?' Filippino may have been only a boy; his name, because of his father, was far more famous than mine. If Filippino came with me no one knowledgeable would be able to forget that we were painters.

'I don't know,' said Filippino. He spoke without interest.

'There's no point moping around here.'

Tommaso gave me a ring, a fine piece of emerald set in gold. 'You'll need something to identify yourself to the Pittis. Tell them to get to the convent by sundown. Are you going to be there yourself?'

I took a piece of the thread we used for binding canvas and tied the ring round my neck. I had probably never touched anything so valuable in my life. 'Of course.'

'Excellent. I'll see you then.'

Filippino and I washed quickly. It was five o'clock, that hottest and stickiest hour of that hottest and stickiest of seasons, when we left the studio for the Palazzo Pitti. Normally the streets are quiet at this time, crossed only by scrawny dogs with their heads hunched low to the ground, but that day there were crowds everywhere. I thought about the ring round my neck; its weight was a constant reminder to worry about thieves and to worry about Florence. Piero had not been well loved, yet he was his father's son, his son's father, and was mourned for that. He had also been a survivor; could those who survived him do so well?

A group of horsemen pounded by, scattering the crowds and my thoughts. 'Do you see the man at the front of the horsemen?' I asked Filippino. I was pleased to be able to identify these notables I had never met; it was a useful bonus to spending time in artists' studios. 'That's Donato Acciaiuolo: his father Agnolo is still in exile for joining Niccolò Soderini's conspiracies. I wonder if Donato is going to oppose Lorenzo de' Medici?'

It was not a long walk from our house to the river. We went through the Piazza Goldoni, and along the river toward the bridge of San Trinità where my father had his shop. The embankment was as busy as the rest of the city. Over the river, on the swelling at the foot of the hill, were the fortifications which surround the Pitti palace, and flying above the palace and the neighbouring, obscuring buildings was the standard of the imperial eagle, which the Holy Roman Emperor in person had allowed the Pitti family to use. Perhaps that flag was the reason the Pitti family were so arrogant: it is probably hard not to be proud when you've the eagle of emperors for your symbol.

We were forced to stand still once more as a carriage drove along the riverside. I recognized Guaspare di Zanobi del Lama, a friend of dead Piero: it seemed every man of wealth and power in the city was on the streets that day. Filippino took hold of my sleeve. 'Sandro?' he asked. 'What do the Medici do?'

'What do you mean, what do they do?'

We stood on the edge of a crowded street. The church bells continued to announce Piero's death. Our destination was the other side of the river; the Pitti eagle blustered and drooped in the hot afternoon. I wanted to get on; Filippino wanted an answer to his question. 'Why are they so important?' he persisted. 'They're not princes.'

'No,' I agreed. 'Florence is a republic.'

'And the Gonfaloniere is leader of the council.'

'That's right.'

'So what do the Medici do?'

Like many questions asked in innocence, this was not easy to answer. 'They're very important people. They have lots of money.'

'But they're not kings or popes, so why do people talk about them as if they were?'

'Well, somebody has to make the decisions. Piero's father Cosimo did that job, and then Piero, and now probably Piero's son Lorenzo will have a go.'

'I hope so. Everyone likes Lorenzo,' Filippino said. 'He pays for jousts and processions. No one'll mind him being in charge.' Filippino's nature may have been serious, priestly, but he had enjoyed Lorenzo's wedding as much as anyone. It occurred to me that Lorenzo had not just got himself a wife with that display, but probably bought himself his succession too. He had seemed shrewd when I met him. But the wife could be a liability.

'He's very young,' I pointed out. 'Only twenty. And not everybody likes his wife. She's an Orsini, a Roman noblewoman. Nobody wants a powerful foreigner in Florence. And some people think the Medici are getting fancy ideas, marrying nobility so they can become nobility themselves. We don't want Florence to end up with a duke like Milan.'

'Oh,' Filippino was thinking; I still wanted to hurry. 'Then what happens if the people decide they don't want Lorenzo after all?' he asked.

'Somebody else will run Florence. One of the other big families.'

'I didn't mean that. What'll happen to Lorenzo? Will they kill him?'

'I shouldn't think so. They might exile him, I suppose, but probably he'd just be a citizen of Florence, like you and me and the butcher and Luca Pitti. Except richer of course.'

'Is he richer than Luca Pitti even?' Despite the extravagant wedding the Medici palace was not as impressive as the Pitti palace, the balls of the gold Medici flag not as inspiring as the Pitti's imperial eagle.

'He's the richest man in the world now his father's gone,' I said, which might have been true and certainly impressed Filippino. 'Now, come on. If we can deliver Tommaso's message we'll have helped Lorenzo, and perhaps he'll help us.'

Filippino pulled me on, as if to ask why we'd been wasting time in conversation.

We crossed the Arno. The stone of the bridge was yellow and threaded with fine white veins. Upstream to our left were the towers and arches of the Ponte Vecchio, where the butchers have their shops. I was glad we were not crossing there: the crush was so great that I saw a man pushed straight over the edge into the brown river. I hoped he could swim. The waters do not go fast, but there is a weir to the west where the city walls end, and no one survives that.

The servants at the gate of the Palazzo Pitti were armed and wore helmets. It seemed that all Florence was on the alert, was waiting for something to happen. I asked to see Luca Pitti and the guard laughed. 'Who do you think you are?'

'I am Alessandro di Mariano Filipepi, and this is my assistant Filippino di Filippo Lippi.'

Neither name meant much to the guards. 'Bugger off.'

'We've brought a message from Tommaso Soderini.'

'Oh yeah?'

'Yes.' I showed them the ring. They probably did not recognize it specifically, but it looked more valuable that anything I could afford so they accepted my story. 'You want Luca. They're all upstairs somewhere.'

We crossed a wide courtyard. The palazzo ahead was defiant and rather terrifying, built of blocks of stone of enormous size. I felt overawed and out of place, but Filippino seemed perfectly relaxed and pestered me with questions when I would rather be silent. Filippino was still curious about Florence's politics; Florence's politics are curious, and I was not sure I could explain them to him properly. 'You know you said we're all citizens,' he said. 'You and me and the butcher and Luca Pitti and Lorenzo and everyone?'

'Yes.'

'Does that mean we're all as important as one another?'

'In a way. Florence is a republic. All the citizens are equal.'

The imperial eagle was curved above the doors of the Pitti palace. The proud curve of its beak denied my words. I had been to the Palazzo Pitti some years earlier, with Filippino's father, but the façade had not been complete then. Finished, it was daunting. 'My father was important,' announced Filippino, as though, reading my mind, he sought to lessen my sense of humility. We climbed the wide steps to the door. Filippino spoke with great confidence, remarking on a rusticated stone to our left of such huge dimensions it was impossible to imagine human hands moving it; for myself, I felt as small, exposed and vulnerable as a fly.

At the door we were stopped again, by a Dominican priest with a superior smile. 'What can I do for you gentlemen?' He sneered as he said 'gentlemen', as though implying that we were not really gentlemen at all and that he only used the word because he was too polite to do otherwise. I did not think him polite at all, but I explained what we wanted and showed him the ring.

'I am Luca Pitti's chaplain,' said the priest self-importantly. His accent was Venetian and I wondered if he was a spy, a connection between the Pitti and the exiles. 'I will take your message.'

'No,' I said. 'I will.' I could not cope with the Pitti palace, but I felt I could manage a jumped-up Venetian priest.

A young man in rich yellow hose came through the courtyard and up the grand staircase. We stepped aside for him respectfully. 'Is my father still here, Fra Ermolao?'

'He's upstairs.'

'Has there been any news? Do we know what the other families are doing yet? Marco Vespucci is coming out for Lorenzo. What about Alamanno Rinuccini, Tommaso Soderini, Donato Acciaiuoli? Do we know where they stand?'

'I've come with a message from Tommaso Soderini,' I announced.

'Oh. Right. You'd better follow me then.'

The Dominican's smile became more fixed and ghastly than before. 'I'm sure the presence of these people is not necessary,' he said.

'Oh, that's all right,' said the young man. 'My father'll want to hear from the horse's mouth. You don't mind being called a horse?' he asked me. He could call me anything he liked if it meant I scored points off the Venetian.

We left Fra Ermolao in the hall, climbed the marvellous stairs, and entered a large room decorated in crimson and gold. The light of the afternoon sun came through the windows in horizontal bands. Marble putti frolicked on the walls. Tapestries of crimson and cream proclaimed the proud history of the Pitti clan, and between the tapestries were religious scenes painted on panel. I recognized some as the work of Fra Lippo.

At the far end of the room a group of people were arranged around a desk. The eldest, a frail old man with grey hair and grey cheeks, was sitting. Last time I had seen him he had been shaking hands with Piero de' Medici, looking nervous and beaten. Today, surrounded by his sons and grandsons, nephews and cousins, he looked assured despite the weakness that comes with age. The family looked up at me. I saw variations on the same pinched cheeks and long nose, as though in front of me were a dozen portraits depicting the same man at different ages. 'Ercole?' asked a man with a thick black beard. 'What's the news?'

'Marco Vespucci is behind Lorenzo,' said the young man in yellow hose.

'I expected as much,' said the old man. 'Anything else?'

'The Barbadori family have sent us a message of support. If we want to challenge Lorenzo they'll be for us.'

'Well, that'll make a big difference,' said a youth in a scarlet jerkin, loading the the adjective with sarcasm. 'What about Soderini?'

'I have a message,' I began, 'from Tommaso Soderini.'

The old man leant forward to peer at me. His eyes must have been weak. The young man in the scarlet jerkin rested his weight gracefully against the desk and nodded his head encouragingly. 'Yes?'

I was slightly embarrassed to be the focus of this attention but after all I had a right to be heard. I was as much a citizen of Florence as any of them. It was my city as well as theirs that they discussed. 'He wants to meet you at the convent of Sant'Antonio,' I told them. 'Tonight at sunset.'

Red jerkin turned to the others. 'I thought as much. We can be sure Tommaso is for Lorenzo.' There was a babble of discussion. Unnoticed but undismissed, Filippino and I waited as the Pitti family argued its options.

'We shouldn't do anything too hasty,' said the thick beard. 'If we join with Soderini we'll have to declare for Lorenzo; if we wait others might join us.'

'Others like the Barbadori, with nothing to offer but their hatred of the Medici?' said red jerkin.

'There are others who hate the Medici as much,' said yellow hose.

'Such as?'

Thick beard answered for him. 'Niccolò Soderini, Diotisalvi Neroni, Agnolo Acciaiuolo.'

'Exiles!' snorted red jerkin. 'Exiles and old men!'

'So what do you suggest, Bernardo?' asked an older man who wore a short blue cape. 'That we just let Lorenzo walk in, walk over us? I thought you'd got more guts than that!'

Red jerkin put his hand to his sword; the seated old man interrupted. 'No fighting among ourselves!' he declared. 'I think

Bernardo is right. People like the Barbadori are of no importance; we needed allies among the bigger families. It grieves me to say it, but Lorenzo is well-liked. I don't think we've any choice. If we don't declare for him we'll be isolated again. We've daughters to marry off: we don't want to be ostracized again; you know what it was like after that business with Niccolò Soderini.' He winced and then turned to me. 'Tell your master that we'll be at Sant'Antonio.' Sitting back, he opened his hands wide to indicate his family, then brought the palms together to show his decision was final. 'All of us.'

Filippino spoke up. 'Tommaso isn't our master.' It was my turn to wince. 'Florence is a republic. All the citizens are equal.' As if this were evidence of his claim, the boy pointed to a painting of the Madonna and Child. 'My father painted that picture.'

'Fra Lippo was your father? Well, well,' said the old man. 'I know some tales about him, I can tell you.' Every man over 50 in Florence knew some tales about the friar. 'Give him my regards.'

'He's dead,' said Filippino, more complacent at having news to deliver than saddened by the bereavement, it seemed.

'Really? When did this happen?'

The rest of the Pitti family were as impatient as I with this conversation. 'Father,' said thick beard. 'I still want to check that the Tornabuonis are going to be behind Lorenzo.'

'His mother is a Tornabuoni. Of course they'll be with Lorenzo,' said the old man. 'But you can do what you like as long as you're at the convent in good time. And you should show a little more respect to the son of the great Fra Filippo.' He smiled at Filippino. 'You'll eat with us, you and your companion? Who are you, by the way?' he said, turning to me. I gave my full name.

'But everyone calls him Botticelli,' said Filippino. 'He's a painter too.'

'Never heard of him,' said Luca Pitti.

'I ought to go back to Tommaso,' I said, 'and tell him your decision.'

'No point. He'll see us soon enough.'

Luca Pitti's relatives left. The afternoon sun still angled across the room, illuminating curlicues of dusty air before falling on the crimson and gold carpet, on gilt furniture, and on an old man who, with his arm round a boy, was pointing out paintings on the wall.

When the meal came it was of good quality but surprisingly plain, a pasta with sauce, goat cheeses, a sharp white wine and white bread. We ate in a vast hall. The old man had taken a fancy to Filippino; the two sat together, and though I can't imagine what they were talking about it was clearly amusing them. I found myself between the Venetian, Fra Ermolao, and one of the Pitti retainers. The retainer was ugly and slovenly. He had few teeth and chewing seemed to take all his effort, all his concentration. Fra Ermolao still looked like a snake, but his table manners were less repulsive than those of my other neighbour and at least I knew his name. I asked him if he had been in Florence long.

'Yes,' he said disdainfully.

I was discouraged but persistent. 'Do you like the city?'

'There are aspects of Florence which are attractive,' he answered.

'Such as?' I didn't like the man and, I suspect, only made the effort at conversation because Filippino, at the table's head, was chattering so happily. The fact was, I felt jealous, and neglected.

'The Duomo is not unimpressive. And the doors to the Baptistery are quite well made.'

'Not unimpressive!' I said. 'Quite well made!' He was talking about two of the wonders of the earth. The dome of the cathedral is unsurpassed, unsurpassable. Brunelleschi designed it, a soaring structure of impossible size that as a boy I watched grow on the skyline. It grew faster than I did. And as for the doors of the Baptistery, even Brunelleschi could not equal them, though he had tried, entering his own designs for the competition which Lorenzo Ghiberti won. Ghiberti's bronze reliefs, so perfectly cast and finished that they don't seem like bronze at all, attract visitors from all Italy and from other countries as well. 'Is that all you can say about them?'

'It is.'

I was angry. I was angry with this Venetian and his sense of his superiority; I was angry with myself for trying to converse with him, and thereby way throwing away the advantage I gained over him when we first met. And I was angry with Filippino for being so comfortable in this fabulous palace and among these fabulous people.

When he meal was finished I saw Luca Pitti send Filippino over to me. The lad came cheerfully. 'Isn't this place wonderful?' he asked.

'Signor Pitti has eighteen of my father's paintings, and lots of drawings; he's promised to show them all to me some time.'

'That's nice for you,' I said. 'What are we doing now?'

'The Pitti are riding to Sant'Antonio. I suppose we could go with them.'

'Them on horseback and us on foot!' I should have thought of this. Painters walk, the *popolo grosso* ride. I looked for Luca but he had already left. Our contribution to history was over. Slowly, through the warm twilight of a late summer evening, we made our way home. There were still many people on the street. I heard questions – 'Is it true Soderini's arranged a meeting of the *popolo grosso*?' 'Will the Pitti oppose him?' – and for once I knew the answers. But I said nothing. I felt bothered by my day, taken for granted, somehow vaguely insulted. Yet at the same time, curiously, I felt smug and privileged. Tommaso Soderini was my friend; I had met Lorenzo; I had met Luca Pitti. The dome of a warm summer's dusk arched high over my city. The swifts returned to their roosts, and the sky filled with bats. I looked to the future with relish.

1498

For two days after his ducking Sandro was delirious, sweating out the waters of the Arno, shivering himself back to warmth. His only surviving brother was summoned: Simone paid for a girl to stay with Sandro and feed him broth, ordered new crutches, and settled up with the boatman. Daily, to get out of the house, Simone visited Sandro. He was there on the third day when Sandro, seemingly recovered, rose from his bed.

It was a clear autumn morning. The hills were russet in the distance and a mist hung over the river. Sandro ran through the events that had nearly led to his death. 'You poor deluded fool,' he said to himself, and Simone cupped a hand behind an inadequate ear to catch the words. 'I wasn't talking to you,' Sandro shouted.

'Are you better?' Simone shouted.

'Much, thank you.'

Sandro dressed and the brothers left the rooms. 'Why don't you come back and live with Gabrielle and me?' shouted Simone.

'No, thank you,' Sandro bellowed back.

They walked together to Simone's comfortable house, parted, and Sandro continued alone. He visited many places that day. He leant on his new crutches outside the Medici palace, looking at the broken shields where the palla had been chiselled off; he thought about Gozzoli's famous fresco of the Medici family, dressed as the Magi on their journey to the infant Christ, under which he had spent so much time, and remembered the conversations and affairs once conducted behind those shuttered, boarded windows. He passed his father's old house and entered the church of the Ognissanti, where

Simonetta was buried and where his fresco of St Augustine in his cell faced Domenico Ghirlandaio's fresco of St Jerome. He limped to Santa Maria Novella and looked at the painting he had done of the Adoration of the Magi, which, like Gozzoli's earlier picture, gave the Magi Medici faces, and at his picture of the Madonna and Child with St John and two angels. At San Martino alla Scala he looked at the rapid picture of the Annunciation he had painted between the April and May of 1481, just before his first journey to Rome. The mists had cleared by the time he returned to the river, looked out to the Palazzo Pitti, and thought about his panel of Pallas and the Centaur which was hanging there. He went to Santa Maria Maggiore and saw his Lamentation and his painting of St Sebastian, to Santa Maria Maddalena dei Pazzi where an Annunciation was displayed, and to San Paolino where there was a different painting of the Lamentation. Gathering darkness, distance, and private property stopped him completing his tour. He did not manage to see the paintings he had done for Lorenzo Tornabuoni, the Young Man Admitted to the Liberal Arts and the companion picture of the girls, nor the Madonna of the Pomegranate tondo in the Palazzo della Signoria, nor the paintings in the Vespucci palace, much less those he had done for Lorenzo di Pierfrancesco de' Medici's villa outside the city or his frescos in the Sistine Chapel, but he had seen enough. He had seen Simonetta's beautiful face in many Madonnas, and he had reminded himself she was dead. He had seen the beauty he could fashion out of paint, and restored his sense of his place in the world.

The world shall end in thunder that rends the tired afternoon. The survivors shall huddle in ruins, clasping one another, caught beneath the cornice of the palace, the fallen masonry of the church, the silent façade of the civic hall. Dogs shall wander the street, lick the feet of the dead. Flies shall settle, undisturbed, to lay their writhing spawn. And when night falls, the rats will grow fat on human flesh. Yet, thought Sandro, I have done something with my life, I have left my mark on my city, on my world. Savonarola may have been right. Vanity may be the Devil's mark. But without pride we are nothing. Caked in shit, tossed in the river, was I humble enought to enter Heaven? It did not feel that way. The world shall end in thunder, my flesh shall feed the rats, my paintings turn to dust, the vanity of all my endeavours shall be exposed. But at the moment I am alive. We are all humbled by death; we need pride to stay alive. We are held together by vanity as we are held together by our seamless pale skin. Pierce either and we bleed. Rip either apart and we die.

He walked back through the dark streets. He felt assured of the city and the world, reassured of his place in both. And then he saw Simonetta again, still dressed as a careless youth, and was humbled, and mad, once more.

1470

In the spring of 1470 I was still living at my family's house near the church of Ognissanti. I had little work to do, just odd jobs for Verrocchio and the occasional design for a flag or a carnival mask. I worked in my room: the light was poor before noon, but later, while the rest of the city took a nap, I could paint without trouble. My assistance to the Medici, like my contact with the Pitti, had so far brought me nothing, and I had not seen Tommaso Soderini for several months. It was a listless period of my life, and I often wondered if I should ever get the chance to prove that I could paint.

One morning, in the time before the feast of the Annunciation, I was at Verrocchio's bottega, delivering a finished canvas which would be carried in the Annunciation day parade, when Tommaso Soderini called. He was looking healthy and cheerful, as though the new regime suited him. After greeting Verrocchio and the others he knew in the workshop, Leonardo and Pietro Vanucci, he turned to me. 'Sandro! It's a lucky coincidence meeting you here. I was going to call on you anyway. How are you coping with life?'

'I get by,' I told him.

'Is this your work?' He looked at the canvas. The colours were bold, the design simplified, as the painting was essentially a banner. 'Pleasant, but I'd have thought you could do better things. Are you busy?'

'Am I ever?'

He looked distastefully at a bowl of steaming hooves. The *garzoni* were making glue and the stench was appalling. Puckering his upper lip as though to block the smell he led me outside. We stood in the busy street for a while getting in the way of Florence's trade – wagons of bundles and barrels, men humping sacks and braces of game, women with milkpails or lengths of dark cloth – and then he led me to a nearby loggia where we could sit in comfort. 'I know I haven't seen you for a while,' he said, 'but I'm not going to apologize. I've been busy.'

'I heard you were at the siege of Prato,' I told him. Immediately after the death of Piero de' Medici the town of Prato had been captured by exiled Diotisalvi Neroni.

'That's true,' he replied.

'You soon dealt with Neroni,' I said, admiringly. 'He won't try to take on Florence again.'

'He was a Florentine himself,' said Tommaso. 'There's nothing glorious about fighting our own kind. I was sorry it had to be done.'

Around the loggia the citizens swarmed, enjoying the June sun. I ignored the sadness in Tommaso's voice. I was young. 'I've never seen a battle,' I admitted, and felt jealous. Tommaso was many years older than I; were I to live twice as long as him I knew I should neither see nor do so much.

'I hope you never do,' he said, which sounded patronizing to me then. 'Your role in life is to create beauty. There's not much beauty in a war.'

'Honestly,' I corrected. 'I should like to see a battle. I love the jousting.'

'Jousting! A battle isn't like a joust, whatever Uccello may paint.' I didn't know the picture Tommaso meant at the time – a picture of the Rout of San Romano which in those days Lorenzo de' Medici kept in his bedroom – so the reference was lost on me. Tommaso looked down at his hands. 'You know Boccaccio's poem, the *Ameto*? That was written in Prato. I doubt he could write of the town with such innocent joy now.' He steepled his fingers and rested his forehead tiredly on the tips. 'Do you know what I always forget until I see a battle?' he asked his hands. 'I forget how very much blood there is in a man.'

I felt younger than ever then, so young I was still unafraid.

A woman staggered by, weighed down by round cheeses wrapped in cloth. Tommaso looked at her with relief, for she was a chance to escape this subject, and feigned the malice with which he spoke.

'Thank the heavens she's not stopping here! I think I preferred the smell at Verrocchio's. I swear Florence stinks worse every year; heaven knows how high high summer will be. You know the decoration for the Court of Mercatanzia?'

'Yes,' I replied, pouncing on the tail of his conversation the way a cat grabs at a mouse.

'I decided I should join the committee in charge of the commissions. You remember that Piero Pollaiuolo won it? He was to paint seven Virtues?'

'I remember,' I said. 'I've seen the picture he was doing of Charity, in his shop.'

'Did you like it?'

'It's all right.'

'We on the committee are a little disappointed.'

'What's the problem? Did he take too long? Charge too much?' These were the main reasons people complained about Fra Lippo; it sometimes seems a good half of my short apprenticeship was spent fending off such complaints.

'He did take a long time, and maybe that's what started people asking questions, but no, it's the painter's skill that's being challenged.'

'That's unusual.' I had three reasons to be surprised. Firstly, Pollaiuolo won the commission in competition against Verrocchio, so the committee had not only liked his drawings but would lose face if they admitted a mistake: this would usually be enough to keep them quiet, for no Florentine can bear to lose face. Secondly, clients, and particularly committees, are usually concerned only with how much the artist has used expensive materials – ultramarine and beaten gold mainly – and what proportion of the work has been left to assistants; they rarely appreciate skill for its own sake. And thirdly, I had seen the painting: it wasn't exactly inspired, but it seemed adequate to me. 'What's the matter with it?'

'There's some suggestion that the original drawings were done by Piero Pollaiuolo's brother, and that Piero won the competition by cheating.'

'I suppose that's possible.' Antonio Pollaiuolo was the better painter in my view: when I had visited their shop last Antonio had been working on a painting of the Annunciation which had, behind the angel's head, the most beautiful little view of Florence seen through a window; in comparison Piero's painting of the figure of Charity might seem a little wooden. 'But even if Antonio did do the original drawings it's hardly cheating,' I said. 'Piero is a competent painter. I'm sure his painting won't be so inferior to the cartoon that anyone outside the trade would notice.' If Tommaso expects me to get excited about a bit of gossip like this, I thought, he's wrong.

'I noticed, and Lorenzo noticed.'

'Lorenzo de' Medici?'

'Who else? He suggested the name of a better artist who could take over the commission, and of course we of the Mercantanzia were delighted.'

And even if you weren't, I thought, you wouldn't say anything. 'So who has got the job now?'

'You have.'

'Me!'

'You,' Tommaso confirmed.

'Thank you,' I said, gasping rather. 'But how did you persuade them to give me the commission?' I wondered. 'I'm not exactly famous.'

'I didn't. It was Lorenzo's doing.'

'I'm surprised Lorenzo remembers me.'

'Lorenzo remembers everyone. That's his secret. He's a very impressive young man. I'm proud to have him for a nephew.' Tommaso contrived to look modest and cunning at the same time, an expression he must have practised often in his trade. 'And of course, I was able to put in a word for you myself from time to time, with both Lorenzo and my colleagues in the Mercatanzia. I've been looking to give you a chance to prove yourself, and one came up.'

At the expense of Piero Pollaiuolo. But I was in no position to be squeamish. 'Thank you,' I said again.

'You're pleased?'

'I'm delighted.' It was, I was realizing slowly, the best thing that had happened in my career so far. 'Thank you,' I said, for the third time.

'My pleasure, believe me. You're too good a painter to waste your time on the second-rate stuff you've been doing. This is your chance to make a name for yourself. Don't waste it.'

The weeks went quickly. On the day after the feast of the Assumption, when the image of the Virgin is fetched from Impruneta and the guilds all march in procession, I met the committee of the Mercatanzia and learnt the details of the commission. Only Tommaso seemed genuinely pleased to see me; the others seemed a little embarrassed, a little hesitant, and I was certain that it was only Lorenzo de' Medici's influence that had persuaded them to employ me, and that they were rather less dissatisfied with Pollaiuolo's efforts than Tommaso had suggested. Confirming this impression, it seemed they were letting Pollaiuolo complete four of the remaining panels and giving me only two, though at least they let me choose which of the available subjects I wanted. Prompted by Tommaso, and remembering my debt to the Medici, I chose Fortitude and Temperance. These virtues, together with Prudence, were associated with the Medici family in those days, and, represented by three peacock feathers, had been Cosimo de' Medici's personal device: it was a reasonably subtle way of saying thank you. The Mercatanzia asked me to set to work at once, and I certainly had nothing better to do with my time.

Although it was a fine commission – the Court of the Mercatanzia remains exactly the sort of place any young artist wants his work to be displayed, for almost all the potential clients in Florence visit it regularly – I was limited in what I could do. The panels were already prepared, about my height and half as wide, tapering to a pointed arch. It was agreed that the figure should be almost life-size, which meant it had to be sitting if I was to include any background. Moreoever, as Piero had already painted Charity in the series, and as I was still inexperienced in many ways, I did not dare do anything too startling. My Fortitude is still in the court for all to see. I received plenty of advice. The fancy chair I designed for Fortitude to sit in, topped by a rounded classical arch and flanked by heavy arms, was Lorenzo's idea, and Tommaso passed the suggestion on to me; Verrocchio proposed that I seat her with one foot firmly in front of the other and a scarlet cloak draped over her knee as a way of showing her determination; even Piero Pollaiuolo helped, suggesting I make the background, which I originally intended to be a landscape, entirely dark in keeping with his own pictures. In fact, the Pollaiuolo brothers were extraordinarily helpful, which was almost distressing, and Antonio supervised the whole of my painting. I learnt why they were so helpful later.

For the reason you will see only my picture of Fortitude, and not my Temperance as well, when you visit the Court of the Mercatanzia, is that while I was finishing my panel the Pollaiuolo brothers went back to the committee and spoke to them. Tommaso reported their argument: Sandro Botticelli is a competent painter, they said, but his picture has only been possible because of our supervision; rather than have said Sandro do any more work on the series, therefore, it seems more sensible to return the whole commission to the man who first won it, namely Piero. The Mercatanzia, who prided themselves on their sense, were interested; Tommaso argued the other way, saying that Sandro Botticelli had proved himself more than merely competent, that his painting of Fortitude was a credit to the Court and the city, and that to prevent him completing his second panel would be a travesty of justice. Which reminds us, said the Pollaiuolo brothers, we'll throw in a painting of Justice for free: you won't have to pay us any more than you are doing already, and can pay Sandro Botticelli considerably less. The sensible businessmen of the Mercatanzia were persuaded.

'I'm sorry, Sandro,' finished Tommaso. 'But your painting will be admired by everyone. You'll soon have plenty of commissions, soon be able to set up a shop of your own and give Filippino a proper apprenticeship. How is Filippino by the way?'

'He studies hard, both at school and his drawings. He's a good boy.'

'You know,' considered Tommaso. 'I can't see what the Pollaiuolo brothers gained. It seems to me they're worse off than before. They get no more money with the current arrangements, and have to paint an extra picture. All that happened was that you lost.'

'Exactly,' I said. Tommaso, after all, was a member of the Mercatanzia and another sensible businessman. I was a painter, and could follow the Pollaiuolo brothers' reasoning. 'It isn't hard to understand them really,' I told him. 'They lost reputation when they lost the commission. It showed them in a bad light, and will make it hard for them to get other commissions in the future if they're not careful. They had to do something. They're painters with a living to make. So am I.'

'You're being very charitable,' he said.

'I'm in a mood to be. I got another commission today. A Virgin and Child for Santa Trinità.'

He looked genuinely delighed. 'That's wonderful!' Fra Lippi had been right: I could not have wished for a better friend in Florence than Tommaso Soderini. 'I just hope you'll have time to do it. I have a commission for you too, for a Virgin with two angels. And Lorenzo asks you to dine with him on Saturday.'

Dining with Lorenzo did not quite mean what it said on that first occasion. There were many people there, though Tommaso, I was disappointed to see, was missing. We ate, as was common when there were many guests, in the fine chapel with Gozzoli's Adoration of the Magi looking down on us; there was a gilded salt cellar to scatter the light round each table. Our host was entertaining an embassy from the duke of Milan, which meant that he ate at a distant bench and retired shortly afterwards for discussions. I would have expected nothing else: the alliance with Milan was vital for the Medici interest; his opponents still favoured the Venetians; the Pitti still had their Venetian priest.

Despite Lorenzo's absence, I had an interesting time. I was sitting between a delicate boy of about 16 years of age and a heavy middle-aged man. The man, though dressed in a peaceful black gown and grey hose, had the look of a warrior. The skin around his eyes was bunched, as though he spent much time staring at the sun, and his hands were large and muscular. My nose had recovered well from being broken: I had no more than a slightly wider bridge than before – and a wheeze when I was tired – to remind me of it. This man's nose had suffered far more. The bridge was flattened completely, with a scar on one side where the bone had burst through the flesh, and the nostrils were of different shapes, one being long and thin, and other short and fat. Nor did his conversation, though we spoke only of peace, do anything to alter my opinion that this was a man of war. He spoke in short, deliberate phrases, often thinking for so long before he had spoken that the talk had moved on to a new subject.

The boy could not have been more different. His skin had the pallor of a scholar or a priest, and his conversation came in smooth passages that seemed as concerned with sound as substance. 'What manner of man are you, sir,' he asked me as we waited for food, 'to sit among this company in darned hose? Are you a scholar?' He said something in Latin. 'No, you are clearly not a scholar or you would have reacted. I suggested that your mother was a female of the species the vernacular has as dog, and that she birthed you out of wedlock which, though I have no doubt is entirely untrue, would, you must agree, provoke a response from any who understood the language of our ancient forebears.'

I laughed, for I did not know what else to do, and regretted my darned hose.

'I am pleased, sir, that you took no offence at my pleasantry. Or perhaps, sir, you are offended, yet do not want to draw attention to yourself and your hose by making a scene. In which case, sir, you will doubtless wish to know my name, as that way you can employ others who can beat me to a pulp one starless night. Sir, I am Angelo Ambrogini, of the town of Montepulciano, from which, in deference to ancestors both local and Latin, I have taken my adopted name of Politian or Poliziano.'

The scholarly man sitting the other side of Politian spoke briefly. 'Don't pester the young man.'

'Pester? I would hardly do that, Marsilio. Now, I might pester a man of wealth, for he might make my life more comfortable, furnish me with books or an income. But I would never pester a man with darned hose. If I speak with such a man as this it is out of interest, no more. And if I speak to such a man, to any man, I expect a reply. So sir, I ask again, what manner of man are you?'

I wanted to be witty. 'I used to be pupil to my pupil's father; now I am master to my master's son.'

'As you would be,' he said, 'for your second statement is no more than a gloss on your first. Had you not been pupil to your pupil's father, you could not be master to your master's son.'

This was true, and quickly worked out. 'I'm a painter,' I conceded.

'Good. Now we have a way of placing you in the firmament of stars that makes of this hungry company. And you, sir?' he asked, leaning over me to address my other neighbour. 'I know you are not a painter, or rather that if you are it is fences that you paint, for you have an outdoor look to you. Are you perhaps a seaman, a Portuguese navigator fresh from the coast of Africa? Or a soldier of fortune returned from distant parts? A farmer of the contado? A merchant who plies the markets of Champagne, maybe? Or a brigand fresh down from the mountains?'

'No,' said the older man.

'No? Is that all you are prepared to say? All to which you dare commit yourself?'

'Yes.'

'But sir, though your mouth speaks so little, your nose is eloquent. That, sir, is a nose which has seen some action.'

'Whereas yours,' said the scholarly man, 'is too long, pries too hard into others' affairs, and will doubtless some day be shortened by a swift and painful blow.'

The youth took our laughter well. 'Allow me to introduce my own master, Marsilio Ficino, a man whose nose is as sharp as mine though his tongue is less blunt.'

I had heard of Ficino. 'I am honoured to meet you,' I said.

'And perhaps he might be honoured to meet you,' said Politian, 'if only he knew your name. Is this perhaps a paradox, that we scholars, who live only for the quiet pursuit of study, should be so forthcoming with our names, while you, who as a painter are constantly pressing your opinions, in the guise of images, upon the reluctant public, should take such pains to hide your identity?'

'I'm not trying to hide anything,' I said. 'But it's hard to speak over your babble.'

'Bravo,' said Ficino, and the grizzled man nodded. But the youth was untroubled. 'My dear sir,' he said, 'I had no notion that my loquacious circumlocutions were interfering with your desire towards expression. Pray speak.'

It was hard to think of anything to say after that. 'I'm Sandro Filipepi, known as Botticelli.'

'And sir,' said Politian, 'I am delighted to meet you too.' He smiled engagingly. 'Your fame has gone before you as that of Alexander in Parthia or of Caesar through Gaul.'

'You've heard of me?' I asked, surprised.

'Our patron and friend Lorenzo speaks of no one else,' Politian assured me.

'Lorenzo has mentioned you once or twice,' corrected Ficino more soberly, more plausibly.

'But always with enthusiasm,' said Politian, looking to his master for agreement.

'That's true,' said Ficino, and I was satisfied.

The Medici chaplain said prayers of thanks, and then the food arrived, gold plates covered with poultry and game, vegetables and fruit. With it came wine and, more surprisingly, glasses. I had never been given my own glass at a table before, and I had to be very careful not to try passing it to my neighbours when I had finished, as would have been polite at more humble meals. Many of the guest had knives to cut their food; some even used pronged instruments to carry their meal to their mouths. I was relieved none of my neighbours was so well equipped.

I was also relieved that Ficino restricted his pupil to one glass of wine. What effect would wine, which makes even a quiet man talkative, have on this athletic tongue?

The proof of the way wine loosens a man's speech was my neighbour. 'I'm Orlando,' he told us. It was hardly an oration but, as Politian pointed out, it doubled the number of syllables he had spoken so far.

'Pleased to meet you,' I said. His speech was northern. 'You're not a Florentine?'

'Milanese,' he agreed.

'Ah, part of the entourage of the embassy of the noble duke of the esteemed city of Milan!' exclaimed a voice I need not identify.

Orlando chewed on a goose wing. Music began, lutes and sweet viols, and a small bear was persuaded to dance.

'I have heard it said that the duke of Milan,' continued Politian, 'who is allied not only to this radiant republic but also to both Louis of France and Charles of Burgundy, is deeply worried that Charles's ambitions on Alsace and Lorraine will lead to war between Burgundy and France, which in turn will demand Milan's involvement on one side, the other side, or both. Is this true?'

'That's right,' said Orlando, but in reply, I suspect, to Politian's first question; he was too busy chewing to even notice the second.

'A perfectly natural concern,' said Politian, which would have baffled Orlando if he'd been listening. 'Since the cessation of their war with England, the French have suggested themselves formidable foes, but maybe even more formidable friends. For them to intervene in the affairs of any Italian state would be dangerous in the extreme; we must not let our natural sympathies with them against the more insidious claims of the emperor or the papacy blind us to the nature of their threat. Yet this duke of Burgundy seems a foolhardy man.'

'Milan's secure,' said Orlando.

'Milan's security, I would say, is that of the largest boy in the school. Just as that boy has nothing to fear from his classmates, thus Milan has nothing to fear from the cities of Italy. But when the schoolmaster walks in he is as ineffectual as the scrawniest runt in the class. King Louis of France wields a heavy cane.'

Orlando looked annoyed, though unlikely to reply. 'I hear Giuliano de' Medici intends you to paint his portrait,' said Ficino, throwing his remark into the pause.

I spluttered into my glass. There were no other painters present. He had to be talking to me. 'Really?' I managed to say.

'You weren't aware? I'm sorry. But no harm done. If I must let slip news, let that news be good.'

Politian, unstoppably, was proceeding with his analysis of the international situation. I heard names that meant something – Paris, Bruges, Cologne – and other names that meant nothing to me then and I forget entirely now. He was a strange young man, I felt, tremendously gifted, and sure of his gifts, yet unsure how to present himself. He wants to be liked, I thought, hates to be ignored, and cannot quite reconcile the two ambitions. He will be formidable, I decided, in a year or two's time.

The other predictions I made that evening proved less accurate. After we had eaten, Jacopo Pazzi, the loud-mouthed head of the Pazzi bank, inevitably wanted to gamble. There were drinking races, running races, even crawling-on-the-knees races. Orlando, who as a foreigner knew none of the participants, kept asking me whom I thought would win. Fortunately no one asked us to place a bet, so all I lost was pride.

I could afford to lose pride. I had plenty. I was a guest of the Medici. I had dined with a famous scholar. I was to paint the portrait of Giuliano. There was dancing that evening too. I had not danced much recently, and was unsure of myself in this sophisticated company, but when the singer began 'De Phyllide et Flora' I had no choice: I believe my feet would have danced without me, leaving my torso fast in the chair. As we stepped and turned to the dances I found myself seeing the women in a new way. I am not a man much given to lust. The whores of the Orsanmichele hold no interest for me. But the women of Palazzo Medici were clean and beautiful. Their figures were kept trim by riding and hunting, and many had all their teeth. We circled in scarlet and black, yellow and blue, green and gold. We danced in lines and squares. Twenty fingers daintily met. Ten male backs bowed low. Twenty heads looked left, looked right. Ten female backs stayed upright through a curtsey, and as I danced, a peacock in darned hose, I fell in love with them all.

I went to the Palazzo Medici often after that. The household was informal, and always busy. Sometimes my visits were social; sometimes I had an appointment to sketch my subject. Young Giuliano de' Medici had a strong face, not handsome exactly, though more conventionally attractive than his brother's, with distinctive features: a firm jaw, hooded eyes, and a sharp nose that seemed designed for looking down disdainfully. Yet despite the arrogance of his expression he was a cheerful and well-bred youth, only a year or two older than Politian, and though often busy – he had an estate of his own, and helped his brother with many family duties – was a patient sitter. I also managed to sketch Lorenzo's distinctive features at this time, as he called for his brother one morning, and Lorenzo promised that one day I should do his portrait too. Lorenzo died in 1492. I am still waiting.

Suddenly I was in demand. News of my popularity with the Medici meant those trying the curry the same wanted me to paint their pictures. I don't generally enjoy portraiture. Sitters want pictures not of how others see them, but of how they see themselves: show a client two pictures, one of himself and one of his friend, and invariably he will say, 'Yes, I see him, but you've not got me quite right.' Most people's conception of their own appearance is the face they see in a looking-glass. That face is reversed. It is also, though few people believe me when I tell them, half-sized: had I kept my painted mirror I could have proved it, but you can prove it for yourself by clearing the space your reflection occupies from the surface of a dusty glass. In fact today, after Savonarola's prohibition on looking-glasses, portraiture has become less of a chore, as people have less misinformation about their own appearances. But in the days of Lorenzo, golden though they were, vanity was not so much a sin as a luxury, well within the reach of the rich.

And we were rich. Even I was rich, by the standards of my past and my family. I took a small shop near Santa Trinità, making use of a building my family had rented some years earlier, and an assistant. I felt wealthy and young then, and youth was a marvellous thing. Lorenzo and Giuliano seemed to gild the city. It was a time when the old men seemed to vanish, either to shove their years into hose designed for much younger men or to shut themselves behind their doors, and only the young seemed to matter. Even in my household this seemed true. I was suddenly earning far more than my father: I moved out, took a room close to the shop, but visited him frequently, and on each visit I brought him a gift in an attempt to wipe out my debt to him; I believe I even, in some perverse way, wanted him to fall on hard times, so I could support him and reverse our roles completely.

Filippino also moved from my father's house, sleeping at the shop and becoming my pupil officially, while Politian took to calling on my studio. His conversation was lively, his energy remarkable, and his intellect humbling. In his company I felt at once cleverer than I really am, for he taught me many things, and more stupid, for he spoke of so much I did not know. Apart from his interest in the writers of antiquity, he was fascinated by, and fascinating on, the political situation around Florence at the time, which was still dominated by the Milanese alliance. Old Tommaso sometimes came to the studio with Politian, and I listened as they spoke, Tommaso grave and measured, Politian excited by everything. I no longer envied Tommaso his experience, as I had before, for his experience seemed to belong to a different age. Politian's enthusiasm was more enticing. A new era was dawning, the era of Lorenzo, and I wanted to be ready for it. The time of our fathers, of Piero de' Medici as much as Mariano Filipepi, appeared crabbed and mean; our imaginations leap-frogged over that time to the grandeur of ancient Rome. There, among the ruins, was our model and inspiration. We sought to make the new from the very old, and what lay between, the recent past, seemed listless, meaningless, dead.

1498

I was wrong. No part of the past is ever meaningless, and even the dead live on in our minds. History is the layered underpainting without which no picture can succeed, the deep foundations without which each building shall fail. It is not so much dead as dormant, and should the sleeper awake then the underpainting will crack, the foundations shift: the paint shall peel from the board and Troy come tumbling down.

Sandro saw Simonetta again. Troy came tumbling down.

1498

She was walking through the Piazza Santa Trinità. She was still dressed in her boy's clothing – Sandro could not help but admire the shape of her leg, the delicacy of her throat – and was still with her friend Bernardo, but she was so lithe, so lively, so lovely, he decided to forgive her the events of the rainy night. To do otherwise would be churlish. He watched her. There were sellers of dried flowers in the piazza, middle-aged women with posies of lavender and violet, and Simonetta ran from one to another, exchanging a kiss for a flower until she had gathered a bouquet, and charming everyone with her gaiety. Sandro stayed in the shadows, fearing brutish Bernardo might recognize him – or his crutches at least – and attack him again, but he knew he need have no fear of Simonetta. Her innocence, and her joy, made her radiant.

He tried to follow her through the Porta Rossa, cursing his useless feet as he swung through the crowds. He was not completely accustomed to the new crutches: they were not yet worn smooth beneath the armpits, and, though he could see no difference between them, he always had the sensation that one was longer than the other and that they were trying to take him in circles. Once, as a young man, he had danced down this street for love of her. This time he hobbled, on wounded legs, crippled love.

The day was overcast. It was the Eve of All Souls. Winter was approaching, mustering belligerently over the hills, and the flocks of migrating birds no longer crossed the sky above the city. Now when he looked up he saw crows, and higher still the broad dark shapes of kites. The carrion birds looked back at him, patiently. There would be snow that night.

Simonetta and Bernardo reached the Via Calimala, the Street of Ill Fame where Sandro had his studio at that time, and turned south towards the Piazza della Signoria; Sandro continued past his bottega, paused for breath at the corner and watched them. Simonetta still had her bouquet, and gave a flower to each attractive young woman she saw. Almost all of them smiled and thanked her. It is so like her, thought Sandro, to give pleasure wherever she goes. All her life she did that, and now she has come back. Even at the onset of the season of long nights she is like Flora announcing the coming of the spring, just as she is Venus risen daily from the waves. He limped his way down towards the Piazza della Signoria after her, panting at the effort but determined not to lose her again. I will confront her, he told himself: she shall know me and her love shall restore me. As Dante was saved from Hell by his Beatrice, so I shall be saved from this place by Simonetta, in whose Resurrection is everlasting life.

Bernardo's broad back, dressed in dark green, was easy to follow even through the crowds of the Signoria. He watched as they climbed the few steps of the Loggia dell'Orcagna to sit on the low wall separating the arched canopy from the piazza below. The Loggia, where the public events take place, the installing of the Gonfaloniere and the announcement of new laws, is for the rest of the time a place to rest or meet with friends. At the moment Michelangelo Buonarroti, who as pupil of my dear colleague Domenico Ghirlandaio has my love, and as usurper of my position as Florence's foremost artist has my envy, is turning a huge piece of marble into a statue of David for our city, and already there is talk of a committee of painters to decide where it should be placed. Despite – or perhaps because of – my acknowledged lunacy I have been asked to join that committee, as has Leonardo. Fra Agostino tells me Leonardo has written from Arezzo, where he draws maps to help Cesare Borgia attack us, recommending the statue should be placed in front of the Palazzo della Signoria; this position is far too vulnerable, and in my opinion the statue should be placed in the Loggia dell'Orcagna, safe from the weather and the crowds. But all discussion is premature. The colossus of David, with its disproportionately colossal hands, is unfinished and likely to remain so. Bernardo's hands were equally disproportionate. He sat with Simonetta on the wall, he lumpen, she the epitome of grace, and Sandro stared at them both.

Taking a quick decision he hurried round the far side of the square, daring not approach directly for fear they recognize him. The traitor's head on its pole above the battlements of the Palazzo had decomposed further. The eyeballs had been taken by small birds, and the cheeks had been attacked too. The skull grinned recklessly.

Dusk and starlings collected in the eaves. Sandro had been sweating when he pursued the young couple; now he was cold. He lifted his stubborn legs cautiously up the steps at the far end of the Loggia. Simonetta was out of sight now, hidden behind the Loggia's pillars, though there were enough people about, youths and priests, gossips and scolds, for the cripple to feel inconspicuous. He made his cautious way to behind the pillar Bernardo was leaning on and sat down on the next section of the wall with his back to the piazza. The pillars were broad, twice the span of a man across, and solid. He was concealed, and, though he could see neither Simonetta nor her friend, he thought he recognized the voices. 'I don't give a toss for any of them,' said Simonetta, using the hard, uncultured voice she had affected before. 'I'm not afraid.'

'I'm not afraid either,' said Bernardo. 'But be sensible. How do we know what we're getting into?'

'Why? What are you scared of? What've we got to lose?'

'A whole load of things when you think about it.'

'Our lives?' asked Simonetta's voice.

'Gentle Christ, I hope not.'

'Our bollocks, then?' said Simonetta, and she said it so unselfconsciously that Sandro almost laughed. She really was performing her strange role remarkably well. He wished he could see as well as hear her, but dared not take the risk. 'I didn't think you were using yours anyway,' she added.

'I told you,' said Bernardo. 'Katerina's coming on strong enough. I'm just waiting till the time's right.'

'Katerina doesn't even look at you and you know it,' returned Simonetta. 'The only reason she talks to you is to get to me.' Sandro could believe this. Bernardo was big but ugly; even as a boy Simonetta was beautiful.

'Well?' asked Bernardo. 'So what? You don't care about her and I do, so if she comes our way what d'you expect me to do? I'm not hurting you any.'

'That's true. You're not hurting me at all. I've already had her.'

'What? Had Katerina?' And if Bernardo was shocked at the notion, Sandro was utterly amazed.

'Of course. She goes some, I'll tell you. And you should see her tits. Oh, but you want to anyway, don't you, and she won't let you. I'd forgotten.'

'You bastard,' said Bernardo, his voice low and dangerous.

'I don't see it changes things for you,' Simonetta said carelessly. 'You weren't going to get any oats from her anyhow. I'll tell you what. Next time I screw her I'll let you come and watch us.'

Sandro could not believe he heard this correctly. He wished he could be absolutely sure it was Simonetta and Bernardo he was listening to. He thought he had recognized the voices, and undeniably they had been sitting there earlier, but perhaps another couple had taken their place. He raised himself up on his crutches as the voice he thought was Bernardo's cried, 'You bastard!' again, more loudly; 'Stick to wanking!' replied the voice he identified with Simonetta. Sandro clung to the pillar and peered round in time to see a back the size of Bernardo's leap from the wall and start running. Of Simonetta, if she had been there at all, there was nothing to be seen. I must have been wrong, thought Sandro. I can't even be sure that was Bernardo, and Simonetta must have gone already. It was a pity he had lost his quarry, and a pity he had wasted so much time eavesdropping on the wrong conversation, but it was a relief too. He limped back across the piazza. The shifting crowd was colourful, a tapestry caught in a breeze. The marks left by the great fires still stained the cobbles and commemorated the recent past.

The eve of Palm Sunday in that year of Our Lord 1498 had been a significant day, for it was then that in distant France King Charles cracked his head on a low beam and died, and that an event of equal moment, equal bathos, took place in the Piazza della Signoria. Savonarola, who had been excommunicated by the pope and ridiculed by a faction of the people, had been challenged to prove his divine inspiration by Fra Francesco of the Franciscan order, and an ordeal by fire had been decided to settle the dispute between the two friars. The city was cleared of foreigners, the streets blocked for fear of riots. In the piazza an avenue of wooden stakes, thirty paces long and soaked in oil, was erected in front of the Loggia. The Franciscan friars arrived first, led by Fra Francesco, and by his side was Fra Giuliano, who was to be the order's representative in the flames.

Fra Giuliano had been shriven that morning, for he expected to die, and looked resigned and outwardly calm. He stood before the oil-soaked sticks and prayed that, though no one could survive the walk through the flames, his death might serve God's purpose, and asked that he might be brave. There was a long wait. Fra Francesco inspected the avenue too. It would be an inferno when ignited, he said, and because there seemed little point praying for Fra Giuliano's body, he prayed for the friar's soul.

The Dominicans arrived. Well organized, they marched in pairs behind a crucifix and chanted a psalm as they marched. Last to enter the piazza, side by side in the cool spring morning, were Fra Domenico, who was to undergo the ordeal by fire on behalf of his prior, and Fra Savonarola, the prior himself. Savonarola, though recently excommunicated by the pope, Alexander the Spaniard, carried the consecrated Host. Sandro, who had been among the crowd, had been shocked by the blasphemy, impressed by the audacity.

Fra Giuliano stepped forward and stood at the opening of the wooden avenue, ready for the moment when it was lit and waiting for Fra Domenico to join him. He stood in silence, a rational man condemned to an irrational act. He had agreed to take part in the ordeal not because he believed that God favoured him above Fra Domenico, but because he wanted to disprove Savonarola's claim that the Dominicans had a special grace. He hoped God would recognize his purpose and his humility.

Fra Domenico showed no such humility, and rather more purpose. He clearly looked forward to the walk through the flames; he did not care if he lived or died. And from his point of view, why should he? If he died he would be a martyr to God and to Savonarola, whom he knew – despite excommunication – to be God's authentic messenger; should he survive then he would be the absolute and living proof that Savonarola spoke the truth. Domenico kissed a crucifix and brandished it but was persuaded that it would be sacrilege to risk Christ's symbol in the flames; no persuasion could separate him from the Host that Savonarola handed him.

At last the two friars, one submissive and the other ecstatic, stood before the wooden gauntlet. The sky darkened ominously. The crowd was silenced. And then the rain began, all prospect of lighting the wood vanished, and the ordeal was postponed. Fra Domenico knew then that God was saving him for some greater purpose; Fra Giuliano was simply relieved. The friars returned to their monasteries.

The citizens were less phlegmatic. Many were tired of Savonarola and his humourless holiness; they had been cheated of the proof that Savonarola was – or wasn't – the bearer of God's stern word, and been cheated of what had promised to be an interesting and exciting spectacle. Sandro had returned to his lodgings, feeling sad and tired, and then sent out for a bottle of burnt wine.

That night the monastery of San Marco, which is next to this madhouse and is where until that night Savonarola was prior, was stormed. To the sound of La Piagnona, the great bell of the monastery, citizens and Dominicans fought in the heavy rain. Many died. Savonarola was captured in his cell, submitting less to the angry citizens than to God's ineffable will. Proud, almost aloof in his certainty of God's favour, Savonarola was led away to the Alberghettino, the prison cell in the tower of the Palazzo dell Signoria. The friars wept as their master was taken; the crowd danced with delight. Sandro in his room was weeping too. His tears were maudlin, flavoured with burnt wine, yet sincere. Florence had lost so much. It had lost Lorenzo de' Medici to death and its pride to an advancing French army which, invading Italy in 1494, had marched into the city without a fight. It had lost Pisa. Many great pictures and books had been consumed in Savonarola's bonfires, and now Florence had lost Savonarola too. Hope seemed to end with the century. Faith was chained in the Alberghettino. Charity was already long dead. It is perhaps no surprise that on the night before Palm Sunday that year Sandro had been confused and drunk and waiting for madness. The only surprise is how long he had to wait.

His crutches stalked across the piazza. The snow began to fall.

1471

A new year began. Though I saw much of Ficino and Politian after that first meal at the Palazzo Medici, I was to see Orlando again only once. In 1471 the duke of Milan, Galeazzo Maria, visited Florence in person. He brought an enormous retinue with him, almost an army: five hundred halberdiers, a hundred and fifty horsemen wearing cloth of silver and mounted on warhorses dressed in cloth of gold, his advisers, his attendants, his servants, his trumpeters, his drummers, his falconers, and his hounds. Drummers were a novelty in those days, and the beat of their mechanical hearts made the soldiers seem even more formidable and even less human than their suits of faceless armour. I saw Orlando among the advisers, his visor raised, his disfigured nose easy to identify even from my place in the crowd; I never, however, spoke to him. The visit was impressive, ostentatious, and brief. Florence enjoyed the spectacle, and our faith in Lorenzo, who had organized the alliance with this spectacular visitor, was confirmed, but most of us felt no great sympathy for these barbaric northern knights. Their arms were impressive; their arts were nothing. Only Leonardo da Vinci, whom I still saw from time to time, showed genuine enthusiasm for the Milanese. 'Real men,' he declared admiringly, 'with a desire to achieve real ambitions. We're too soft and feminine in Florence. We should eat more meat.' Perhaps he was right. We are not a warrior people – though Niccolò Machiavelli, the secretary to the Ten of War, is demanding we sack our mercenaries and replace them with a local militia – and perhaps we have suffered for this. But I could not help remarking that, as Verrocchio's catamite, Leonardo was hardly in a position to judge 'real men'. He smiled wolfishly. 'Who better to assess manliness than a man who loves men?' he asked.

Shortly afterwards, Lorenzo had business outside the city. At that time, though recognized as the head of the Medici and therefore the most important individual in Florence, Lorenzo was accorded no special status, and the Signoria appointed him one of the delegation sent to Rome to congratulate the new pope on his elevation. 'It's a bore,' he said. 'Still, this new man must be an improvement on the last.'

The death of Pope Paul II had caused me no tears either. I had admired his predecessor, Pius II, the pope of my adolescence: although Pius was from Siena, and therefore had no love for Florence, he had seemed a clever and broad-minded man; more importantly I admired him because, although he was physically weak, as I had been at that time, he was courageous and determined. Paul, a Venetian, may have shared the courage, but he had shown himself far from clever, anything but broad-minded. By the time he died, in 1471, I had become part of the Medici circle. I had started joining them regularly, for supper and conversation. My chatter could never compete with the convoluted method of expression affected by Politian at that time, the pithiness of Ficino, or the depth of Landino's learning. Nor did I have the authority of the Medici brothers and their wealthy friends such as Alamanno Rinuccini and the Acciaiuoli cousins. But I enjoyed the meetings. They showed me a world I had known only through my fragment of Virgil, a world of gods and goddesses, satyrs and nymphs, that seemed at that time more relevant, more alive, than the familiar round of prayer that was our usual spiritual diet. It was not heresy we discussed. We did not believe in the gods of the ancients, much less worship them. But sometimes, as I listened to the scholars talk of their reading, I felt like one reminded of a marvellous dream, a dream remembered only in fragments, yet each fragment so pure, so bright, that it seems the whole shining truth is within reach could but the rest be recalled. The Roman Academy was a similar group to ours. In 1468 Paul II had ordered it to be closed down, and its leading members were imprisoned and tortured for beliefs identical to our own. Florence was outraged. Yet had we known what the future would be, had we been able to foresee how his successor, Sixtus IV, would damage so many lives, then I believe we would have wept even for Paul.

Sometimes the conversation at the Palazzo Medici was in Latin. This was galling to me as my grasp of that tongue is imprecise, but it was impressive too. The Roman republic, the Rome of Cicero and Virgil, of Horatio and the first Brutus, was being brought to life in Florence. We were the apex of a golden tradition, for there had been an interest in antiquity before the time of Lorenzo. My friends spoke of earlier Florentines, the divine Dante who conversed with Virgil in Hell, the immortal Boccaccio who complied mythologies as well as writing so many glorious tales of his own, the noble Petrarch who presented us with the lives of the great ancients, the great Bruni of Arezzo whose tomb in Santa Croce had been built by my collaborator on the wedding arches, Bernardo Rossellino. And there were others almost as well known, some who had been tutors to my friends, and all of whom who, though dead, still influenced the Platonic academy: the temperamental Poggio Bracciolini; Lorenzo Valla whom Poggio had tried to have murdered; the Greek known as George Gemistus Plethon; his compatriot John Argyropoulos; the aristocratic Florentine Niccolò Niccoli.

Vespasiano da Bisticci, not yet as famous as he was to become, nor as rich as he had been in Cosimo's day, had a bookshop near my studio, and one day he called on me. 'I envy you painters,' he said as I worked on a small and intricate cartoon of Judith's return to Bethulia for one of the Ridolfi family. 'When I write I need silence. In your trade friends drop in and chat and you're undisturbed. It must be marvellous.'

I'm sure it is, but I was too busy to reply. He carried on. 'Not that writers need be unfriendly. I hear you know a few yourself, Ficino and Landino. And of course, there's Lorenzo, who somehow finds time to write poetry despite everything.'

'Filippino!' I called. Filippino was ready to do more important work, and, once I had the Judith painting begun, I wanted him to take over. 'Are you busy?'

'I was going to prepare this gilding,' said Filippino. The shop was not large, just a single room with a curtained alcove for Filippino to sleep in, but the light was good. He came over. 'How can I help you?' he asked. He was beautifully polite, unless he had a drink in him, all his life.

'What do you think?' I asked in turn, indicating the cartoon.

'I like it,' said Filippino. Despite his youth he was beginning to grow hairy, as his father had been, and soon I would have to pay for a barber.

'Do you think you could paint it?'

'I don't know. I could try. You'll help?'

I put my arm round his shoulder and squeezed. 'Of course I'll help.'

'It's wonderful to encourage the young,' said Vespasiano, which made me feel old. 'You've heard of Niccolò Niccoli of course? He was a great collector of manuscripts: I wish Florence still produced his like. And a great friend of Cosimo de' Medici too. As I was, of course, as well as being the great man's book-buyer. Anyway, I was talking of Niccolò, who one day saw Piero de' Pazzi – that's Jacopo's older brother – when Piero himself was just a youth. In those days Piero was a waster, rich as you like but with no purpose in life, spending his money on gambling and women.'

I wasn't really listening. The picture of Judith was to be a panel of a small diptych; the other half, which I would begin once Filippino was safely embarked on painting Judith, was to show Holofernes lying dead. The commission had specified that the two pictures should be as different as my skill could make them, and I was wondering about colours. 'Greens and yellows for Judith, and plenty of red for Holofernes,' I said aloud.

'Sorry?' said Vespasiano, as Filippino nodded thoughtfully. 'Anyway, Niccoli came across young Piero out on the street outside the Palazzo del Podestà, one morning after the youth had spent a long night drinking, and saw how unhealthy the young man was looking. Niccoli asked Piero who he was, and who his father was, and what his work was. "I enjoy myself," replied Piero. "That's all very well," said Niccoli, "but you are a good-looking young man from a rich and ancient family: don't you think you should do more with your life than just fritter it away? Now, in the flower of youth, your pleasure-seeking doesn't seem to do you too much harm, despite the black rings round your eyes this morning. But pleasure is only lent, never given, and one day must be paid back. By the time you are a man you will be worthless, dissolute and ugly, your youth and health as spent as your money." Piero didn't like the sound of this. "What do you suggest I do?" he asked. "Learn Latin," Niccoli replied, "and learn from the ancients how best a man should conduct his affairs." So Piero did! Niccoli found him a tutor, books, everything. And Piero became a great scholar.'

I was still only half listening. 'Piero de' Pazzi's dead, isn't he?'

'That's right. Jacopo's head of the Pazzi family now.'

As a friend of scholars I suppose I was meant to have been impressed by the story of Piero's conversion, but I couldn't help thinking that Piero had died young while Jacopo, the most committed gambler in Florence, survived. If there was a moral there it was an unpalatable one. 'A pleasant story,' I told him, deciding that the picture of dead Holofernes should be essentially blue and red, and wondering if I could raise the price to cover the expense of the highest grade of Levantine ultramarine, which is drawn from the first soaking of the powdered lapis lazuli.

'I know more about the scholars of this city than any man alive,' boasted Vespasiano. 'Perhaps you could remind your friends of that. I'm sure it's an accident, but I fear they have overlooked me when sending out invitations to the city's scholars.'

That explained why he had visited. I was becoming a route to patronage. I smiled graciously. 'I'll do my best,' I said, while continuing to puzzle over my cartoon of Judith.

When I thought of Dante, Boccaccio, Petrarch, Niccoli, and all the others who had been interested in antiquity before us, I knew that what we did at the Medici palace was not new. Yet I still believe that it was under Lorenzo that the movement to rediscover the past became most popular and exciting. While the Portuguese explored the coast of Africa, Florence was finding an empire of her own, in history. Our empire proved the more profitable, so we gave it all away.

Today, in the noisy security of the madhouse, with the monkey-man whooping in his tree and my enduring city sprawled around us like so many dregs in the cup of the hills, I often think of how much we have lost. Lorenzo gave us our empire of the past; we exchanged it for Savonarola's promises for the future; and then we burnt Savonarola. The walls of this place are thick, yet sometimes they disappear, and city and madhouse are one.

1498

So much was lost, so much given away. So much was consigned to the flames.

The snow began to fall, and Sandro continued across the piazza. The marks of the great burnings earlier that year were left on the flagstones still, undisturbed by the rains, not yet hidden beneath the snow. The larger stain was left by a Bonfire of the Vanities: that year, as the year before, Fra Savonarola had ordered a pyre as the climax of the carnival and a pyramid of wood had been built in front of the Loggia dell'Orcagna where the abortive ordeal by fire was to have been staged. On the bottom steps masks, false beards, hairpieces and carnival costumes were arranged; above these were books and manscripts, Boccaccio and Petrarch as well as Aristotle and Plato; higher still scent bottles, pomade pots, rouge, mirrors and jewels; at the top were paintings of beautiful women, pictures from classical mythology, even religious paintings their artists or owners considered might threaten their souls – Piero di Credi, Fra Bartolommeo and I had all donated pictures of our own to the flames in an excess of humility. The bonfire had been fierce and had consumed many things of great beauty but the fire commemorated by the smaller ring on the piazza, though it had destroyed little that might be considered beautiful, had been fiercer still. Savonarola had burnt in its flames, tied to a post which had the arms lopped short to stop it resembling a crucifix. The decision to execute him had been taken quickly, for there was danger of an uprising in support of the prior; he was killed on 23 May. Fra Domenico and another of his followers, Fra Silvestro, were bound beside him. They had been partially hanged beforehand,

and may have felt little pain from the fires; whatever the case, they made no noise, and after a few hours their flesh was so thoroughly cooked that their arms and legs dropped off. The crowd threw stones at what was left of their bodies, until these fell too, and then, to prevent these remains being taken as relics, more wood was brought and the three friars became ashes; as a further precaution the ashes were carefully swept up, loaded on donkey carts, and taken to the Arno near the Ponte Vecchio. Borne and dispersed by the river, they had disappeared within minutes. But the marks the flames had scorched on to the piazza remained visible, though the first snow lay across them like a gauze, and the citizens, whether they had been supporters or opponents of Savonarola, and whether they acted from reverence or superstition, scrupulously avoided them. Only Sandro in his madness, dragging his bent body behind him on his crutches, scraping a track through the damp layer of snow, dared cross where the stones were stained.

1472

The new year began, not at the end of December as the Julian calendar dates it, but in the middle of March in accordance with the Florentine system, and though Filippino was making a good job of the small picture of Judith, my painting of Holofernes' headless corpse was proving difficult. It is easy to induce a model to lie flat on his back, harder to persuade him to have his head removed. Certain painters in Florence at the time made regular visits to the mortuaries. Antonio Pollaiuolo was one; later Leonardo and the master of Cordona, Luca Signorelli, spent much time peeling the flesh off corpses. The bodies of executed criminals are the favourite model: unlike those who die of natural causes, or in accidents, they are usually in good condition, and less often reclaimed by their families; many a dead Christ or martyred saint has been modelled on a larcenist or murderer. I contemplated going to a mortuary myself, though the notion did not appeal much, until a more interesting idea occurred.

Florence had acquired control of Volterra, to the south, a century before. Volterra had never been comfortable under Florentine rule, however, and certain intrigues, involving a consortium which mined alum in the neighbourhood, led to bloodshed. I did not know the details – in addition to the awkward Judith and Holofernes diptych for Sirigatti Ridolfi, I had just been commissioned to do a tondo of the Adoration of the Magi by the Pucci family, and, as the Pucci were still largely responsible for tax-gathering in Florence, I was giving this job a lot of my time – and only later learnt that two of the consortium, Inghirami and Riccobaldi, the latter of whom I had once met at the shop of Verrocchio, had been killed by the citizens. Inghirami had apparently been thrown out of a window into the square.

Lorenzo's reaction to this was uncharacteristically determined. In Florentine affairs he was normally prepared to let things take their course, interfering as little as possible; it was only when dealing with the subject cities that he behaved harshly. His reason to intervene in Volterra was slight though legitimate. The consortium had been protected by Florentine law; the death of two of its members was an affront to Florentine dignity. He employed the army of the condottiere Count of Urbino – Federico Montefeltro, father of that duke of Urbino who led the Venetian invasion at the time of Sandro the Mad and who as I write defends his city from Cesare Borgia's tyranny – and ordered that Volterra be taken. There was a siege that lasted a month, and then the city fell. Lorenzo and Florence rejoiced at the news.

I was at the Palazzo Medici when the next news arrived. I was not with Lorenzo when he heard the messenger, but shortly afterwards he came into the courtyard, where I had been listening to Ficino and a young man called Jacopo Naldi discussing epic poetry. 'Virgil is a pessimist, essentially,' claimed this Naldi.

'He is neither a pessimist nor an optimist,' said Ficino. 'The vagaries of his mood, the moments of bleakness and the moments of light, simply reflect the variety in the world. At every moment in the history of the world, however tragic, however dreadful, children are being born and couples are falling in love. At every moment also, someone else dies. Truly great art is informed by a single mood, perhaps, but never fails to acknowledge the sheer contrariness of the world, the singing of caged birds, the sting of the summer bee. To lable a poet " pessimist" is to limit unnaturally what you can find in what he has said; to label the great Virgil that way is to reduce his genius to your own meagre level.'

Lorenzo strode across and broke into the conversation roughly. 'Marsilio!' I had never seen him so agitated before. 'Listen to me. I need someone to talk to. Volterra's been sacked!'

Ficino bowed his head respectfully. 'Isn't that what you wanted?'

'I wanted it captured, not razed to the ground.'

Ficino's capable mind examined the problem. 'You are certain your information is correct?' he asked.

'There's no doubt, I'm afraid. And, oh God, it's my fault. There's been a massacre. I didn't order that. The count must have gone mad.'

'What do you intend to do?' asked Ficino.

'I don't know. What do you think? Have the authors of antiquity any suggestions?' He sounded bitter.

'In antiquity Volterra was nothing,' said Ficino, equivocating on behalf of his books. 'But if I can make a suggestion, you should go to Volterra, see the extent of the devastation, try to remedy some of the damage by a personal visit of atonement.'

'I'm just going to have to go there, see how much damage has been done, see what I can do to put things right,' decided Lorenzo, as though this was his own idea. As perhaps it was: perhaps Ficino had only confirmed what he had already thought. For myself, I was uncertain why the sacking of Volterra was such a disaster: Volterra was meant to be our enemy after all.

Naldi spoke. 'Sire. Could I travel as part of your company? Marsilio and I have just been discussing epic poetry. Perhaps this might be a suitable subject.'

'The glories of war?' Lorenzo was contemptuous. 'But yes, you can come if you like.'

'And could I perhaps come also?' I asked hesitantly.

'Are you a ghoul too, Sandro?' asked Lorenzo. 'But I suppose you can come along if you want. I can see no reason why not. I can see no reason in any of this.'

I had barely left the city before this occasion. Sometimes my brother Giovanni, whom I still saw as often as I could, invited me on hunting expeditions in the hills north of the city, but I generally declined. The walk was hard, the hunt rarely successful. Likewise, my father had taken a podestà, a small villa and some fields, in the foothills, but I found the place drab and cold. The only time I had left the gates out of choice was to sketch flowers in the meadows by the Arno. The prospect of a journey to Volterra excited me and frightened me in equal measure but, having committed myself, I had to go through with it or lose face; on a hazy summer's morning in 1472 I joined Lorenzo's company, behind the gold banner of the palla, and left the city by the Porte Romana on the road towards Siena and the south.

Around the city, the countryside is reasonably tame. It has been claimed that the reason Florence is so rich is that its climate is more suited to producing people than food: we have to work hard just to live, and the habit extends into the rest of our lives. This might be true, though if Florentines are really more hardworking than others then there must be some lazy people on this earth. Certainly the comment about our climate is fair for, as we climbed into the hills and looked back over the city, at a Duomo the size of a pea and San Miniato standing on its hill to the south of the walls like the last bastion of civilization, the land we journeyed through was barren and inhospitable to my eyes. We climbed past small houses, walled against nameless threats, and dingy hamlets where the children gawped at our passage. A single olive tree was often enough to signal a farm. Behind us Florence grew smaller, receding to that vanishing point all painters are taught to find, yet swelling in my heart as it finally disappeared from view.

The hills around Florence seemed huge and imposing to me then. Since that time I have travelled further, even to Naples where our boat diverted to see the great fiery volcano of those parts, and twice to Rome where the road goes through many mighty mountains and in winter the wolves have control. In comparison our Tuscan hills are nothing. Yet they dominate our city and our lives, augment our city walls, count the passage of the seasons in the setting of the sun, and save us from the cruellest of the winter winds. Seen from the safety of the city they were guardians and friends; when among them the hills became sinister and strange.

Perhaps I should have felt better had I been a more capable rider. My mare was complacent and the road quite good. But my inexperienced back jarred with every step, and I could feel the flesh inside my thighs heating up with the movement. I have never had much need to ride. For the *popolo grosso* it is a necessary accomplishment; for soldiers and merchants it is a prerequisite of the trade. But for Sandro Botticelli a horse, a rather large animal after all, with excessive teeth, is a creature best avoided.

We followed the Siena road as far as Poggibonsi. Poggibonsi is little more than a resting place: a day's ride from Florence, it is also where the road crosses a tributary of the Arno. It was evening when we arrived. The citizens came out to greet Lorenzo, and the local notables argued as to who would entertain us. I did not want to be entertained. We slept in an old-fashioned castle. I heard the sounds of a party downstairs, and the music of a dance. But – a measure of my distress – I could not be persuaded to dance. It was all I could do to walk.

We were up early again the next day. Our route took us through Colle, where we stopped for food. Here the citizens, though carefully polite, were more suspicious than welcoming, and our soldiers stood picket duty around where we stayed. Aching, I decided to use my unwanted proximity to a horse to make some sketches. Verrocchio loves horses, and those trained in his bottega have all drawn flayed horses to learn about the musculature; in Fra Lippo's studio a flayed angel would have been more use. I did my best though, despite my tiredness and my distaste, to produce something worthwhile, and was helped by one of Lorenzo's attendants, Gentile Guicciardini, who held the bridle for me. When we rode on Gentile stayed near me, but I barely had the breath to talk. He found it amusing that I should be so put out by what he called a gentle ride; I asked him if he could draw a horse, he replied that he couldn't, and I suggested that perhaps God had given each of us roles and life and the gifts whereby we could carry them out. But then we saw smoke that stained the clear horizon, and the company was urged to a canter.

Volterra is in broken, hilly country, and as we approached we tried to make out details. The smoke came from the church, and from another large building near the gate which was burning too; the city walls had been breached in several places, and a large section was missing entirely; the streets seemed curiously fashioned. Growing closer, we realized that the wall was less missing than buried, and the streets were awash with mud, for to compound the Volterrans' misery there had been a landslip, which had buried many of those who had survived the massacre, yet exposed many of the victims.

I have described already some of what I saw in that place at that time, the skewered babies, crawling women, mutilated corpses. The babies' bodies were mottled, a delicate pale blue and white. Dangling between the exposed thighs of the women were webs of scarlet that dragged in the mud. The mud and blood on the naked bodies dried in intricate patterns. The troops had left three days earlier, and then the mud had come. What attempts had been made to clear up after the first disaster had been buried by the second. I saw many headless bodies ideal for my purposes, and drew none.

Lorenzo was energetic, organizing shelter for those who had lost their homes and paying for food to be brought in from the contado. Some countrymen, to their credit, were already delivering what food they had to the citizens of Volterra though they knew they would not be paid for many years to come; most just altered their prices, swapping grain for a chair, a woman, a boy's bottom, a drinking cup. Only one of Lorenzo's suggestions involved me. 'I am going to rebuild the hospital,' Lorenzo announced, 'and I should like you, Sandro, to decorate its chapel.' I did not feel mine would be a significant contribution, but how much can anything signify when a city has been destroyed? Lorenzo did what he could, and even he admitted it was not enough.

We understood how he felt. We functioned in that raped city. Our throats drew air; we ate and drank. But we could not think we were genuinely alive. This was not a place of life. It was a place of death, and I was reduced to a hand and an eye, sketching yet barely daring to think for all the short time we were there. The crows gathered, and buzzards. Dogs came in from the contado. At night wolves howled in the darkness and interrogated the moon. I too was full of questions. Was Troy like this when it fell? Did Ulysses sanction such violence?

'It doesn't make sense to me, this destruction, this killing,' I admitted. 'The Count of Urbino is a civilized man, a patron of artists and scholars.'

'Try telling that to the folk of Volterra,' said one of our soldiers. I looked at him carefully. He seemed as distressed as any of us, yet had he been among the count's troops, instead of Lorenzo's, would he have behaved better than they? His mouth seemed slumped with grief; would the same mouth have grinned in lust had it been present a few days earlier? I started to sketch him in charcoal.

'None the less, what I say of the count is true,' I told him as I drew, more to keep him near until I had finished than for the pleasure of his company. 'He is a man of famous taste and learning. Luciano Laurana is building him a palace at Urbino; he has employed Piero della Francesca, the Flemish painter Giusto da Guanto, and the Spaniard Pedro Berruguete, to portray his family in paint; a bookseller who lives near me keeps writing to him, because he is such a famous patron of the arts, in the hope of getting work.' I drew as quickly as I could. 'Why should such a man permit this?'

'Most likely he couldn't stop it.'

'Yet he's a famous condottiere, an experienced general,' I said. 'Surely his troops obey him?'

'Well, I've been talking to some of the folk here. There's several different tales. Some say that it was mercenaries meant to be working for Volterra itself that started it, that they opened the gates to their mates outside, and it was just a free-for-all. Hey, what you drawing?'

'Is that likely?' I asked, showing him the picture because I did not want him to move.

'Is that me?' This was not a man who preened himself daily in a looking-glass. 'I like that. Can I have it?'

'I'll need it for a painting, I'm afraid.' I made the shadow beneath his eyes more intense, and the line of his lips, to emphasize the grief and shock he displayed. 'You were telling me whether it was likely that the Volterran troops betrayed their employers.'

'Things like that have happened,' he said. He was keeping more still now he knew he was being drawn, which was a shame. I neither wanted nor needed him to pose. 'Perhaps you could do me another picture, for my girl in Imola? And there are other stories doing the rounds. I've heard tell that the count found a sort of Bible, you know the sort, in Greek and Latin and Jewish.'

'Polyglot,' I said, with the authority of one who has overheard the expression.

'Aye. He found one of these Bibles and was so pleased he just left his lads to it, some say. Or there's others tell it that he hanged one or two of his men at the start but nothing was going to stop them once they'd the taste of blood on their lips. That's your choice of reasons why.'

I put down my charcoal and showed the sketch to the soldier. He seemed pleased. 'I'll be famous,' he said, and laughed. I briefly did a copy, capturing only the likeness, not worried by the expression, and gave it to him. Although I could not dislike him and his naïve enjoyment of my art, my fear of him and his kind did not diminish. A soldier is probably only worse than any other man because he is exposed to worse temptations – I have never had the opportunity to rape a city or sack a church and perhaps would do the same as the mercenaries given the chance – but that knowledge only made me feel sadder. One of the saddest thoughts I know is that, throughout history, not even the most vicious and debauched tyrant has ever had the slightest problem finding people to work for him. After my sitter had gone I turned back to the drawing, added a scourge in one of the soldier's hands and a crown of thorns in the other. Tyrants don't have recruitment problems.

That soldier is still there, on my picture of the discovery of Holofernes' body; he's the Assyrian soldier who is standing to the right of the picture and resting on a sword. But I don't think he ever became famous.

We returned to Florence. My friends remarked how quiet I was after my trip, and it is true I found it hard to talk to them. The only man I knew that I felt might share my distress was Tommaso, and he had been out of the city for some months, in Milan and Ferrara on business. So I tried to put it all into my little picture of Holofernes' death. The painting wasn't a success, to my mind, though others have said they admire it. I tried to express everything Volterra meant to me on a panel no bigger than the seat of a chair. That's why the open wound of the neck faces the viewer, why there are so many figures in different attitudes of grief, why there are two at the back who look frankly unconcerned, as several of our soldiers looked even in the ruins of Volterra. It is even why those two are on horseback, though the scene is set in a tent, for I wanted to cram all my experience, even my mistrust of the horse, on to the panel. It was too much for such a small panel, I know, yet I felt better for having painted it and began to live again.

It was as well. I had many commissions that year. I had the paintings for the Volterra hospital to do for Lorenzo. I did a portrait for Gentile Guicciardini and a Virgin and Child Enthroned for his father, though both were destroyed soon after in the fire at his family home. I completed the tondo of the Adoration of the Magi for the Pucci, adding – as my master Fra Filippi had often done before me – a large peacock overseeing the events as a comment on human vanity, and explaining it away to my vain tax-gathering clients as a symbol of eternal life. I had to paint another version of Judith returning to Bethulia, not because there was anything wrong with

Filippino's version but because – my carelessness – the first was too large for the frame. And finally I painted a panel for myself, without commission or client, of a woman weeping by a closed door. The woman is small: the bleak wall of the building behind her dominates the scene. I have called this picture La Derelitta, and when Filippino did a copy I suggested he tell people it is Mordecai weeping in front of the palace gate of Ahasuerus, because such a title seemed to give a picture more authority, but in truth it is Volterra I depicted there.

1473

My prosperity continued into the following year. I had to take on another assistant to supplement Biagio, and chose a young lad who had earlier worked for my old friend Jacopo del Sallaio. My new assistant's name was Sandro, like mine, so we called him Jacopo after his previous master. The original Jacopo, sadly, was not doing well. After completing several Madonnas for Luca Pitti, who had a particular liking for representations of the Virgin, he found himself out of work, and talked often of leaving Florence to try his luck elsewhere. He was not, perhaps, a great painter, yet he was eager and honest and I was sad to see him in trouble; I tried to help by putting his name forward for various jobs, but it did no good, and in the early summer of 1473, when Florence looked its most beautiful, he left the city. He did not return for nearly twenty years, and then came home only to die.

I also had an opportunity to leave. The canons of Pisa cathedral wanted a fresco of the Assumption. I had not yet worked on a fresco, though I had learnt the theory from Fra Lippo, and in that sense the offer was attractive, especially as I had heard that Pisa cathedral is a fine setting for any artist's work, but despite this I wasn't tempted. In Florence I had friends, family and clients. My friends I would miss, as my family would miss me; my clients I would doubtless lose. So I wrote to the canons, claiming that pressure of work prevented me from accepting their more than generous offer, added several similar honeyed phrases, and thought no more about it. I had other things on my mind.

My tondo of the Adoration had proved successful. The Pucci

family had used it as a *desco da parti*, a table on which presents for a woman at childbirth are displayed, which meant many influential people, delivering their gifts, got to see at least those parts of it not covered by the gifts of others. Two things seemed to appeal to them in particular: that I had modelled several of the participants on members of the Pucci family, and that I had shown the stable in which Christ was born as a ruined classical temple. The first was hardly an original notion. Even old Gozzoli, in his fresco of the Adoration in the Palazzo Medici, had represented the kings as members of the Medici family. But I believe I may have been the first to paint a ruined temple as the place of Christ's birth, even though the original idea had been Ficino's. 'What our philosophy seeks,' he had said one evening as we sat in the gardens of the Medici palace and tried to ignore the mosquitoes, 'is to emphasize the continuity between Christian and antique thought. Dante said Virgil was condemned to hell because although he was a good man, Virgil knew nothing of the Messiah; I beg to differ, and suggest that any God worth worshipping would recognize that though he could not be redeemed by the Blood of Christ, Virgil and many like him were redeemed by their poetry and philosophy. Were I a painter, Sandro, I would have Christ born in a ruined temple of the Greek kind, not because I believe that he was born in such a place, but rather to show how Christianity is a continuation and not a denial of ancient thought. And,' he added, 'should anyone say that it is a contradiction to paint the stable as an antique building, you can reply that it is no more a contradiction than to place antique authors such as Virgil and Homer into our Christian hell.' In the event there were no objections; on the contrary, the Pucci tondo was seen as the very essence of modernity, and the Puccis, ignorant money-grabbers though they are, were anxious to show my picture off to all who came to their palace. I was asked to paint several similar pictures – the Adoration of the Magi does not just combine the antique and the religious, but, dearer to Florentine hearts, combines wealth and piety – and had to choose between commissions. I did not want to become known as a man who can paint only Magi.

A better commission was for an almost lifesize St Sebastian for the church of Santa Maria Maggiore. At the same time Tommaso Soderini, though his business remained unfinished, had come back to Florence briefly, and introduced me to his godson and nephew Antonio Tornabuoni, asking me if I would do a portrait of the young man, in the red cap of a councillor and with a hole in it that would bear a portrait medal of Cosimo de' Medici. I agreed to paint this slightly unusual panel, on condition that Antonio, a handsome if rather foolish youth, would pose for my Sebastian.

At that time the Pollaiuolo brothers had recently completed a picture of St Sebastian which had attracted a lot of attention. It showed the saint on a tall stake, surrounded by archers. Antonio Pollaiuolo was responsible for the archers, which I have to admit are rather fine, and Piero painted the saint. I did not like the saint. He holds his head back in the attitude of one less agonized by the proceedings than bored, and I was determined that my Sebastian would outdo theirs. The pose I chose was languid, partly because that was the only way Tommaso's Tornabuoni godson knew how to stand, but also because I wanted to show Sebastian indifferent to the arrows piercing his flesh. Volterra had shown me the damage an arrow can do, but I was not painting Volterra now, I was painting a Holy Martyr, and the attitude I sought to portray was one of philosophic detachment and noble calm, as though the saint is aware of his importance yet chooses not to advertise it. Around his head I placed not a solid halo such as Fra Lippo would have painted, but a ring of light. This is another innovation I claim as my own, though Leonardo brags he used it first: as Leonardo claims responsibility for every invention of man since the wheel, this boast is no surprise.

I was working so hard on this picture, and its companion, the portrait of Antonio Soderini, that I even missed the visit of the princess of Naples, who passed through Florence on her way to marry the duke of Ferrara, but the reception St Sebastian received made the effort worthwhile. The princess's visit had been spectacular, but my picture of the saint made nearly as big a sensation. For several days there were queues to see it, and even after those queues had gone people still queued to employ me. I started to get commissions from people who did not care at all whether I was friendly with the Medici, and perhaps this was as well, as I had been working so hard that my visits to the Palazzo Medici had virtually stopped once the Volterra hospital panels were out of the way; at the same time Politian had been appointed tutor to Lorenzo's sons, which meant he was too busy to visit me. For several months the only news I received from the palazzo came through Antonio, and that was only gossip, as befitted an empty-head. Though one piece of news he brought, that Naldi had indeed written his epic poem, which he called the *Volterrais*, and presented it to Lorenzo, did interest me: the young poet had been in Volterra with us after all; he must, I thought, be remarkably insensitive if he thinks such a gift will please. Hearing this, I decided it was time to renew my acquaintance with the Medici household.

There was straw in the courtyard to muffle the hooves, a symptom of sickness as unmistakable as pockmarks, for Lorenzo's grandmother, the Mona Contessa, was ill and not expected to see the summer out, but despite this the palace was as full of life as ever. Children played between the arches. Embassies waited at doorways. Servants fetched and carried. Unchallenged, I strolled past the attendants and waiting petitioners into the great chamber, exchanging greetings with those I recognized. Cristoforo Landino was there and beckoned me over to him. 'Have you ever seen anything like this?' he asked, handing me a bound book.

I took the book and looked at it. 'I don't understand,' I said. It was an odd volume, written entirely in black ink and in letters of remarkable regularity.

'It is printed.'

'Printed?'

'Exactly! A press has opened here in Florence. I'd seen printed books from Venice. Now we can produce them ourselves. What do you think?'

'It seems rather plain.' Frankly, it seemed ugly; though we have grown used to printed books today they will never compete with an illuminated manuscript for beauty.

'That's because you're a painter. A scholar doesn't care about decoration and colour. He finds colour enough in the words.'

'I take it you like it.' I was surprised. Landino in most ways was a conservative man; he generally dismissed anything more recent than Cicero as vulgar.

'Like it!' he cried. 'I think it's marvellous. Soon everyone will be reading my works!'

I studied the book in my hand again. The first few pages were blank, and then I saw what I was looking for. 'Commentary on the Odes of Horace. By Cristoforo Landino, professor of poetry and rhetoric. Printed for Vespasian Bisticci, Florence, MCDLXXIII, by Bernardo Cennini.' I looked up. 'Vespasiano di Bisticci?' I asked. 'The bookseller?'

'It's wonderful, isn't it! Have you seen Cennini's press at work? It's like a loom, but makes books instead of cloth. And at what a rate! The press can produce forty books in a day! Think of it! It takes a copyist half a year to produce four hundred leaves. Consider how many copyists it would take to do the work a press can do in a day! And pictures as well as words can be reproduced: think of that, my writings, your drawings, in every house in Florence!'

I thought about it. It did not seem very likely. 'A charming idea,' I said.

Giuliano de' Medici walked by, lost in thought. I greeted him; he gave me a sad smile and moved on. 'I suppose his grandmother's illness must be preying on his mind,' I said, commenting on his melancholy.

'Sandro,' cautioned Landino, 'it is time you learned the difference between grief and love. He adores Simonetta Cattaneo.'

'I've heard of her, haven't I? Isn't she married to Marco Vespucci?'

'Have you ever seen her?'

'No.'

'If you had,' said Landino, 'you would realize that the presence of a mere husband, and particularly a husband like Marco, would not be enough to stop men loving her.'

'I had heard she was attractive.'

'She's beautiful. I confess, even at my age I feel stirrings when I see her. You should paint her.'

'I should like to,' I said politely.

Lorenzo entered the chamber, with a handful of attendants including Politian who, pen in hand, was noting down something his master said. Lorenzo saw us and led his party over. 'Cristoforo,' he said, 'are you still showing off your book? And you, Sandro. Where have you been hiding? I wanted a word with you. I forget what about.'

'Pisan canons,' said one of the attendants. I knew this man was called Gasparino, and did not yet know what he meant.

'I've been busy,' I apologized.

'I'm sure you have,' he soothed. 'All Florence talks of you now. You'll soon be more famous than I, and with better cause!' He smiled his winning smile, and I was won over; he turned to Gasparino, and smiled an identical smile. 'I hear your reputation has even reached Pisa,' he said, addressing me again.

'I've been asked to do some work there, yes,' I said.

'Are you going to take it?'

'I don't think so. I've plenty to do here.'

'I think you should.'

I was surprised, and annoyed. The Medici had no official position, so their orders were not officially framed, but they were orders none the less. I did not want to go to Pisa; Lorenzo thought I should. Ergo – even my thoughts were becoming latinized – I was going to Pisa, like it or not. 'Why?' I asked. I was not disputing the veiled command, but I did want to know the reason.

'Pisa is something of a nuisance. Florence gives Pisa protection, and instead of being grateful they call for liberty, whatever that means. The liberty to be attacked by someone else? The Pisans are like the Volterrans. We defend them against Siena – though of course sometimes it is necessary to use a little persuasion to make them see it that way – and in return for our expense all they can do is moan. But here we have a situation where the Pisans want something from Florence that they are prepared to pay for: your skill. And I think it would be a pleasant gesture if you were to paint the fresco in the cathedral that the canons have requested. You'll get paid, Florence'll get praised, and everyone will be happy.'

It was hard to dislike Lorenzo, with his charm and his smile, but I came close to it then. Perhaps Naldi hadn't been so foolish when he wrote his ridiculous, unnecessary verse; perhaps turning the massacre at Volterra into an epic poem had made the affair seem less ugly than it had been in fact. For here was Lorenzo, urbanely talking of Volterra as though events there had been just a normal part of diplomacy. His argument too seemed flawed. Why should Pisa or Volterra be grateful that we stopped some other city dominating them when we dominated them ourselves? If things were reversed, if Pisa controlled Florence, I can't see us being grateful that it was Pisa rather than Siena. We wouldn't care: we would fight Pisa first, worry about Siena later. And finally, I resented Lorenzo's knowledge of my affairs. How did he know the Pisans had been in touch, much less the details of the commission I had been offered? I did not like to feel I was being spied upon. I looked at Politian to judge his views, and Politian looked away.

'I don't know,' I began. But I did know: my objections were unrealistic. All that really counted in this was that he was son of Piero the Gouty, grandson of the great Cosimo, and married to an Orsini, whereas my father was a tanner. 'I'll pack my belongings,' I said.

'Not so fast.' He laughed. 'I know you're busy. I told them that they would have to wait until the autumn.'

So even that was arranged. Had he arranged a fee as well? 'The autumn?' I asked.

'That's right. Give you time to sort out things here.'

'Is Pisa cathedral well lit?' I asked.

'Do you know, I can't remember. I've visited of course – a rather impressive building, though a bit old-fashioned, with a very curious bell-tower. You'll like it there. But the light? Sorry.' The magnificent smile flashed again. 'Why do you ask?'

'Because I'm a painter. I can't paint in the autumn if the light is bad. And I can't paint frescos in the winter at all.'

'What's this? Some ridiculous ordinance laid down by the guild?'

'The guild has nothing to do with it. I'm not even a member. It's a purely practical problem. A fresco is painted on to wet plaster. When the plaster dries the paint is sealed. You can't do that in a frost.'

'That's a blow,' said Lorenzo. 'Oh well. You'll just have to explain it to them when you get there. You'll dine with us tonight?'

I wanted to go home. 'Of course,' I said.

It was the usual large gathering. For privacy Lorenzo retired to one of his villas; in Florence he was a public figure entirely. Politian came to sit with me. 'You didn't want to go to Pisa.' As he had grown older and more confident, his speech had grown more direct, though he was still capable of flights of verbal extravagance when the mood took him.

'Not much, no,' I replied. 'But what can I do?'

'Exactly. What can any of us do? Our talents are just commodities. And Lorenzo is very concerned about Pisa.'

'Why?' I asked. 'I've not heard of any trouble there.'

'That's because nothing has happened, yet. A politician's skill, if not his fame, can be measured as much by what he prevents as what he achieves. It is because nothing has happened in Pisa that Lorenzo is concerned. His reputation was badly damaged by the events in Volterra, you know. Before, he was considered a smiling, pleasing, educated young man, a rather charming and friendly figure even to our enemies. Suddenly he has the reputation of a ruthless murderer. Ruthlessness is a virtue in a prince. But Lorenzo is no prince. He rules by consent. He needs to be popular, and especially in the dependent cities. Don't forget, Florence has no army: all we can do is employ mercenaries.'

I picked Politian up on that last word. 'Isn't that the point, though? Surely the massacre wasn't Lorenzo's fault. The count of Urbino led the mercenaries. Lorenzo tried to make amends to the Volterrans.' I thought about my paintings in the hospital there. 'All right, it was too little and it came too late. But the count should take the blame.'

'The duke is a soldier. He obeys orders.'

I did not notice at the time that he said duke for count. 'You mean Lorenzo commanded the massacre?' I was horrified.

'No.' He shook his head to drive away the suggestion. 'There were no orders in this case. That, however, although a fact, is irrelevant in this instance. I'm talking not about how things happen but about how they are perceived. In politics a fact is significant only if it is accepted as evidence. The fact is that the count had just heard that his wife had died, and therefore took no interest in the behaviour of his troops. Perhaps, in his misery, he even took a delight in the misery his men inflicted on others. But the facts do not matter. Lorenzo is perceived to have been responsible, and must do all he can to win back his reputation. At least now he is able to tell the Pisans that he has managed to persuade the popular artist Sandro Botticelli to work for them: it is not a major achievement in terms of international diplomacy perhaps, but it is a least in accord with his previous benevolent reputation. And you can't complain too much. You'll be well rewarded here, as well as receiving payment from the Pisans.'

This was true. 'I suppose you're right,' I conceded.

'Of course I am. It's time to enjoy the party.'

Why not? 'Isn't that Vespasiano da Bisticci?' I asked, looking round. 'He was trying to get me to introduce him here. It seems he managed on his own.'

'Or with his printing machine,' corrected Politian. 'Though in all honesty I think he'd have got his feet under the table one way or another. He's quite shameless, that man, when it comes to currying favour.'

I studied the other guests present that evening. 'I'm disappointed that the beautiful Mona Vespucci is not here though. Landino was full of her praises.'

'Guiliano even more so.'

'That's a point. Where is Giuliano? I saw him earlier.'

'He only eats with us when the Vespucci are here. Otherwise he takes his meals in his rooms, and pretends he has eaten nothing. He wants the world to believe that he is pining away for love. But what makes you ask about the lovely Simonetta? Are you in love with her too?'

'Just curious. I don't think I've ever seen her.'

'You'd remember her if you had. I have to agree with everyone else, though consensus runs contrary to my nature: she is a woman of remarkable beauty. But as it happens I'm sorry you're not in love with her. I've been worrying about you, Sandro. You must be the most continent man in Florence. The monks of San Marco show more lust than you, considerably more in some cases. Your master was Fra Lippo Lippi: did he teach you nothing?'

'He taught me a great deal, including that to live a life of relentless debauchery requires a good deal more energy than I shall ever have. Besides, as our Vespasiano once said to me, "Pleasure is only lent, never given, and one day must be paid back."'

'That sounds remarkably pithy for Vespasiano,' Politian commented.

'He was quoting someone else.'

'That makes sense. He is incapable of originality, but quick to recognize it. Landino was describing the printing press to you, I believe. Invented by some German, who doubtless died in poverty, it will make Vespasiano's fortune.' Politian leaned back on his bench. 'But we were talking of you. I must say, Sandro, you're the first man I have met who has used laziness as a reason for chastity. Tell me the truth. In public you seem uninterested. But in private, don't you even have one little mistress?'

'Not even a tiny one,' I said.

He shook his head. 'Then it must be boys you're interested in. Perhaps your inclinations go the same way as Verrocchio's, and you are madly in love with that Leonardo de Vinci who joined the painters' guild last year.'

'You couldn't be further from the truth.'

'No mistress, no little boys! What do you do for pleasure?'

'I paint.'

Politian shook his head. 'I'm mystified. Were I in your position I should surely take advantage of it. You use models?'

'Of course.'

'Surely they are available? And attractive too, unless every painter in the city lies. I've taken quite a fancy to several women I've seen in paintings. There's a Madonna that Fra Angelico painted for the cloth guild that sends me weak at the knees. Don't you ever get the urge to poke the Virgin Mary? If I had the chance I know I would.'

'You've been to my studio. A model is a model. They're not even all that clean, often. They're just bodies. I often borrow someone else's face.'

'Just bodies!' Politian put his face on his hands, as though he might weep. 'You dress them as the Virgin, or Judith, or St Anne, and then say they're just bodies. They are objects of fantasy and beauty. If you won't stick your prick into them I'll do it for you!'

'If you like. But not while they're posing if you don't mind.' I tried to speak lightly but the conversation bored me. I would have changed the subject if I could, but Politian was always relentless.

'Oh Sandro! Your case is worse than I thought. It's time someone showed you what fun you are missing.'

'I expect I'll find out one day. When I fall in love.'

Politian looked relieved. 'Ah. Perhaps all is explained. Tell me, Sandro, what are your views on love?'

I always had to be careful in my conversations with Politian. His monologues could be fascinating, but once he started an interrogation I had to be on my guard. 'I believe that love is very beautiful,' I said. 'I believe in faith, hope and love, and that the greatest of these is love. Don't you believe the same?' In dialogue with Politian it was always as well to throw the question back if possible, to find out his well-considered views before blurting out my own half-baked opinions.

'I most certainly don't,' he replied. 'Faith, hope and love; God is Love: these notions are irrelevant to what we are talking about. God's love is a blanket which protects us all, but what we're talking about is getting Cupid's arrow up your arse, the specific attraction of one human being for another.'

'And you don't believe that occurs?' I asked.

'Oh, I know it can happen, that Cupid's dart can pierce any human flesh. But belief in love, if I understand your meaning, implies not that I believe it exists but that I believe it benevolent, and I do not believe the latter at all. I believe in love in the same way I believe in the plague: I cannot deny that either exists, nor that they produce tangible results, but that is not to say that I would welcome either of them. On the contrary, I fear both.'

'So you fear love?'

'Certainly. And so, if you will permit a younger man giving advice, should you. God is love, certainly, but remember this: love is frequently cruel.'

1499

That Florence is the centre of the universe is a fact all Florentines know. 'Why on earth do you want us to leave?' asked Matteo, one of the reborn Simonetta's pack of vicious friends.

'Why on earth not?' replied Simonetta. 'Next year is a jubilee year. A hundred thousand people will visit Rome. Pilgrims make easy pickings, we've already proved that, because no one knows they're missing till it's too late. A few'll pass through Florence, but Rome's the place we ought to be.'

'Even so. Rome has its own gangs. They'll not appreciate outsiders muscling in on their business.'

Simonetta smiled and raised the wine cup to her lips. 'We won't be outsiders,' she said. Wine on the rim of the goblet gave her a ghastly painted smile. 'I told you, I've connections.'

'Yeah, you've told us.' Matteo spoke loudly. 'But how can you expect us to believe it? The pope's son! And I suppose the pope himself will bless us for our crimes?'

Simonetta's reply was quieter. 'Why not tell everyone?' she asked. 'My only worry is your big mouth. Rome's no problem: I've been useful to the Spaniards and they'll not forget me; I'll not let them.'

'How did you get to know Borgia anyway?' asked Bernado.

Simonetta simpered. 'He likes a bit of arse. Everyone knows that.'

'You'll do anything, won't you.' Bernardo sounded more admiring than critical.

'Anything except pray,' replied Simonetta. 'Anything except that.'

Sandro sat as quietly as he could in the shadows of the tavern, sipping their conversation.

It was the third time that he had seen Simonetta in this place. The first time had been mere chance. He had been on his way home from his shop when he had seen Bernardo's lumbering figure coming from the tavern; Sandro had waited a long while in a neighbouring doorway, ignoring the suspicious glances of passers-by, until eventually Simonetta, her beautiful face flushed by drink, had come out supported by Matteo and another young man she had called Tonio. He watched enviously the way Tonio's arm wrapped his beloved's waist, the way she rested her head on Matteo's shoulder, but even as he stepped from the doorway for a better view Simonetta had straightened, slipped free of her companions, and started crazily down the street, screaming snatches of obscene songs as she ran. It was all Tonio and Matteo could do to keep up; Sandro never stood a chance.

After that Sandro had been a regular visitor to the tavern, calling in each night. The second time he had seen her there had been less than a week ago. The day was a holiday and Sandro, who had little enough work to do anyway, closed the shop early; he stopped at the tavern more from habit than expectation, but had no sooner settled at his bench with his bottle of aqua vitae than Simonetta and her gang had come in. He kept his face down, fearing confrontation, but his eyes darted towards Simonetta of their own accord; the group shared a single bottle, a single goblet, and then left noisily and without paying. 'Oi!' the landlady shouted, ripping off her apron.

Matteo had paused at the door. 'Got to see a man about a horse. I'll settle up later.'

Now they were back again. Matteo had presumably kept his word, for there had been no ugly scene when the group had returned. Sandro finished his second bottle of burnt wine and ordered a third. Simonetta apart they were an unprepossessing lot, he thought as he looked at them. Bernardo was big and simple. Matteo was smaller, with the broad shoulders and tight waist of a Tuscan youth, and with an incomplete set of strong white teeth that he grinned regularly and villainously. Tonio was a few years older than his companions, and had a badly scarred lip which a full beard failed to disguise. Each wore a Soderini scarf round his upper arm, a quilted black doublet, and black hose. Except for the changing fashions – we wore no quilting when I was young – Angelo could have passed for one of this group without question. He had the same look in his eye, truculent and arrogant at once, always ready to answer a word with a blow, always ready to enjoy another's misfortune, and Sandro, remembering Angelo's fate, wondered if this three would end the same way.

In that group Simonetta, her gracefulness imperfectly hidden behind her man's clothing, her beauty radiant despite the sneer so often on her lips, was a flower in a midden. Yet clearly she was their leader and inspiration. Sitting with his back to them as they discussed their trip to Rome, emptying another bottle of strong burnt wine, Sandro marvelled once more at God's mysterious purpose.

Matteo stood up and ordered more wine for his group. He seemed to have more money than the others, and threw a silver florin contemptuously towards the landlady. 'Something decent,' he ordered. 'Something the rats haven't pissed in.'

The landlady spat on the flagged floor, and, having no teeth, tested the coin in her gums. 'Maria!' she called. 'Get this lot a bottle from upstairs.'

'Maria!' Simonetta echoed. 'Let me join you upstairs.' She flourished a suggestive finger.

'You can keep your hands to yourself!' said the landlady, though the girl seemed willing enough. 'I've seen the women you go with. More paint on than a picture by our Botticelli and riddled with pox like worms in a grave.'

Sandro swallowed the strong wine the wrong way and had to be helped back on to his bench. 'Are you all right?' asked a face that was too close to his head.

He focussed. 'I think I'd better have another drink,' Sandro said.

The landlady had turned towards him when he fell. 'No you don't,' she said. 'You've had enough and more. Come on. Let's be having you out.' She was a big woman, he was a skeleton badly wrapped in a skin. She picked him up by the neck of his jacket and half pushed, half carried him to the door. Many people were looking at him, including Matteo and Bernardo, but neither seemed to remember him. Simonetta was looking away, winking at Maria.

'You got any money on you?' the landlady asked.

'I might have,' said Sandro, defiantly.

'You'd best leave it with me.'

'You what?'

'I'm serious. There's men in this neighbourhood would slice you for the price of an empty purse, much less for the coin inside. There's plenty in this tavern would do it, come to that. But you're a regular customer here. I'll look after your money for you.'

'Thank you,' said Sandro. The strings tying his purse to his belt seemed to be more knotted than usual; the landlady got tired of his fumbling. 'I'll do it,' she said, and did.

He leant against her. 'Tell me,' he said. 'Did I hear you mention the name of Botticelli? The painter?'

'I might've done. Why?'

'Oh, no reason. I used to know him, wondered what'd become of him.'

'Don't know,' she said. 'Dead, I should think, by now.'

She left him then, and when she went he fell over.

For a while he lay there, dozing. It was a warm night in August. In the north the French under Louis XII were invading Italy once more. A cat strolled out of the tavern and walked across Sandro's back. He was oblivious of both events. He barely stirred even when frisked and then left by two children. A watchman lifted his head by its thin grey hair and held a lantern to his face. 'What do you think you're doing?'

Sandro considered this but could come up with no reply.

'You'd better come with me.' The watchman was officious but not unfriendly. 'Been drinking, have we?' He spoke like a countryman.

'Fell over,' Sandro decided.

'I'll bet you did,' said the watchman. 'Can you walk?'

Sandro thought again. 'Need my crutches.'

'And where are they?'

Sandro couldn't remember.

'Lean on me. Where do you live?'

The questions were getting harder but Sandro refused to be tricked. He raised an arm and waved it up the street. 'That way,' he said.

'You sure?'

'Yes.'

'I'm not,' said the watchman as Sandro's head slumped back on to the pavings. 'I can't carry you, that is for sure. But what am I going to do with you?'

Sandro felt sick, and no longer really cared.

The watchman gave it one last try. 'Have you any mates, anyone who'll come and get you?'

'Lorenzo,' said Sandro.

'That's more like. Lorenzo who?'

'*The* Lorenzo. Lorenzo de' Medici, the Magnificent.'

'Shhh,' said the watchman urgently, bending down and speaking quietly. 'There's some would call that kind of talk treacherous. Not that I'm one of them, mind. I'd wave the palla again no problem given half the chance, even for that fool son of Lorenzo's, Piero. And for his dad I'd have given both ears. But there's not so many think like that, or dare admit they do any road. So you'd better watch what you're saying.'

The watchman's friendly warning worked its way through the burnt wine. 'All right,' Sandro agreed. Lorenzo is dead, he remembered. Lorenzo is dead, Domenico is dead, Politian is dead. Tommaso is dead, Landino is dead, everyone is dead except Marsilio Ficino and dear Filippino. And Filippino is in Rome.

'Rome!' he said aloud.

'What?'

'I've got to go to Rome, see my old friend Filippino.'

'You're going nowhere, believe me. You couldn't make it off that paving slab without help.'

'I've got to go to Rome.' Filippino is in Rome, he thought, and soon Simonetta will be there too. He felt a rush of love. 'Filippino and Simonetta: it'll be like old times.'

'Tell you what,' said the watchman. 'You sleep it off a while, and I'll do my rounds. And then I'll get a lad to help me and we'll get you back where you belong.'

Sandro slept, and when he woke he was being lifted. 'Which way?' asked the watchman. Another watchman picked up his useless feet.

'Across the river,' said Sandro. 'On the Lungarno.'

'I said he was a gentleman,' said the first watchman to the second. 'Even if he is pissed.'

'At least he isn't heavy,' was all the other could reply.

They carried him to his door. The key was in his purse. His purse was with the landlady. 'I'd rather be in Rome,' Sandro told them as they propped him in his doorway.

'Sod that,' said the second watchman. 'I've carried you far enough for one night.'

'I thought you said he wasn't heavy,' said the first.

'He wasn't. To begin with.'

Sandro looked round. The sun was coming up. So was something else.

'Wish he'd chucked that lot a bit earlier,' said the second watchman, stepping back to avoid the widening pool of vomit. 'We could've done with the loss of weight.'

The watchmen left, to return to their homes and families; Sandro went back to sleep, and returned to his distant past.

1474

Lorenzo had not foreseen the amount of work my fame would bring and, despite his chiding, I could not set off for Pisa until the beginning of winter. The day I left was cold and icy, the very worst sort of weather for fresco painting. The sky was flat and white, while the road, like a tempered sword, had been soaked in water and hardened. I took Biagio and Jacopo to Pisa with me, leaving Filippino in charge of the shop. Filippino had grown into a good-looking young man of middling build by then, with a serious face and a beard that needed to be shaved twice daily, and never was. He was ready to take on commissions in his own right but I hoped he would not leave my shop. I had known him a long while. It pleased me to believe he looked to me as I had looked up to my brother Giovanni.

Once more I was outside the city walls, in the contado, the vast bleak unknown area that lies between cities. We followed the same river that runs through our city, rode through the fields that provide Florence with its grain, passed the hills that provide it with protection, and yet were in a land as remote and alien to me as any discovered by Cristoforo Columbus. The frost drained the colour from the land. Hills, trees, outcrops of rock, all became pastel; wicker fences, mills, white churches were wrapped in a haze of ice. Everything took on the colour of our winter breath. Noon was as cold and quiet as a city dawn. A mist feathered the hills, isolating them, turning them to mysterious islands, to the place where birds go to die.

Sometimes we saw people, huddled figures with dogs and black pigs, dressed in clothes that were brown as the earth, black as the boles of the trees. Their feet were bandaged, their hair unkempt, their faces red and creased; there were children among them, but these infants were not like children of the city, where even the poverty-stricken *popolo magro* in the Santa Croce slums learn to play gutter games, but were instead like smaller, weaker adults, the first to die in times of hunger or plague, with none of the vitality the city breeds. Each of us is shaped, I believe, not only by God who in his wisdom apportions our gifts at birth, but also by our surroundings. Within the city walls all vitality is contained, channelled down the narrow streets, forced upwards by the towers and the cathedral's soaring dome; in the contado human energy dissipates, spreads across open fields and pours unused over the distant horizons. This is why country people are so different, so slow of thought and speech; this is why they are so unlike us.

We were accompanied on our expedition by a Genoese who rode a large black warhorse. He wore armour and carried a lance. A painter has to know a little about many subjects. He has to be familiar with the iconography of the saints, the symbolism of flowers, the stations of the Cross and the various ways the Virgin can be depicted without causing offence; he has to know something of architecture; he should be conversant with the various trades of his city, with the ways of the cloth guilds and the bankers; he must learn the lives of men and beasts, and how they are to be depicted. For a painter is always judged by all but the few not for his skill but for his accuracy. A swallow sitting in a blackbird's nest, a cloak slung over the wrong shoulder, a bridle hanging incorrectly, and the painter is dismissed as a fool or worse. Armour is a particular problem for many painters. Painting is rarely a warlike activity, yet we are often expected to paint warriors, or to make our subjects look like warriors: Donatello's statue of St George outside the Orsanmichele was paid for by the Guild of Armourers, who insisted on fidelity; Piero de' Medici, Lorenzo's inglorious son, ingloriously allied now to the foul Cesare Borgia, always insisted he was painted in armour, as though the image could compensate for the man. Therefore we painters have to learn not only how to paint the sheen on armour, to make the metal gleam as if burnished although we use no more than matt pigments and skill, but also the technicalities, the visor pierced by the sight and the air-holes called breaths, the gorget that protects the throat, the paudron and besagew at the shoulders, the lower arm protection of couter, vambrace and gauntlet, the way the tassets fall over the thighs, the correct design of a leg armour that consists of four articulated parts, cuisse, poleyn, greave and sabaton. Without such knowedge our work will be ridiculed, and is. When I looked at our Genoese, whose shoulder armour was spiky and fluted in the German style, yet whose helm was rounded and stamped with the crossed keys of the Negroli workshop in Milan, I knew I was not looking at a single bespoke suit of armour, but rather at the surviving parts of several. He wore not the armour of a knight, but the armour of a miscellany of knights. This was reassuring. If I must travel, let me be accompanied by the sort of man who can kill several knights and strip off and steal their armour, for such a man knows his business.

The journey to Pisa can be done in a single day, but we took two. My dislike of the contado is great, and grows at night when the wolves howl at the moon, but my dislike for hard riding is greater. When we arrived at Pisa it was the afternoon of the second day. The Arno, which we had followed for the whole journey, dropped down a noisy weir. Rising above the cream city walls was the cathedral – though what I took to be its dome was, I soon learnt, its Baptistery – but there were no other buildings of note there; indeed, in comparison with Florence, Pisa is a small and unexciting place, and its constant struggle for independence, which continues to this day, is surely a product of the heart rather than the mind, for the minds of the Pisans cannot but acknowledge the supremacy of Florence in all things. We even build better. The Pisan bell-tower, though famous and not unattractive, is falling down and will not survive long.

We rode into the city through the eastern gate. There was a small party from the cathedral to greet us, two priests and a lay clerk. Our Genoese companion left us there: his instructions had been to make sure we arrived safely, and having done that he was to go back to Lorenzo, who had hired him as our escort. I did not envy him that return journey alone, for all that I felt homesick, yet I watched him leave with a certain bitter fascination, and when the gates were shut behind him I did not know if I felt relief, secure at last from the wildness of the contado, or trapped in this alien city.

The welcoming party, to begin with at least, was hospitable and polite, though they speak the Tuscan language curiously in Pisa. They led me to my lodgings, near the cathedral, and servants were found to help Biagio and Jacopo unpack our equipment while I went to the cathedral to discuss the commission. Even to my Florentine eye, the interior of the cathedral, I have to admit, is rather fine. Despite the winter the cathedral was full of light. Two lines of antique columns receded into the distance like an illustration from a textbook, and the vanishing point of their perspective was the altar, so that my eye was drawn immediately to its cross and the ancient Byzantine fresco Cimabue had painted above it. The roof was high and modern, a series of gilt panels ornamented in the classical style, and made all the more beautiful by the starkness of the walls that supported it. The apse, painted by Gozzoli, was rich in colour though his figures, characteristically, lacked animation. The pulpit was magnificient. All in all I began to feel honoured to be employed there.

I met the committee of canons responsible for the commission. I knew from their letters that they required me to paint a fresco of the Assumption for the chapel of the Impagliata, and had already prepared some drawings, but what had not been made clear was the size and shape of the area they wanted painting. As soon as I saw it I knew my drawings would have to be altered radically, for there was more to be covered than I had been led to believe, and the shape was awkward. I mentioned this to the canons.

Fra Giusto, leader of the committee, was immediately on the defensive. 'I assure you that the dimensions we sent are accurate in every detail.'

'It's the arch of the wall that's the problem. I planned my composition in the belief we were dealing with a square.' I indicated the curve of stonework that marked the top of the wall. It turned the space I was meant to cover into a sort of large shallow niche, and meant I would have to rethink the composition entirely. 'Now it appears I've got to find some way of filling the upper area too.'

'That's not our fault,' said Fra Giusto.

'I'm not saying it is. I'm just saying that it means more work.' I showed them my drawings. 'I need to think of something else.'

'I hope this will cause no delay,' said Fra Giusto.

'I hope you realize – ' I began. I had been going to explain that no fresco could be painted in the winter when another of the canons spoke up.

'Perhaps angels,' a canon, whose name I soon learned was Fra

Michele, said loudly. 'I have seen the fresco of the Deposition by Giotto in Padua. The angels are extremely handsome.'

'And I haven't seen them,' I said, tired by my journey and tired of this meeting.

'Perhaps you should,' said Fra Michele. 'This is the problem with employing an inexperienced artist, of course.' He was talking to his colleagues. 'But you wouldn't listen to me.'

It was getting dark anyway. We left the subject and the cathedral, and went our separate ways.

On Matins bell of the next day Fra Giusto called on me at my lodgings. I was out, being shaved, but he waited and was there when I got back.

'Sandro Botticelli,' he said. 'The committee of canons sends its greetings and wonders if you have thought further about the fresco of the Assumption.'

It seemed a formal, rather cold way of phrasing it. 'I've thought about it,' I said.

'Perhaps if you came to the cathedral again we could discuss the matter further.'

I went with him. I did not look forward to meeting the canons again. I still did not know if they understood the problems the winter would cause.

We met in the Baptistery. As things turned out the disagreement was even worse than I had expected. The committee had already decided what alterations they wanted to my drawings: in the square area I should paint my Assumption, as I had already planned; in the arch I was to paint a choir of angels. This not only meant much more work, but also irrevocably weakened my original composition. I had intended Christ, on the hill, to be the apex of my design; instead he was to be topped by a crowd of angels, which would destroy the upwards thrust of the work. I tried to explain this to them; they were not interested. 'When can you start work?' they asked.

'I can begin on the new cartoon immediately, and my assistants should begin copying the design on to the wall in ruddle within a week.' I prayed they knew enough about fresco painting to understand what I was to say next. 'But of course, I can't begin the painting until the weather is warmer.'

Clearly, they were ignorant entirely. 'Why not?'

I put my hand on the wall of the Baptistery. 'It's cold; it's damp. The walls of the chapel are the same. No fresco will take to that.'

The canons looked at one another. 'Do you mean it has to be spring before you can begin to paint?' asked Fra Michele. 'That you must wait three months?'

'I mean exactly that.'

'Ridiculous!'

Fra Giusto was anxious rather than explosive. 'We can't wait that long, I'm afraid. There is much work that needs to be done.'

'Much work,' agreed Fra Michele. 'We need the whole thing complete by the feast of the Assumption. And I don't just mean your fresco; I mean the whole decoration of this chapel. If you don't start until spring there'll be no time to do the rest of the work.'

'I'm sorry,' I said. 'I'm only a painter.'

'We were told you were the best young painter in Tuscany,' said Fra Michele.

'If that's my reputation,' I said carefully, 'then I don't want to jeopardize it by producing inferior work.'

'Inferior work!' Fra Michele was outraged. 'Are you insulting us? Look around you. Is this an inferior place?' He turned to his companions. 'I said we should have hired a local painter.'

'This man was recommended to us,' said another of the canons. 'You know that. The donor didn't think your brother-in-law was sufficiently familiar with modern styles.'

'Recommendations!' snorted Fra Michele. 'What use are they when this painter in front of us thinks the cathedral deserves inferior work and can't begin until spring? At least my brother-in-law Gozzoli is a Pisan. He wouldn't have shilly-shallied about like this. Even if this young man is the donor's choice, how's the donor going to react when he discovers how far behind schedule we've fallen? Answer me that. And what about this young man's disrespect? How dare a Florentine offer Pisa his second best work? Any man should be honoured to work in our cathedral.'

'You misunderstand,' I began, intending to explain that while the cathedral might be second to none, a fresco painted in winter certainly would be, when Fra Michele interrupted with a second snort.

'I misunderstand! No, my Florentine friend. You misunderstand.

You are employed to paint a fresco, which must be complete before a certain date. It is to be of the highest standard. If you cannot manage that then we will find someone who can.'

'Let's not be hasty,' said Fra Giusto, hastily. 'I'm sure it needn't come to that. All we want,' he said, addressing me, 'is that the fresco is done in time for the feast of the Assumption. We have certain obligations,' he explained, 'and would find it most embarrassing if there were to be a delay.'

He did not elaborate, but I had a fair idea what he meant. Behind this committee there was a rich man, the donor, who was putting up the money for the decoration of the chapel. The canons were probably already behind schedule because I had delayed in taking up the commission, and the donor had set them a deadline; doubtless the rich man in turn had pressures. Rich men have daughters they need to marry off, visitors they need to impress. The days before the feast of the Assumption are often used for negotiating marriages.

I was not surprised. It is the way of the world that artists are only one small factor in the production of art. I have become familiar with printing machines. Many cogs must turn before the page is printed. Likewise, the artist is just one cog in the machine that makes art. I had no choice. 'I'll begin at once, but I make no guarantee. The drawing will be of the highest quality, I can promise you that. But the paint may not take because of the cold.'

'Excuses already!' said Fra Michele, but they really had no choice either. They would find no other artist at this notice – unless it were Fra Michele's brother-in-law Gozzoli, whom apparently the donor did not want – and they knew it. I began work in earnest and, as I had promised, Jacopo and Biagio were soon transferring the design to the wall, pushing styluses through the paper of my cartoon on to the underplaster and painting the broad outlines of my figures in ruddle.

Some people argue that fresco is the most important work an artist can do, and certainly many of the most important commissions – including the work I was later to do for Pope Sixtus – are for fresco, but I do not agree. The advantage of fresco is that it is permanent. The paint is applied to wet plaster; the plaster dries; the paint is sealed. The disadvantages, however, are fourfold. First, a panel, and even more a canvas, is portable and can be painted in the bottega; a fresco has to be painted where the client demands and in what light that room allows. Second, the paint has to be applied rapidly, before the plaster dries. Third, it is not really possible to retouch a fresco, for although the plaster when dry will still take a tempera paint, which ought to allow a certain amount of repainting, the tempera will never be as durable as the fresco nor the finish as smooth: the retouching shows for what it is. And fourth, because metal reacts with the plaster, only earth and vegetable-based colours can be employed when painting in fresco, which means that our favourite biacca white, made from lead, and the useful sulphur-based yellows and reds, cannot be used; the limited palette can lead to attractive effects, but it denies other, equally attractive, possibilities. His attempts to get round these restrictions have made Leonardo a laughing stock among those who understand fresco painting; I, less ambitious, have worked within the rules, yet feel I have never done myself justice in this medium.

I did my best at Pisa cathedral, but on top of the usual problems of fresco work I had two more, for the time of year was wrong and I was inexperienced. It was Jacopo's job to apply the plaster to the wall, never covering more than I could paint in a single day, and to prick out the design on the fresh plaster to give me something to work to; it was Biagio's job to mix the paints. Jacopo, who had worked with his previous master on one or two frescos before joining me, was at least efficient with the plaster and sensible about how much work he expected of me, but Biagio was useless, sometimes mixing the paints too thickly for me to use them, and often producing them so slowly in the numb cold weather that we covered only half the amount of plaster we should have done. When this happened we had to chip off the plaster from parts we hadn't painted, which made a dust that dried into the still moist parts we had. Worse still, because we were in the cathedral, a public place, people could witness our problems. During services our chapel was curtained off so we would not disturb the devotions, but for the rest of the time we were mere spectacle. Most people are either sympathetic or uncomprehending – one advantage of fresco is that the parts that are painted are complete, which means that a half-finished fresco does look better than a half-finished panel painting and the artist's skill is appreciated at once – but Fra Michele, while probably the latter, was never the former. He seemed to take pleasure in my mistakes, laughing at me and complaining to the committee, and there was nothing I could do to keep him away. I endured him for two laborious months. But one day in early February, when it was particularly cold and the plaster ran with water, he pushed me too far.

'You haven't done much today,' he said.

'Look at the state of the wall!' I said. 'You can't expect paint to hold to that!'

'I'm not interested in your excuses.'

'And I'm not interested in your opinions.' I put down my brushes and rested the pot of ochre I had been using in the crook of my arm.

'Finished already, I see,' he said.

'This plaster won't be fit to use before Easter,' I said.

'More excuses.'

'At least my opinions are based on knowledge,' I replied.

'You can't take criticism,' he jeered.

'I can't take criticism from an ignorant priest like you, no.'

'You? Call me ignorant? I'm surprised you've heard of the word. But then, all Florentines talk big: it's converting words into action they can't manage.'

I inverted the paint over his head. Ochre streamed down his face and on to his habit. 'An action,' I explained.

I was arrested of course. Not only had I assaulted a priest, I had done so within the cathedral. Worse crimes occur in cathedrals – a crime far worse was to occur in Florence cathedral only a few years later – but I was a foreigner there and Fra Michele a well-known preacher. No one seemed sure what my punishment would be, but it was agreed it would be heavy.

There was no trial. Nor, thank the Heavens, was there any torture. I was simply thrown into the common gaol, where the food was bad and the company worse, while Biagio and Jacopo were expelled from the city and, penniless, expected to make their own way home.

The prison was an unpleasant place, though not as awful as I had feared. The spring months are the best time to be in prison. In winter the cold kills many prisoners, and summer is the time of disease. I was in a long low-vaulted corridor of a room, some fifty feet by twelve, and chained to a wall. There were perhaps thirty men and boys in there, though numbers shrank and swelled with the moon, and they ranged from children of no more than ten years of age to derelict old men with neither hair nor teeth. At either end of the prison's long tunnel were bars as though this were a cage, and beyond the bars to my right I could see the tilting tower of the cathedral, mocking me.

I have heard it said that it is in extremity we get to know ourselves best. So far as I had thought of imprisonment in the years before, when I was in constant fear of arrest for treason, I had assumed I should hate prison and that it should send me mad. I cannot say I actually enjoyed prison. I did hate the parasites, and the way we had to shit where we were chained, and wait for a working party to shovel it up as they did once a day. But the experience of being in prison itself was not so dreadful. Indeed, I found it almost soothing. I was far more worried about Jacopo and Biagio, cast penniless into the contado, than I was about myself. At least in the prison I had walls around me and a roof over my head; at least in the prison I could survive, though at night rats ran over my legs.

Events moved slowly, but with comforting predictability. A month went by. I was regularly visited by a representative of the Florentine Capitano who, through a cloth he held over his nose to keep out the stench, introduced himself as Donato Trissino. 'Look, I'm dreadfully sorry about this,' said Donato. 'But you must look at the broad situation. The Capitano has a difficult job at the best of times. I know that in Florence he's considered to be the ruler of Pisa, but in Pisa he's considered more like an ambassador, influential certainly, and not to be unduly provoked, but certainly not in charge of the city's day-to-day affairs. We're doing everything we can to get you out but we can't demand they release you, I'm afraid. We've been having a bit of trouble with the archbishop. Still, at least you're keeping cheerful, and that's the main thing.'

I had become, it seemed, a sort of hostage in their political games. I could not be treated too badly because I was a Florentine and Florence ruled Pisa. But I could not be released because Florence was afraid of a Pisan reaction. Oh well, I thought, at least now I have official confirmation that I'm keeping cheerful.

I think the situation could have gone on indefinitely had the Pisans not overstretched the mark. The canons of the Cappella Incoronata, for whom I was meant to be working, delivered a rather formal decree to the effect that Sandro Botticelli, painter, had breached his contract and was liable to repay all monies he had so far received; as all monies so far received had long since been spent on food and paints and lodgings I was unable to comply with their demands. I told this to Donato when next he visited; he looked disturbed, went away, and came back later the same day with the Capitano in person. The Capitano, a weathered man whose face resembled a damaged portrait of Tommaso Soderini, said he would do all he could and then replaced the cloth over his nose.

A day passed, then another, and Donato returned. 'Wonderful news!' he announced. I was released immediately and all charges dropped: the means to release me had, I suppose always been there; the question in their minds was whether or not I was worth the effort. I had, after all dyed a priest; I assumed that was what Donato meant when he had spoken of 'a little trouble with the archbishop'. But when money became involved, the Capitano did too. Florence has always put money before the dignity of clerics; even Savonarola could not suppress that trait for long.

I had been in the same unpleasant room for eight weeks. My body was covered in sores, and I expect I stank. Outside it was late spring. Pisa was brilliant in sunlight. Butterflies danced among flowers. Swallows swooped from the eaves. I wanted to go back inside. But the gate was shut again, I needed a wash, and I could barely walk on my own, so I was supported by the soldiers of the Capitano and led to his residence. Much to my surprise, as the feast of the Assumption had already passed, I was expected to go back to work on the fresco. A carpenter had built me a scaffold – or perhaps it was just converted from the one the canons had ordered for my hanging – and new assistants had been found. I worked another month, painting as quickly as I could, because I needed the money if I was to return to Florence, and then slipped out of Pisa on the night I got paid. It was a quick decision quickly regretted.

Outside the gates of Pisa, as outside most cities' gates, were the huts and shacks of those who, though not citizens, live off the city's wealth. The men are often halfway to banditry, the women little more than whores: unaccompanied, on foot, and with a month's salary in my purse, I did not relish spending the night with such people, and was starting down the road away from Pisa's walls when the first wolf bayed.

In theory, valour is commendable, but in practice it often hurts. There seemed little point at the time in being both brave and torn apart by wolves; I have since learnt that there are few wolves in that country, and none in the summer months, so what I heard was probably a chained farm dog, but as things turned out, returning was a wise decision. For among the vagabonds were several who knew me from prison. I was almost lionized, and with the help of a few lire and a fireside sketch, in charcoal fresh from the embers and drawn on a piece of rough wood, I earned myself a popularity I have rarely achieved elsewhere, as well as a bed for the night and drink to warm my stomach. The price of fame, I discovered, was a thick head the following morning, but a few more soldats got me the hire of a livery horse from just within the gates, and unpursued, if uncomfortable, I set off for my home.

One of the messengers that in those days regularly passed between Pisa and Florence, carrying instructions and money-orders, soon caught up with me. I explained who I was and he promised to take care of me; he rode fast and I had trouble keeping up, but this time I did not worry that I rode my horse hard and opened many sores. I wanted to be home, and wept when I saw the Duomo in the distance. I rode into the city along the Borgo Ornissanti, passed where my father lived and worked, and stopped to tell him I was back. He seemed surprised to see me. 'You look thin,' he said. 'You need a new cook. And why are you walking like that? Have you got piles?'

'I've been in prison in Pisa. Didn't you know?'

'Why should I know? I haven't seen you in months.'

'That's because I've been in prison,' I explained with impatient logic. 'But I'm out now.'

'I can see that.' He looked at me. 'You'd better eat here on Sunday. You need fattening up.'

'All right, Father,' I said.

Always he cared for me more than he cared to show.

Next I went to the bottega. It was open and Filippino was at work on an attractive painting of San Lorenzo. 'Hello,' he said. 'Everything's sorted out then.' He had grown a thick beard in my absence, which made him seem older than his years.

'You'd heard I was in prison?' I had been greeted far more joyously by the vagabonds. Here I had expected to be a hero; it seemed I was yet to be missed.

'Jacopo said you'd been arrested,' Filippino confirmed.

'Is he back? And Biagio?'

'They're working for Cosimo Rosselli now. I hadn't enough work to justify keeping them and he wanted extra assistants. He's doing some frescos in the church of Santissima Annunziata.'

'Marvellous. So now I've lost my *garzoni*.'

'Why are you looking so glum?' He smiled through the new beard. 'I thought you'd be pleased to be home.'

'Home?' I asked him. 'I felt more at home in a prison cell in Pisa. What's the matter with everyone? Did nobody worry about me?'

Filippino shrugged. 'Poliziano came here once or twice, told me you'd been arrested and asked if I'd heard anything. But I hadn't of course, except what he already knew, so he went again.'

'I'm glad somebody noticed I'd gone,' I said. 'I'll go and see him.'

'All right. I'm a bit tied up now, but drop in later and we'll have a drink.'

'Maybe,' I said. 'Though I might be eating at the Medici palace.'

'Oh, I shouldn't think so. They'll be a bit busy I should imagine.'

'Why? What's going on?'

'I don't know the details. It's to do with the pope and things, but don't ask me what. I've been working; I haven't had time to follow the details.'

I went to the Palazzo Medici. The courtyard was busier than ever, and there were several fine horses tied there that carried the crossed-keys livery of the papacy; I tried to go through to the hall, as usual, and my way was blocked by two guards. I recognized them both. 'What's the news?' I asked.

'Sorry. You can't go in. Lorenzo's meeting the Papal Nuncio right now.'

'The Papal Nuncio? What's going on?'

'What do you mean, what's going on? Everyone knows.'

'Everyone but me. I've been away.'

A voice I recognized made me turn round. 'Piero! Come back!' A scholarly man in black was shouting at a boy of about 3 who was running loose across the cobbles. 'Piero!' he called. 'Piero!' The child ran fast; the scholar, though young, was unsuited to this sort of exercise and looked hot and red when he caught his quarry and tucked it under his arm. 'If it wasn't for the fact that my contract specifically states you are the legitimate son of people I know well,' he was saying to the boy, 'I would be quite convinced that your mother and father were strangers who met but once.'

'Politian!' I said.

'Sandro!' The boy in his arms was struggling. 'When did you get back?'

'Today.'

'Nice to see you again. Give me a hand with this will you?' He passed his charge to me. 'Sandro, meet Piero di Lorenzo de' Medici, heir to the world.'

On hearing who the boy was I turned him the right way up. 'I'm going to tell my father,' the boy spat as I put him down.

'Your father, fortunately, is too busy to listen,' said Politian.

The child ran off again; Politian took a half-hearted stride in pursuit and then stopped. 'Forget it. The child wants to grow up an ignoramus; who am I to thwart a Medici?'

'Not an easy task then, being tutor to the house of Medici?'

'The girls are fine. Not much expected of them, of course, except a smattering of culture to make them acceptable brides. But the words I could use for young Piero I dare not utter in the home of his ancestors for fear they rain vengeance upon me. How are you?'

'I'm fine. But what's been going on? I seemed to have missed it.'

'Missed it? Dear Sandro. You've been in Pisa. You've been at the heart of it. In a manner of hyperbolic speaking.'

'Meaning?' I asked.

'Earlier this year our esteemed archbishop of Florence, Piero Riario, died. Not an event which need have made much impact on the Florentines, as the noble archbishop, whose uncle, by a pure and unfathomable coincidence that could not have been further from base rumours of nepotism, was Pope Sixtus, held also the benefices of' – he counted out on his finges – 'Patriarch of Constantinople, Abbot of St Ambrose, Bishop of Treviso, Mende, Spalto and' – he had to use the other hand – 'Senigallia. Naturally holding so many offices meant there were many demands on his time: hunting and whoring, drinking and dicing, for instance.' Politian smiled modestly. 'It's been my business to compose certain letters on these matters,' he explained. 'Anyhow, the archbishop's death, though no great blow to the spiritual authority of the Church, did leave a number of vacancies, so naturally Lorenzo thought at once of his Orsini brother-in-law, Rinaldo. Rinaldo would be an ideal candidate for the bishopric of Florence. Unfortunately though, relations between Florence and Rome have not been good recently. Another of the pope's Riario nephews – "nephew" being here a polite euphemism, you understand – called Girolamo wanted to marry Caterina Sforza and in the process purchase Imola, so he asked the Medici, as bankers to the papacy, for forty thousand ducats. But when the news came that Imola was for sale Lorenzo tried to buy it for Florence – it lies on the road between Rimini and Bologna – rather than for the pope, so he made excuses; the Pazzi were happy to lend the money to Sixtus instead.'

'But the Pazzi are Florentines too,' I said. Jacopo de' Pazzi, after all, was a frequent visitor to the Medici palace.

'They're businessmen. The papal account is worth a fortune. And so is papal support, which sadly it seemed our esteemed Lorenzo has lost. Never underestimate the papacy. At the moment Sixtus is trying to marry off another nephew, to the daughter of the duke of Urbino. You've heard of course that Urbino is now a duchy?' I shook my head. 'That's the pope's way of saying thank you – Federico Montefeltro is now duke of Urbino. This not only gives the pope yet another foothold on the territory to the east of us, but means we are going to lose the services of the count, or duke as he should now be styled, to a man who is going out of his way to be hostile to us.'

'I'm not sure that's much of a loss,' I said. 'I wasn't much impressed with the count of Urbino's work at Volterra.'

'Naturally not. But on the other hand, no one can deny that the man is successful. He does no less than he is asked or paid to do; at Volterra he did more, that's all.' Politian shrugged. 'He's by far the most reliable condottiere Florence has employed in recent years. He won't be easy to replace.'

'And it was because of all this that I was abandoned in Pisa?' I asked. 'It isn't flattering to find I was forgotten, even if things were getting busy here.'

'You weren't forgotten,' he said. 'Naturally, as Lorenzo had got you there, you felt the least he could do was get you back. Unfortunately the same pressure that led to you being sent, namely the need to keep Pisa sweet, meant we didn't dare intervene on your behalf. Particularly as by all accounts including those of your assistants you'd frescoed a prelate. Were you drunk? Not that it matters. The point is that Lorenzo has applied all the pressure he can to have Rinaldo Orsino made archbishop of Florence, and seems to have succeeded, except that now the pope has named Francesco Salviati as archbishop of Pisa. Lorenzo's daughter has married a Salviati, but Lorenzo and Francesco have never liked one another, and anyway the pope had agreed that no appointments would be made anywhere in Tuscany without consultation with our Signoria. That's why the Papal Nuncio is here: Lorenzo has refused to let Salviati into Tuscany; the Nuncio is trying to negotiate so that Salviati can take up his post, or rather the income that goes with it. And that's why you were kept imprisoned in Pisa: we needed Pisan support for our actions, because if they rose up and said they wanted Salviati we'd be in a mess.'

'So why was I released?'

'You were lucky. There are more ways to win support than by being nice, and when the Pisan authorities started making silly demands on you, and making it look like they didn't fear us, it was time to intervene. The donkey will work for a carrot, but it needs to be guided with a stick.'

'Oh, wasn't I lucky,' I said, but Politian heard the tone in which I spoke.

'Don't be like that,' he said. 'These things happen.'

'Not to me. Never again. Next time Lorenzo wants a picture painting outside Florence he can get someone else to do it.'

'I'd reserve judgement on that,' said Politian. 'We live in an era of mutability. Everything changes, even the subject of conversations. Have you managed to meet Simonetta Vespucci yet?'

'The famous beauty? Not yet. '

'Then now's your chance. She's here at the moment, sewing with Donna Lucrezia.'

'So?'

'Aren't you aching to feast your eyes on this paragon of feminine pulchritude?'

'Not especially.'

'Come on, you've been in prison. You need reminding of the pleasures of the world. Besides, you're an artist. I'd be fascinated to learn what your professional eye makes of the lovely Simonetta.'

'We can hardly disturb them if they're in Donna Lucrezia's chambers.'

'Naturally not,' said Politian. 'But fortunately they're taking advantage of this charming spring weather; they're in the gardens. Actually, today is a good opportunity. Were Giuliano de' Medici here then the beautiful Simonetta would be absent, for his attentions, though presumably flattering, are undeniably excessive. Such sighing and sobbing must prove wearisome, especially for a married woman. But Giuliano visits his estates above Prato and isn't due back until nightfall.'

The day was indeed charming, and though the grounds of the Palazzo Medici in those days were not as extensive and attractive as those Rucellai is currently laying out north of my birthplace on the Ognissanti, neither were they as bleak as they have become since Rucellai appropriated the Medici statuary. We strolled down graceful walks past shaded arbours. Late spring blossomed in the bushes, flowered delicately on the lawns. The trees still wore the pale green haze of new leaves. Birds sang; butterflies flopped drunkenly from flower to blossom, sipping the warmth of the day. We passed antique statuary, old Cosimo de' Medici's collection, and Politian conjured zephyrs and fauns in the city's midst as he discussed the statues' subjects. The air was sweet, and at last I was convinced that liberty was a prize worth attaining. I was half in love already – with the butterflies and skies, statuary and flowers – when we came upon Lorenzo's mother and Simonetta sewing in the shade of a broad chestnut tree. And then I was in love entirely, and the beauty of the day was irrelevant. I would have loved her had we met, as we might yet, in the second circle of Hell.

1499

Sandro was lost in his past but the present, unperturbed, continued without him. In the second week of August 1499 Florence rejoiced. It seemed Pisa was almost recovered at last: the wall near the Porta a Mare had been breached; the Stampace tower had been stormed; Sandro got his purse back. Preparations began for the victory parade, and Sandro was commissioned to engrave a broadsheet to commemorate Florence's triumph. But then the news changed. Our mercenary generals, Paolo and Vitellozzo Vitelli, had apparently stopped the attack and, though Florence urged them on, nothing would persuade them to pursue their advantage. They were in the pay of the Pisans, it was rumoured, or even of the French. The French were meant to be our allies, but in September while the Vitellis procrastinated and Florence wept with frustration the French army, under the Milanese renegade Giangiacomo Trivulzio, captured Milan: it was in the French interest that Florence should continue to be distracted by the Pisan war.

Shortly afterwards, thinking himself invited to a banquet, Paolo Vitelli instead found he was arrested. Sandro never got paid for the broadsheets. Nor did any further commissions come his way. His career flagged, and he had too much leisure, too little sense, to stop his mind pursuing Simonetta. He thought of little except how he might meet her again or how he had met her first. His mind viewed and reviewed their first meeting, the Medici gardens, the birdsong, the warmth of the spring, the warmth of her smile. He had painted her so often, in so many guises – idealizing her beauty into Venus coming from the waves, recording her serenity where Venus sits with

Mars, catching both her poise and her playfulness in the double portrait that has become known as *Primavera* – that her features were as familiar, as much part of the landscape of his mind, as the Duomo. Yet, both when he analysed her features on first meeting or itemized them in his memory, he found it hard to explain what made their beauty exceptional. The face was well-shaped, certainly, with firm cheekbones and a narrow chin. Yet wasn't the chin a little too pointed? The lips were full, and full of promise, and the mouth rose always at the corners, not to laugh at the world but to laugh with the world. Yet perhaps the mouth was a touch too much, a jot too wide? Then there was the nose, slender and delicate. Yet the underside was rounded slightly when seen in profile, and though this gave it, when viewed from the front, a childlike, endearing quality, was the nose not also a little turned up, almost snub? The eyes of course were faultless, large and of the clearest blue; they tilted slightly, to emphasize the rise of her mouth, the curve of her cheekbones, the feline languor of her body. Even the most exquisite gem however loses its lustre in a flawed setting: surely even those eyes should not compensate for the limitations of the rest of her features? Yet even as she looked up, politely, demurely, to greet him, and Sandro returned her modest gaze, he found that what should have been flaws were blended into perfection. Her features had the irresistible logic of music. Each, like a note in a harmony, contributed to her beauty; each, like notes in a tune, led effortlessly to the next. The imperfections of detail only underlined the beauty of the whole, so that seeing her, instead of questioning her beauty in terms of standard notions of what a mouth or a nose should be like, he rather questioned the standard notions. Any notion of beauty that could not appreciate Simonetta's exquisite features was, it seemed to Sandro, redundant; any criterion for beauty which did not recognize her supremacy was invalid.

But what had she seen as she looked up through long lashes to where Sandro stood? A thin man was before her, of such extraordinary paleness that he looked as though he had seen no daylight for months; his hair was that colour that is no colour, neither brown nor fair. His prison skinniness seemed to enlarge his features. It emphasized the bone of his nose, the way it had been broken and had reset well, but not perfectly. It hollowed his cheeks beneath the bones and exhibited the swell of flesh around his generous mouth. It drew attention to eyes that were both dark and cheerful, hooded by lazy lids. It was not quite a handsome face, she thought as she looked, but it was an honest one.

As a young girl Simonetta Catteneo had been, in her own eyes, like a colt, with bones too big for grace, and she had thought herself ugly. Yet since she had grown into those bones men had pestered her constantly. She came of an old Genoese family which had more connections than wealth. Her father owned land near Pisa, and she had dined with fat men who had pawed her. Her mother was from Florence, and she had stayed with aunts whose husbands had stroked first her hair then her breasts. As she reached her nubile years she had found herself with suitors, admirers who had promised her love and her father money, but by then she was afraid of men and hoped, though she told no one, that she might be allowed to retire to a nunnery. Then Giorgio Vespucci had visited her father, with a retinue of men and an eligible son. The Vespucci were rich and distinguished, with their own palazzo in Florence and lands in the contado, and Giorgio was well-known and respected for his study of astronomy and mathematics. Old Cattaneo gave the son, Marco, his permission to court his daughter.

Marco was not a conventional lover. As a boy he had been robust and boisterous, but a fall from a horse in his 15th year had cost him his teeth and damaged his neck. That night Catteneo held a banquet for his honoured guests, and sat Marco next to his daughter. Simonetta was impressed by the young man, who was still handsome until he opened his mouth, which he did rarely, and who held his head so stiff and proud. He hardly seemed to notice her, and on the occasions when he did he turned his whole body towards her as if giving her all his attention. There was dancing after the banquet, and although Simonetta enjoyed dancing with her friends and with the women who attended her, she liked less to dance with strangers. She was relieved when Marco did not ask her to dance, and pleased at his reserve. Too many men had forced their attention on her. One who held back was a pleasant change.

As for Marco, he too was satisfied with his companion. She was undeniably attractive, apparently modest, and above all quiet. Marco loathed talkative women. He wasn't all that fond of any women, in fact, and preferred the company of grooms. But his father had threatened to disinherit him, leave everything to his cousin Amerigo, if Marco didn't marry, and Marco had no desire to be poor. This Simonetta would do, he decided.

They married in the autumn of 1463. The wedding had been the usual combination of high ceremony and low farce, and on the wedding night the couple, in their shifts, had sat in bed while their guest encouraged them to the act of love. Their performance had not been particularly inspired, despite Amerigo's enthusiastic commentary and her father's cheerful encouragement, but Simonetta's nurse had taught her the noises she should make under these circumstances, and Simonetta dutifully made them. Both husband and wife were grateful when it was over and their guests had gone.

Neither of them considered their awkward lovemaking a problem; indeed, both were relieved to find their partners demanded so little. Nor did either feel that their marriage was anything less than a success. As a married woman, Simonetta hoped at last to be free of the lust of men; as a married man, Marco intended to indulge in lusts of his own.

It could have been an ideal situation, and perhaps would have been, had Simonetta been just a little less beautiful. There were beauties in Florence already, Lucrezia Donati, Bencina, Lena Norella, Bina and Maria de' Lenzi. But none was ethereal as Simonetta, none so demure or remote. She had been in Florence no more than a week before well-dressed young men began to gather at the door of the Vespucci palace, no more than two before she attracted the notice of the glamorous Giuliano de' Medici.

Giuliano recommended the young woman to the attention of his sister-in-law Clarice. Clarice was not a beauty, though she had a gentle mind and a kind heart, and I believe that despite his many mistresses Lorenzo always loved his wife first. Clarice's greatest attribute was that she was incapable of jealousy. She was never jealous of her husband's mistresses. She was never jealous of Simonetta's beauty. She took the shy young woman under her wing, much to Giuliano's delight.

Even more delightful, from Giuliano's point of view, was that his mother, Donna Lucrezia, also took a fancy to Simonetta. Normally a Medici would not compromise his family's honour by bedding the wife of a member of the *popolo grosso*, but with his mother's blessing Giuliano believed that anything was possible, and pursued Simonetta relentlessly. His mother was a formidable woman, and the look she gave Politian and Sandro as they approached through the glade was penetrating and ironic. 'Ah, Poliziano!' she commanded. 'Entertain me!' The young woman at her side returned her modest eyes to her work.

Dearest Simonetta. The disease of the lungs which was eventually to kill her showed itself in the first winter after her arrival in the city. She had never been strong, and the Palazzo Vespucci is a dour and old-fashioned place, draughty in winter and airless in summer. She had a fever, and then coughed blood. For a month she was not expected to live, and then with the coming of spring she was, like the trees, reborn. The rumour of her recovery spread through the city, and when she went to chuch, at Santa Trinità, to express her thanks to God, a crowd lined up to see her. Even her husband, who was fond of her despite his general dislike of her sex, arranged a banquet in her honour, and people had to be turned away at the door. If anything, it was considered, her illness made her even more beautiful, reddening her lips, making her skin so pale it was almost translucent, giving an additional lustre to her eyes.

She was belladonna, she was the virgin moon. She was irresistible, she was adorable, and she was sitting in front of Sandro, needle poised above a pretty sampler, while he gawped his clumsy love.

Politian broke the silence. 'Mona Lucrezia, do you know Sandro Botticelli?'

She extended her hand elegantly. 'I believe we have met. You're a painter? Is that right?'

'It is,' I agreed.

'And,' continued Politian, 'this is the Donna Vespucci, wife of Marco.'

'I am honoured,' I said.

'Sandro has just returned from Pisa,' said Politian. 'I believe your family are from that city.'

Simonetta continued to look at her embroidery, though her lovely fingers, white and shapely, were still. 'My family is from Genoa,' she corrected, and then, perhaps thinking she had been rude, 'but I was born and brought up on my father's estates near Pisa. To that extent I am a Pisan, yes.'

'Sandro doesn't like Pisa,' Politian said.

I tried to think of something to say, some witty denial of his charge maybe, but nothing came to mind and anyway Politian was still speaking. 'He complains of their curious habits. It seems that in Pisa artists are put in cages.'

'Really?' said Lorenzo's mother. 'So you're that artist?'

'I am honoured you have heard of my troubles,' I said, horribly aware that I had not been brought up a courtier, trying to adapt my speech.

'Honoured balderdash,' said Lucrezia. 'We should have released you earlier. There's no point trying to appease these people. It is necessary to be firm.' She was, after all, a Tornabuoni, a noblewoman.

'I do not suppose I came to any lasting harm,' I said, believing neither what I was saying nor that I was saying it. 'If I have been of some service to your son I will consider myself amply rewarded.'

'Do you hear that, Simonetta?' Lucrezia laughed. 'You had better watch this one. He has a silver tongue in his head.' I blushed.

'Silver, not gold,' Politian confirmed. 'We must not let Sandro get big-headed. He might take up oratory and cease to paint: Florence would lose twice from the exchange, for we have too many second-rate orators and too few first-rate painters. Besides, despite his manners at the moment, I have to tell you that beneath this mask of gallantry lies a crude and lecherous man who whores like a market porter and swears like a market porter's wife. You see him now weakened after his period in gaol. When his health is recovered you would find him less the gentleman.'

Lucrezia smiled at me. 'Don't worry. I don't believe a word this young scoundrel tells me. His tongue is neither silver nor gold, but mercury, ever moving and impossible to catch. Isn't that so, Poliziano?'

'Madame, I am what you decree,' he replied. 'For times when your stomach demands I am your man of letters. I can converse with ease on matters alchemical, archaeological, astrological, botanical, geographical, mathematical, philosophical, scatological and theological. I can give chapter and verse from a dozen ancient authors, with vernacular glosses for those who cannot cope with the tongue of the learned. Yet: should the occasion demand, I am your jester, madame, with a smile and quip suitable for all occasions, all company. For you, my lady Simonetta, a chanson d'amour to lighten your young heart. For Sandro here, a bawdy tale from Boccaccio. And for you, adored and esteemed lady, a story from the divine Dante would seem approriate, a tale of how the lovely Beatrice led him from the pit of Hell just as you, my lady, lead me from all temptation into a life of purity and contemplation.'

Lucrezia laughed. Even Simonetta smiled. 'You're a rogue,' said Lucrezia. 'And I expect to see you hanged some day. But he has a certain charm, Simonetta, don't you think?'

'I think,' she said, speaking carefully, 'I think he is like wine. A little can make you feel happy, but too much can make you giddy.'

'Too much can make you sick, I expect,' agreed Donna Lucrezia. 'But fortunately he has work to do. Shouldn't you be stuffing my grandchildren with grammar or something?'

'Your grandson, alas, is more interested in the sword than the pen. He is, I would imagine, inspecting the soldiers who accompany the Papal Nuncio, or stabbing them, or similar.'

'I don't know where Piero gets it from,' said Lucrezia. 'Not from the Medici line, that's for sure. Bankers and talkers to a man, though I fancy Guiliano would fight over you, eh Simonetta?'

Simonetta made no reply. The same observation could never be made of Politian. 'Of course he would,' he said, 'as would half the blades in Florence. Though I fancy our Giuliano would fight harder than most. He suffers a familiar fate, the penalty of the younger son, the combination of high blood and low aspirations which leads to a heart chock-full of passion; he leaves us in no doubt of the depth of his feeling for the lovely Simonetta here, boasts daily of his misery, yet I wonder whether he would feel the same if Donna Vespucci were available. I wish no disrespect to your justly famed beauty when I suggest that he is in love with loving you, that he is animated not by the hope of consummation but by the delicious misery of the hopelessnesss of his condition.'

'Sir, far from disrespectful, I find your words reassuring,' said Simonetta. 'The pain I have caused has caused me great pain.' Such wisdom! Such humility!

'This is getting a bit sophisticated, though,' said Lucrezia. 'Are you saying my son Giuliano wouldn't give Simonetta a tumble given half the chance? Because if you are you're speaking tosh.' Simonetta's lovely face blushed; her eyes turned down once more.

'Sir Giuliano would doubtless give any woman of such beauty that which you so expressively describe as a "tumble" should the opportunity present itself,' said Politian. 'This is not the issue. What I am suggesting – and remember, I was his tutor before I was your grandson's, and, though I can never have a mother's intimate knowledge of his mind, I do have a contemporary's intuition – is that "tumbling" is not the only object of his behaviour. I would go so far as to suggest that his behaviour is its own object, and that being in love is an end in itself.'

'He might as well love his horse then,' said Lucrezia.

'Not exactly: in Giuliano's case – and, let me say, his case is by no means unusual – the object of passion must be worthy and unobtainable. It is generally agreed that Simonetta is the most beautiful woman in Florence; ergo, she becomes a candidate. She is demure and pious; this elevates her above the other contenders. And she is married, which makes her superb. Donna Vespucci, may I say this: it is as if you were put on the earth, in God's ineffable fashion, to be the object of young men's passion, to inspire them to poetry and courage. You are the perfect object of that perfect love which, seeking no satisfaction, is fuelled and fulfilled by frustration. Your bearing, your manner and your beauty would be enough to provoke desire, but it is the knowledge that you are unobtainable which converts desire into that maudlin joy we witness in Guiliano. Such happy misery could not survive consummation; such love is a beautiful moth which, if grasped, turns to powder in the hands.'

There were moths around my heart, and they fluttered. 'You're being very quiet, sir painter,' said Lucrezia.

'There's rarely any option in Poliziano's presence,' I replied.

'I know,' she said. 'You know how you just can't stop when you've started to piss. His conversation is like that. The words just stream out of him.'

'A fine analogy,' said Politian, apparently admiringly, though I was rather embarrassed by the older woman's bluntness. 'For, like a stream of piss, which in a certain light unravels in a glamorous golden arc, my flowing words have beauty, though contained within them is the sharp bitter stench of humanity.'

'What you say stinks,' said Lucrezia. 'Is that what you mean?'

'I mean only what my lady wants me to mean. I am your humble and obedient servant.'

'And yet,' I told them, once more amazed to hear myself speaking, 'there is truth in his words. For such beauty and modesty as Simonetta displays can only cast its light upon all who observe it.'

'Oh dear,' said Donna Lucrezia. 'You've won another admirer, Simonetta. How boring.'

1475

I did not speak with Simonetta again for many months, though I often contrived to glimpse her by waiting in the shadows outside the Palazzo Vespucci or following her to her husband's church of Ognissanti. I had time for this: I had been right about my visits to Pisa, for I had lost many clients, and now a new man, younger, called Domenico Ghirlandaio, was on the scene.

As I sit in my cell in the madhouse I cannot help but wonder who shall read my words. Fra Agostino, certainly. But after him? I have imagined some future scholar who will scan these pages, but will he – or even she, for in the unimaginable future perhaps all women will be as educated as the delightful Isabella d'Este, whose recent reluctance to employ me has confirmed my decision to retire from my trade and the world – recognize the names of those of whom I speak? Some of those I have written about are surely destined for everlasting fame, yet others just as surely face oblivion. There can be no doubt of the immortality of Lorenzo il Magnifico of course, nor of Savonarola. Pope Sixtus, the duke of Urbino, and the infernal Cesare Borgia are other names here mentioned whose fame is assured, for without them the course of history would have taken a different route. It is not these political figures I wonder at. It is the fame of the artists. Will enough of Leonardo's work survive for him to be anything more than a footnote? Will the work of Fra Lippo, already considered old-fashioned by the ignorant, be remembered by future generations? Or what of Gozzoli, whom even the discerning call old-fashioned? Will Michelangelo, who was Domenico's pupil, develop in his master's footsteps, or have we seen his best work already? And what will become of the reputation of Sandro Botticelli which, even as I write, has turned to dust, leaving me stranded, like a moth with damaged wings who flounders beneath the flame?

But one painter whose reputation is assured is Domenico Ghirlandaio, whose short life saw so many magnificent paintings, largely in imperishable fresco, that he cannot but be remembered as the paragon of our age. It may seem, to that future scholar, that I have been less than charitable towards Leonardo, whose reputation as I write is so high, but let me demonstrate that my antipathy is not based on professional jealousy by adding my own contribution to Domenico's apotheosis. We first met in the late spring of 1475. Tommaso Portinari, who was the Medici bank's agent in Flanders, as well as being a distant relative of Dante's famous Beatrice, had commissioned a big triptych of the Nativity by a painter from the Low Countries. This painter was called Hugo van der Goes, and I have already mentioned him among the many painters who went mad; I ought to add that in his case, as in mine, madness may have been a personal tragedy, but it led to remarkable art, and that, though I have seen only this single canvas, I believe Hugo also will rank among the finest of our time. The painting was exhibited in Florence. The populace visited it out of curiosity, for it is undoubtedly different from any painting an Italian could produce; the painters also visited it, and discussed it. I went to see it with Filippino, and it was while waiting to see it that I came across Domenico for the first time.

Domenico was a tall man, a few years younger than I, who stooped to disguise his height. Filippino, who had a gift for knowing everyone, introduced us, and I was pleased that, although Domenico had already achieved a certain reputation with his portraits of the fashionable, he was far from arrogant. 'Have you seen the altarpiece yet?' he asked as we queued.

'Not yet, I look forward to it.'

'It's a r-revelation,' he said, stammering his enthusiasm. 'I've been here every d-day since it was unveiled. A revelation!'

And so it was. The central panel in particular caught my eye. The colouring, in a more sophisticated oil paint than Florence had then used, was subdued yet quite magnificent. In front of what I am told is a typical Netherlandish city scene, solid buildings of gables and arches, the Madonna gazes down at a naked infant lying on straw.

Arranged around her, obeying the rules not of mechanical perspective but of the spirit, are various groups of angels, delicately painted, and a group of totally convincing lifesize rustics whose simple devotion before the Christchild is both comic and moving. In the foreground are two pots containing plants, white lilies for innocence, red lilies for the Passion, and a strange dark plant which I cannot identify yet which speaks volumes about the darkness to come. Domenico was right, it was a revelation. Over the years he was to use many of its motifs in his art. I took but one, I believe: there is a hovering angel in the top right of the central panel whose simple grace informs and inspired my last and most perfect Nativity.

We stood in front of the huge triptych and marvelled until those waiting behind us became impatient and jostled us out of the way; together, the three of us went for a drink. 'I m-must say how m-much I like your Adoration for the Pucci,' Domenico told me. 'I think the way you put the scene into an antique ruin is w-wonderful.'

'Not entirely my idea, I'm afraid,' I replied, having to take care not to mimic his stammer. 'Some of my friends at the Palazzo Medici suggested it. Perhaps you know them, Ficino and Poliziano.'

'N-not exactly. Though I should love to meet them. I am fascinated by ant-antiquity. As you perhaps know, I've only just begun to paint for myself, and I've so much to learn.'

'You seem to have acquired a reputation already.' And a studio, I nearly added: his bottega, which was attached to his goldsmith father's workshop, was larger than mine.

'It's n-nothing, believe me. Those who praise me are very kind, but they flatter me. I have so much to learn. I envy you, Filippino. Your father and your master are both such fine painters. How could you f-fail to be a fine painter yourself?'

'Don't envy me,' said Filippino, who sometimes got argumentative on wine. 'I'll tell you what, you can have Sandro, and my father too if you like, if I can have your father and the workshop he's provided you with. My father, God rest his tormented soul, gave me nothing.'

'Come on, Filippino,' I said. 'That's not fair. Do without me if you like, but not your father. He was a great painter.'

'He was a great painter, but a lousy father.'

'I didn't know you felt like that.' I was drinking burnt wine, which made me sentimental: Filippino's words made me sad. 'I always believed, sincerely, that you loved and admired him.'

'Oh, I do. But when I see our friend Domenico, who is only ten years older than me and yet who runs a workshop kitted out by his father, with all the best modern equipment, don't you think my father could have done the same for us? All right, I was too young at the time. But you wasted ages working at your father's house, scratting around. If my father had left us in better shape we wouldn't have had so much difficulty getting started.'

'He tried,' I said, reluctant to elaborate. 'But it didn't work out for us.'

'He could have at least got you a place with Verocchio or someone,' insisted Filippino. 'Instead of leaving you in the lurch. What exactly did you get? I'll answer that, you got me. You got the old bastard's bastard, that's what you got.'

'I know you'll f-find this strange,' said Domenico. 'But believe me, Fillippino, I would make that swap tomorrow if it were possible. Not that I don't love my father, nor appreciate how he has helped me. But when I hear you talk with such familiarity about the great masters, about Fra L-Lippo and Verrocchio, I can't help envy your experience, your background. I was brought up amongst g-goldsmiths, not painters.'

'I was apprenticed to a goldsmith once,' I said, feeling generous in my wine and wanting to comfort this young man. 'Well, a gold-beater anyway. My brother Antonio. It's a good training. It's a good trade.'

'More secure than painting,' said Filippino. 'And a better guild to belong to. I wouldn't mind being a goldsmith sometimes and be in the silk weavers' guild.'

'Sometimes?' I asked. 'You mean times like now when you've had too much wine and are feeling sorry for yourself. Listen, Domenico, when Filippino was a lad – and I know he's not much more than a lad now, for all the hair on his face – but when he was younger he spent every spare minute visiting bottegas. He's welcome in workshops I've never even visited, like Rosselino's.'

'Things haven't changed so much then,' said Domenico, 'for the first day I opened my d-doors he came round.'

'Exactly,' I said. 'He's addicted to the smells of gesso and size.'

'All right,' agreed Filippino. 'I admit it. I wouldn't exchange my trade for all the wealth of the Pazzi.' And we continued to agree all evening.

I have sometimes found that people who are agreeable when you are drinking with them seem strangely reticent next time you meet. I am probably the same, a little embarrassed about the enthusiasms the wine made me reveal, a little worried by the indiscretions the wine might have made me let slip, and, in this case, totally unnerved by the eulogy on the subject of Simonetta I remembered delivering. But with Domenico I felt none of that. He called round late the next day, by which time the little man who had been quarrying stone in my head had downed tools; Domenico was as friendly and open as the night before, if somewhat less slurred in his speech. Giuliano was there, with Politian, and I introduced them. 'D-delighted to meet you,' said Domenico.

'You've arrived at a good moment if you want to learn the more sordid side of a painter's life,' I told him. 'These two have just arrived with a commission, but not one to make me excited. This is the bread-and-butter part of our existence.'

'Our friend Sandro has grown cynical,' said Giuliano. 'It wasn't so very long ago that he would have been delighted to do any work for the Medici. And now, when I offer him the honour of painting my banner for a joust, he is unimpressed. Well, Sandro, I'm sure there are other painters who could do the work.' He smiled as he spoke, to suggest he was not serious, but the smile was deceitful, for he was.

'I'm sure there are. But I would do it best.'

'What Sandro means,' said Politian, 'is that he knows that the tournament will be a major event, and that, with the adorable Simonetta Vespucci guaranteed to be there, he cannot afford not to make a contribution. Isn't that right, Sandro?'

'Er . . .' I said.

'Isn't that the woman you were talking about last night?' asked Domenico. 'The one whose voice is as soft as m-moonbeams on a lake and whose smile is as radiant as the sunset?'

'Thank you,' I said.

Giuliano and Politian were laughing; Filippino was trying not to. 'Another rival for the heart of the fair Simonetta?' asked Giuliano. 'We may have to fight for her.'

'That should be an interesting combat,' said Politian. 'I can picture it now. The scion of the Medici on his fiery warhorse, bearing down on Sandro who valiantly, if somewhat foolishly, defends himself with a loaded brush. The gasp of the crowd as Sandro defiantly reaches up and touches Giuliano's shield with a dab of red paint, followed by the louder gasp as Giuliano, with a single blow, lops Sandro's head off and sends it rolling into the gutter. It should be a fascinating spectacle. I think, Giuliano, you should seriously consider how we can incorporate this novelty into the tournament.'

'You can laugh,' I said giving my permission to what they were doing already. 'Is it my fault the woman is so beautiful?'

'Not at all,' said Giuliano. 'I respect your good taste.'

After they had gone Domenico apologized for causing me embarrassment. 'That's all right,' I said. 'I deserved it.'

'Is she really so lovely, this woman?' he asked.

'She really is,' I confirmed.

The tournament of 1475 is famous, immortalized by Politian's charming poem, the 'Stanze della Giostra di Giuliano de' Medici' which did so much to elevate his status. Politian's stanzas are beautiful and extravagant, but not inappropriate to the subject. It was that sort of affair. My contribution, the standard Giuliano bore, depicted Pallas, goddess of war and wisdom, and forever through the pun on the palla – the discs on the Medici shield – associated with that family. I dressed her in a golden tunic, armed her with a shield and a spear, and showed her looking at Cupid who was tied to an olive tree, his bow and arrow broken at his feet. The design was partly of Politian's suggestion, but I wanted also to imply to Giuliano that wisdom and love could vanquish war. I did this not because I believed it, but because I wanted him to believe it. All right, so Politian was correct and Simonetta was beyond any of our reaches, but I still wanted to remove my most distinguished rival for her love.

I might as well not have bothered for all Giuliano or Simonetta noticed; I would have fared better in single combat. Lucrezia Donati was crowned Queen of the Tournament, as she had been at Lorenzo's tournament in 1469, but Simonetta was crowned Queen of Beauty and Giuliano, who bore her favours in his helm, was proclaimed victor of the joust. Perhaps this was no surprise, as the whole affair has been arranged in his honour, yet I still resented the long, lingering kiss he planted on her lips as she placed the laurel on his head. 'Your banner's come out well,' commented Filippino, who stood by me.

The banner was of plaited material, a method I had devised myself which allowed both sides to be painted at once. It certainly looked bold and effective as Giuliano, circling the tourney ground outside the church of Santa Croce in his triumph, bore it aloft. 'Bollocks,' I replied.

There was a banquet that night in the Palazzo Medici. I was placed at a distant table, well below the salt, with grooms and squires and the men who had dragged away the fallen knights. Even Verrocchio, who had designed Giuliano's helm, was closer to Simonetta than I was. I could barely see her, though I noticed she ate little.

After the eating and the tumblers came the dancing. I watched as Giuliano led our Queen of Beauty to the floor; he danced with her many times until she complained – in the sweetest, gentlest way, naturally – that she was exhausted and could dance no more.

It was then, when she sat slightly removed from the banquet, that I had my chance to speak with her again. She was not alone – I doubt she was ever alone save in the privacy of her chambers in the Palazzo Vespucci – but Giuliano, who was strutting in his victor's laurels and generously patting the bruised backs of all those he had beaten, was being fêted by his brother; the thought of being close to Simonetta again made my heart beat hard, but her admirers, Giuliano apart, did not worry me in the least.

She was reclining on cushions in an alcove. Around her were four men. I recognized them all as sons of good families, though only Tommaso's godson Tornabuoni recognized me. 'I say,' Antonio declared, 'it's good old Sandro Botticelli. Don't I look splendid in the picture he painted of me as Sebastian, eh? You have seen that painting, Simonetta, haven't you? You must have. I look terrific.'

'He was very patient when he posed,' I said. 'There are few models thick-skinned enough to let me pierce them with arrows.'

My attempt at wit foxed Antonio completely, though his friends laughed. More worryingly, Simonetta did not appear to have understood. 'I have seen the painting,' she said. 'I always assumed the painter invented the arrows.'

'So I did,' I said, a little desperate, pressing home my disadvantage.

'Twice. Once when I painted them, and secondly when I spoke of them just now.'

She nodded, comprehending but unimpressed. 'You look rather more healthy than last time we met,' she said.

I wished I could say the same for her. Though her beauty was breathtaking still, there was a darkness around her eyes that spoke of a long day, a difficult year. 'In that case I must thank you, for after bathing in your beauty that lovely afternoon I was invigorated entirely.'

'As I remember, you expressed a dislike of my place of upbringing,' she said. Could eyes so lovely mock, I wondered. If so they were mocking me then.

'As I remember I said very little,' I replied.

She waved a small Venetian fan over her face. 'I remember one thing you said,' she told me.

My mind was blank, all memory pushed aside by her smile. What had I said? I remembered it was something embarrassing, that had caused Lucrezia to tease me.

'There's no need to blush,' she told me. 'And nothing to blush for. A little sincerity is pleasant among so many courtly sallies.'

Perhaps I had been going about things the wrong way? I had been trying to behave like a courtier, to display my wit and independence of mind; perhaps my independence was best displayed by being honest to my feelings? But even to think that way was to assume that she already liked me, and I did not dare assume that.

I left her then. I do not think I even said goodbye, and anyway she was being regaled by some silly youthful anecdote about hunting. Politian found me later, so he says, face down in a plate of cold meats, a goblet of burnt wine spilling down my doublet. He replaced the plate with a cushion and left me to sleep if off.

I was not particularly busy that year. No major commissions came my way, nor indeed fell to anyone else. The situation was very much as it is today. The bastard son of a pope was trying to make a kingdom for himself in the Romagna to our east, and his ambitions threatened Florence. The only serious difference between then and now is that Pope Sixtus's son, Girolamo Riario, was essentially incompetent, whereas the son of our current Pope Alexander is the

Antichrist. The result of the tension was that people stopped spending money. All through my career I have noticed the way that the demand for paintings reflects political stability. In times of peace we have much to do; in times of war, nothing. Fortunately, until the end of my long life, open warfare has been unusual, and now we are truly at war, fighting against the pope's son and Lorenzo's son for our very survival (an unholy alliance indeed), I am too old and infirm to suffer directly. Or perhaps not: I dread that my city might fall into the hands of the Antichrist.

Whatever the relative danger, certainly in those years I was desperate for money. Perhaps things would not have been so bad had I the ability to save. I certainly earned enough in the fat years to tide me over the lean ones. But somehow this talent has always been beyond me. What I earn gets spent, not in deliberate extravagance, I believe, but rather in innumerable small ways. To some, such as dear Filippino, money sticks. I expect he will die a wealthy man. But to others money is as hard to grasp as water, and even when we have bucketsful it seems to slop about or leak through the staves. That year of 1475 was a lean year, and had it not been for a few uninspiring portraits I might have had to close the shop.

What was perhaps most odd was Medici patronage, or rather, the lack of it. For despite the fact that I became known as a Medici painter – which did my later career no good at all, as you can imagine – I received exactly two commissions from them directly, the small portrait of Giuliano and the decorations of the Volterran hospital. The cadet branch of the Medici line patronized me: Lorenzo's cousin, Lorenzo di Pierfrancesco de' Medici, who has changed his name to de Populi in order to escape the stigma now attaching to the House of Medici, was undeniably a good client of mine. But direct patronage from the direct line occurred only twice, even though the painting that salvaged my career from the doldrums, the painting that finally established me at the forefront of Florentine painters, was of the Medici family.

The commission came, shortly after the feast of the Nativity, from Guaspare di Zanobi del Lama, who had decided he wanted to commemmorate his friendship with the late Piero de' Medici in a painting for the church of Santa Maria Novella. I was in a subdued mood when Guaspare called on me. It was a cold winter afternoon, and that morning, thinking walking would be a cheaper way of keeping warm than lighting a fire, I had wandered round the open area to the west of the city. This is the district that the Rucellai family are currently turning into magnificent gardens, but in those days it was just open common lands, enclosed by the city walls but featureless except for two roads, and where the roads crossed was a scaffold. The frosted grass was a pattern of silver blades, the abandoned arms of a vast yet minute army, the scattered bones of a tiny horde, and the ruts in the road were smoothed by sheets of ice. I passed quickly under the scaffold, crossing myself conventionally as I went, and was appalled to hear my name in the rusty creaking of the chains that bound the villain executed there. 'San-dro,' said the iron as the dead man swung in the wind. 'San-dro.' I looked up and was even more appalled. Dangling above me, his feet at the level of my head, was Angelo. His nose had been split, his ears cut off, but his scarred face was unmistakable. Pinned to the body was a sheet of cream paper bearing the single word 'Murderer'. As I blanched and turned away my foot cracked through a sheet of ice and my velvet boot was soaked; when I returned to my bottega I was cold, wet and miserable.

None the less I had to be hospitable to Guaspare. I was glad my wet foot had forced me to light a fire, for at least the bottega was warm; I was glad too that I had been given time to recover my composure, for this was an important commission. Although not a large picture, Guaspare, a wealthy man without connections, who was anxious to ingratiate himself with the *popolo grosso*, was eager that I should include likenesses of all his friends in the Medici circle, in the guise of the three Magi and their attendants. 'I want the best, mind,' he told me. 'And I'm prepared to pay for it. I've not employed a painter before, but I've heard you're good.'

'Thank you.'

'And I want to be able to recognize everyone. I know some important people, and I want everyone to know I know them.'

I assured him that I could fulfil his commission. 'Right then,' he said. 'Here's a list of them I want shown.'

I glanced at the list. Some of those I was required to paint, such as Cosimo and Piero de' Medici, were dead, but many others, such as Filippo Strozzi and Lorenzo Tornabuoni, were undeniably alive, which meant that if I was to capture a genuine likeness I would have to draw them from the life. Accordingly I would have to make appointments to visit them at their palaces. Many of those listed seemed to be Lorenzo's friends rather than Guaspare's, I noticed, which meant that some of them, Politian and Ficino for instance, were my friends too. I began to look forward to the commission. And then I came across a name that made me start: Marco Vespucci. I admit I trembled when I realized I should soon be calling on Simonetta's home.

The dark weeks after the winter solstice found me, therefore, engaged on a circuit of many great houses, and anticipating, fearing, desiring, my inevitable visits to the Palazzo Vespucci.

1503

Time passes, even in the madhouse, and a new year has begun. The days are getting lighter, getting longer. To our east, abetted by Leonardo, the bastard son of our Holy Father daily confirms what I already knew. We have just had news of his latest infamy: he has slaughtered his own captains. One of those captains was the brother of Paolo Vitelli, the treacherous condottiere who refused to lead our troops against Pisa. He fell for the same trick by which Florence captured his brother, was invited to a banquet that sealed his doom. But Cesare's inhuman delight in pain, so different from the justice meted out to Paolo Vitelli, meant that Cesare's captains were given no trial, no warning: they were slaughtered as they ate. Surely even Leonardo must be disgusted.

In Florence feeling about these events is mixed. Cesare is clearly a man to fear but, because he is allied with Piero de' Medici, many Florentines refuse to believe all they hear. I understand this; I too feel nostalgia for the glorious days of Lorenzo. But I have seen Borgia's actions, whereas they have not, and understand, as they do not, that this is no man but a monster. Rather than engage in politics, however, I take refuge in my past. Sometimes, accompanied by Fra Agostino, who has read all I have written so far and tells me he finds it fascinating, I leave this place for a while, to refresh my memory of the rest of my city. Always, however, it is a relief to return, to come back to a place where madness is recognized and, being recognized, is contained. Out there in the streets there is madness, undiagnosed and uncured, which will bring my city to its knees.

I went to see my painting, the Medici Adoration of the Magi, yesterday. The figure in the saffron robe at the far right of this painting is a self-portrait. My eyes are golden brown, much the colour of my hair, and look out, questioningly, beneath heavy lids. My jaw is full, my nose Roman though a little too broad to be handsome, my upper lip is a disdainful Cupid's bow. I painted myself as an arrogant son-of-a-bitch, but why not? The painting shows the incomparable Medicis, in the roles of the three wise men and attendants, presenting their gifts to the infant Christ. Cosimo, the patriarch, the virtual ruler of Florence, kneels at the Madonna's feet in the guise of the first king. The other two kings are depicted by Cosimo's sons, Piero and Giovanni. Lorenzo the Magnificent, still young, stands at the left with a sword in his hand; his brother Giuliano, eyes cast down, stands at the right in a black cape striped with red. Not bad company for a tanner's son, and I put myself there, literally, metaphorically, with the talent of my brush.

Yet there's more to this self-portrait than arrogant complacency. I look out of the painting, meet your eye: somewhere in the twitch at the base of my nose there's a smile, an invitation for you to smile too. Which is fair enough. Giovanni de' Medici died thirteen years earlier, in 1463, Cosimo in 1464, Piero in 1469; I'd been working on the portraits of dead men. I put Lorenzo de' Medici, heir to this lot and their city, opposite my self-portrait. Like me he does not seem to be interested in the devotion to the child that takes place in the background. He looks bored, impatient, as well he might: he recognizes that this is a charade.

The picture is kept at Santa Maria Novella. It was painted as an altarpiece, but now it's behind a curtain: neither the Medici nor I are much in favour any more. I had to ask permission to see it. The priest in charge is a young Franciscan, no older than Fra Agostino, who did not recognize me. When I asked that the curtain be moved he was dismissive. 'If you like,' he said, implying that it can do no harm, no good. 'It's an old-fashioned piece but well painted. We have better.'

I did not particularly like this young priest, but his judgement is sound. The painting, well painted, is product of a different age, both for Florence and for me. Growing old has vanities of its own – the greatest is believing we grow wiser with the years – but it does not have that self-satisfied smugness of youth. I look at the picture before me. One of my vanities as a youth was to believe I was clever. It seems to me now I truly believed that I could outwit God.

The painting was conceived as a joke at the expense of old Gozzoli, who had painted a similar scene some fifteen years before. In his fresco – I have mentioned it before, and you can see it for yourself, for it survives in the Palazzo Medici – those who attended the Council of Florence, the stern-bearded Greeks, the politicians and churchmen, a single Moorish slave, are turned into the processsion of the Magi, and at their head, in isolate splendour astride a white horse, is the most unlikely and flattering representation of Lorenzo imaginable. Gozzoli has turned Lorenzo – our swarthy Lorenzo, with his thick hair and thicker nose – into an angel. Even Lorenzo, who generally accepted flattery graciously if rarely gratefully, found Gozzoli's picture silly, despite the fact that his father Piero had commissioned it; when Guaspare del Lama wanted a picture as tribute to his dead father and grandfather he consulted Lorenzo, who in turn consulted Politian; Politian suggested we continue the processsion to its conclusion. I was happy enough with the idea. I was 32 years old, starred enough to be friend of the Medici; old Gozzoli, a quarter-century my senior, still hung around, as he continued to do for many years, as forgotten as I am today.

That my painting had to exceed Gozzoli's goes without question. Not only my pride but that of my patron demanded that. And technically this was not hard. Gozzoli had his abilities – he filled the wall well; his horses are good – but his work was old-fashioned even then. I haven't seen the Medici frescos in several years but I remember well enough the stiffness of pose, the awkwardness of recession, the concentration on design at the expense of nature. All I had to do was paint people who looked like people, in natural arrangement, in the fashionable setting and costume, while paying such attention to perspective as was required, and I had achieved my first aim.

Equally, I had to praise the three dead Medici, Lorenzo's father, grandfather and uncle, in whose honour my painting was commissioned. That was what del Lama was paying for.

At the same time however, to show how clever Lorenzo, Politian, the rest of us were, I chose to distance my friends from the scene. Lorenzo carries a sword, disdaining to watch the proceedings as his predecessors present their offerings to the infant Christ; Politian, heavy-lidded, is making some typically smart comment; Ficino, gloriously attired, is the figure to the immediate left of the kings; the bookseller Vespasiano, miraculously youthful, hangs from Lorenzo's shoulder, giving, as always, a long-winded explanation of all that he sees; finally there's the portrait of the artist, catching the viewer's eye, and there's irony in my glance.

In addition I included a small jibe, one I had to be sure Lorenzo would not mind. I wanted to distance myself one step further from the – let's face it – rather theatrical idea of presenting three undeniably dead old men as the three wise men, the oriental magi, the kings who travelled from afar to view the infant Son of God, so to show up the vanity of the whole Medici notion I gave prominence to only one creature in the picture. As in the similar painting I did earlier for the Pucci, in this nativity there are no lambs, no humble donkeys, but there is a peacock dancing his pride.

Even at that I had not finished being subtle. Lorenzo de' Medici is flattered in my picture, and so am I; I did not flatter Lorenzo's brother Giuliano, and for what seemed at the time good reason.

In short, this wonderfully clever picture by this wonderfully clever young man overlooks only one thing: this is meant to be a picture of the Adoration of Christ, and Christ here is marginalized. A religious picture, I am now sure, should be of no time, no fashion. Christ is above time, above fashion. And my wonderfully successful picture of Lorenzo and his family now hangs behind a curtain, where it belongs.

Marco Vespucci, incidentally, is the stiff-necked young man whose profile is to be found just above my head.

1475

I left my portrait of Marco almost till the last, for reasons of superstition or trepidation, but I let it be known among his circle that I would be painting him soon: I hoped that, when I finally made a formal request for him to sit for me, he would be prepared; I also hoped, and dared not admit the hope, that his wife would hear I was coming, and arrange to be at home that day. I had to spread the message freely for I rarely saw Marco in person. His young cousin Amerigo, who later went to work for the king of Spain, was quite popular in the group around the Medici, but Marco had his own tastes, his own friends. Simonetta still visited Donna Clarice, naturally, but apart from once passing her on the stairs of the Palazzo Medici, and a dozen times seeing her from afar, she remained as distant as ever, more vision than woman, more lovely than either should be.

Eventually, however, when I had almost completed my sketches of all the other characters who would appear in my painting, I sent a note to Marco asking if I could call one Tuesday morning. The note went via a boy I sometimes employed. He was more trustworthy than most, but still I didn't pay him his soldi until he had returned and described the response. Messages disappear in Florence. They are sent off with the best of intentions, the best of mesengers, but somewhere between you and the delivery they vanish, sucked into the Arno or dropped into the city of the dead which rumour has built beneath the city and populated with demons. I do not know if such a city exists beneath Florence; I have visited the catacombs of Rome, with dreadful consequence as I shall relate, but Rome is different for, even above ground, Rome is a city of the dead.

Marco's reply was concise – 'Yes' – so I waited anxiously until the appointed day. I was sketching Ficino at the time. He had a proud, rather noble head, which I wanted to capture in silhouette, but was a lousy sitter, forever fidgeting and complaining. I never did capture his eyes properly. Yet the fault was more mine than his, because my mind was already in the Vespucci palace.

At last my Tuesday arrived. I had deliberately not specified a time for the appointment, and arrived as early as I decently could to eke out my visit. The door was huge and wooden, with a smaller door set into it. I tugged the bell cord and heard a distant ring. Set into the door were vicious metal spikes bearing the mark of the wasp, a pun on the Vespucci name.

A retainer answered and opened the small door a crack. I explained my mission and he opened the small door further. A member of the *popolo grosso* would have been admitted through the large door. I was not sure I needed such reminders of my humble status, my insolent aspirations.

Marco it seemed was still in bed. I enquired, casually, after the lady of the house. She was apparently feeding the chickens, an unlikely occupation for the wife of the Vespucci, and even more unlikely for a woman who looked like a goddess. Left to my own devices by the servant, I spent no time looking round the anyway rather dull hall, but instead went to the windows that overlooked the courtyard. The servant had been right. There, dressed in a hooded cloak, was Simonetta feeding the chickens.

I watched as she bent to toss the corn across the frozen cobbles. Even the cloak could not hide the beauty of her figure, its grace and elegance. Her breath made fragile ghosts. The cold wind tugged at her cloak from time to time, revealing neat shoes, slender ankles, the swell of a calf. When the chickens were all fed she came indoors.

As I had hoped and prayed she came through the hall. 'Sandro Botticelli!' she said. 'I heard you were coming. You're too early. Marco won't rise from his bed for another hour yet.'

'Perhaps the lady of the household would entertain me then?' I asked.

She smiled. 'Not unless you want to curry horses.'

'Why ever not?' I said.

She led me through to a scullery where she exchanged the corn basket for two sets of stiff curry-combs. 'Do you always do all this work?' I asked.

'I was born in the contado,' she replied. 'I tried to accept that in the city it is not considered proper, but I found I woke early anyway. Tending the few animals we have – my father has farms – keeps me busy until Marco comes down from his room.' She looked at me sharply. 'Don't you approve?'

'I find it charming.'

'In that case you have no idea what you've let yourself in for,' she told me. 'Feeding the chickens isn't charming, because chickens have no charm; currying horses is hard work.'

'I'm used to using a brush,' I said.

She coughed, a harsh and ugly sound. 'The fresh air does me good,' she explained, though the cough suggested otherwise.

The horse snorted plumes of steaming dampness. Isn't it strange how animals sense when we fear them? I did not want to show fear: I wanted to be brave and manly and perfect. Unfortunately, the black mare she gave me to rub down first wanted me to look a fool, and succeeded, letting me into her stall and then pinning me to the wall.

The black flank, the fine hair short enough to let me see the veins that patterns its leathery skin, pushed against me. I could feel the ribs as separate joints of pressure on my chest. 'How are you getting on?' called Simonetta.

'Fine,' I gasped.

I tried shoving the brute off me, and then beating it. It did not move at all to begin with, and then it lifted a foot, which looked like progress until it stamped down on my shoe. I let out a cry of pain.

Simonetta was there in a moment, expertly shooing the horse away. 'Are you all right?'

I was lying on the floor, covered in sweat despite the cold. One of my shoes seemed crushed flat. 'I'm fine,' I said, not daring to think what my foot must look like.

'What happened?'

'He trod on my foot.'

'She,' she corrected automatically, and then looked at my shattered boot. 'Oh my goodness. We need a surgeon. Wait here. I'll send for one at once.'

She left me in the stall with the black mare. The mare stood on my foot and she left me with it. The mare came over and nuzzled me sharply between my shoulder blades. 'I can't get up,' I told it.

Almost ten years had passed since last I saw this surgeon, but when he arrived I knew him at once. 'Pettro Negro!' I exclaimed. The pain was not too bad at that time. I believe I was in a state of shock. 'What are you doing here?'

The sleek fat of his middle years had been replaced by a saggy grey authority, as though his portliness had become patrician. 'Shhh. I am Piero del Negroni now, physician. I am a member of your guild, I am a respected man. Pettro Negro, he is dead.'

'Is he all right?' asked Simonetta, kneeling on the straw beside me. 'You're being very brave,' she said to me as Pettro, or Piero, cut away my boot. She was talking to me as though I were a child. I did not mind. She was talking to me.

'The damage is not severe, though there is always the danger of poison growing in the wound,' Pettro said cheerfully. 'He must rest and be bled regularly.'

His prodding had woken the pain. I was determined not to scream while Simonetta was watching, so I fainted instead.

When I came round it was dark and I was lying in a large bed. The bed was moist, perhaps with my sweat though the room too was damp. The sheets smelt musty and little used. I did not know where I was but hoped it was the Palazzo Vespucci. There were no clues in that shuttered room.

To start with I thought I might get out of the bed, but that proved impossible. I could not move my foot at all without a searing pain that all but knocked me cold again. I lay still for what seemed like an age, listening to bells chime over the city at infrequent intervals, and probably dozed.

A candle appeared at the bedside, and I looked up, hoping for Simonetta's lovely face. Instead I saw an old woman, a crone, who looked down at me past the beak of her nose in a critical fashion. 'Where am I?' I asked.

'Mistress asked we bring you here,' she said, explaining nothing.

'But where is here? Am I still at the palace?'

'You are.' She had a rustic voice that croaked like the threshing of corn.

'And your mistress? Is she here?'

'She asked I bring you food. It's by the bedside.' Her clothes were black. Her face was grey.

'What time is it?'

'Late.'

She went. I could not reach the food. I went back to sleep and awoke in Heaven.

Simonetta was kneeling on the bed, cradling my head on her lap, stroking my hair. 'Calm down, calm down.' She breathed through her teeth as she stroked, as though she still curried a horse. 'You were crying,' she said. 'You have a fever.' I put my hand to my hair, felt moisture, touched her cool fingers. By candlelight her face was more lovely than ever, and all she wore was a shift with a cloak thrown over it. I became aware of the swell of her breasts an inch above my eyes, an inch away from my hand, separated from my longing by no more than a layer of thin white cloth. 'Are you awake now?'

'No,' I said. 'I'm dreaming.' It was an honest reply.

'You're awake,' she said. Her hair was loose, copper shot with gold in the light of the flame. She coughed several times then, each cough shaking me, confirming I was awake.

'Are you all right?' I asked.

'You're the invalid,' she said. 'Not me. It's nothing. I always cough at night. It stops me sleeping: I don't sleep well, I'm afraid, and was walking round when I heard you whimpering.' She was apologizing for being in my room! Did the Archangel Gabriel apologize thus to Mary, I wondered. 'I thought you might be ill. Negroni said there might be a fever. You've had a nasty wound.'

'It doesn't matter,' I said. Nor did it, any more than it does now, even though as the years have gone by the trouble that wound has caused me has never gone away, until now when I go about on crutches, tapping the earth each step I take as though asking to be let in, with my useless leg swinging beneath me like a club. For without that wound I should have been without that moment, and without so many other moments. Without that wound I should have been without the most important thing in my life. She coughed again. 'You're cold,' I said. 'Get under the covers, get warm.' Had I not been a virgin myself I could never have made such a suggestion. My member was certainly aroused, but then my whole body, reacting to the combination of her proximity and my fever, was shot through with unfamiliar sensations like a piece of Spoleto stone. Had she not been almost as pure she would never have accepted the invitation. As it was, she slipped beneath the heavy covers and thanked me. 'It's your house,' I reminded her. 'Are you warmer now?'

'Much, thank you. And are you feeling better?'

'Yes.' I was 32 years old, a virgin and in love; next to me, her shift rucked up her body from when she had climbed into the bed, was the most beautiful woman the world has seen since the ancient nights of Cleopatra and Helen. The candle burnt out. We did not touch, yet I felt her presence as though it pressed tight against me. Nor, for some time, did we speak, yet our silence was no more than the peace that comes with trust.

What is innocence? It is more fragile even than love. I had read Boccaccio. I knew that lovers met in bed like this – though I swear that, for all the bawdy tales I had heard, I had only the sketchiest idea what they did there. And she was a married woman. Yet we were innocents then, wholly and holy. Holy innocents, holy fools, our ignorance more precious than the libraries of the pharaohs.

'It's getting late,' she said at last. 'I should go now.'

'Of course.'

She climbed from the bed in the darkness. I heard her delicate, desperate cough. 'Simonetta?' I whispered. I had never called her by her name before.

'It's nothing. Goodnight, Sandro.' Nor had she used mine. 'Rest now.'

She left.

I was still trapped in bed the next day. I had hoped Simonetta would visit me, but instead it was the old crone. She brought me food and emptied my bedpan. I asked after her mistress but the reply, 'Here somewhere,' was too vague to be of use to me.

Pettro Negro bled me in the afternoon. 'You're doing well for yourself,' he said, indicating the ageing finery of the chamber with its heavy furnishings, the bed with its heavy hangings. 'Friends of yours?'

'Clients. You seem to be doing all right yourself. Working for the *popolo grosso*: a bit better than the back streets.'

'Made myself respectable, didn't I,' he said as he inserted a knife that was like a tube with an angled mouth deep into my leg. The pain was atrocious. 'I was making a bit of money and putting it aside. I already knew I was better at my work than most of the fancy physicians that had studied in Geneva, so when my old mother died I took a shop near the horse market, bought a bit of paper that said I'd a degree from Paris, never looked back.' My blood belched up the tube and he caught it deftly in a porcelain bowl. 'I've a wife now, one of the Cellinis from Santa Trinità, and I'll be looking for a good match for my daughters. That's the way it should be. Look at my family. My mother, God rest her weary soul, worked day and night to feed me, make sure I lived up to my talents. Now I work day and night for my children, who have no talents to speak of but a better start in life than I ever had. With luck, their children'll marry better still. These are good times for an ambitious man. I just wish I'd had a son.'

He bound my leg violently above the wound, withdrew the knife, bandaged the hole. He left on his waddling bow legs while, weakened by the bleeding, I fell into a kind of trance; I barely moved when the crone came to fasten the shutters.

Simonetta returned that night, setting the candle by the bedside and climbing in beside me without speaking. The candle behind her, her head on the bolster was a dark shape framed by a fraying halo of hair, and I heard her lips quivering. 'Are you still cold?' I whispered. The flame stabbed and feinted at a draught.

'A little.'

I put a slow arm over her, held her far shoulder, pulled her closer. 'Is that warmer?'

She put her face against my neck. 'Thank you.'

Once more I felt that strange sensation in my loins, that uncomfortable swelling. I too wore only a shift, and I pulled it up with my free hand to check the state of my member. 'What are you doing?' she asked.

I did not want to lie. 'I'm a little uncomfortable,' I said.

She moved away from me. 'I'm sorry,' she said.

'Come back!' I whispered urgently. 'It wasn't your fault!'

She moved back to me, nestling in the crook of my arm, returning her head to my neck. She wriggled her lower body. I felt her naked thighs next to mine, and then felt them press on my member. She put her hand down and held it tight. 'Shhh,' she said to it. 'Go to sleep.'

If she thought stroking it was going to make it sleep she was even more innocent than I was. Instinct was suggesting answers that my deficient education could not provide. But then her hand, though still holding my member, stopped moving, and she was asleep. I must have slept too, for I remember waking, though I was awake and in exquisite pain for most of the night.

When I awoke she was still next to me, though facing away now. I still had my erection, or perhaps it was a new one, for I have often noticed that I am so formed when I awake, under any circumstances. There was light making lines round the shutters. The pain in my foot was much less.

'Simonetta?'

She stirred. In the soft winter light that slipped round the shutters I could see no more than a suggestion of her features, yet they were so beautiful that I felt I must die. 'Sandro?' she asked, and my heart beat as she spoke my name. She was so comfortable with it, and with me. 'What time is it?'

'First light, I think. I've only just woken myself.'

She started to cough, quietly at first and then with increasing violence. I pulled myself up in the bed, pulled her up too. Beneath us the feathers shrugged. She rested herself against me as I stroked her back, and at last the coughing subsided, became gasps. 'I'm sorry.' It seemed we were forever apologizing, forever thanking one another, forever checking how the other felt. But perhaps that was right. We were treading carefully over the thin ice of our innocence as it thawed beneath the heat of our bodies. Like travellers in a dangerous land, we had to keep reassuring ourselves.

She lifted her head from my chest. On my white shift was a gout of blood, black in the inadequate light. 'Darling!' I whispered.

'I'm so sorry,' she whispered again.

'Are you truly ill?'

'It's nothing. It happens. I'll be all right soon. Hold me.'

I had to take off the soiled shift. Naked, I lay next to her, holding her slight body against mine. Her breath was short, a rise and fall of her breasts against my chest, a tightening of her shoulder blades beneath my hands. The pain I felt from my foot, the greater pain from where I had been bled, were diluted among many other messages my body was sending me. Her shift had ridden up to her waist: I could feel the slight rise of her lower stomach pressed beneath my erection, and the soft secret itch of tightly curled hair against my balls. Her calves, cooler than mine, were round my good leg, and her thighs squeezed mine gently. Her arms wrapped around my back, and I could feel the pressure of each of her fingers gently kneading me, and the exact place where the sleeves of the shift exposed her naked forearms. I needed a barber, and my furzed face was too harsh to rest against her; I needed a wash, and from the bedclothes rose many smells, a roasted spice like rare Indian cumin, a rough bitterness like onion, the warmth as of cooking garlic. I was sensation only, my bound and naked body pierced through by shafts of hesitant desire.

Her breathing settled, and then I kissed her, once, on a closed eyelid. Her fingers pressed my back with just a little more intensity; my member seemed to swell ever further, as if threatening to burst. I kissed her again, on the other eyelid, and was ashamed at the bristle on my chin. Her elbows squeezed the flanks of my stomach. I moved my head and laid my mouth on hers.

Her lips were dry and slightly parted, closing slightly at my touch to draw mine closer and then opening, drawing me closer still. Our teeth scraped clumsily and I angled my head. The flesh within her mouth was warmer and more moist, and our mouths opened together with a gasp. There was an unknown flavour of woman to her, and of mortality. Her narrow tongue teased mine, drawing it into her mouth, thrusting back at it. I tasted her illness and her desire; my desire set my hands to work, slowly tugging at her shift, and she raised her hips to help me.

Now her shift was no more than a collar and a pair of sleeves. Her breasts were small yet full, her nipples a tidy hardness against my ribs. I stroked at her spine, touching each descending vertebra, reaching the narrow cleft and spreading my hand before clenching a smooth hemisphere of muscle as though trying to pull her closer yet. Our lips still moved together, our tongues still darted. My other hand was drawn there too, pressing and caressing, and my thumbs slipped into a moistness that was downed with faint hair.

Fingers joined the thumbs. Her mouth released mine and she

leant back, eyes closed, lips parted, tongue slightly protruding as she pushed my head almost roughly to her chest. My fingers danced. My lips puckered over the apple stem of her breast. The flesh between her thighs was silk, then there were the folds where legs met torso, and then the deeper unfathomable fold in the midst of the hair, guarded by warm wet lips and topped by a tough button that made her body twist marvellously each time I stroked it. From beneath her arms came a tense, hot aroma. The nipple poked between my lips and my tongue greeted it until my mouth gaped to take in more and more of her, as though all I wanted was to devour her.

She pushed my head further down and the bedclothes followed me, the increasing light of an early year morn showing off her white flesh, darker nipples. The nipples were more raw sienna than pink, a ring of dark flesh two fingers' width topped by a stalk that divided at the end and hinted a redder flesh within. My tough chin scraped at her stomach and still she forced my head down. I tasted salt, a delirious bitterness, as my mouth reached the unfathomable hole. The mouth learns intimately what fingers can only guess. She held my head with both hands. The firm button above her wet opening had a cowl like a monk's that my tongue could force back, licking until she writhed; the sentinel lips that guarded her were soft dewlaps, tough and dry at the edges, warm and welcoming within. She held me there and I heard her breathing, a summer gasp in spring. Then suddenly her body was jerking, four or perhaps five times; she called out my name, and hands that had clutched me so tight seemed now to be fighting me off. I drew back from her, dismayed, though still relishing what lay splayed and displayed beneath my face, the hairs parted, the guardian lips a purple brown outside, vermilion within, and the dark entrancing shadow at the centre of the design.

She lay on her back, upper teeth biting lower lip, a grimace of pain on her face. 'Darling,' I whispered. 'Are you all right?'

She did not reply. Instinct told me exactly what a man should do in these circumstances, how I should impale her on my swollen member and stab her till I won relief. But she was so fragile, so much damaged already, and in my mind's eye were the torn women of Volterra. I pulled the bedclothes back over her, covering her as reverently as I might a corpse; I wondered what damage my passion had already done, and cursed myself for a fool. For such was my love that I would rather not have touched her than ever caused her pain. I waited, anxiously, and hoped she would recover.

At last she opened her eyes, reached out to me, and kissed me more tenderly, more lovingly, than ever. All I could think of was to ask the perennial, 'Are you all right?'

'Oh, Sandro,' she said. 'Oh Sandro.' But she was smiling and it seemed the pain had gone.

I stayed at the Palazzo Vespucci another five days. Negro attended me each day, Simonetta visited me each night. Negro caused me regular pain; with Simonetta, though we pressed our naked bodies together and talked much, I never dared touch her depths again – even though, in her desire to please me, she sometimes seemed to invite me – for fear of the damage I might do. After five days was up I could walk, with a stick, and could think of no excuse to stay longer. I left and returned to my rooms, confused and elated, and only then remembered I had not even seen Marco, much less drawn him.

Guaspare del Lama's painting came easily despite that. I worked in a kind of frenzy of love. Even Marco's unsketched profile semed to slide unforced from my brush to the panel, as though the time I had spent with his wife had somehow made him familiar to me. I worked hard. I worked for Simonetta, and at night she filled my dreams; often, to my disgust, I woke sticky and wet, or with a crust of dryness on my bedclothes.

News of my painting spread. I had many visitors to my shop. Those featured in the painting were naturally anxious to see what I had made of them, but a large number of other people came to look too. Among them was Lorenzo's wife Clarice, and with her came Simonetta; following Simonetta, it seemed, were half the blades in Florence, and they crowded my studio and made work impossible.

But could I have worked with Simonetta there, even had she been quite alone? I doubt it. It was a cold month and she looked weak, her strength hardly improved by our sleepless nights. Yet she had never been more lovely than she was that season, with her hair tied back in the antique style as was the fashion and her cream gown high-waisted, gathered beneath he small full breasts. She did not speak to me, did not have the chance, yet her modest glance and smile were eloquent, and I knew that, although our secret place – feather mattress for an island and our innocence cracking like ice – could hardly be recaptured, I should not be without her for long.

I had more desire than opportunity, however, and much work to do. The Medici altarpiece was almost completed but other commissions were arriving. The church of Santa Maria Novella, where the altarpiece would be displayed, wanted me to paint a fresco of the Nativity, while Ficino and Lorenzo's cousin, Lorenzo di Pierfrancesco de' Medici, had some complicated notion for a series of paintings on mythological subjects for a villa Lorenzo di Pierfrancesco hoped to buy. Meanwhile Politian, pleased with the small picture of himself on the Medici altarpiece, wanted a lifesize portrait, and though I had other work to do I could find no way to refuse him.

Because I was so busy, particularly on the fresco, with all the work that type of painting involves, I chose to paint him in his room at the Palazzo Medici, where we could not be disturbed, rather than in my shop. And, perhaps also, I wanted privacy so I could ask him certain questions. He raised the subject. 'Florence has been intrigued by your sojourn at the Palazzo Vespucci,' he began. 'There can be no question but that, for all the pain your injury may have caused, any wound which results in time spent with the lovely Simonetta will always provoke more envy than pity among the ardent and anxious lovers of this city.'

'I've a crushed bone in my foot,' I said, steering the conversation away, despite myself and my wish to discuss my adventures.

It seemed I would have little choice anyway. 'And did you see the famous lady during your time there?' Politian asked.

'She was a great comfort, though she's unwell herself.' Still I was reluctant to commit myself.

'Really? And how many nights were you there?'

'Seven.'

'So you shafted her fairly regularly then,' he said. I must have looked angry, or shocked, because he smiled weakly. 'Only a joke,' he apologized.

Yet in a sense this was a conversation I wanted. 'It's all right,' I said.

'I'm sure it is. Wouldn't mind fucking her myself, who wouldn't.'

He looked at me. 'Well come on then. No secrets from your old friend. Did you or didn't you?'

'Well. Not exactly.'

'What do you mean, not exactly?' He stopped all pretence at posing for his portrait and came over to me, put his arm round me. 'Sandro, what are you saying? It isn't possible to fuck inexactly, unless you entered by the wrong hole. My mind is turning tricks at the thought!'

'Are you trying to make me angry or something?' I threw down my brushes.'Because if that's your intention you're succeeding. Here I am trying to tell you about something important and intimate and loving and you're talking like some schoolboy!'

He looked serious, and penitent. 'I'm sorry,' he said. 'Go on.'

I hesitated, uncertain how to phrase my next statement. 'I wanted to do that thing with her, but I couldn't.'

He nodded. 'Don't worry. It's a common problem. Everyone has it from time to time.'

'Really?' It was a relief to know others shared my scruples. All I had learnt thus far about coupling suggested it was a pretty ruthless business.

'Certainly,' confirmed Polition. 'Has it ever happened before, this problem?'

'What do you mean? How could it have happened before? I've never had to chance to be with her before.'

'Not with her, obviously. With anyone?'

'Well, I've never . . . I mean, it's not.'

'Are you telling me you've never done it? A pupil of the famous Fra Lippi and still a virgin – incredible! But that explains everything. Too much tension I guess. But I've got the solution.'

I learnt what he had in mind later the same day. The sun was setting when I met him outside the Medici palace, and we walked together past the Duomo towards the Orsanmichele. He took me to the Grand Brothel, a house on the Via dell'Oche, decorated with frescos of hanged traitors. The establishment I believe still exists; the frescos have been scraped off the walls. Some of my own work met the same fate: after the Pazzi conspiracy, when Giuliano was killed in the cathedral during Mass and Lorenzo nearly so, I was commissioned to paint the execution of the traitors on the walls of the Palazzo della Signoria, to commemorate their infamy; the portrait of the last to be hanged was painted by Leonardo, as I was in Rome at the time. But once Piero de' Medici had fled Florence, those who had conspired against the Medici were no longer considered traitors; their likenesses were chipped from the plaster and their reputations officially altered. Such is the fate of these who meddle in history: one day notorious, the next praiseworthy; and, should the vile Borgia return Piero to Florence, then doubtless the Pazzi conspirators will become notorious once again. At least an artist never becomes notorious: the worst that can happen, and has happened to me already, is to be neglected.

We entered the brothel and Politian, greeted familiarly by several of the denizens, draw the hag in charge to one side. A few words were exchanged, and then she came over and embraced me, which was unpleasant. The smell of Arabian oil, noticeable when first I entered, came from her in almost overpowering waves, yet somehow didn't overpower the deeper, dying smells that lingered in the folds of her clothes. 'I have just the thing!' she said. 'Beatrice, come here!'

Beatrice was a plump, pretty girl of about half my age. 'Yes, Donna Lucinda?'

'Beatrice, the gentleman here needs a little instruction in the arts of love.' Donna Lucinda whispered something and the girl nodded intelligently. 'If you'd take the third room? It's the only one free.'

Beatrice led me down a dark corridor. The rooms were small, with no more than a straw mattress in each. 'Do you want to undress me?' she asked.

'Not really,' I replied.

She shrugged and slipped out of her bodice and skirt. She wore a short shift beneath, slit to allow her nipples a chance to watch the proceedings. 'Are you going to sit here?' she asked, sitting on the mattress herself.

When I sat down she started to tug at my hose, pulling my member out. Meanwhile she was flapping her inquisitive nipples in my face, and though her breasts were much heavier and softer than Simonetta's and the ring round each nipple was larger and more dark, simply by making the comparison and therefore thinking about Simonetta's beautiful nakedness made me reach out and touch Beatrice. 'That's better,' she said. 'You can play with them if you like.'

This too was enough like my experience with Simonetta to make me comply. 'Oh, you're growing,' said Beatrice. 'Well, that was easier than expected, I must say. I thought you'd got problems. Steady now, and don't bite.'

She positioned me on top of her and held my erect member in her hand. 'That's it,' she said. 'Steady now.'

I felt her slide me into her. The fit was surprisingly good: I raised myself up on my arms to check what was going on, and then lowered myself, astonished at what I saw. 'That's right,' Beatrice encouraged me, and I found a rhythm occurred naturally, a sort of bounce of the hips, which made me feel strong and good. 'That's it,' she told me. 'That's the way!'

As my body bounced I shut my eyes, imagined Simonetta beneath me, and stretched my neck to kiss Beatrice. 'No you don't,' she warned me. I did not mind. I doubted her lips would taste like Simonetta's anyway.

I carried on bouncing for a few moments longer and then felt something give, something spurt, and was suddenly tired. 'Is that it?' she asked.

Unsure what she meant I tried to lie inside her a while, letting my member slowly grow limp, but she was having none of that. 'Off with you. You've nothing left and I've a busy night,' she said, pushing me from her. She sorted out her clothes while I tucked myself back together, and then led me back to Politian. 'That didn't take long,' he said to me, and then turned to Beatrice. 'Any problem?'

'None at all. Hard as you like. Came a bit quick but what can you expect?'

'What indeed,' agreed Politian. 'I'll settle up, Sandro; you can knock it off the price of my portrait. You see, it was just tension making you impotent. Nothing to worry about at all.'

'Impotent? What are you talking about!'

Politian looked up from counting his money. 'Your problem of course. The trouble you were having.'

'It wasn't impotence!' My Tuscan rebelled at the suggestion. 'I had a prick like a watchman's truncheon, if you must know. But she was so fragile, so lovely. And I saw the ravished women of Volterra. I couldn't do that to her.'

Politian looked at me in amazement, and then laughed. 'I got that wrong, didn't I,' he announced cheerfully. 'Still, we may still have solved the problem. Did Beatrice look damaged when you went inside her?'

'No.' A bit bored perhaps but that was all.

'There you are then. Calm your qualms. A good fuck hurts no one – though making babies can be a bit of a nuisance. Problem solved?'

'I suppose so,' I said, and I walked through the antechamber on my own while Politian arranged his next visit. As I thought about it I realized Politian was right. Beatrice had not been harmed. And with Simonetta it would be an act of love, an act of worship, a celebration.

As I stepped out of the door and into the Via dell'Oche I met Leonardo de Vinci, who was crossing the street with a handsome young man I recognized as one of Verrocchio's models. 'Ah, Sir Sandro!' he called. 'I knew you lacked taste and preferred women but I thought even you would draw the line at paying for your pleasures. By the way, have you met my friend Jacopo?' He wrapped a long finger through the model's hair. 'Had you the inclination I'm sure Jacopo would find time to service you for free. So much more pleasant than banging some hag from the contado, I should have thought, and so much more civilized.'

I walked away without speaking. I felt soiled; I felt elated. Leonardo called some other pleasant insult at me but I was no longer thinking about him. I thought only of Simonetta, of our next meeting, of our love. I could hardly wait. And despite my broken foot, despite my stick, I danced the length of the Porta Rossa in my joy.

1499

As the year of Our Lord 1500 approached there was a sense of doom, of the passing of ages and the clash of planets. The head of our erstwhile captain, Paolo Vitelli, mouldered on a pike above the walls of the Palazzo della Signoria. During the autumn of 1499 French armies occupied Milan and, to stop Florence joining the league of Italian states opposing them, offered to help us recapture Pisa: the irony of this, considering they had lost Pisa for us in the first place, was not lost. And at the same time, for the first time, we began to hear the name of Cesare Borgia who, on some pretence to do with tax-returns, had captured Imola to our north, and besieged Caterina Sforza in Forlì for a month before even that brave lady was forced to submit. Warfare was breaking out across the peninsula, and the Antichrist was expected daily. Some saw it in the unlikely figure of the French king Louis; others in the equally absurd shape of Piero de' Medici, who was still attempting to raise an army and recover his patrimony; I was soon to learn the identity of the Antichrist only too well.

Political events were not the only portents of some disaster to come. A lion had given birth on the streets of Naples. In Germany it rained blood, in Paris frogs. And Simonetta walked the streets of Florence and made plans to go to Rome.

Sandro saw little of her in those months. In Florence the new year begins on the Feast of the Annunciation, 15 March, when the days begin to be longer than the nights and new life bludgeons through dead soil, but in Rome, where they date the year from the Nativity, from the first coming of His light into the winter darkness, the year

1500 had already started. The world survived three months of the Roman new year, but we worried that Armageddon was waiting for the Florentine calendar to catch up. But the coming year was not only the demimillennium but also a jubilee year, when all Christendom is invited to Rome for absolution, and many pilgrims from France, Germany, an even the Low Countries and England, paused in our city on their way south to Rome and marvelled at the wonders they saw there: their mouths were frequently as wide open as their eyes as they witnessed the beauty of my city. Yet Florence was but the limping survivor of what it had once been. Its fortune was squandered, its powers sapped. Our city state had become a battledore in the manoeuvres of nations: in February Ludovico Sforza, deposed duke of Milan, recaptured his city from our 'allies' the invading French, which had caused rejoicing throughout Italy, but in March, as the pilgrims thronged and jostled in Florence, Sforza's Swiss mercenaries laid down their weapons and the French, masters of north Italy once more, were ready to repeat their march south. Gascon and Swiss troops in French pay arrived to help us against Pisa and were greeted by jeers or silence, while Florence saw many re-enactments of the political events in the north. Milanese pilgrims fought Swiss, and were themselves soundly thrashed on our streets by Gascon mercenaries. German pilgrims attacked the French. There was a touch of plague that spring, and of the sweating sickness brought by the English, as well as many more cases than is usual of that French pox which is contracted by unclean fornication. Pettro Negroni had died many years before but his son-in-law, Cosimo, did good business in a bad season.

Sandro, in contrast, did no business at all. He spent his time hunting out Simonetta. Sometimes he received invitations to dine with his brother Simone, and once or twice he dined with Ficino. But he was no company. On rare occasions he opened up his shop, but his *garzoni* had given up on him and so had the clients. He saw Doffo Spini, one of the Signoria at the time Savonarola had been condemned, and had to listen as Doffo anxiously told him, as he anxiously told everyone, the reasons they had ordered the friar's execution. 'We had to do it,' claimed Doffo. 'The friar had done no wrong except anger an impious pope. We didn't kill for any offence he'd committed. We killed him because if we'd let Savonarola go

Florence would have killed us instead. It was him or us: he was in our power and not the other way round, so it had to be him.' Sandro had nodded vaguely at this. Once he would have been surprised, dismayed at this callousness, this calculation of political advantage at the expense of human life, but not any more. He was not the innocent he had once been. Savonarola had taught that life is a prologue; then comes the time of purgatory; finally, if we have deserved it, we awake to God's presence. Savonarola was the most convincing preacher, yet Sandro was never convinced, though his own conclusions about life were so tentative, so imprecise, that he never dared argue them. None the less, it did seem to him that life was too complicated to be only a prologue; life, like the pointless self-indulgent love Politian had once described, always felt like an end in itself. But he agreed with Savonarola on one point. Innocence must be defended, for it can never be restored.

On another day in that confused period he had passed Ficino's house and discovered it in mourning. The old scholar had at last died. 'Now there's only me left, and Filippino in Rome,' Sandro thought to himself. He tried to get in, to say farewell to Ficino, but was stopped at the door. 'You can't come in here,' said the servant blocking his way.

'Marsilo was my friend. We were together at the Palazzo Medici. In the good days.'

'What! You at the Palazzo Medici! Come off it! Your'e a stinking drunkard with daft ideas, that's all.'

'I am Sandro Botticelli, painter of Florence.'

'Painter of Florence! Go on, bugger off. You'll offend the family.'

Sandro had limped away.

He was reflex only, afraid to think, afraid of the dark places his thoughts might lead. It was jubilee year. Rome was a lantern to the world. Sandro was a moth to its flame. And why not? He had painted what seemed his last painting, a maudlin Crucifixion. He had lost his last Florentine friend. Rome offered more than a papal blessing for him. It offered Filippino. It offered Simonetta.

He had visited Rome only once before. The city, with its magnificent ruins home now to rabbits and weeds, its population of prostitutes and clerics, and its tawdry beauty, had fascinated and disgusted him in equal measure. Now the fascination was all Sandro could recall. He spent the last of his florins on a broad-hooded pilgrim's cloak, new sandals and a cross made of reed, and joined a party of pilgrims at the gate. These were mendicant pilgrims, travelling with no money and begging alms on their journey, which suited Sandro. They were also mostly Flemings, speaking little or no Italian, and that suited him even better. Head down, handles of his crutches concealed within his cloak, he shuffled with the pilgrims through the gate. No one objected to his presence; no one took much notice.

The journey was a long one for a man with crippled feet, diseased legs. To begin with Sandro had no difficulty keeping up, despite his lameness, for the pilgrims walked slowly and spent much time in prayer, but after a few days his hands started shaking, his eyes hurting, and he needed a rest and a drink of burnt wine. A rest was easy, for there were many as old and crippled as he in the company, people who sought cure or death in the Holy City; burnt wine was not to be had, and the shaking lasted a week.

After that the going seemed easier. Sandro's head cleared. Even his lameness, one foot damaged at the Palazzo Vespucci, the other more recently weakened by a fall down Simone's stairs, was never so bad in the summer. The pilgrims were on the road to Rome for a month. Sometimes they were overtaken by other groups. Sometimes they passed bodies by the wayside. Yet Sandro felt relaxed, refreshed. Certain only that he wanted to go to Rome, uncertain what he would do once he got there, he concentrated on the journey, and the simple act, balancing the crutches, swinging his legs, had a rhythm that cured many ills.

The pilgrims' route took them through Orvieto, high in the mountains. Many of them visited the cathedral, where Luca Signorelli was painting the walls, and Sandro looked with interest at the man's work. He had met Signorelli at the Medici villa of Castello, owned by Lorenzo's cousin, Lorenzo di Pierfrancesco de' Medici, and the two painters had found much in common. Sandro decided to stay the night in Orvieto, meet Signorelli again.

He found the painter the next day, intercepting him at the doors of the cathedral as Signorelli made his way to work. Fifteen years had passed since last they met, and Luca Signorelli had worn no better than Sandro. They studied each other with surprise and concern, and then embraced. 'Sandro Botticelli!' cried Signorelli. 'You look terrible!'

'The effects of pilgrimage,' Sandro admitted.

'At least that gives you an excuse,' said Signorelli. 'We're getting old. I was wondering about making the trip to Rome myself, but I've too much work to do here. Have you been busy?'

Sandro shook his head. 'Not at all.'

'That's terrible. I remember the paintings you did at Castello: *The Birth of Spring* and *Venus Rising from the Waves*. Quite beautiful, both of them.'

Sandro bowed his head, pleased by this expert opinion. 'Lorenzo di Pierfrancesco was a delightful client,' he said.

'Wasn't he just!' Signorelli agreed. 'I wish there'd been a few more like him. Delightful mistress he had too. What's he doing now? I hear he's changed his name to Mr Popular and is trying to pretend he was never a Medici at all.'

'That's more or less true,' said Sandro. 'The Medici are out of favour. And so am I. I did some drawings for Lorenzo di Pierfrancesco, illustrations from Dante, but I've done no more paintings for him.'

'Dante.' Luca Signorelli relished the syllables. 'You've seen my frescos here in the Duomo?'

'I spent yesterday admiring them.'

'Then you'll see how much they too owe to the Divine Comedy.' The most striking fresco showed the Damned in Hell. Many writhing naked figures, tortured by demons with grey and green skin, suffered eternity's agonies, while above, floating effortlessly on pastel wings, three angels in French armour distributed God's justice and God's vengeance. 'I'm glad you are here. It's good to see someone from the old times, the good times; these times are bad, the worst.'

'Your angels look like French soldiers,' said Sandro.

'It's no accident. The French invaded, invade again. Always they sit in judgement on Italy's affairs. But though they were the model, they are not the subject.' The two painters walked into the cathedral together. 'Do you believe the world is ending?'

'I don't know,' Sandro said.

'It sometimes seems it is. The world has grown old with us, the patrons are all dead or impoverished. Yet my work keeps me going.'

'If the world is ending,' Sandro began.

'I know. If the world is ending, why paint at all? To record the world I knew, I suppose. To capture the world and the world's worth.' He drew Sandro's attention to a monochrome tondo set high in the walls. 'Dante and Virgil entering Purgatory,' he explained. 'Mankind is base, yet capable of so much. Purgatory is where we shed the baseness, go on to Heaven. Yet I want to show both: the baseness and the achievement; the Inferno and God's Grace. And while I work, I find I no longer care if the world is dying or not. The work itself is the thing.'

'I envy you,' said Sandro. 'You have found work to make the labour worthwhile.'

'You envy me?' Signorelli was incredulous. 'I envy you! Your art, its beauty, have been my inspiration.'

'The world has no use for beauty,' said Sandro sadly.

Signorelli shook his head. 'The world may have no time for beauty, but that's a different matter. Beauty is more necessary than ever in these times. I wish I had your gift: I would give them beauty! But I haven't, and instead you see the poor tormented souls of the damned on that great wall. When you get back to Florence you must paint again, paint a scene of beauty, show you don't despair.'

'But I do despair,' said Sandro. 'Often. And anyway, I have no clients.'

'Then paint it for yourself. What else can we do except paint? And now, I must get on. It has been delightful meeting you again, delightful. Good luck with your pilgrimage, and remember me to Pope Alexander if you meet him.'

Luca Signorelli left him then, and, with the assistance of his *garzoni*, mounted the high scaffolding that climbed to the roof. Sandro watched the painter make his way upwards. Signorelli was stiff with age, yet in his eagerness to resume work he seemed almost agile, a man climbing towards Heaven. Sandro breathed in, heavily and uncomfortably. 'A lucky man,' he thought.

Yet when he looked again at the painting of the damned which occupied the east wall he was not so sure. Such torment could only come from a man himself tormented. Signorelli was right: despite the easy association between the invading French and the figures of the angels, this picture is not about the French. This is the punishment of sin. Sin existed long before the French arrived, would cope with their occupation, would survive their leaving. Sandro had not given much thought to sin, for all that Savonarola had harped on the subject. He had never been a sinner in the determined way that some men are, a fornicator, a lover of boys, a lover of money. Yet when he looked at Signorelli's painting he saw in the faces of the damned not the hardened features of the habitual sinner but the shocked faces of those who have sinned but once and thought their sin forgotten. Sin is never forgotten, Savonarola had taught. God will forgive, but he will not forget, and only the truly innocent are sure of salvation.

Sandro knelt, as many did, before Signorelli's grim vision. Bones in his legs clicked irritably as he bent. He thought of Signorelli, high above him, trying to capture in paint the world in all its glory and horror. He thought of his own works, spread thinly across Tuscany, lacking the unity of Signorelli's masterpiece, yet another record none the less of the world and the world's worth. And he thought about innocence, and the day he lost his. 'Innocence is like ice over a pond,' he whispered to himself and to God. 'Christ could walk on water. But Christ was truly innocent. For the rest of us, when the ice cracks we drown.'

I lost my innocence.

Simonetta drowned.

1476

She drowned on 26 April. She drowned in her own blood. It welled from some hole in her chest, burst through her gorgeous throat, spewed from her perfect lips. Filippino was hesitant when he delivered the news, as though he feared my reaction. Yet my initial reaction was calm, for I did not believe what he said. Filippino was neither malicious nor macabre, so I did not think him the author of this sour joke, but Florentines have long had a reputation for jests that marry death and love.

'Don't be ridiculous,' I said.

'Sandro. Sandro, she's dead.'

I humoured him. 'Come on then. How do you know? Who told you?'

'Everyone knows. I heard it from Domenico.'

Domenico would not think this a joke either. I thought of her sad cough, the one ugly aspect of her beauty. 'It isn't possible.'

'Sandro. It is.' Filippino could not meet my eye. 'They say Giuliano is searching Florence, looking for the physician who was in attendance, looking to whip him.'

'Physician?'

'A man called Negroni.'

Might she be dead? The thought was treachery and I fought to dismiss it. 'It can't be true,' I insisted.

'It can be.' Still Filippino avoided my eye. 'It is.'

The next day there was no doubt. The flag above the Vespucci palace was lowered, and the drapes were drawn. Giuliano and his braves caught Pettro Negro on the road north and beat him viciously.

Old Giorgio Vespucci, the star-gazer, appeared in black and cursed the Heavens that had taken his daughter-in-law before she had borne a child. These were public displays. Florence marries love and death; Florence turns life into theatre. The city is designed for performance: each district has its piazza, each palazzo its courtyard. We have poets to give us our lines, tailors to dress us, artists to touch up the scenery. As long as we are acting out a role we are happy. Any occasion occasions display. The death of Simonetta was the excuse for a new play.

There was extravagant mourning for the loss of one so lovely. The flags at the other palazzos were also replaced by gaunt black cloths and black ribbons trailed from the windows. Ashes were spread in the streets outside. The braves wore black to signal their despair. Politian put his verses celebrating Giuliano's tournament aside and wrote graceful epigrams celebrating Giuliano's grief. Marullo too wrote epigrams, as did Bernardo and Luigi Pulci. Florence turns life into theatre, and death too; the mourning was universal, yet brief. Within a couple of days she was dumped in the family crypt, to rot on a block of stone until the stone was needed for another Vespucci; then her remains, brittle bones, would be swept away and left in the cold ossuary to blend readily with all the rest. April's promise of full fields and full streams was a mockery that year, and the wind brought ice from the north, until Giuliano fell in love with Fioretta Gorini and that performance was over. Then the actors found new parts to play, the chorus changed its costume. As long as we are acting out a role we are happy. But I had no role in the mourning for Simonetta. I, who had loved her best, had been given no lines, no part in the grief. All I had was the loneliness of a tired heart, the emptiness of a world which no longer held my love. Her absence was as tangible as her presence. There was a silence at the core of every noise, a void in the midst of every prospect, and that silence, that void, was Simonetta. For some weeks I did not go to church even, did not wish to worship a murdering God, and when at last I went I wept.

There are vices, there are virtues. Which is grief? I believe that Simonetta loved me and that, looking down from heaven, she would have been saddened to see me so sad. My misery, my private misery so different from the public mourning which first surrounded her death and then abandoned her poor sad corpse, ate me from within as might jealousy. It was not a pleasant grief, for it was shot through with regret, spliced with bitterness, brimming with the awareness of all that might have been and never was. It was an angry grief, a wailing and bewailing, a cursing of all fates, all men and all gods. It was an agony to live with, that grief, and so was I. Yet it was all I had left, and I could not put aside, for to do so would be to relinquish what little of Simonetta I had left.

I did meagre work for the remainder of the year. It was not difficult to borrow money – it was easy – as the fame of my Medici Adoration of the Magi spread through the city and beyond. The bankers were happy to advance me florins, ducats, crowns and lire, and I spent without pleasure or plan. She died in April. Flowers opened, birds built nests. The sun travelled the heavens. I passed a hot summer walking the meadows by the Arno, imagining the waters' cool embrace. The moon waxed; the moon waned. The harvest was gathered and prayers were said. The landscape became ruddy, and suited me better, for autumn is a time when the world admits death, when the leaves leave the trees and the birds gather like flies around meat. And then it was winter, the time of little light and many candles, and each candle was a candle for the dead.

Or perhaps it was always winter.

My friends tried to help, but they were busy while I was idle. Politian completed his famous stanzas on the joust and ensured his eternal fame; Domenico Ghirlandaio, with his brother David, was establishing his marvellous studio; Filippino had commissions of his own. Each of them visited me regularly, though I was lousy company. Politian was full of talk of papacy and policy. Pope Sixtus was still angry that Lorenzo refused to allow the archbishop of Pisa into Tuscany, and was still raising armies in the Romagna to our east. In the north the affairs of the duke of Burgundy were causing concern. Tommaso Portinari, who had sent the wonderful altarpiece by van der Goes to Florence, was apparently lending the duke vast sums of money, and the duke was spending the money unwisely. Politian spoke with great insistence on this and I wondered if he was hinting something about my own increasing debts. He was capable of subtlety when he thought it appropriate; he was capable of anything. But perhaps he was simply relishing an interesting tale about an interesting man. 'A curious figure, this Duke Charles of Burgundy. When his father, Philip the Good, was alive Duke Charles was then count of Charolais. One day he learnt that his father had stopped all his allowances, which was something of a blow as you can imagine. But he retained his dignity. He gathered all his followers around him and spoke of the respect and love he had for his misinformed father, and then of his worries about the welfare of his retinue. "Let those who have the means to remain with me do so, until my fortunes improve; let the poor go away freely, in the knowledge that they will be welcomed back with open arms on the day I can once more afford to protect them." To which, of course, the entire body of men swore they would stay with him until death if necessary, while the richer of his followers gave him what money they could, so that the count and his court continued to live as well as before. That's the proper way for a prince to behave. But a prince is still a man, for all that, and it is in the nature of all men that they continually strive for more. For example: our duke of Urbino has sold his soul to the pope for a duchy; Charles of Burgundy wants to be elevated to king, and his ambitions are doing him no good. A ruler needs pride, but pride can get out of hand. Charles's pride is getting out of hand. He's going to war, spending Florentine money, and in doing so stirring up hornets. The advantage of Lorenzo de' Medici, Sandro, is that Lorenzo likes what he's got. Lorenzo doesn't want to become count of Florence or duke of Tuscany because he's happy being Lorenzo de' Medici. He's a banker's son, after all. Florence's prosperity was won in peace rather than war, and so was Lorenzo's prestige. A noble potentate owes his position to his own valour or that of his ancestors; our Lorenzo owes his position more to prudence than valour. Lorenzo will attempt to keep the peace because he prefers peace to war: he's no ambition to set off on some chivalric quest like the noble Burgundian, for all that he has a taste for jousts and tourneys. The only danger in his policy, as I see it, is that pacifism can appear weakness. Lorenzo will try to preserve the peace, but others may want to go to war. I don't like the pope's nephew, or bastard more likely, Count Girolamo, on our borders. The man has ambitions which threaten us all.'

We think of the past as of something we have lost, yet our knowledge of the past comes from what is recorded on tablets and documents, dug from the earth on antique stone, recalled in our heads and our conversations. History is not what is lost but what remains, not what has vanished but what survives. The rest, the spaces between the records and the artefacts, we fill with conjecture, illuminate with connection. The patterns we make of the past are like the patterns I make with my paints, showing not reality as it is or was but rather reality as perceived, as digested and passed through the human system almost like bread or burnt wine. It is my vanity to make designs, of paint and of my past. I cannot see with God's eye, see the wholeness, the entirety of eternity. I am the fly on the canvas, skirting the pennon and the woman's foot. Yet I am also human, and therefore touched with the divine, albeit in corrupt and adulterated form, so I still try to make my patterns, still try to make five senses make sense. My life is an arrow's flight, a trajectory, an arc that will end in my death; my life is my city's life – growth, splendour and decay. And the history through which I move, that too can be granted design and shape, as though, touched with the divine, I can grasp the edge of the divine pattern. Thus, while I mourned my Simonetta one pope's bastard was carving an empire in the Romagna; while Sandro the Mad chased his moth as far as Rome another's was doing the same. But patterns do not necessarily repeat. The first bastard, Girolamo Riario, was overcome, whereas now, as I write, that second bastard, that Cesare who is become duke of the Romagna, has with Leonardo's help turned to attack Florence, and seems unstoppable.

Filippino mentioned Leonardo once when he called. 'An old friend of yours has got himself in trouble, I hear. Leonardo's been charged with sodomy.'

This stirred my interest rather more than Politian's news. 'Who charged him? Anyone we know?'

Filippino lifted a finger to his lips. 'I've an idea, but the charge was anonymous, a written accusation posted into the box outside the Palazzo della Signoria.'

'All right. So who charged him, in your opinion? And what's he done?'

Filippino chose to keep me in suspense. 'He's been screwing one of his models, a youth called Jacopo Saltarelli. And he's left Verrocchio's studio.'

'One thing doubtless led to the other,' I said. 'Perhaps our Leonardo tired of always being underneath?' But such crudity didn't sit properly on my lips even in those desperate days. 'Is he going to trial?' I asked.

'There's already been a trial, but no witnesses turned up. Now there's going to be another one.'

'Well, well. And now are you going to tell me who the accuser was?'

'Verrocchio,' said Filippino.

I was astonished. 'Are you sure?'

'No one's sure. But a thwarted lover is a dangerous beast.'

I had been thwarted by Death, cheated by God. In my case there was little chance of revenge. 'What's Verrocchio doing now?' I asked.

'Working off his fury with a statue of David for the Council.'

'Well, well,' I said again.

When Domenico visited we usually discussed art. Few painters like to talk about their work, and of those who do many, like Leonardo, are opinionated: they do not so much discuss as lecture. But Domenico was not only a great painter, he was also a great enthusiast. He took me to see Verrocchio's bronze David. 'It's quite b-beautiful,' he stammered at me. 'The moulding is so smooth, so lovely, yet the nobility and p-passion are remarkable. When Donatello sculpted David he made him a playful naked boy; V-Verrocchio's David is still a boy, but a dangerous one.'

When I saw the statue I saw what Domenico meant, and what Filippino had meant too. This was a mean, unforgiving David, standing proudly over the severed head of Goliath and staring challengingly ahead. This was a furious David, tense and alert, with each vein and muscle defined. This was a jealous David, with the potential to betray Uriah and bed Bathsheba.

Domenico was horrified when he learnt about my debts. 'You're the best p-painter in Florence,' he flattered. 'You shouldn't be living like this. Why, at this rate, however much you earn, you'll never be clear of the money-lenders.'

'Exactly. So it doesn't much matter how much work I do, does it. I may as well die lazy and poor as exhausted and poor. I'll certainly never be rich.'

'Why not? I run a studio on what I earn, and still make a profit. You earn more per painting tham me, have no c-commitments, yet still can't make ends meet.'

'Don't preach at me,' I warned him. 'I didn't try to get into this mess. It just happened.'

He was silent, and hurt, but too generous to be either for long. 'Look, why don't you borrow from me? I don't charge interest. How much do you owe?'

I wasn't sure. I never have been. 'Too much.'

'A single f-florin is too much. But I've got some savings.'

'Keep them. Please.'

'Just tell me how much we're talking about. Twenty florins? Th-thirty?'

'Much more than that. I owe the Medici bank fifty alone.'

'And others?'

'I don't know. Soderini I owe thirty-five to. Pazzi I think it's twenty. I haven't paid my rent for two months, or my tailor for six.'

'We're t-talking about more than a hundred florins! It'll take you six months to earn that even if you spend nothing! And a ma-ma-man's got to live!' In his horror his stutter grew worse. 'Wh-what are you going to do?'

'Hang myself, I expect.'

'No!'

'Why not? What have I got to live for?'

He struck me, once, back-handed across the cheek. I was in pain, yet he was the one who was crying. 'For art, you f-fool. For art. Live for the paintings you haven't yet painted. You've lost the woman you loved. All right. Recapture her in paint. Make her live not just for a few more years, as a physician might, but for ever. That's what an artist can do. That's what he owes the p-people he loves. That's what he owes to himself. That's what he owes to God.'

'God!' I exclaimed.

'God gave you eyes and a hand. He gave you the mind to understand what you see, the dedication to learn the techniques, the skill to transcend them. You talk as if throwing that away counts for nothing. You're wrong! It counts for everything. God gave you the g-gift of life, and then gave you extra gifts too. And it isn't just God you're indebted to. What of Man?'

'Oh, I'm indebted to him all right. Up to my ears.'

'I'm talking of Man, not men. You hold, as a baton, the skills of our craft, to p-pass on to others by your teaching and example. You have the gifts to celebrate life, to celebrate Man. Instead you want to s-squander them on some s-self-indulgent s-self-pitying stupidity? Do that, and you forsake the right to be called a Man, and Simonetta, in heaven, will despise you.'

The last argument struck home first, and I began to weep too. 'But what shall I do?' I asked. 'I still owe more than I earn.'

'There's nothing else you can do. You'll have to work, and p-pay off your debts over the years.'

'Everyone'll want paying soon.'

'Then paint them f-foreclosing on you.'

'I'll be thrown in gaol again.'

'Paint the gaol.'

'The more I earn, the more I seem to borrow. I'll never get free.'

'Then paint your captivity. Paint anything. But paint, paint, p-p-paint. It's hard to be a painter, harder still to be a g-good one. But remember, you're a p-painter because to do anything else would be harder still.'

'I live in the gutter. I stare at the clouds. That's why I'm a painter.'

'Pardon?'

'Just something someone once said. Someone wiser than I realized.'

I visited Leonardo shortly after. The charges against him had been dismissed. There had been no witnesses at his second trial either, and his accuser still failed to reveal himself, so the case was dropped. 'Good morning, Sir Sandro,' Leonardo said. He had grown a beard since last I saw him, and his hair, though thinning at the front, fell in outrageous waves down his back. If he was surprised to see me he did not show it. 'What can I do for you?'

His bottega was small and evil-smelling. I was not sure why I was there. 'I just thought I'd drop in, congratulate you.'

'Oh what? On this place? It gives me the privacy I need, but little more.'

I wondered if this was a hint. 'If you want me to leave . . .'

'No, now you're here you might as well stay. There are some things here that might interest you.'

'Actually, I was congratulating you on your acquittal.'

'Silly business. Why should anyone care where I push my prick?

Still, torture would have been an interesting experience.'

'They might have hanged you.'

'Well, that would have been interesting too. Now, what was it I was going to show you?'

His bottega was unlike any I have seen. There was a desk in the centre of the sort used by scribes or copyists. The entrails of some large animal – a horse perhaps, or a cow – sprawled over a pile of books and spilt on to the astrolabe beneath. A series of cogs from a mechanical device had been arranged on one corner of the table. Various drawing instruments, compasses and squares as well as the more familiar styluses and chalks, were scattered among the mess. A quill lolled from the eye of a skull.

Leonardo pushed some of this aside and pulled out something corrupt that looked and smelt suspiciously like the bladder of a pig. 'Watch,' he said, and blew into the bladder, distending it. I wouldn't have put my lips near it. 'You see?' he asked.

I didn't, and didn't like to say I didn't.

'Now,' he said, plugging the end. 'Watch this.'

He took the bladder to a tub of black water in a corner of the room. The bladder bobbed on top. 'You see? It floats. Now watch this.'

He unfastened the plug. Suddenly the room was sprayed with water and the bladder had disappeared. I was wet but Leonardo was soaked. 'That wasn't supposed to happen,' he said.

'No,' I agreed. 'I was the one meant to get wet.'

'It wasn't a practical joke,' he insisted. 'It was a demonstration. What did you see?'

'You blew air into it, put it in the water, and when you unplugged it instead of air coming out, water did. Then it disappeared.'

Leonardo nodded, then shook his head. 'No. That can't be right. Last time it just went round the tub tremendously fast, hardly splashing at all. No water came out of the bladder then. So what happened this time?'

'Perhaps there was a hole in the bladder and the water got in that way?' I suggested.

He looked at me scornfully. 'The air wouldn't have stayed in then.'

'No. I suppose not.'

'Wait a minute. I've got it. The bladder should be . . . There it is!'

Without pushing his sleeves out of the way he fished into the water and fetched the bladder from the bottom. A little water dribbled out when he squeezed. A lot more dripped from his sleeves. 'Now. Watch.' He blew into the bladder once more – at least it was clean this time – and without bothering with the plug forced it into the water before releasing the air. Again we were splashed, though less violently. 'You see? There was no water in the bladder. The air forced the water out of the tub. Fascinating!'

'Marvellous.'

'Don't you see what this means? Already, gunpowder has changed the way we fight our wars on land. Soon, perhaps air and water could revolutionize sea battles. At first I thought of the bladder as a way of making a ship move: you'd have thousands of bladders on board, and open them when necessary to shoot the ship forward. But perhaps it could also be used as a siege weapon.'

'Does everything have to be a weapon?'

'War is what makes a state great. I'll show you some drawings.'

These were mostly diagrams of curious guns and defences, admirably drawn in red chalk but otherwise, as far as I could tell, completely pointless. 'Florence's prosperity is based on peace, not war,' I said, paraphrasing Politian.

'Then I'll have to go elsewhere. The dukes of Milan and Urbino are more warlike: they might be able to find a use for my talents.'

'I thought you were a painter?'

'So I am, and the best. But painting does not exhaust me.'

'Then you're not working at it hard enough.' Water still dripped from him. His vanity seemed more comic than offensive.

'I work at everything with the whole of my soul,' he corrected. 'When I paint, I paint with an intensity that leaves other men wanting. But you're an adequate painter yourself: answer me this. Does painting satisfy your every want, your every need? Can you honestly say that all your talents and faculties are involved when you paint? What of your ears? Can you paint noise? Your sense of smell or of taste? What do they contribute to your art? A general paints with men. His canvas is a battlefield and all his senses are involved.'

'Nobody dies in a painting,' I pointed out.

'That's because no one lives in a painting either.'

'Do you believe that?'

He thought for a moment. 'No,' he decided. 'No, I don't.'

'Then there's hope for you yet,' I said.

We parted on good terms. We would never be friends, but I no longer felt we were rivals. Leonardo had a route of his own to follow. I was glad he had been acquitted.

I walked through the streets. The cool March sun inspected the city. The Florentine year was ending. It would soon be Easter and spring, the renaissance of our Lord and his dear earth. Yet, in the dry crypt beneath the Ognissanti, flesh became parchment, bones turned to stone. A perfect kiss withered on bloodless lips. Rats made a nest of her rib-cage. Death is the grin beneath everyone's skin. It is the rattle of rats among bones.

1500

To paint, to paint, to paint again: the dotted rhythm of his limp took on words as he travelled. The second part of his journey took them from the high lands to the valley of the Tiber. Sandro travelled among the Dutch in companionable mutual incomprehension. His crutches tapped their way along a damaged antique road, a surface of displaced bricks and cobbles. At the wayside were many shrines.

They first saw Rome from the north, the metropolis revealed as a vista of open spaces and broken buildings; they fell to their knees to thank God, then made their slow way towards the gates. The city, obedient to the laws of perspective, grew as they approached, and Sandro sketched it in his head. But though perspective is an adequate measure of what one stationary eye sees, a city of receding planes where parallel lines – streets, walls, windows – converge as they get further, it seemed to Sandro that such conventions had little to do with the messages his eyes were actually receiving. Everything he saw as he made his way into Rome seemed more complicated than a mathematical scheme would allow. Perspective shows a single view, but Sandro saw many views, many Romes, and all were of equal value. The pilgrims began to chant in bastard northern Latin as they descended. And perspective limits our art in other ways, thought Sandro: perspective paints time into a picture, because perspective depicts distance and distance is measured in the time it would take us to reach such or such a place. But Rome is the Eternal City and Sandro, entering the extensive ruined outer regions, where grass sprouted high on abandoned walls and columns supported only air, suddenly understood what eternity means. Eternity is not all of time, from past to present and future, as he had previously imagined; eternity is a place where there is no time at all, just as darkness is a place with no light. Time is a function of life, he decided. The living need time in which to live, just as they need water to stay alive. But, just as he had heard of places in Africa where there was no water, so he could imagine a place without time. It would be a place of the dead, of course, a city of the dead. It would be Rome, city of bones, city of death. And to paint such a place would mean abandoning the rules of perspective.

And then he laughed at himself, for taking himself too seriously. Rome may be a city of the dead, he thought, but just at present it is thronged with the living. Several hundred thousand people, it was reported, had gathered to earn the Pope's benediction. It did not matter that Rome was a charnel house. It did not matter that the basilica of St Peter's was surrounded by scaffolding and was being dismantled, slowly, to make way for a new building. It did not even matter that the pope was a corrupt old Spaniard who openly acknowledged his vicious son. Rome, the Eternal City, the Holy See, the resting place of Apostles, was the centre of the earth. The pilgrims were sucked through an open gate and then they dispersed.

The weather was warm. There were few lodgings available, less still for a cripple with no money, but the ruins offered shelter of a kind. Like the Virgin and child in one of his tondos, Sandro slept beneath a shattered colonnade. For several days, exhausted by his journey, he did nothing more than beg a little food, but as his strength returned so did his strength of purpose. He wanted to see Filippino. He needed to see Simonetta. And he needed remission of his sins, for his soul was as confused as his mind.

He had no address for Filippino. It was only the reliable rumour of the Florentine bankers that told him his friend was still in Rome at all. But he trusted to luck that he would find him.

Of Simonetta's whereabouts he was equally ignorant. The city was vast, and though two-thirds of it was ruins that were normally home only to foxes and weeds, in this time of pilgrimage it seemed that every inch had been colonized. But Sandro was unconcerned. He trusted to more than luck in this case. Fate had brought Simonetta back into his life, albeit surprisingly disguised, disturbingly transfigured. Fate would lead him to her again. He sat on an overgrown stone step near his meagre shelter. Fate would lead him to her again. He found himself listening to garbled chatter, familiar conversations recorded in unfamiliar tongues. Equally unfamiliar was his sense of contentment. 'I must paint again when I get back to Florence,' he told himself. 'Meanwhile, Filippino will prove no problem, Simonetta will prove no problem, and remission of my sins has been won already.'

He had been talking aloud without realizing it. 'You've got the patent then?'

'Pardon?' Next to him, Sandro saw a small dark man with a withered face, a Sicilian by his accent.

'You've bought a patent? A piece of paper that says your sins have been remitted?'

'Bought? I haven't bought anything.' Remission of sin is the pilgrim's reward: I came here as a mendicant, he thought, not a customer.

'Then you haven't been remitted, not properly,' said his companion on the steps. 'Pope Alexander talks of ambitious plans for rebuilding the basilica of St Peter, and demands hard cash in return for God's favours. But don't worry about it. There's no shortage of salesmen. Make sure you get the genuine article though. There are plenty of forgeries about too.'

'Has it come to this?' asked Sandro.

'What do you mean?'

'Isn't it enough we're here? Some people have crossed seas to get to Rome for the jubilee. Do we have to pay as well?'

'Yeah,' sympathized the Sicilian. 'I've heard others say much the same. But it's a hard age we live in. Everything has its price. Why not God?'

Sandro hoisted himself to his feet. He thought of Signorelli's painting of the Damned. It was powerful, but there was something missing. Jesus was missing. 'Jesus lived in poverty,' he announced. 'Money has nothing to do with it.'

'If you like,' said the Sicilian. He was bored with the conversation, bored with the cripple. 'I could see from your boots that you'd just arrived, was just trying to let you know how things were. I don't want an argument.' He stood too. 'But I'd rather have my bit of paper than all the conviction in the world, when it comes to getting through Purgatory.'

Sandro hobbled away.

There were many processions through Rome that dry season. He saw strange creatures he had not seen since Lorenzo's day, and was now able to give them their beautiful exotic names, tiger, leopard, antelope, gazelle, rhinoceros, elephant, zebra, giraffe, names that spoke of distant worlds. His friend Amerigo, in the service of the Spanish monarchs, had travelled across the ocean, seen the New World, written back to Florence with excited and fabulous descriptions. The old world might be ending, as so many believed, but there was a new world coming, and Amerigo was already there.

Another procession celebrated Cesare Borgia, the pope's bastard, who rode through the streets on a triumphal chariot in the guise of Julius Caesar. Cesare was a powerfully built dark man, his Spanish blood evident, his face composed in arrogant disdain as he looked at the pilgrims queuing to watch the pageant.

The most striking procession, though, was that made by the pope on St Bartholomew's Day: Alexander, though much smaller than his son, was a fabulous figure in white and gold, held high on a golden chair, and all around him men and women, whether in finery or rags, fell to their knees and begged for his blessing. But Alexander was unimpressed, and when he held out his hand it was a gesture of command, not benediction. 'Christians, beg not, for it is not by your words but your deeds that you shall be judged. The church of St Peter in Rome, which should be the most wondrous in all Christendom, the mightiest building beneath the stars, must be rebuilt. By the power of St Peter, by the Apostolic succession of St Paul, I tell you this: Purgatory will indeed be crowded, with your souls and your children's souls, until the work of rebuilding is done. I ask not your labour, I ask not your skills. Masons and craftsmen we have. I ask for your donations, that the church of St Peter may rise to its proper glory, the heart and centre of the world.'

Sandro vowed immediately to buy his patent of remission.

Finding a salesman was not difficult. There were salesmen everywhere. Finding the money took rather longer, but still, though he was twice robbed, because he was a cripple it took only a month before he had begged enough. The salesmen had portable stalls, a box like a small wooden pulpit topped with a placard; there was one at every important crossroad. There was no queue at the one he chose. He paid his money, a tied cloth full of small change that was the equivalent of two papal sovereigns, and took his piece of paper. He read it carefully, knowing enough Latin to recognize that Pope Alexander, in the name of God, was promising this or that to the bearer, not knowing enough to decipher the whole printed document. He had no way to tell if this was a forgery. He wondered if God would mind if it were. Sandro had made his contribution and his sacrifice. Perhaps God would recognize that. And surely God would not miss two sovereigns.

It was only as he limped away from the crossroads that he realized he knew the salesman: Matteo, Simonetta's friend. The face was thinner, paler than it had been in Florence, but the look of uneasy contempt it gave to the world was the same. Sandro turned round. It was late in the day and Matteo, with the help of a boy, was dismantling his booth. Sandro stood in a sparse crowd and watched.

Matteo and the boy took the pulpit apart and strapped the pieces together. Matteo picked up the bundle of planks and boards, while the boy carried the placard, still on its poles; together they took a road that led, not towards the Vatican as Sandro expected, but in the other direction, towards the viaduct and the entrances to the catacombs. Comfortably anonymous in this alien city, Sandro followed. To paint, said his crutches on the paved Roman road: to paint again.

1477–92

They were right of course, Domenico and Signorelli: the only thing a painter can do is paint. The years that followed Simonetta's death were busy and successful, yet the only meaning they had for me I found in paint, just as the only story they have to tell I told in paint; I have little to add with words, and that little is of a historical rather than a personal nature.

Two years to the day after Simonetta died Florence was again plunged into mourning, for Giuliano de' Medici was slain in Florence cathedral and Lorenzo almost killed with him. Yet this time the mourning was buttressed with anger. The Pazzi family was responsible, but they had been encouraged by Pope Sixtus. First there was a massacre of the Pazzi in Florence – recorded on the walls of the Palazzo della Signoria by Leonardo and me, as I have mentioned – and then came war with Rome and Naples: Girolamo Riario built his empire in the Romagna to our east, and the forces of Rome and Naples helped him. It seemed Florence was lost. But Lorenzo had been blessed with courage and good fortune. His courage took him to Naples where he negotiated with King Ferdinand for an end to the war. I was with him, a long and uncomfortable voyage followed by a longer period of inactivity while the rulers wrangled and I sought out my brother Simone, then resident in the city. Lorenzo was more successful than I was: Simone was away on business and his wife a little too anxious I should stay with her; Ferdinand was stubborn but intelligent, and saw that Lorenzo would be more use to him as a friend than an enemy. On returning to Florence I painted Pallas Athena taming the minotaur, a tribute to Lorenzo's diplomacy. But if courage is useful for a ruler, good fortune is an even more necessary ally: Naples had drawn back from the attack on Florence, but Rome still threatened until a Turkish horde landed at Otranto in the south-east and devastated Italian soil; there was unlikely peace among the Italians as we faced the greater threat.

Again I was involved in a minor way, paid to provide another oblique record of the events. As a consequence of this peace I was sent to Rome, with Domenico, Pietro of Perugia and Cosimo Rosselli, to work on the chapel in the Vatican that Sixtus was building to glorify himself. This work in the Sistine chapel should, I suppose, count as the greatest moment of my career. I painted several large frescos in such a place that princes and potentates would know and appreciate my work; I was universally acknowledged as the foremost painter in Italy. Yet Sixtus was not only a despicable man but also a poor patron. He had no discrimination: Rosselli, the least skilled painter among us, sought to disguise his limitations by decorating his pictures with excessive gilt, enriching them to the point where all meaning was lost, and we laughed at his pretensions; when Sixtus saw Cosimo's work he was delighted and ordered that all the frescos were to be similarly cheapened. There was much honour but little satisfaction to be gained from that work, and my father died while I was away.

Landino's fantastic idea that one day all Florence should read books made from his words and my pictures was another scheme that promised more than it produced. He wrote a commentary on Dante, for the Cennini's presses in Florence, and asked me to illustrate it. But the book was not a success. The Divine Comedy was inspired, but Marsilio, the engraver who turned my drawings into plates, was not, and the illustrations did justice neither to me nor to Dante. I had more pleasure in those paintings mentioned by Signorelli which I did for Lorenzo's cousin, Lorenzo di Pierfranceso de' Medici; though hanging in a private villa, and therefore seen by few people and winning little fame, I none the less agree with the verdict Signorelli gave when we met in Orvieto. In some way these, and similar paintings of Venus and Mars and Venus bathing which I did for Marco Vespucci, of all clients, are my favourite paintings. Most patrons have a purpose when they offer a commission. They want me to elevate them among their friends, or demonstrate their wealth to the city; they wish me to commemorate some treaty or marriage, or to praise some individual or institution. But Lorenzo di Pierfrancesco when young had no interest in these things, and Marco was too vapid to be truly corrupt. They wanted pretty pictures, and so did I. I painted a world where innocence was repaired by a daily dousing in the waves, where the cycle of the seasons restored purity to the year, where the warrior Mars could sleep and sleeping be the butt for children's pranks; I painted a world still inhabited by Simonetta, and she was the face and the body that inspired my most beautiful figures. Some of the few people who have seen these paintings, in Castello, in the Palazzo Vespucci, or in the Piazza della Signoria when my *Toilet of Venus* was consigned to Savonarola's flames, have commented with surprise both at the strange subject-matter and the use of Simonetta as a model: they should realize that very often portraits are painted posthumously, for clients rarely think of recording faces they see daily, yet often commission a picture of those they have lost.

During that period I painted many altarpieces too, and earned more money than at any other time. Lorenzo de' Medici's mother's family commissioned an important picture, and the Vespucci became regular clients. I became a friend of Amerigo, and even Marco became an acquaintance, visiting my shop and chatting merrily enough as I worked. I sometimes like to think Marco knew of my affair with his wife and was grateful for the brief joy I gave her; though I know this is unlikely, the thought makes him less the cuckold, me less the villain. I have never wanted to be a villain, never even shown much talent for it. I am not a cruel man, I believe, though I live in a cruel world. A particularly convivial commission was in the church of the Ognissanti, my neighbourhood church and the place where Simonetta lies, for not only was I in a place of many memories – memories which grew less bitter with each passing year – but I was also working alongside Domenico, who painted a St Jerome while I worked on St Augustine. The punters of Florence saw this commission as a competition – who would produce the finer work? – but it was comradeship, not competition, which fired us there.

And then came a new decade, and Lorenzo de' Medici, Lorenzo the Magnificent as he is already becoming known, abandoned us for death.

1500

What goes through the mind of a moth as it finds itself drawn to a flame? Sandro had a comforting sense of inevitability, as though all that happened and was going to happen was ordained and could not be avoided; the instinct he obeyed was so strong and pure that he did not, could not, but believe that his behaviour was sanctioned by God. Somewhere among these ruins, he imagined, would be the subject for his final and greatest painting, his last statement, his last record.

Sunset is a poignant time in Rome. The alum mines spew a fine white dust that filters the evening light, and the sun becomes a ball that balances on the horizon and splashes the ruined columns with orange and black. Sandro looked for the Holy Spirit in the alum powder, angels in the setting sun. Despite his lameness it was not hard to keep up with Matteo. The collapsed pulpit was obviously heavy, and he and his boy made frequent stops. When they stopped, so did Sandro; when they continued, he did too. Sandro's madness became a great certainty in his mind: he was climbing, as Jacob had climbed, as he had seen Signorelli climb, the ladder that leads to Heaven.

The way was necessarily steep. The road they followed was ancient and rutted, hard going for a man on crutches but hard too for a man with a burden. The rests became more frequent. The last stop was by an olive grove. A rutted track led through the trees, and Sandro let Matteo and the boy get well ahead before creeping after them. Ahead was a mound of stone, jutting the height of the trees, that formed a kind of arch, and protecting the arch was a rough lean-to formed of trimmed branches and roofed with straw. It was apparently a shelter for animals, judging from the many droppings all around. Sandro stood in the twilight shadows of the olive trees and watched his quarry. The boy rested the placard against the wooden frame and Matteo paid him off. 'Tomorrow at the same time,' he said. He grabbed the lad roughly and shook him. 'Don't be late this time.' The lad hurried away and, as Matteo looked around carefully, Sandro drew further back into the shelter of the dark trees.

The leached light was almost done. Sandro remained quite still with the dowsed sun's glow behind him; he rested on his crutches and was unobserved. Matteo turned, entered the arch, raised his right arm to the inner wall, and tugged.

There was nothing, no lock, handle or hinge, to suggest a door within the arch, yet as Matteo pulled with his hands something within the arch seemed to shift noisily. The opening must have been wide enough to admit a man, for Matteo lugged his pulpit into the hole before following himself. The noise repeated; the hole was sealed.

Sandro remained silent. The shadows linked and spread. Behind him was Rome, lit by many tiny fires. It is only at night that Rome shows its true self. Rome is the city of the dead, the city of our dreams. Many of the buildings seemed half buried, rooted so deep in the past that their foundations could not bear the weight of their years, and in front of him, Sandro guessed, was a mouth to the catacombs beneath, another City of the Dead like this one on the surface, though better preserved. Rome is the city of our dreams, the setting for my nightmares. Sandro went forward as stealthily as he could and tried to find the latch that opened the door. His fingers found nothing more promising where Matteo had groped than a cleft the width of his hand: he put his finger in the cleft and tugged, experimentally at first and then with all his strength.

A whole stone pivoted and a hole appeared. The moth does not fear the flame it embraces. Sandro stood for some time pretending he had a decision to make. This was not yet Heaven. He thought of Signorelli's tondo of Dante and Virgil entering Purgatory. They too entered through an arch. This is the entrance to Purgatory, he decided, and beyond Purgatory is Heaven, where Simonetta awaits. He went in.

He had no way of closing the hole again, and no desire to do so.

Ahead was an absolute dark, and a cold that caressed his bones carefully, as though weighing them up. He shivered and wished he had a torch, yet at the same time knew he was a spy and accepted that spies must always travel in darkness. At least he could use his crutches to prod a way through the dark.

His way twisted, descended and forked. The sides of the passage were treacherous. His hands were encumbered by crutches yet compelled by his blindness to grope for the walls: it seemed to those flailing hands as though they clutched first the crutches then air. His knees encountered stone; his hands encountered nothing. A moth is discouraged by the heat of the flame: it veers wildly away, reminded of its mortality, and then the craziness perseveres and it returns. It seemed to Sandro that the walls were hollowed out from some point above ground level, a series of cavities not wide enough to be thoroughfares yet wide enough often to deceive him. Sandro started off slowly. Rather than follow the walls he had to rely on the floors, on the faint tapping of his crutches on stone, on the imperfect sensations he received from his feet. He went through Purgatory slowly, sweating in the chill, and sometimes something crushed beneath a testing ferrule, something that gave grainily, something that shattered like a tiny bone. At last he turned a corner and saw a faint flamelight flushing the side of the passage ahead of him. The light came from a chamber cut to the left of the main passageway, and explained the treacherous walls. They had indeed been hollowed out, and each hollow contained a heap of catalogued bones, here a heap of jaws, there a pile of thighs, ahead a collection of craniums. The piles had settled, no longer filling the niches, and sometimes bones had fallen, lying on the floor of the tunnel. Sandro paused. The catacomb was silent. The only sign of life was the flickering of the flame and a trickle of oily smoke from the chamber.

Eventually he crept forward. The tunnels played tricks with sound. From where he had stopped he had heard nothing, yet a few furtively limped steps on he could hear the conversation within the chamber clearly. He recognized Bernardo's bass at once. 'What's Paolo doing with the food anyway? I'm starving.'

'I don't know,' replied a lighter voice Sandro did not recognize. 'He arranged it with the Spaniard. Anyway, he didn't take the lot. There's bread still.'

'Black bread,' said Bernardo in disgust. 'Black bread and water. Every day he has us out there flogging these damned things, earning a fortune, and what do we get from it? Black bread and water!'

'It's only for a week or so now,' said the unfamiliar voice. 'Until we've made enough money. He said so.'

A new voice laughed. 'What's the matter, Bernardo? Your stomach or your balls?' It was Matteo's voice. 'Come on, cheer up. Has Paolo let us down before?'

'That's right,' urged the stranger. 'Be fair. I've not known him long but the kid's done us all right in the past.'

'Since Tonio was killed – ' Bernardo began.

'That was his own fault. And you know it,' said Matteo. 'He ignored what he was told.'

'Sod that,' said Bernardo.

'Take no notice of Bernardo,' suggested Matteo, presumably talking to the stranger. 'He's always bad-tempered when he's hungry.'

No one spoke for a while, and then Sandro heard Bernardo again. 'I've had enough of this. I'm off!'

Sandro worked his way back rapidly into the shadows, hoping he would make no noise, and could no longer hear the conversation in the chamber. But then the conversation began to follow him. 'I don't give a toss, I want a drink, a meal and a woman,' announced Bernardo. 'You've still got today's takings, Matteo. Are you coming or what?' Shadows fell across the light. Sandro retreated further. An unsuspected side passage opened behind him and he stepped into it gratefully.

'What are you going to do if I don't?' demanded Matteo. 'You've no money of your own.'

'Take my share back from you, that's what.'

'Yeah?'

'Yeah.'

There was a scuffle and a lull. 'All right, let me go,' said Matteo grudgingly. 'Take your portion back. But the kid'll not like it.'

'Paolo can shove what he likes and doesn't. I've had it with being cooped up. Might as well be in prison!'

'Have it your way,' said Matteo, and then, as an afterthought, 'have a woman for me.'

'I'll do that,' said Bernardo. He sounded sincere and determined. 'I'm sorry about threatening you.'

'Forget it,' said Matteo. Sandro saw Bernardo's bulk pass down the tunnel towards the exit, and heard Matteo mutter, 'He probably will, fat ox,' under his breath.

Matteo's shadow receded from the wall; Sandro waited, then carefully re-entered the main passage. If Simonetta was there she was being very quiet. Sandro suspected she wasn't, and that she and the absent Paolo were one, but this knowledge was of little help. He decided to return to the surface, and followed the way Bernardo had led. Bernardo had moved rapidly, despite the darkness, which suggested he knew the tunnels well; Sandro was incapable of moving fast at any time, yet he was confident of his route. Few painters I have known get lost easily, except when careless or distracted, for painters, like guides, are concerned with significant landmarks and the relationship between things, but when he reached the place where he expected the entrance to be Sandro's confidence failed. There was no exit, no lighter darkness of open air to greet him. Instead there was just more black, and that seemed to go on for ever. He lurched a step forward on his crutches, and swung his legs straight into stone. Bernardo had shut the hole behind him.

For a moment Sandro cursed, and then he was grateful it had been Bernardo who had passed that way. Bernardo was the only one who would not wonder why the hole had been open in the first place. He knew, from watching Matteo, that there had to be some mechanism for opening the hole on the inside too, and started to grope round the edge of the opening. His progress was slow, hampered by the dark and the need to prop himself on his crutches, but at last he supposed he had found the mechanism, though he felt nothing give, for the hole opened once more. When he looked up, however, he learnt he was wrong. Simonetta was standing outside. Simonetta had opened the door.

For a second she stared at him with shock. She recognizes me, he thought, and his heart leapt. But even then she would not acknowledge her recognition, and pretended instead that it was merely his presence that had startled her. 'Who are you?' she demanded in the voice she was using. 'How did you get in?'

'Simonetta,' Sandro began.

Simonetta shook her head, as though denying her identity, and drew a narrow-bladed knife. 'Someone's cocked up,' she said. 'You come with me. Down the tunnel.'

Sandro began to limp back towards the chamber. Simonetta was just behind him. He felt her presence, more real than ghostly, just behind him, and her irresistible beauty seemed to bite through his back, gnaw at his stomach and heart. 'Simonetta,' he said again.

'Just shut up and keep walking. Can't you go any faster? Left here.'

Clearly Simonetta did not know he had already been this way. He wondered whether to tell her, and decided against it. He could not tell what game she was playing but he did not dare upset her, jeopardize her love when she was at last so close.

They reached the chamber. 'Look what I've found!' said Simonetta, and she shoved Sandro through the opening.

Sandro looked up from the floor. The chamber was red-eyed from the smoking fire but he could see Matteo and the stranger, an ugly young man who wore his skin too tight across his skull. They looked up in surprise. Sandro made an unimpressive prize. 'Who's he?' asked the stranger.

'Just some beggar. Who left the entrance open, that's what I want to know? I found this cunt sheltering inside.'

'That'd be Bernardo,' said Matteo. 'He went out. Not long ago.'

'Stupid bastard,' said Simonetta. 'It had to be him, didn't it? He left the sodding entrance open. What did he go out for anyway?'

'He said he's had enough of being cooped up here,' said Matteo, reclining on a pallet of straw and fur. 'He took his share of today's take to spend.'

Simonetta stepped over Sandro and kicked Matteo viciously in the ribs. The smile left Matteo's face. 'Hey,' he said. 'How was I meant to stop him?'

'I'd have stopped him,' said Simonetta grimly. 'We've got enough trouble making an impression on the Spaniards without this sort of balls-up. They barely trust us as it is. What are they going to think if they hear Bernardo's been out without my permission?'

'I don't know why you're so worried about the Spaniards anyway,' said Matteo, nursing his ribs.

'That's because you're as stupid as Bernardo, for all your education. The Spaniards are the real power in this city.'

'But who wants this city anyway?' said the stranger. 'What was wrong with Florence?'

'Florence!' Simonetta spat her disgust in a globule that gathered dust on the chamber floor. 'That's small-time. Florence is finished. Borgia's the man.'

'Borgia! You can't get past that Don Michelotto. You never get to see Borgia.'

'Don't I though!' Simonetta sounded young again. 'And where do you think I was last night? Not chasing bats, that's for certain.'

'All right,' said the stranger wearily. 'Maybe you've met the pope's son. That doesn't mean he's going to give you anything except maybe a shafting.'

'Simonetta!' said Sandro from the floor.

'What's up with the old man?' asked Matteo.

'Soft in the head,' said Simonetta. 'All he can say is this girl's name.'

If that's how she wants it, thought Sandro, that's how it must be.

'What we going to do with him?' continued Matteo. 'Kill him?'

'I don't know,' admitted Simonetta. 'It'd be hard to get rid of the body. The air's bad enough down here with all these old bodies. We don't want a fresh corpse stinking the place out.'

'Hey, old man.' Matteo stood and walked over to Sandro. 'What's your name?'

Perhaps Simonetta would react to his name at least, betray herself by that. 'Sandro Botticelli,' he announced.

But it was Matteo rather than Simonetta who showed recognition. 'Sandro Botticelli? The painter?'

'Yes.'

Simonetta pretended impatience. Perhaps she wanted the subject changed for fear she gave herself away. 'So what?' she asked.

'Come on,' said Matteo. 'Even you must've heard of Botticelli.'

'Maybe I have, maybe I haven't,' said Simonetta evasively.

Matteo thought it was ignorance she was hiding; Sandro knew better. 'My God,' said Matteo. 'And you call me stupid!'

'Don't come that with me,' said Simonetta. 'So what if you were at some arsehole university? Lot of good it did you.'

'At least I recognize the name of Florence's most famous painter when I hear it!'

'And how do you know he's telling the truth? He doesn't look like Florence's most famous painter!'

'Maybe he's fallen on hard times,' said Matteo. 'Maybe he was robbed, beaten up, left for dead.'

'And maybe he's just lying.'

'Easy enough to test.' Matteo helped Sandro to a sitting position. 'You're the painter, right?'

Sandro nodded. 'Fat lot that proves,' said Simonetta.

'I haven't finished yet,' said Matteo. He went over to his straw bed and from a leather bag pulled out a book and a pen. 'He can draw something for us.'

I took the book and, on the inside of the cover, began to draw Simonetta's beautiful head. Matteo was triumphant. 'What did I tell you?'

'Famous, is he?' asked Simonetta.

'We might get a good price for him,' said Matteo as Sandro continued his drawing. 'Someone'll want him back, I expect.'

Sandro paused in his drawing for a moment, wishing that might be true, then began again.

'It wasn't ransom I was thinking about,' said Simonetta dismissively. 'Do you think Cesare Borgia will have heard of him?'

'Of course he will.' Matteo looked at the picture. 'Hey! That's you, Paolo!'

Simonetta looked unconcerned, unimpressed.'Shut it. I'm thinking.' She walked the length of the chamber and back. Sandro watched her calves, surely more muscular than in the days before, and the way her hair frayed in the firelight. Her shadow waxed and waned on the walls. 'The old man's a famous painter, right? And Cesare will have heard of him, right? There must be some advantage we can get from this.'

The stranger stirred. 'I don't see it.'

'Nor do I,' said Simonetta. 'But there must be some way we can use this. Wait a minute. Umberto! Go down to the lower level and speak with the Spaniards. Ask Don Michelotto to come up here. Tell him I've a present for Cesare.'

'Why me?' asked the stranger. 'Why can't Matteo go? Or go yourself.'

'Are you frightened the ghosts will get you?' mocked Simonetta.

'I'm frightened the Spaniards might.'

'I've told you, they're all right. They respect me and trust me.'

'Then you bloody go!'

'I'm sending you.'

Umberto went, carrying a tar-brand he lit from the fire, and muttering. Sandro put down the pen and the book and waited for whatever might happen next. 'Picture not bad,' admitted Simonetta. 'But the old man's nothing to look at.'

'What's it matter what he looks like?' Matteo countered. 'He's a painter, not a catamite.'

'First impressions count. If we're going to present him to Borgia we want him to look better than this.' She prodded Sandro's travel-worn clothes with her toe.

'More fancy dress,' said Matteo scornfully.

'Cesare likes it.'

'You know your trouble?' Matteo asked. 'You're obsessed. You've managed to wheedle your way in with this guy and, just because his dad's the pope, you think he's wonderful. When as far as I can tell he's no better than the rest of us.'

'Never!' Simonetta was outraged, Sandro jealous. 'You've not met him. No better than you?' He's a hundred, a thousand times better than you! He's a real man. He's afraid of nothing. Look what he's done already in the Romagna: he's going to rule all Italy before he's done.'

'Bollocks.'

'You wait and see.'

They all waited. The fire burnt low. 'Get some wood,' said Simonetta.

Matteo was lying down. 'Where from?'

'I don't know. Just find some.'

'Why don't we burn the painter's crutches?'

'Don't dare touch him!'

Sandro, eyes pricking from the smoke, felt gratified. She cares for me after all, he thought.

Umberto returned. 'Where's Don Michelotto?' asked Simonetta.

'He wouldn't come.'

'You told him I wanted to see him'

'He just laughed. "Tell pretty boy he comes to me, not the other way round," is what he said. Word for word.'

'Bastard! All right, I'd better go. But he'll pay for that some day. Painter! On your feet!'

She took the torch from Umberto and led Sandro down steep passages. The higher tunnels had been dry; deeper the walls were damp. Torchlight picked out water that beaded like perspiration on the displayed skulls, and showed stylized fish painted in red on the walls. They reached a blind tunnel. Simonetta knocked against the far wall. The knock sounded hollow; the wall opened.

'It's Paolo here,' said Simonetta. 'I want to talk with Don Michelotto.'

'Do you know what time it ith?' asked a heavily accented voice. 'He'th athleep.'

'Wake him up then.'

'For you?' The accent was a clearing of throats and a lisp. 'Thuck yourthelf.'

Simonetta squeezed through the opening. 'I want to see Don Michelotto. Come on, painter.'

Sandro followed with difficulty. Simonetta had to tug him through. It was the first time they had been so close for nearly twenty-five years.

They were in a cavern. Torches in brackets lined the walls. The floor was streaked with bat droppings. There was a sound of running water. Off the cavern were many small curtained openings. Simonetta left Sandro with the Spaniard and walked confidently over to one of the curtains. 'Michelotto, you Spanish bastard. Wake up.'

A young girl, perhaps 9 years old, looked out from behind the curtain; Simonetta grabbed her by the hair and pulled her out. She was naked and struggling. 'Michelotto. I've got your little mistress.'

'So I saw.' The Spaniard emerged. The torchlight showed him fat, his skin greased. 'What do you want?'

'I'd like you to meet somebody. A painter.' She turned to Sandro. 'What d'you say your name was?'

That was clever! 'Sandro Botticelli,' Sandro answered.

'That's right,' agreed Simonetta. 'Best painter in Florence, in the world.'

'I don't care much for painters,' said Don Miguel.

'But Cesare might, right?' Simonetta suggested.

'All right. What do you want?'

'Go back inside and I'll tell you. I'll bring the girl with me shall I?' Simonetta, Don Michelotto and the girl retired behind the curtain. 'A bit of pleasure to go with the business?'

The lisping Spaniard turned to Sandro. 'You'd better thleep. I find you a plathe.'

Despite the girl's giggles, and later her screams, Sandro slept. Purgatory is a place of waiting. There is little to do there save sleep.

He was woken by the same Spaniard. 'Time to go. Don Miguel, he thayth you should have a wash, wear theeth cloth.'

The Spanish, well-equipped, organized as though for a long stay, even had servants in their cave. Water was fetched and heated, and though it was still not warm at least it was warmer than the cavern. Sandro washed his face and hands before stripping off his outer garments and his hose, then climbed carefully into a new knee-length jacket, new black hose. The bandages round his legs stank but he did not dare remove them too. He had not changed them for several years. He feared what he might find beneath.

Don Miguel's child-mistress trimmed his hair and beard. She had a serious face and bruised eyes. Pity was not part of Sandro's purpose yet he pitied her. But then a red hat, like those worn by the Florentine council, was found for him and he was led away.

Their route this time was a single tunnel that had neither turnings nor side passages. The walk was long and Sandro slow. 'I don't know how you make a pilgrimage when you cannot walk,' observed the Spaniard.

'God helped me,' said Sandro.

The Spaniard flinched in the torchlight.'Don't mention Hith name down here,' he said.

The tunnel was narrow and fearful; Sandro was possessed by a new certainty. This was not Purgatory, the ante-chamber to Heaven. He had passed through the gateway to Hell.

1492–8

The final decade of the century was a time of many farewells. My youngest friends left Florence: Filippino went to Rome to work; Amerigo found Florence too confining, entered the service of the king of Spain, and has gone to the New World, a place more strange to us than the Kingdom of the Dead. Not that the Kingdom of the Dead was remiss in collecting my older friends. My generous and much loved brother Giovanni was first to go, leaving a widow and three healthy sons. Next, my colleague from Fra Lippo Lippi's bottega, Jacopo del Sallaio, returned from his self-imposed exile only to die at my dinner table; made unhappy by that event, I moved house to the home of my brother Simone. Lorenzo was already dead, as was Ficino's exotic young nephew Pico della Mirandola. And finally, devastatingly, Domenico and Politian were killed the same week by the fever that comes with the river mist. It sometimes seems I have never smiled since.

After Lorenzo's death Florence turned naturally to his son Piero. But, as Politian had recognized, Piero lacked the application to be a good ruler. He enjoyed the banquets and the tournaments, loathed the work. When the French king Charles entered Italy, as had been foreseen by Savonarola, Piero was totally unprepared, utterly overawed. He made some kind of pretence at negotiation and in the process, the numbskull, gave away more than Charles had asked for! There was no doubt: Piero was a fool. He was chased from Florence, and into the void he left came Savonarola.

Perhaps Savonarola never wanted power of the temporal kind. Certainly he never enjoyed the trappings that go with power, continuing instead to live in his cell at the monastery of San Marco. But, as the most respected man in Florence, he was given little choice.'Tell us what to do!' we begged him, and he replied the only way he knew how. 'Make Florence the City of God on earth,' he said, for the City of God was the only city he could imagine.

And what a New Jerusalem we built! It was a city where beauty was consigned to the flames, a place where children had their hair shorn, spied on their parents, were praised for their treachery. My brother Simone loved it, and his wife came to my room in the night with excuses, and was sent away with more. Savonarola was a prophet who saw the future and stole our city's past; while he tried to make Florence a Heaven on Earth, I took refuge in Dante's Hell. Lorenzo di Pierfrancesco was again my client: the drawings I did for him have beauty, though they earned me little; they are my tribute to Dante, who understood, as Savonarola never would, never could, that in this world as in the heavens, perfection is a dangerous and icy blade. Savonarola never recognized this, any more than he realized that, as Politian had said, God is love but love can be cruel. I believe Savonarola was indeed a saint. But, though his life spoke of nothing but virtue, in his sermons he spoke only of sin. He thought that beauty was a sin and must be punished.

It was with this in mind that, at the height of the fervour, Marco Vespucci came to me. His face had fleshed out; his mouth had collapsed into the gap left by his teeth and become a slit in a turnip; he had contracted the French pox and his flesh was failing on his bones. 'Sandro,' he said, gasping. 'Will you allow me to burn Simonetta?'

I knew what he meant. Of all the paintings of Simonetta I had done, the most straighforward likeness was the one which showed her as Venus, naked, washing before a gilt looking-glass. 'Why?' I asked. He did not have to ask my permission, it was true, but neither did he have to burn the painting. Or so it seemed to me.

'I am dying, Sandro. The acid has got into my blood. I'm dying for my sins. You've heard what Savonarola has asked. We must take everything we love, everything that has beauty, and throw it in a pyre on the Piazza della Signoria. Your painting of Simonetta is the most beautiful thing I have. It should burn.'

'Why do you come to me? The painting is yours: you paid for it.' I felt I was being unsympathetic to a man in desperate need of sympathy; I felt that I should offer reassurance or some memory of the past. I understood what he was saying: he wanted to do the right thing, whatever that might be. But I had nothing but coldness to offer, for I was cold inside.

'You know why I need to ask,' he said, but he was wrong. Did he know of the love I had shared with Simonetta? Or perhaps he simply did not want to destroy one of my paintings without my blessing, for fear that this too would be a sin.

'Do what you like with it,' I said. 'It's nothing to do with me.' This was unfair. He sought a different answer, sought to share the burden of destroying the painting, sought to share the loss. And instead I was being legalistic.

Yet I shared his burden and his loss only too well. The painting was placed high on the scaffold. The flames reached it late, and oily smoke obscured the destruction. Yet still I could see Simonetta's beautiful features. A black patch appeared on the panel and the paint seemed to writhe as if to avoid the darkness. But the darkness spread, became a hole fringed with a line of fire, and Simonetta was consumed. Then there was a shrug of damaged timbers, a velvet cape fell on to my panel, and the painting disappeared.

Simone congratulated me. 'You have conquered another vanity,' he told me. 'With the destruction of that lascivious work you have stepped a little nearer to Heaven. Are you coming to the Duomo with us to pray?'

I did not utter the reply that first came into my head. 'I don't think so,' I told him instead. I stayed where I was in front of the dying flames; I was still there in the morning, watching the embers fanned by the breeze, and in the overcast dawn saw barefooted children pick their way through the ash as they hunted for something of value. An urchin boy prodded a charred velvet cape with a stick. Lifting the cape revealed a piece of painted panel. I thought I recognized Simonetta's image as reflected in the looking-glass, but the boy recognized nothing and tossed the fragment away to the edge of the circle of ash. A slow rain began, turning the ashes to mulch. A carter drove his horse across the square. One wheel trundled over the margin of the ash, over the shards of a perfume jar, over the fragment of Simonetta. The wet panel bent and fastened itself to the metal rim of the wheel, and was pulped with each revolution. The carter drove on to the north. I imagine him on the road towards Prato, climbing past the wheatfields. The painting, unnoticed on his wheel, is no more than a smudge of pigment squashed in a mat of mud. And then the wheel goes through a puddle, the fragment is loosened, and the next turn of the wheel deposits it, unrecognizable, in a fresh shallow rut. The sun comes out, smiling on the puddles and the road. The carter begins to whistle. The horse plods on.

Savonarola thought that beauty was a sin and must be punished, which is why, when we had burnt everything else of beauty, we burnt his beautiful soul; Savonarola was right, for I followed Simonetta's beauty, and it led me deep into Hell.

1500

As they approached the centre of Hell the air suddenly freshened. Sandro, matching his journey against Dante's verses, wondered how far he had gone. The tunnels where Simonetta had her headquarters, he reasoned, must have been the first circle, where the unbaptized but worthy pagans spend their time: he had seen them in the alcoves of the tunnel. And he had not yet reached Cerberus, he was sure, for he would have recognized that awful dog, and therefore had not reached the third circle. So I am in the second circle, he thought, which is the circle of the lustful. For a while this did not seem appropriate, for he had shown less lust in his life than almost any man he had known, but as the air cleared so did his head: my lust for Simonetta has brought me to this place.

The reason Simonetta had returned was apparent to him now. She had come not to bless but to test him. And he had failed, miserably. Instead of showing strength he had fallen for the temptation; God forgives those who repent, but Sandro had not repented, and had repeated his mistakes.

A patch of orange light ahead showed that the tunnel was about to end. Sandro and his companion emerged into a steeply walled pit with a roof of stars; although they had been descending for the whole journey they seemed to have reached open air. Have we reached the bottom of the hill I climbed, he wondered, or is this just another torment of the Devil's devising?

It was the sort of pit used for bear-baiting, circular, with two small chambers off. A ring of candles on tall tripods explained the fiery light, and behind the candle-flames' glare he could see nothing. He stood at the edge of the arena of candles until his companion gave him a push, and then he was in the middle of the ring and aware of shadowy figures in the darkness beyond. The candles guttered in the draught, then the door was closed and the flames were still. There was an odd scent in the air, an incense he had never smelt before, and another, more ancient smell beyond.

One of the figures beyond the tall tripods spoke. 'Welcome, painter.' The accent was cultivated, Roman.

'Welcome, painter,' chorused other voices, but their words were a response to their leader rather than a greeting.

'We are glad you accepted our invitation,' added the first voice. 'It was so kind of you to come.'

Sandro said nothing. Where is Simonetta; is she here to share my torment? That wouldn't be too bad, he decided, but the voice – it was to his right, Sandro realized – continued suavely. 'You are perhaps wondering why you have been brought here.'

Sandro nodded. He could be seen and could not see, and smelt fear rising from his clean clothes and filthy legs.

The voice continued. 'Tonight my friends and I will be performing certain rituals. I hope you have a strong stomach, painter: we have an interesting commission for you. Although we derive great pleasure from our performances down here, there is something unsatisfactory about our current arrangements. We have no record of our rites. Your function will be to provide that record, to draw our performance. We know your skills.'

'You want me to draw for you?' asked Sandro. Had he not known his lips were moving he would never have recognized that thin small voice as his own.

'That is your profession, I believe.'

It was appropriate. On earth Sandro's function – his only function – had been to draw and paint; it was the same, it seemed, in Hell. 'Yes,' he said in his novel tight voice.

'Good. We are ready to begin.'

'I have no materials,' said Sandro quickly. 'No pens or chalk.' Even as he spoke he wondered whether this was an excuse, an attempt to get him out of this sinister employment, or an apology to the unseen authority in the Devil's voice.

'Materials are provided. Prepare the altar.'

The last was an instruction to others, it seemed. Two figures in black stepped into the circle of light carrying a rolled cloth. Their hoods were pulled over their heads and Sandro gasped when he saw not a face but a skull in the shadows within. Someone laughed at his discomfort. He risked a second glance at the awful face. It was no reassurance to find that the skull was a mask.

The cowled figures started to unroll their bundle on the floor and Sandro had to step aside. He moved reluctantly, fearing he had left a puddle of urine, even more frightened to commit himself to the shadows beyond the candles. The cloth was circular, and fitted neatly into the ring of tall tripods; it bore the design of a five-pointed star, and was carefully positioned so that each point aimed directly at a candle. There were thirteen candles, one at each point of the star and two between each of these, except by the door where there was a space.

Out of the ring of light Sandro could see more clearly. Anonymous figures in dark cloaks busied themselves in the gloom. Someone presented Sandro with black German chalk and a sheaf of paper tied to a board, but he was otherwise ignored. The paper, he noted, was also German, and of the best quality. He stepped further back as the figures, the necromancers, prepared for whatever the ritual was to be, and his legs felt weak. One necromancer, wearing a gold chain, stepped on to the cloth. Sandro felt this must be the man who had spoken, the one with the Roman accent, the leader, the Devil. Or perhaps not Satan himself but some other demon, Beelzebub or Baal. In his hands the Roman carried a long curved knife. The knife was oriental, vicious, rather beautiful. The Roman shook back his cowl. He too wore a skull mask, a piece of white linen that covered all his face save his lower jaw, with black circles around the eyes, an ugly black triangle over the nose, and black lines which represented teeth at the lower fringe. That the mask was crude made it no less fearful.

Sandro sat down just behind a tripod. He needed to be as inconspicuous as possible, yet also needed enough light to be able to draw. He felt the cold of a midsummer midnight. The chalk was comfortable in his hand, reassuring, yet it was a reminder of the world of God. Such reminders were an agony here in Hell. Yet he put the chalk to the paper and began to draw. What else can an artist do?

He drew the demon stepping from his discarded coat, naked except for his mask and a large gilt phallus, bound in brass and with brass testicles beneath, which was strapped over his groin. He drew a thin Moorish woman, apparently unconscious, being dragged by two acolytes, and indicated with a flick of the chalk the heavy muscles in the men's arms. He drew the Moorish woman, tossed roughly to the floor, penetrated by the metal phallus, and had trouble with the foreshortening of her prostrate body. Her living body was replaced by a corpse, not particularly fresh. The body was naked, scrawny, and had sores on its legs which must have been troublesome when it was alive. He drew the demon as it carefully slit the corpse's chest from throat to belly.

Several of Sandro's colleagues were interested in anatomy. Sandro was reminded involuntarily of the stench in Leonardo's studio; of Verrochio's flayed horses I have spoken before; Antonio del Pollaiuolo and his brother frequently dissected the bodies of hanged criminals; Luca Signorelli had spent so long at the dissecting table that the nude figures on the walls of Orvieto cathedral looked almost flayed. But Sandro had never shared this interest. Volterra had been terror enough. Some might call his fastidiousness a weakness, a preference for surfaces, an ignorance of what lay beneath. He did not think of it that way. He considered his preference was simply for beauty, and there was little enough beauty to be found beneath even the most lovely flesh.

A coil of purple sludge slid from the corpse's chest and confirmed Sandro's distate. He stopped drawing, breathed deeply to check the nausea, and then resumed, sketching a cockerel with a damaged comb, tucked under the arm of an acolyte. He sketched the laughter of the demon as the cockerel, decapitated, scampered in tight circles. He drew the bird's body, its feathers barely stained by the blood, as it throbbed fatuously for a while before dropping. And then he stopped drawing again, and stared in horror. A youth, bound and gagged but otherwise naked, had been brought into the circle, and despite the gag Sandro recognized the face at once. 'Simonetta!' Yet the body was that of a man.

The demon was grinning. 'Hello, Paolo,' he said politely in his Roman accent; he touched the young man on the chest with the point of the knife and drew a neat line of blood. 'So nice of you to join us this evening. I hope you've enjoyed the entertainment so far. The girl was disappointing, wouldn't you agree? We drugged her too much: it's so much more pleasant to get a squirm when you penetrate, I always say. And the old man was predictable. In fact, my handsome young friend, it appears that if the night is to be a success you'll have to provide the entertainment.' The Roman traced the lines of the bonds with the knife, pushing slightly now to cut through muscle. 'I do hope you're feeling up to it. Not too cold, are you?'

The knife came to a halt too, resting on the young man's stomach. 'You know why you're here, I suppose? You're a pretty boy, I grant, but importunate. The Devil gave you a charming face, charming body; a shame he made such a mess of the mind, eh? For you're a fool, Paolo. You gave yourself to me. And I never want what I can have. That's my secret. That's why I am who I am.

'Not that I'm criticizing. The painter was a clever idea, I'll grant you. But did you really expect me, the son of the Vicar of Christ, to treat you as an equal just because you could bully a small gang of Florentine cut-throats? That's hubris, Paolo. That's unnecessary pride.

'I am, however, granting one great big favour. You're pretty, I don't deny. And we have the painter here to record you: isn't that right, Señor Botticelli?' The voice raised to ask the question but the demon son of the Vicar of Christ did not move his face from just in front of his victim's. Sandro felt no need to reply, and was glad, but he was prompted to start to draw Simonetta's desperate gagged features, the mouth stuffed with a black rag, a ring of white orbit showing round the iris of each eye, and the unfamiliar male body beneath. His hand shook badly and the drawing was poor.

The Roman leaned even closer to the young man, put his weight on the knife, and forced it into Paolo's belly. The young man whimpered and closed his eyes at the pain. 'Oh dear,' asked the Roman pleasantly. 'Does that hurt? Better pull it out then.' He twisted his wrist as he withdrew the knife, widening the hole, and then let the knife drop to the ground. It fell on the cloth with a muffled clang.

'I suppose he wants a rest now. Lower him a few inches: that's right; that looks much more comfortable.' The magus took his metal penis in his hands and pushed it towards the knife-wound; he slid the phallus into his victim's guts and embraced the naked man. 'Are you drawing all this, artist?' he asked over Paolo's shoulder and Sandro, clutching at the one thing he knew, continued to draw. The magus pulled his victim up by the hair and jerked him up and down. Blood and excrement ran from the young man's bowels. Simonetta's face, dangling from Paolo's neck, was contorted beyond anything Sandro could capture; the magus's mouth was open in a kind of pleasure, and one of his front teeth was merely a stump.

The skin on Paolo's stomach ripped from within, and the gilt phallus, festooned with damp pale strands and stained with blood, slipped out. The son of the pope let go his victim's hair and the body slumped. 'What a shame,' said the Roman. 'I think he's dead.'

'Oh God!' Sandro whispered. 'Oh Simonetta!' Neither answered. Neither heard.

1501

The performance was over. Someone took the drawings from me. They tried to prise the chalk loose from my hand but I would not let go. The chalk snapped in my hand.

And then I started to weep. Dawn was beginning, and above us the sky lightened. The birds sang of peace and love. The birds lied. Though her pain was dreadful and her shame so much worse, the Moorish woman tried to comfort me. Her father had wept like that once, she whispered, when telling her of his life before slavery. A man weeps like that but once in his life, she said, for after such tears the world in his eyes, the only world he has known, has been washed away and drowned. She said prayers for us too, for we expected to die, but instead we were simply left, and the gates to the pit were fastened. Crows sat on the rim of the pit, and waited.

Alone, I would have abandoned myself to the crows, but the Moor was stronger and called out, regularly, for many hours. Rescue came with the noon: a couple of Venetian women heard her cries and fetched the city watch, who lowered a rope ladder, climbed down and carried us out. To begin with they wanted to know how we had got into the pit, but when we mentioned the name of Cesare Borgia they lost interest and wanted instead to know more about us. We were taken to the fortress of Castel Sant'Angelo and led down separate dark dank tunnels. My crutches were still in the pit: I was hauled and tossed like a sack of beet.

I was left, apparently forgotten in my cell, for two days, but on the third I was interrogated. They did not believe I was who I claimed, did not dare hear a word about Borgia, and would have thrown me back in the cell, I am sure, had I not mentioned Filippino's name.

The captain stared at me. 'Filippino Lippi the painter?'

'I was his father's apprentice and Filippino's master.'

'That's easily checked. He lives just by here, on the Borgo Sant'Angelo. I'll have him fetched. Boccacello, you say your name is?'

'Botticelli. Sandro Botticelli.'

'We'll send word to him. Mind, he's an important man: if you're wasting his time I'll have you flogged.'

I waited in a cold room and warm light streaked past the window. Eventually Filippino came to me. At first we hardly recognized one another. It seemed he had acquired the weight I had lost, for whereas I was no more than bone wrapped in skin he had grown a belly to rival his father's. We stood looking at one another. 'Sandro? Is it you?'

'I'm afraid it is.' I moved my lips into what, toothless, is the closest thing I can get to a smile. 'I'm sorry you've been troubled.'

'Sorry! Nonsense! Oh, Sandro, what have they been doing to you?'

'Nothing to do with us,' said the captain primly. 'He was like that when my men found him.'

'It's true,' I said. 'I'll tell you about it.'

'Of course,' said Filippino. 'But we must get you home. Look at you!'

'Before I go,' I said, 'There was a Moorish woman brought here with me. Is she all right? Can she be released too? She saved my life,' I added to Filippino. 'I'd never have been found without her; I didn't have the strength or the will to be found.'

Filippino studied me. 'This is serious, isn't it.'

'It is.'

They fetched the Moorish woman. She was hardly more capable than I of walking so we had to wait until Filippino's *garzoni* could be fetched: we were carried on large unfinished panel paintings. 'The perfect bier for Sandro Botticelli,' said Filippino.

That night I told him it all, from the first sighting of Simonetta to her violent, hideous end. I wept often, and Filippino looked concerned. I thought it was my health and sanity that worried him, but his fears were more immediate. 'You mustn't breathe a word of this to anyone else,' he said. 'And you must get out of Rome at once. You too,' he told the Moorish woman. 'I'm surprised Borgia let you live.'

'I hear them talking,' the woman said. Her Italian was strange, accented with Spanish and something more alien, more fabulous. 'They decide we not worth killing, is more fun let us live – who would listen to us, who would care?'

'It's true,' said Filippino. 'Borgia revels in his reputation for infamy. Yours is just one more tale among a lot of tales. But still.' He didn't finish, nor need to.

'You have to live here,' I said. 'You can't risk sheltering us.'

He stared ahead, out of the window of his bottega at the busy Borgo Sant'Angelo beyond. 'What sort of world is it when I dare not shelter my oldest friend?' he asked. 'Of course you must stay here.'

'No,' I said. I had been to Hell and had seen the Devil's vengeance. 'We must go.'

Filippino nodded, and then his face brightened. 'But not at once; you must recover your strength, both of you. And not tonight! We must celebrate our meeting!' I had the sensation that it was the father and not the son that I was with. 'Do you still dance? Sorry, of course not. But we must have a feast, a banquet for Botticelli. And when you are stronger, then you can leave.'

And so we had a banquet. I tried to be good company, and probably failed, but Filippino understood and, before the feasting was over, had me carried to my bed. The Moorish woman joined me and we slept chastely side by side.

A week passed. The Moorish woman recovered more quickly than I, although she had suffered more, and as she recovered she seemed to become younger. I could never become young again, I knew now; my past was gone, laid out in lines of perspective, receding to a vanishing-point. The last of my innocence had been impaled in a bear-pit, and all I had was the future. 'Now would be a good time to leave,' the Moorish woman told me. 'Many pilgrims are leaving Rome. We can go with them.'

'You're coming with me?' I asked.

'Where else for me to go? I was born some place I cannot remember, across a sea. I cannot go back. Now I am slave, which is next to nothing, and if I am slave no more then I become only nothing.'

'What is your name?' I asked.

'Sbella,' she replied.

Filippino paid for asses to carry us, and offered us money. 'I can't take this,' I said.

'Why not?' asked Filippino. 'You've lived off other people's money before. I know, I've watched you.'

'But – '

He offered the money to Sbella instead, and she took it. 'Why not?' she asked me. 'Giving make your friend feel better, eating make us feel better. We take the money, say thank you.'

I embraced Filippino warmly and we left. We rode out of Rome the same way I had entered, and I did not look back. As I rode my ass, Sbella at my side, it was as if most of my mind had been closed off, like a room that hides a dreadful secret, and I inhabited only that small portion concerned with the here and now.

Even the here and now brought problems. Autumn was coming; the weather was worse than usual for that time of the year. On our second day out, as we entered the mountains, it began to snow. The snow stole the horizon and everything horizontal from the landscape, leaving us with ice and black stakes that jutted from the ground. Sbella prayed loudly, as she had been taught, and in the desolation I learned to need prayer too; in that cold that fingered my bones I learned once more the hunger for God. Slowly, as we travelled, I began to explore the closed-off parts of my mind, throwing light in shuttered rooms, unlocking heavy doors, preparing for my final painting. We travelled for three cold weeks.

Florence was unchanged. I was the one who had altered. I had lost everything. The world I had held in my eyes was drowned. Familiar streets seemed alien and strange. My rooms had been let, but my bottega was still open. We slept there and I planned my last painting, while the news spread through the city that Cesare Borgia was on the march and had captured Pesaro and Rimini.

Without Sbella there would have been no painting. She fed me and made me sleep while I sketched and planned. We used the inferior panels for firewood, but I had one good panel left, not large but of excellent quality, which I knew would suit the painting I was assembling in my imagination. I began to plot out the design.

What was left of Filippino's money I spent on colours, and especially on gold, for not only did I want my picture to be rich and magnificent but, in that cold season of heavy snow, I wanted to celebrate colour. The painting was to be a Nativity, I decided, because the Nativity is the most perfect moment of all, imperfectly repeated with each new birth on to the earth, but it would be a Nativity unlike any I had painted before. In the centre of the painting the Christchild lies on straw; he is the naked light of the world, guarded by the ox and the ass. Hunched Joseph looks at the child; gentle Mary prays for Him. But in this painting the manger is no longer in some ruin of antiquity, as in my earlier paintings. It is in an arch of rough rocks in an olive grove, sheltered by a crude wooden lean-to. For where was Christ born if not over the mouth of Hell, which his tiny radiant presence innocently defies.

Around the manger, on either side, angels direct shepherds who gaze at the child in wonder, while above them more angels are dancing. Their dance is a vortex of gold where, holding hands, they rejoice at the coming of the Lord, while below, in the foreground, the tombs spring open and the dead return to life. There are three angels there, to embrace three corpses who are restored and returned from the dead, while a demon, vanquished, slinks into an opened grave. All is calm. The resurrected figure in the middle of the three is a boy who wears Simonetta's face.

There is no perspective in the picture, for time does not function there. This is the Nativity, but it is also the Judgement Day. The figure of Mary is far larger than those of the angels and men in the foreground. Perspective, the regular mechanical recession, is a man's-eye view. It accords prominence according to position in space: a dog in the foreground is far larger than a distant prince. I no longer wanted to paint what men see. Such a view had been washed from my face in a torrent of tears. I wanted to paint what God sees. I had no client to flatter, was not working for some merchant or banker who wanted assurance that God was indeed a man and therefore man could become a God. I was painting for myself. I was painting for God.

I had forsaken Him. He had not forsaken me. That was the lesson of my troubles. That was the lesson of my final painting. Yet, though I painted for God, I did not forget that I am a man. A man must live in time, needs time to live just as he needs food or water. Above the picture, in Greek letters, I wrote an inscription from the Book of

Revelation. It was a prophesy. God be praised, my prophesy is proving correct.

I was absorbed in my painting, barely speaking and never leaving the bottega. Sbella provided the little I required: food and heat, company in the evenings when the light was too poor to work. I did not notice until the painting was finished, and by then it was obvious. She was with child.

The child was not mine of course. Our relationship had never been of that kind. But I felt tender towards her and asked who the father might be. She would not reply. 'Not Borgia!' I asked in horror. Had the Antichrist sired a new demon to be born in my own bed? But she smiled and shook her head. 'A young man,' she told me. 'Of Florence.'

It seemed the young man was a servant of the Rucellai family, and that she saw him often and liked him greatly. 'But he asks I will marry him,' she said. 'And I will not leave you.'

I was touched by her loyalty. I was an infirm old man who had painted his last picture; her lover was a good-looking chap of her age. Yet she chose to live with me rather than marry him. I was touched, but no longer with madness. If she would not leave me, then I must leave her. My painting was done, so I waited until she was out, and left. For several days of pleasant spring I walked the streets on crutches I had fashioned myself, sleeping in the gutters, staring at the stars. I crossed Florence many times, seeking the familiar places. I was at peace with the world and with God, an unnatural condition in this world of ours; the watch found me and asked who I was.

If I gave my name they would return me to Sbella, who would forsake her young man to look after me; if I failed to give my name they would throw me from the city as an alien, and I did not want to leave. I have learned two things in my life: painting and madness. My city has tired of my painting, so I feigned madness and was allowed to stay. Fra Agostino took me in, to this place where the monkey-man shrieks. It is safe here.

1504

And that, my inquisitive scholar of some imagined future age, is where you find me, in this place where the monkey-man swings in his polished boughs and the madmen cry out in my sleep. I have sensed Heaven in a feather mattress, found Hell in a bear-pit. I have talked with princes and suffered with beggars. And I have painted some pictures.

Only the pictures matter, of course. None of what I have written matters, save to me and to your curiosity. Not a word of it changes the world. But the pictures? I believe they do matter, and I have just had confirmation for my belief.

At the top of my final picture, as I have described, I wrote an inscription from the Book of Revelation. 'I Sandro painted this picture at the end of the year 1500, showing the troubles in Italy during that crisis described in the 11th Chapter of the Book of St John, when the Devil is loosed for three and a half years and before he is chained as described in the 12th Chapter and as shown in this picture.' The month after I had finished painting, the first month of the Florentine new year, Cesare Borgia captured Faenza and was made duke of the Romagna; in the next month he threatened Florence itself, and Leonardo da Vinci offered him impractical advice. While Sbella grew fat with child, and I left her and walked the streets, Cesare became ruler of Arezzo; as I listened to the madmen and wrote this manuscript, Borgia captured Urbino, had his own captains murdered at Senigallia, and became ruler of half Italy. But on 13 August 1503 his father died, and now at last I am in a position to guarantee the truth of my prophecy. For on the day following the feast of the Nativity that year Duke Cesare was captured. His reign lasted three and a half years. He is chained still. This is the only painting that bears my name.

Much of my life has been based on misunderstanding. What prophecies I have made have generally proved untrue, what patterns I found in my life have generally proved illusions. I never found out where the dead birds lie. Yet when I painted, when I touched the panel with my brush and made a world of pigment, perhaps then I knew a special truth. Perhaps my life is all lies. Perhaps even this manuscript lies. But when I painted I told the truth. The truth is not measurable in inches and miles. The truth is not just what our senses record. The truth is the whole of it, not just what we see but what we make of what we see. If you seek the truth of my life look not to my words but my pictures.

And now the words are all done, and there is nothing left for me to do but to grow yet older and die. I do not relish death, nor do I dread it. The monkey-man is in his tree. He hurt his arm in a fall but is better now, thank God. And though I am sad that my tale of love is done and I have nothing to do now but die, I have some comfort left. For somewhere in my past, Sandro Botticelli, painter of Florence, raises his brush to the panel; somewhere in the past, Botticelli paints. It is little enough. It is enough.

A NOTE ON THE AUTHOR

Richard Burns is the author of *A Dance for the Moon* (one of the winners of the 1985 Cape/*Times* Young Author Competition); *The Panda Hunt*; *Why Diamond Had to Die*; *Khalindaine*; *Troubadour*; and *Fond and Foolish Lovers* (runner up for the 1990 John Llewelyn Rhys Award). He is now head of the Department of Creative Writing at Lancaster University.